THE FEAST
OF LOVE

THE FEAST
OF LOVE

CHARLES BAXTER

FOURTH ESTATE • *London*

First published in Great Britain in 2001 by
Fourth Estate
A Division of HarperCollins*Publishers*
77–85 Fulham Palace Road,
London W6 8JB
www.4thestate.co.uk

10 9 8 7 6 5 4 3 2 1

A catalogue record for this book is available from the British Library.

ISBN 1-84115-637-X

Printed in Great Britain by Clays Ltd, St Ives plc

Yes, there were times when I forgot not only who I was,
but that I was, forgot to be.

—SAMUEL BECKETT, *Molloy*

BEGINNINGS

PRELUDES

THE MAN—ME, this pale being, no one else, it seems—wakes in fright, tangled up in the sheets.

The darkened room, the half-closed doors of the closet and the slender pine-slatted lamp on the bedside table: I don't recognize them. On the opposite side of the room, the streetlight's distant luminance coating the window shade has an eerie unwelcome glow. None of these previously familiar objects have any familiarity now. What's worse, I cannot remember or recognize myself. I sit up in bed—actually, I *lurch* in mild sleepy terror toward the vertical. There's a demon here, one of the unnamed ones, the demon of erasure and forgetting. I can't manage my way through this feeling because my mind isn't working, and because *it*, the flesh in which I'm housed, hasn't yet become *me*.

Looking into the darkness, I have optical floaters: there, on the opposite wall, are gears turning separately and then moving closer to one another until their cogs start to mesh and rotate in unison.

Then I feel her hand on my back. She's accustomed by now to my night amnesias, and with what has become an almost automatic response, she reaches up sleepily from her side of the bed and touches me between the shoulder blades. In this manner the world's objects slip back into their fixed positions.

"Charlie," she says. Although I have not recognized myself,

apparently I recognize her: her hand, her voice, even the slight saltine-cracker scent of her body as it rises out of sleep. I turn toward her and hold her in my arms, trying to get my heart rate under control. She puts her hand to my chest. "You've been dreaming," she says. "It's only a bad dream." Then she says, half-asleep again, "You have bad dreams," she yawns, "because you don't . . ." Before she can finish the sentence, she descends back into sleep.

I get up and walk to the study. I have been advised to take a set of steps as a remedy. I have "identity lapses," as the doctor is pleased to call them. I have not found this clinical phrase in any book. I think he made it up. Whatever they are called, these lapses lead to physical side effects: my heart is still thumping, and I can hardly sit or lie still.

I write my name, *Charles Baxter,* my address, the county, and the state in which I live. I concoct a word that doesn't exist in our language but still might have a meaning or should have one: *glimmerless.* I am glimmerless. I write down the word next to my name.

ON THE FIRST FLOOR near the foot of the stairs, we have placed on the wall an antique mirror so old that it can't reflect anything anymore. Its surface, worn down to nubbled grainy gray stubs, has lost one of its dimensions. Like me, it's glimmerless. You can't see *into* it now, just past it. Depth has been replaced by texture. This mirror gives back nothing and makes no productive claim upon anyone. The mirror has been so completely worn away that you have to learn to live with what it refuses to do. That's its beauty.

I have put on jeans, a shirt, shoes. I will take a walk. I glide past the nonmirroring mirror, unseen, thinking myself a vampire who soaks up essences other than blood. I go outside to Woodland Drive and saunter to the end of the block onto a large vacant lot. Here I am, a mere neighbor, somnambulating, harmless, no longer a menace to myself or to anyone else, and, stage by stage, feeling calmer now that I am outside.

As all the neighbors know, no house will ever be built on the ground where I am standing because of subsurface problems with water drainage. In the flatlands of Michigan the water stays put. The storm sewers have proven to be inadequate, with the result that this property, at the base of the hill on which our street was laid, always floods following thunderstorms and stays wet for weeks. The neighborhood kids love it. After rains they shriek their way to the puddles.

ABOVE ME in the clear night sky, the moon, Earth's mad companion, is belting out show tunes. A Rodgers and Hart medley, this is, including "Where or When." The moon has a good baritone voice. No: someone from down the block has an audio system on. Apparently I am still quite sleepy and disoriented. The moon, it seems, is not singing after all.

I turn away from the vacant lot and head east along its edge, taking the sidewalk that leads to the path into what is called Pioneer Woods. These woods border the houses on my street. I know the path by heart. I have taken walks on this path almost every day for the last twenty years. Our dog, Tasha, walks through here as mechanically as I do except when she sees a squirrel. In the moonlight the path that I am following has the appearance of the tunnel that Beauty walks through to get to the Beast, and though I cannot see what lies at the other end of the tunnel, I do not need to see it. I could walk it blind.

ON THE PATH NOW, urged leftward toward a stand of maples, I hear the sound of droplets falling through the leaves. It can't be raining. There are still stars visible intermittently overhead. No: here are the gypsy moths, still in their caterpillar form, chewing at the maple and serviceberry leaves, devouring our neighborhood forest leaf by leaf. Night gives them no rest. The woods have been infested with them, and during the day the sun shines through these trees as if spring were here, bare stunned nubs of gnawed and nibbled leaves casting almost no shade on the ground, where the altered soil chemistry, thanks to the caterpillars' leavings, has killed most of the seedlings, leaving only disagreeably enlarged thorny and deep-rooted thistles, horror-movie phantasm vegetation with deep root systems. The trees are coated, studded, with caterpillars, their bare trunks hairy and squirming. I can barely see them but can hear their every scrape and crawl.

The city has sprayed this forest with *Bacillus thuringiensis,* two words I love to say to myself, and the bacillus has killed some of these pests; their bodies lie on the path, where my seemingly adhesive shoes pick them up. I can feel them under my soles in the dark as I walk, squirming semiliquid life. Squish, squoosh. And in my night confusion it is as if I can hear the leaves being gnawed, the forest being eaten alive, shred by shred. I cannot bear it. They are not mild, these moths. Their appetites are blindingly voracious, obsessive. An acquaintance has told me that the Navahos refer to someone with an emotional illness as "moth crazy."

ON THE OTHER SIDE of the woods I come out onto the edge of a street, Stadium Boulevard, and walk down a slope toward the corner, where a stoplight is blinking red in two directions. I turn east and head toward the University of Michigan football stadium, the largest college football stadium in the country. The greater part of it was excavated below ground; only a small part of its steel and concrete structure is visible from here, the corner of Stadium and Main, just east of Pioneer High School. Cars pass occasionally on the street, their drivers hunched over, occasionally glancing at me in a fearful or predatory manner. Two teenagers out here are skateboarding in the dark, clattering over the pavement, doing their risky and amazing ankle-busting curb jumping. They grunt and holler. Both white, they have fashioned Rasta-wear for themselves, dreads and oversized unbuttoned vests over bare skin. I check my watch. It is 1:30. I stop to make sure that no patrol cars are passing and then make my way through the turnstiles. The university has planned to build an enormous iron fence around this place, but it's not here yet. I am trespassing now and subject to arrest. After entering the tunneled walkway of Gate 19, I find myself at the south end zone, in the kingdom of football.

Inside the stadium, I feel the hushed moonlight on my back and sit down on a metal bench. The August meteor shower now seems to be part of this show. I am two thirds of the way up. These seats are too high for visibility and too coldly metallic for comfort, but the place is so massive that it makes most individual judgments irrelevant. Like any coliseum, it defeats privacy and solitude through sheer size. Carved out of the earth, sized for hordes and giants, bloody injuries and shouting, and so massive that no glance can take it all in, the stadium can be considered the staging ground for epic events, and not just football: in 1964, President Lyndon Baines Johnson announced his Great Society program here.

On every home-game Saturday in the fall, blimps and biplanes pulling advertising banners putter in semicircles overhead. Starting about three hours before kickoff, our street begins to be clogged with parked cars and RVs driven by midwesterners in various states of happy pre-inebriation, and when I rake the leaves in my back yard I hear the tidal clamor of the crowd in the distance, half a mile away. The crowd at the game is loudly traditional and antiphonal: one side of the stadium roars *GO* and the other side roars *BLUE*. The sounds rise to the sky, also blue, but nonpartisan.

The moonlight reflects off the rows of stands. I look down at the field, now, at 1:45 in the morning. A midsummer night's dream is being enacted down there.

This old moon wanes! She lingers my desires and those of a solitary naked couple, barely visible down there right now on the fifty-yard line, making love, on this midsummer night.

They are making soft distant audibles.

———

BACK OUT ON THE SIDEWALK, I turn west and walk toward Allmendinger Park. I see the park's basketball hoops and tennis courts and monkey bars illuminated dimly by the streetlight. Near the merry-go-round, the city planners have bolted several benches into the ground for sedentary parents watching their children. I used to watch my son from that very spot. As I stroll by on the sidewalk, I think I see someone, some shadowy figure in a jacket, emerging as if out of a fog or mist, sitting on a bench accompanied by a dog, but certainly not watching any children, this man, not at this time of night, and as I draw closer, he looks up, and so does the dog, a somewhat nondescript collie-Labrador-shepherd mix. I know this dog. I also know the man sitting next to him. I have known him for years. His arms are flung out on both sides of the bench, and his legs are crossed, and in addition to the jacket (a dark blue Chicago Bulls windbreaker), he's wearing a baseball hat, as if he were not quite adult, as if he had not *quite* given up the dreams of youth and athletic grace and skill. His name is Bradley W. Smith.

His chinos are one size too large for him—they bag around his hips and his knees—and he's wearing a shirt with a curious design that I cannot quite make out, an interlocking M. C. Escher giraffe pattern, giraffes linked to giraffes, but it can't be that, it can't be what I think it is. In the dark my friend looks like an exceptionally handsome toad. The dog snaps at a moth, then puts his head on his owner's leg. I might be hallucinating the giraffes on the man's shirt, or I might simply be mistaken. He glances at me in the dark as I sit down next to him on the bench.

"Hey," he says, "Charlie. What the hell are you doing out here? What's up?"

ONE

"HEY," HE SAYS, "Charlie. What the hell are you doing here? What's up?"

Sitting down next to him, I can see his glasses, which reflect the last crescent of the moon and a dim shooting star. In the half-dark he has a handsome mild face, thick curly hair and an easy disarming smile, like that of a bank loan officer who has not quite decided whether your credit history is worthy of you. His eyes are large and pensive, toadlike. I realize quickly that if he is sitting out here on this park bench, now, he must be a rather unlucky man, insomniac or haunted or heartsick.

"Hey, Bradley," I say. "Not much. Walkin' around. It's a midsummer night, and I've got insomnia. I see you're still awake, too."

"Yeah," he says, nodding unnecessarily, "that's the truth."

We both wait. Finally I ask him, "How come you're up?"

"Me? Oh, I found myself working late on a window in my house. The sash weight broke loose from the pulley and I've been trying to get it out from inside the wall."

"Difficult job."

"Right. Anyway, I quit that, and I've been walking Bradley the dog, since I couldn't fix the window. Do you remember this dog?"

"His name is . . . what?"

"Bradley. I just told you. Exact same as mine. It's easier to call him 'Junior.' That way, there's no confusion. He's my company. But you're not sleeping either, right?" he asks, staring off into the middle distance as if he were talking to himself, as if I were an intimation of him. "That makes the two of us." He leans back. "Three of us, if you count the dog."

"I woke up," I tell him, "and I was seeing things."

"What things?"

"I don't want to talk about it," I tell him.

"Okay."

"Oh, you know. I was seeing spots."

"Spots?"

"Yes. Like spots in front of your eyes. But these were more like cogs."

"You mean like gears or something?"

"I guess so. Wheels with cogs turning, and then getting closer to each other, so that they all turned together, their gears meshing." I rub my arm, mosquito bite.

In the shadows, one side of his face seems about to collapse, as if the effort to keep up appearances has finally failed and daylight optimism has abandoned him. He sighs and scratches Junior behind the ears. In response, the dog smiles broadly. "Gears. I never heard of that one. I guess you *don't* sleep any better than I do. We're two members of the insomnia army." He stretches now and reaches up to grab some air. "A brotherhood. And sisterhood. Did you know that Marlene Dietrich was a great insomniac?"

"No, I didn't."

"Do you know what she did to keep herself occupied at night?"

"No, I don't."

"She baked cakes," he tells me. "I read this in the Sunday paper. She baked angel food cakes and then in the daytime she gave them away to her friends. Marlene Dietrich. She looked like she did, those eyes of hers, because she couldn't sleep well. Now me," he says, rearranging himself on the bench, "I just sit still here, *very* still, you know, like what's-his-name, the compassionate Buddha, thinking about the world, the one you and I live in, and I come to conclusions. Conclusions and remedies. Lately I've been thinking of *extreme remedies*. For extreme problems we need extreme remedies. That's the phrase."

" 'Extreme remedies'? What d'you mean? And don't go putting me in your brotherhood. I'm just on a neighborhood stroll."

" 'A neighborhood stroll'! Man," he says, pointing a revolver-finger at me, "you'll be lucky if a patrol car doesn't pick you up."

"Oh, I'm respectable," I tell him.

"Listen to yourself. 'Respectable'! You're dressed like a vagabond. A *goon*. It's illegal to walk around at night in this town, didn't you know that?" He stands up to give me an inquiring once-over. He apparently doesn't like what he sees. "It makes you look like a danger to public safety. Vagrancy! They'll haul your ass down to jail, man. They don't allow it anymore unless you have a dog with you. The dog"—he nods at his own dog—"makes it legal. The dog makes it legitimate. *I* have a dog. You should have a dog. It's best to have an upper-class dog like a collie or a golden retriever, a licensed dog. But any dog will do. Believe me, the happy people are all at home and asleep, snuggled together in their dreams." He says this phrase with contempt. "All the lucky ones." He sits down but still seems agitated. "The goddamn lucky ones . . . What's your trouble?" He grins at me gnomishly. "Conscience bothering you? Got a writing block?"

"No. I *told* you. I woke up disoriented. It happens all the time. Thinking about a book, I guess. I have to walk it off. Anyway, I already have a dog."

"I didn't know that. Where is it?" He glances around, pretending to search.

"Sleeping. She doesn't like to walk with me at night. She doesn't like how disoriented I am."

"Smart. So what you're saying is, you don't know where you are? Is that it?"

"Right. I know where I am *now*."

"Maybe you're too involved with fiction. Well, don't mind me. But listen, since we're here, tell me: how does this new book of yours begin? What's the first line?"

I start to pick some chewing gum off my shoe. "Nope. I don't do that. I don't give things like that away."

"Come on. I'm your neighbor, Charlie. I've known you, what is it—?"

"Twelve years," I say.

"Twelve years. You think I'm going to steal your line? I would never do that. I *don't* do that. I'm not a writer, thank God. I'm a businessman. And an artist. Go ahead. Just tell me. Tell me how your novel starts."

I sit back for a moment. " 'The man,' " I recite, " 'me—no one else, it seems—wakes in fright.' "

He kicks the toe of his shoe in the dirt and tanbark, and Junior sniffs at it. Now Bradley tries out a sympathetic tone. "That's the line?"

"That's the line. It's still in rough draft. Actually, it's just in my head."

He nods. "Kind of melodramatic, though, right? I thought it was a cardinal rule not to start a novel with someone waking up in bed. And what's all this about *fright*? Do you really awaken in terror? That doesn't seem like you at all. And by the way I believe the word is *awakens*."

Irritated, I stare at him. "When did you become Mr. Usage? All right, I'll revise it. Besides, I *do* wake in terror. Ask my wife."

"No, I would never do that. What's the book called?"

"I have no idea."

"You should call it *The Feast of Love*. I'm the expert on that. I should write that book. Actually, I should be *in* that book. You should put me into your novel. I'm an expert on love. I've just broken up with my second wife, after all. I'm in an emotional tangle. Maybe I'd shoot myself before the final chapter. Your readers would wonder about the outcome. Yeah, the feast of love. It certainly isn't what I expected when I was in high school and I was imagining what love was going to be, honeymoon jaunts, joy forever and that sort of thing."

I glance at the dog, who is yawning in my face. I bore this dog. "Aren't you going out with a doctor now? Some new woman?"

"That's private."

"Hey, you came up with the title, and then you decide I can't have it because it's a metaphor? And you want to be a character in this book, and you won't give me the details of your love life?"

"Metaphor my ass. I don't know. Call it *The Feast of Love*. I know: call it *Unchain My Heart*. Now there's a good title. Call it anything you want to. But remember: metaphors mean something," he says, sitting up. Junior also sits up. "You remember Kathryn, my ex? My first ex? When Kathryn called me a toad, which she did sometimes to punish me, I'm sure she chose that metaphor carefully. She took great care with her language. She was fastidious. She probably searched for that metaphor all day. She went *shopping* for metaphors, Kathryn did. X marked the spot where she found them. Then she displayed them, all these metaphors, to me. After a while it became her nickname for me, as in 'Toad, my love, would you pass the potatoes?' They were always about *me*, these metaphors, as it turned out. She got that one from *The Wind in the Willows,* her favorite book. You know: Mr. Toad?"

He says this in his low voice and surveys the gloom of the playground, and now, in the dark, he does sound a bit like a toad.

"It could have been worse," he informs me. "A toad has dignity." He looks around. Then he breaks into song.

> *The Clever Men at Oxford*
> *Know all that there is to be knowed*
> *But they none of them know one half as much*
> *As intelligent Mr. Toad.*

"Anyway, I got on her nerves after a while. And of course, she was a lesbian, sort of, a little bit of one, a sexual tourist, but we could have handled the tourism part, given enough time. At least that's what I thought. The real problem was that she didn't like how inconsistent I was. She thought I was the man of a thousand faces, nice in the morning, not so nice at night. Men like me exasperated her. She once called me the Lon Chaney of the Midwest, the Lon Chaney with the monster light bulb burning inside his cheekbone. *The phantom,* she called me, *of the opera.*" He waits for a moment. "What opera? There's no opera in this town."

He stares up into the night sky, then continues. "Well, at least I was a star. You know, women admire physical beauty in men more than they claim they do." He says this to me conspiratorially, as if imparting a deep secret. He sighs. "Don't kid yourself on that score."

"I would never kid myself about that," I tell him. "This isn't Diana you're talking about? This is Kathryn?"

"No," he sighs angrily, "not Diana. Of course not. No, god-damn it, I told you: this was my first. My starter marriage. You met her, I know that. Kathryn."

"No," I say, "I don't remember her. But you weren't married to Diana so long either."

"Maybe not," he mutters, "but I loved her. Especially after we were divorced. A fate-prank. She loved someone else before I married her and she loved him while I was married to her, and she loves him now. The dog and I sit out here and we think about her, and about the business that I own, the coffee business. I don't actually know what the dog thinks about." A little air pocket of silence opens up between us. I hear him breathing, and I look down at his clasped hands. One of the hands reaches into his pants pocket for a dog treat, which he hands to Junior, who gobbles it down.

"You shouldn't do that. Get lost in nostalgia, I mean. But Diana *was* beautiful," I say.

"She still *is*. And I'm not nostalgic."

"But she was unfaithful to you," I tell him. "You can't love someone who does that."

"I almost could. She was powerful. She had me in a kind of spell, I'm not kidding." He looks straight at me. "Nearly a goddess, Diana. I could let her destroy me. In flames. I'd go down in flames watching her."

Just as he finishes this sentence, some noise—it sounds like a crow cawing—filters down to us from very high in the nearby trees. Odd: I cannot remember ever hearing a crow at night. At the same time that I have this thought, I hear a man laugh twice, distantly, from the houses behind us. A horribly mean laugh, this is. It makes the hair on the back of my neck stand up.

"Oh, by the way," I say, "I just came from the football stadium. Guess what I saw."

"They're going to put a big fence around that place." He laughs. "Didn't you know that? A *big* fence. With a gigantic new Vegas-style scoreboard. People like you keep trying to get in."

"There's no fence around it now," I tell him.

"I can see where this is going," Bradley snorts. "Walking around at night, you're soaking up material for your book, *The Feast of Love,* and what to your wandering eyes should appear? I know *exactly* what appeared. You saw some kids who'd snuck into the stadium and were actively naked on the fifty-yard line."

"Well, yes." I wait, disappointed. "How did you know? I mean, I thought it was rather sweet. And you know, I was touched."

"Touched."

"It's hard to describe. Their . . ."

His curiosity gleams at me from his permanently love-struck face.

"Oh, you know," I say. "The waning moon was shining down on them. Like *A Midsummer Night's Dream,* or something of the sort."

"All right, sure. I know. Love on the field of play. Happens all the time, though," he says in a calmer and possibly sedated voice.

For a moment I wonder if he's on Prozac. "Didn't you know that? I grew up around here, so I should know. Kids sneaking in, it's a big deal for them, they can point to the fifty-yard line and say, 'Hey, man, guess what I did down there with my girlfriend? *That's where I got laid, Bub, right down there where that big guy is being taken off on a stretcher.*'"

"Well," I say, "I gotta go."

He grabs my arm in a strong grip. "No you don't. That's the most ridiculous claim I ever heard. It's two in the morning. You don't have to go anywhere."

"My wife's expecting me back."

He sits up suddenly. "Listen, Charlie," he says. "I've got an idea. It'll solve all your problems and it'll solve mine. Why don't you let me talk? Let everybody talk. I'll send you people, you know, actual *people,* for a change, like for instance human beings who genuinely exist, and you listen to them for a while. Everybody's got a story, and we'll just start telling you the stories we have."

"What do you think I am, an anthropologist?" I mull it over. "No, sorry, Bradley, it won't work. I'd have to fictionalize you. I'd have to fictionalize this dog here." I pat Junior on the head. Junior smiles again: a very stupid and very friendly dog, but not a character in a novel.

"Well, change your habits. And, believe me, it *will* work. Listen to this." He clears his throat. "Okay. Chapter One. Every relationship has at least one really good day . . ."

TWO

EVERY RELATIONSHIP HAS at least one really good day. What I mean is, no matter how sour things go, there's always that day. That day is always in your possession. That's the day you remember. You get old and you think: well, at least I had *that* day. It happened once. You think all the variables might just line up again. But they don't. Not always. I once talked to a woman who said, "Yeah, that's the day we had an angel around."

I DON'T THINK that Kathryn and I had been married more than about two months when this event I'm about to describe occurred. About five years ago, we were living in a little basement apartment, and we both were working two jobs. She had a part-time job at the library during the day and she was waiting tables at night. I was the day manager at a coffee shop—not the place where I am now—and getting headaches from the overhead lighting, and I was also doing some house painting, but it was late autumn and the work came in fits and starts.

Kathryn was strong and spirited, she once even threw a chair at me, but she had one fear. She was profoundly afraid of dogs. And not because she had ever been bitten. She claimed she *hadn't* been bitten. No: it was just that when she saw one of these animals, on or off a leash, walking toward her, the hair on the back of her neck stood up. What you might call primal terror. She had no idea of the source of this fear. She just wanted to run away. I once saw her gallop down a steep hill in the Arboretum to escape a dog, a German shepherd puppy that had trotted up to her, its tail wagging, for a head pat. When I caught up to her, she was crying. "I don't ever want to come back here again," she said. "I can't bear it."

"It was a *puppy*, Kathryn," I told her.

"I don't care what it was. None of that matters," she said. I had my arms around her, but then she turned so that she broke free of my embrace. She ran back to our car and locked herself inside, and I had to beg her to let me in. Man, I had to *beg*. And I ain't too proud to beg. She had had her hair pinned up, but in her panic it had fallen down around her face, little tendrils, and her face was blotched with her crying. God, you know I hate to say it, but she was gorgeous like that, and I would have liked to help her. You need to do something for people when they get terrified, but terror is usually so vague, you can't *talk* it out of anyone. What are you going to do when it doesn't matter what you say?

But it's a funny thing about other people's phobias, when you don't share them: you pick at them, like a scab. You want to remove them.

So on this day I'm telling you about, we were both free of our jobs, Kathryn and I, one of those late autumn midwestern Sundays, with a few golden leaves still attached to the trees, you know, last remnants, leaves soaked with cold rain and sticking to the car windshield or clinging to the branches they came from. She woke up and we made love and I said, I'll make you breakfast, and I did, my specialty, scrambled eggs with onions and hot sauce, and then I made coffee, while she sat at the table, smiling, with her legs tucked under her. That was something she did. She sat in chairs with her legs tucked under her like that.

We lazed around and read the Sunday paper and I massaged her neck and then we made love again, and then she said, "I want to go somewhere. Toadie, take me somewhere today, please?" So I said, Okay, sure. We got dressed for the second or third time that day, and we cleared off the pizza boxes from the front seat of my car, do you remember it? that old Ford Escort with the bad clutch? and we drove off. By this time it was about noon, maybe a bit after that.

Without considering what I was doing, I found myself driving up toward the Humane Society, and I thought, the Humane Society? No, I really *shouldn't* be doing this, but I kept driving because I was distracted by the leaves and by a knocking noise from the engine, which turned out to be the lifters, though I only discovered that later.

"Uh, excuse me, but where're we going?" Kathryn asked.

"Up there," I said in my cryptic secretive way. I did have those kennels and cages in mind but thought I should keep quiet about it. You can't tell some women everything. You just can't. Once we arrived, we parked in the lot, close to this animal bunker that the Humane Society is housed in, and you could hear the barking echoing off the walls and the trees. My God, could you hear it. A deaf person could hear it. It's constant and unrelenting. When they're in that condition, dogs have a kind of howl that's close to human, and it makes your body grip up; your nerves get restless and uneasy, listening to dogs crying out, carrying on. The old alarms seep down into your bones, right into the marrow where fear is lodged. And what I did in the car was, I sneezed, and Kathryn watched me sneeze without saying anything. No gesundheit, no God bless you, no nothing. She let me sneeze. Then she waited some more. I waited, too.

"Is this what I think it is?" she asked. "Is this your great idea of where to take me on Sunday, our day off? Because, the thing is, I'm not going in there."

"Kathryn," I said, "it's the Humane Society. They're in *cages.*"

"No, Bradley," she said. "I won't. You probably mean well, *probably,* I'll give you credit, but, no, I won't go in there."

"I'll hold you," I said.

"Hold me?"

"Honey, I'll hold you around the shoulders. And I have an idea. Kathryn, I have an idea about what you should do when you get inside."

"I don't *care* what your idea is."

"I know it. I know you don't care. But let's try. Come on, honey," I said, and I took her hand for a moment. After we got out of the car, I could tell she was terrified because her knees were shaking. Have you ever seen a woman's knees in a spasm? From fear? It is *not* a sight that lifts you up.

In the anteroom, which I remember because the floor was covered with green-mottled linoleum and also because the air was fragrant with a mixture of Lysol and Mr. Clean, the receptionist asked us what we were there for, and I said, well, we, that is, Kathryn and I, thought it was a little early to start a child, but maybe we could manage a dog. We were contemplating adopting a dog, I said, and Kathryn made a little sound, a sort of glottal grunt of apprehension, or a groan, but quietly, so that only I heard it. Guttural. And the receptionist, this young red-haired woman in a yellow jumpsuit, said, Well, it's fortunate for you that these are visiting hours, so you can just go through that door *there,* and then turn to the left, and proceed down the hallway, and you'll see them, the dogs I mean, because they'll be on both sides. And if you want anything, you just come back and let me know.

So I put my right arm around Kathryn's shoulders, and we went in through that door and down the hallway. It wasn't very well lit. Bare bulbs screwed into the ceiling showered raw light downward so that the place looked like an aging army barracks. I don't know what I was expecting. The floors were cement, so they could clean them easily of waste matter, and our shoes, our running shoes, were squeaking over that surface.

You can't imagine the noise. They were all barking and howling and yapping, these dogs of every size, pure dog-desperation, mutt-mania, an army of refugee dogs, and we marched down that hallway between the cages, being roared at, like these dogs were screaming *Save us save us,* and I held on to Kathryn, and then we walked back, with me still holding on, and then we walked down the hallway a third time, and Kathryn said, "You can let go of me now," so I did. I let go of her.

We kept walking back and forth. We weren't about to *get* a dog. No. That wasn't ever the idea, despite what I had said. We were just there, walking up and down that aisle at the Humane Society, for Kathryn's benefit, and after about the fifth time it felt as if we were on inspection, in the dog barracks. Not all the dogs quieted down, but some of them did, and when they did, we began to peer at them, which we really hadn't done before when they were making a racket and they were just generic dogs.

It's when you start looking at dogs that you begin to notice their faces. Is that the word? Faces? Muzzles? And after all in a Humane Society they're mostly mutts, so you don't have anything like a breed to distract you, except for Dalmatians, because people are always buying Dalmatians, thinking that they're cute, and then they get rid of them because they can't stand how difficult and dumb they are. You do notice all the Dalmatians in the Humane Society.

Kathryn was still a bit scared, but by this time she was noticing their expressions. I didn't prompt her. I didn't say anything. And soon she said, I'll bet that one likes a party. And I'd bet that one's a bully. That one's kind of stupid but has a good sense of humor. And that one, he's a recluse. That one's a pack animal. That one there, she's stubborn and independent. That one likes to ride in cars. That one thinks all day about food.

She had her index finger pointed at them. And then she started to name them.

You're Otis.

You're Sophie.

You're Lester.

You're Duffy.

You're Gordon.

You're Daisy.

You're Waverly.

And you, you handsome fellow, she said, pointing down at a dog on the other side of the bars, *you,* you're Bradley.

There *was* a dog there, I admit it, that looked a lot like me, like my brother or cousin, these sort of eyes I have, and its voice was just like mine, a rumble, phlegmy, you know, but strong and commanding like my voice is. Brownish fur like mine, and friendly, like me, but prone to harmless manias, also like me, you could just tell.

And the thing was, as Kathryn was doing this, as she was naming the dogs, going up and down the aisles, something quite amazing happened. One by one, the dogs stopped barking. They just quit. At first I didn't think it *was* happening, I thought it had to do with my hearing, you know, what do they call it, tinnitus, but it wasn't that. The dogs were really going quiet. Kathryn would point at them, one at a time, at one dog, and give it a name—*you're Inez*—and the dog would look at her, and after a moment or two it—Inez the dog—would clam up. And before very long, it grew *really* quiet in there, maybe a yip or two now and then, but otherwise no sound. As if, all that time, all they had wanted was a name. It was spooky.

"I think we had better leave now," Kathryn said. I took her hand and we went back out to the car.

But before we got to the car the red-haired receptionist in the jumpsuit said, "What happened? What the hell did you do in there?" and she went rushing back toward the kennels, and the dogs started howling again, crying out to heaven as we unlocked the car and backed out of the parking lot and pulled out onto the road. We were gone, we were erased from the Humane Society. Meanwhile, the sky had mottled over with clouds.

We lived in a cheap place in one of those student neighborhoods, an old building, really antiquated, one cigarette would have set it afire instantly. I was driving, rushing back to our old building and that apartment, feeling gleeful, and at first Kathryn was annoyed that I had taken her there to see the dogs, you know, paternalistic or patriarchal or something equally criminal, but then she changed her mind, and in her excitement was actually bouncing on the seat, her legs tucked under her, and she said, "I'm still scared of them, but, Jesus, Brad, I was inspired. *Those were really their names!* I gave them the right names. I knew *exactly* what to call them."

"There's no such thing as the right name for a dog," I said. "It's all arbitrary. A name is arbitrary."

"No, it isn't," she insisted. "There are okay names, approximate names, but there's one correct one, and I hit it every time."

And I thought: Well, I dunno, who cares, maybe she's right, why argue. We got home, and we sat down on the sofa together, and she looked so beautiful in the blue sweatshirt and the blue jeans she was wearing, no socks, just her sneakers, these rags, these gorgeous rags that she had made beautiful by wearing them, and the cap she had on, her gray eyes, the delicate way she moved, and in a sudden heedless rush I said, "Kathryn, I love you," and she nodded, she acknowledged it, she didn't say *she* loved *me* but I didn't care and didn't even *notice* that she hadn't said anything in return until about four weeks later when she moved out. But on *that* day, she leaned into me. We held on to each other. Clutching. We must have stayed together in one posture just holding each other, there on the sofa, for maybe an hour. When you're in love you don't have to do a damn thing. You can just be. You can just stay quiet in the world. You don't have to move an inch.

Then eventually she said, "Look. It's snowing."

We disentangled ourselves and got up together and walked over to the window. The air had been abruptly filled, every square inch, with snowflakes, and I thought of how peaceful it was, even though the snow was just this humble artifact. "This is our first snow," I said aloud, thinking that we would have many more years of seeing it together, that we would stand in front of windows year after year, watching the first snow, the two of us, watching the wind swirl it, then watching the spring storms, watching the snow melting and the water rushing down into the storm drains. From now and then onward into forever, this would happen. We would watch our children playing in the melting snow, splashing in the puddles. After we died, we would still be seeing everything together, Kathryn and me. Into eternity, I thought. Death would be a trivial event as long as I loved her.

She must have thought she loved me, too, because she wanted to cook a dinner for me, which she did, a quick Stroganoff, and then afterward, while I was doing the dishes, she was still sitting at the table, and she started to sing.

I had never heard her sing before. I didn't know she *could* sing. I don't think she knew that she could sing. She had a small, a *very* small, but a sweet voice, and in this small sweet voice she sang two songs, I guess the only ones she could think of at that moment, very slow and sultry, "You Are My Sunshine" and "Stairway to Heaven."

Then in bed, later, she sang the Michigan fight song, "Hail to the Victors." Softly and slowed down, in my ear. As a love song. You know: the way you'd sing to a winner. Because after all, I had won her, somehow.

Outside, the snow went on falling.

For days afterward I went back secretly to the Humane Society. I went back there and gazed at the dogs in their pens. I would look at all the dogs that Kathryn had named. Also I was looking for the Labrador-retriever-collie mix she had named Bradley. After *me*. Finally I went in and said I wanted him, and they turned him over to me, but only after they neutered him and gave him his shots. I persuaded my sister, Agatha, and her husband, Harold, to keep him for a while until I had convinced Kathryn about the wisdom of having a dog. I just knew I could talk her into it. I took Bradley up north, wagging and slobbering in the backseat, and left him with Agatha.

Back at the Humane Society week by week the other dogs were gone, one by one they disappeared, replaced by new dogs. The old dogs—the dogs that Kathryn had named—had found homes, *I liked to think,* where they were fed and housed and taken care of, but where they were occasionally unhappy about one thing, which was that they had the wrong name. The name they were supposed to have had been lost, and their owners had given them bogus names, childish names, lousy standard-issue dog names like Buster and Rover and Rex. The only dog who had the right name was Bradley, a name that he and I had to share.

Once in a while I would see a dog out on the street, and I would recognize it from the Humane Society, and I knew that it had seen us, Kathryn and me, two people in love, walking up and down between the cages, holding each other. It had seen that but didn't or couldn't remember. I was the person who remembered.

Now there's Bradley the person, me, and Bradley the dog, him.

You know, that day was perfect. A breath of sweetness. That's a phrase I would never use in real life, but I just used it. You can laugh at my wording if you want to, you can laugh at the names I have for things, I know you do that, but I'll think of that day from now on as a perfect day. A breath of sweetness.

What I'm saying is: that day was here and then it was gone, but I remember it, so it exists here somewhere, and somewhere all those events are still happening and still going on forever. I believe that.

THREE

"DID HE TELL YOU about the dogs?"

"Well, yes. He did."

"And he said that I was afraid of dogs and that he drove me to the Humane Society?"

"That was the gist of it."

"Did he make fun of me?"

"Oh no, Kathryn, he didn't. Certainly not. No—he didn't do anything like that at all."

"Well, you wouldn't tell me if he had. Anything else? Did he tell you anything else about us?"

"He said you two were broke in those days. You worked in a library part-time. He said that you gave names to the dogs, the ones at the Humane Society. You named the dogs one by one, he said. The way he described it, what you did sounded like a blessing."

"He told you that? I don't remember naming anybody or anything. I believe that he may have imagined the entire episode. We did go to the Humane Society once. I do remember all those animals. The barking. But I think we just walked in and then walked out without anything like an event, any sort of story, happening there. We had both been at the Botanical Gardens and we heard the dogs making a ruckus nearby, and we went over to investigate. The rest is probably imaginary. I'm *certain* he made it up."

"I suppose he might have," I tell her.

"This is all so weird," she says. "Your calling me out of the blue and asking me about some encounter that Bradley and I had years ago. Aren't those matters personal? I think maybe they should be. I realize that nothing stays hidden anymore but I'd still like to keep a few domestic particulars private. Especially when it comes to my love life. Such as it is. I can't imagine why anybody else would be interested in who I love or how I loved them."

"Oh, everyone's interested in that. Besides, I'd change your name. You could retain your privacy."

"That's not quite what I'm getting at," she says. "My marriage with him failed. So it's not a matter of pride exactly. I switched partners, but doing that is very difficult and taxing in ways you don't anticipate. Especially when you do it the way I did. It changes your views of yourself and who you are. You said you're a writer. Have you ever read Schnitzler's *La Ronde*?"

"Yes, sure."

"Then you remember what it's about. Changing partners. You should reread it. I acted in it once when I was a sophomore." She waits for a moment, as if imagining it. "I played a housemaid. There was a pantomime lovemaking scene on stage between me and 'the young gentleman.' That was fun."

"Well, maybe you have a story of your own," I suggest. "About what happened to you."

"I have lots of stories," she says. "But they're not the sort you give away, you know . . . and I don't tell them to just anybody. What did you say your name was again?"

I tell her.

"I honestly don't remember ever meeting you. I've never heard of you. Did we ever meet? And this is for a book you're writing, Charlie?"

"Sort of."

"You aren't going to post this whole deal on the Internet, are you?"

"No."

"Thank God. Who are you anyway? Could you please explain that again, that who-you-are thing?"

I try to spell out to her who I am. It's not easy, summarizing yourself on the telephone to a stranger. Before I'm finished, she breaks in. "All right. I think I get the idea," she says. "Okay. That's enough. You want a story? I'll give you one. But then you have to promise me not to bother me anymore. Are you writing this down?"

"Yes."

"Oh. The thing is, you're appealing to my vanity. I suppose I always wanted to appear in someone's book, and I guess this is my chance. I can be a literary entity. Up there with Mrs. Danvers and Huck Finn and imaginary people like that. But you'll just have to understand that I'll only do this *once*. Then you can't call me again. I'm going to check on you before I talk to you again to make sure that you really are who you say you are. A woman in my position has to be careful. To start with, I don't remember you from my Bradley days. You could be anybody."

"Of course. That's right. I could be anybody."

"But if you check out, this is where I'll meet you." And she gives me the name of the coffee shop where Bradley is the manager, Jitters, and she also gives me a time.

When I get there, I am served by a woman whose name tag identifies her as Chloé. Kathryn orders a café latte, sizes me up, then begins to speak.

CHARLIE, I'LL START with a generalization here that maybe only applies to me. Maybe. Please don't be too offended. I always found it a challenge to love men. At first I just thought I had to, that I had no choice. I thought that men in general—I'd really rather not say this—were unlovable. But I mean, look at them. If you're a man you probably may not realize how they are. Amazing when any woman can stay married to one of them. Most of the ones I've known are bossy, or passive and obsessive, the men I mean, and after the age of twenty-five or so they are by most standards *not* beautiful. If one of them happens to be easy on the eyes, he gets hired by the photogenic industry. Beauty is not part of the show they do, most of the ones I've known. So you have to cross that off the list of accountables right away. And you're left with their behavior.

They sulk, men, so many of them. They bear grudges and they get violent almost as a hobby, the ones I've known. Didn't you realize this? Ask around. As a gender they're—you're—always scheming or at least they seem to be scheming because they never ever tell you what's on their minds. The sample I've had. They just sit there day after day and they *brood.* After the brooding, then the firepower. Well, I know these are generalizations, but I don't care, because they're my generalizations, so I don't have to prove them, which is exciting.

I will say that the one feature I like about men is that they can usually figure out how small appliances work. They're good at fixing this and that. But that competence doesn't lead to passion, just to gainful employment. Of course I'm only using the case studies here of the men I have happened to know in my brief lifetime. But a sample is a sample and what I'm describing to you is what I have observed.

They get to you in the small ways. They have their little bag of tricks. You take Bradley. In high school he sat behind me or next to me in English and biology. He was above average whenever he studied, which wasn't that often because Bradley wasn't and isn't particularly studious. While everybody else was taking notes or being rowdy, Bradley was drawing sketches in his notebooks. Of *me.* Day in and day out he did pencil drawings of me *in detail* on paper. Even if his eyes were too large or too direct, he was a good-looking boy in those days when he remembered to comb his hair and to shave, and you should have seen the sketches he did of me. A few of them were confiscated by the teachers. Whenever they managed to steal a peek at what he was doing, the other girls were agog that he loved me so much. Everyone thought we were terrible sweethearts. Jesus. I never knew what I had done to attract his attention. In his hands a picture of a woman could often be more beautiful or arresting than the woman herself. It was hurtful, how beautiful he made me. I thought: that's me? I was just Kathryn before but in his sketches of me I was a miracle. I was extraordinary. I just couldn't get over what he did to me.

Do you understand what I'm saying? He confused me in the way that a lot of women get confused. He had a system going with these sketches so that if he happened to be distorting my beauty by making me more attractive than I actually was, I never had the brains or the wit to notice it. These pictures pretended to be mere records of my looks, standing or sitting or gazing downward in thought, but they undermined me. If somebody makes you beautiful or says you're pretty and then repeats it insistently, you become his victim. He wasn't always detailed about my eyes but I didn't notice that at the time. That was my mistake. I should have noticed. Remember Picasso's trouble with Gertrude Stein's eyes in that portrait he did of her? Rembrandt's portrait of himself in old age—I saw it in London—is as terrific as it is because of what he knew about his own eyes. Go look. Bradley didn't know anything about my eyes and therefore avoided them. They're not really in the pictures.

But because these Bradley-drawn pictures were celebrating me I fell in love with the pictures and then in a standard move I fell in love with the guy himself as the creator of the images in which a beautified version of me appeared. He drew one very elaborate sketch of me riding a horse that just about took the breath out of me. I was both beautiful and muscled, like the horse. A naked woman on a horse, two animals. I thought: if he can see me this way, then what else would I ever need?

Well, much else *is* necessary, believe me. He only loved his love for me and the pictures he was drawing. He loved those two. He loved the feeling he was having. I was a mere accessory to the feeling.

Loving him was extremely tricky because he was inaccessible in a sort of wacky way. Like so many of these twenty-something guys he was a perpetual traveler in outer space. What are you guys looking for out there? Trysts with aliens? I don't get it. Never have. He was one of those men who could talk articulately about anything—food or movies or music or current events—but you could discern in the middle of his conversation that he had commenced to brood about something else that was not making its way into the mix. Right at the table he'd disappear on you and you couldn't get him back. When he made love to me, he had this absentminded sex mannerism going on that eventually drove me crazy. And I don't mean how, with sex, personality has to give way to your desire. That's why it's so hard to talk when you're engaged physically.

Silent physical passion would have been just fine. But I felt insulted after a while: he made love the way you would drive a car to work. Autopilot stuff. Short-little-span-of-attention stuff. What I mean is that he was hardly in the same room with me when we were in bed together. He didn't notice enough how I was reacting. It was boorish. He *hummed* while he was doing it, as if he were changing a light bulb. If he could concentrate on me in the pictures, then why couldn't he concentrate on me in person when I was naked for him between the sheets? It made no sense. I assumed that this elemental problem with his absentminded love would improve, would go away, would dissolve.

I kept reaching for his heart and finding nothing there to hold on to.

Gradually I lost my confidence. That was about when he proposed to me and I said yes. Some mistakes are both simple and huge. The worst mistakes I've made have been the ones directed by sweet-natured hopefulness.

After we were married I realized that I had no particular idea who he was. I once called him the Lon Chaney of Ann Arbor, and instead of being hurt, he was pleased. At least I'm a star, he said. Days would go by without an endearment. He was too young to be a sleepwalker, so I'd try to wake him up. We'd have a nice dinner and we'd rent a movie and then we'd go to bed. We'd kick back the sheets and frolic like a good modern couple, and he would gradually fade on me, he'd look like he was thinking about the stock market. His distance took the wind out of me. And then I got this idea that the trouble I was having wasn't just with Bradley but was a generic trouble. It was with men. He wouldn't share his heart with me. He was preoccupied with the unspoken and would be all his life.

Believe me, most women know what I'm talking about.

AND THEN SOMEONE walks into your life and takes control of the situation.

This was a few weeks before he took me to the dog pound, this episode I'm about to describe. About at the end of the summer, the last week of August. He was correct about the two jobs I had and that he and I were married by then.

Oh, I should tell you one other story about that period. My grandfather was dying. He was getting Alzheimer's and living in an assisted-care facility. I'd go over there to visit him. And one summer afternoon I drove over to see him and went up to his apartment and knocked and went in, because the door wasn't locked. I heard the water turned on in the shower.

"Grandpa?" I asked. He wasn't in the living room.

"I'm in here," he said, calling from the bathroom.

"Okay," I said.

So I waited for him. But he stayed in there. Stayed and stayed. So eventually I stood up, because I was worried and anxious about him, and I went into the bathroom where he had said he was. I looked in through the translucent glass of the shower stall and saw my grandfather in there, and I could also see that he had all his clothes on. Naturally, I was alarmed. I reached over and pulled aside the glass divider.

There—inside the shower—was my grandfather wearing his three-piece suit. He was standing under the spray of water, his wet hair hanging like seaweed down the sides of his head. Even his shoes were on. "Grandpa," I said, "what are you doing in there?"

He looked at me. "The stars," he said. "The stars are so beautiful."

"The stars at night?" I asked.

"What other stars are there?"

I took his hand and led him out of the shower and took his clothes off and toweled him dry and into his pajamas. Then I went downstairs and told the attendants that they would have to take better care of my grandfather, that they would have to watch him more closely.

BUT BACK TO BRADLEY. In those days he had an idea that he was a painter. Of course he *was* a painter. That's not what I mean. He labored as a house painter but his real love consisted of a variety of sly and very odd expressionism on canvas. He became proficient at it. He understood the ironies of his existence, painting houses during the day and making eerie images at night. When you're as young as we were you have a strong sense of the pranks of fate. He had to prove that he could be a *real* painter and not a pretender, just the way that a lot of men feel they have to prove they're *real* men. I've never known what that was about. I don't think that most women have to prove that they're real women. You live long enough, you graduate to being real.

Bradley comes on as a know-nothing but he really admired

artists like Diebenkorn and Jennifer Bartlett and Hockney and all the other painters who knew how to use a light luminescent blue. He loved representational art that was full of problems you couldn't solve just by looking. He loved stylization and stasis and pale pastel color, color that appeared to be temporary or about to fade, colors that might be in danger of becoming obsolete any minute now, blues that were endangered and inadequate. Did he mention that? Probably not. Because he had sold so few of his own works, he grew killingly modest. The more representational his art was, the more abstract *he* became. You couldn't find him anywhere. He turned himself into the greatest abstraction.

As for his paintings, they filled up all the space we had. It was really tricky for me to adjust my attitude toward his accomplishments because I really wasn't sure whether his work's self-consciousness was intelligent or just gawky and shy. He had given up hyperrealism and had gone in for social commentary in faded hues. I remember that he splashed Tip of the Andes coffee on one of his canvases as a judgment against the proliferation of big coffeehouses like Starbucks, but how would you ever know that unless he told you, since the painting was of a window? All his canvases required an explanation or a commentary. They accumulated in the house. They even occupied the bathroom. And his art took up most of his free time. So when he was painting I found other diversions.

I had squeezed in some softball as my one evening sport. I'm a bit of a jock. As a girl I swam constantly and played basketball when I could. I used to love to watch gymnastics. I would rather watch the women gymnasts than the men. I would rather watch women playing basketball than guys. When sports are played by women it speaks directly to my condition. I like to watch their fierceness and the animal pride of female physical movement.

Our softball team was doing pretty well that particular summer. We were blowing everybody else into the ash can. That week—the one I'm telling you about—we had this night game with the Bruckner Buick Devils. They were another women's team and supposedly our rivals. What I liked was simply getting out on the field under the lights during those summer evenings, playing the game, watching the evening come down to earth, the moths flittering in front of the floodlights. I was psyched for it. I had let Bradley know how much the game meant to me.

So on this occasion it was the bottom of the eighth inning. We were ahead, five to four. Bradley sat in the stands watching. He cast his husbandly gaze on me and maybe paid more attention to me as a softball player than as his wife and lover. He had a curious budget of attention, Bradley did, maybe it was the painter in him, maybe he thought of softball diamonds as geometrical abstractions. I was up to bat. Their pitcher was throwing some skillful stuff and they were concentrating hard in the infield and I could hear Bradley from the stands clapping and encouraging me. That was sweet. Give him credit. I had my patient husband the Toad in my corner. So I thought I'd show them, and on her next pitch I connected with what I thought was a line drive.

Their shortstop was a sort of lanky woman. She had that specific appearance of physical confidence as if she never thought twice about making a move before making it. All her moves were ones she did purposefully. First thought, best thought. She did them quickly. Body and mind together. It was certainly beautiful to watch. As an athlete she had no hesitation of the kind that sometimes hobbled me. After my hit, I was two steps off for first base when she ran backward and leaped to her left for the ball. She extended herself and went airborne and caught the ball smack in her glove. *Thmp. My* line drive.

I was out. I was absolutely out and out. What she had done was there and then the most amazing physical move I had seen for I don't know how long, in its concentration and certainty and grace. Most people would have been crushed that they were put out in a game that close. Not me. Not that time. I am telling you it was heart-stopping. To watch that goddess in her ponytail doing that one leap caused me to halt in my tracks. I was almost irrelevant to what she did. I did the hit. She did the move on it. She had *conviction*. God, I loved that. So I stood there like a waxwork. I stayed right on that spot halfway between home and first base. They could have put me into Madame Tussaud's, I was so unmoving. She got up from the ground and dusted herself off. She rubbed her forehead with her forearm. She held the glove up and then threw the ball to the pitcher. She smiled at her teammates and girl-whooped the way you do when you're the *champ* of one particular action that you can do in front of other people. Then she smiled at me.

If a guy did that smile to another guy it might be a challenge to him and an insult. But not hers. Not her spun-steel-and-stardust smile. She was displaying what she could do for me. A very pleasing and smiling woman. And I thought: *this certainly ain't your regular sort of day.* Or your regular sort of game either. Because that night with the moths clustering in front of the lights, when she smiled at me I felt that smile go down through me and out the other side. Some sort of competitive drive in me gave way to something else. As if I was transparent. A burning. Permeable to her smile.

We ended up losing that game. Six to five. Even while it was happening the game was already a quickly fading memory. Losing. Winning. Who cared? Because by that time I was watching her stealthily. I was trying to recover that moment by sheer willpower.

AFTERWARD THEIR TEAM and our team went out for beers at the King's Armor Bar. As it turned out her name was Jenny. I'd seen her before. She worked as a meter maid. Almost like a song: Lovely Jenny, meter maid. Pitchers of beer circulated all around the table. I was the pretty woman in a baseball uniform sitting with her husband and surrounded by other girl-jocks. We were smoking and laughing and consuming the beer. I was being cool. My husband—Bradley—was scrunched up against my left side where I could lean into him and he was talking to the other husbands and boyfriends and girlfriends who happened to be stringing along. Jenny the meter maid had taken a seat on my right. I had not the slightest clue what I was going to do next. Except for my involuntary stomach flips it might have been any night at all. I was ignoring the stomach flips.

Peanut shells all over the floor. Smoke everywhere. Hubcaps decorating the walls. The cap-gun clang and bonk of pinball machines. People saying "Fuck" every five seconds and then laughing *haw haw haw* after they pour beer down themselves.

After all, I was just married. Some women never even get that far. The wedding ring felt *new* on my finger. That little diamond? I could still feel it planted against my skin all the time. When you've got it there for the first few months it feels a little bit like a gender award that you can carry around and display. It has clout. My ring—outside the mitt—broadcast its glitter as if I had just won it in a small-town raffle, the only prize most women get. He had gazed at me fixedly for hours on end and then he had just made me princess of some personal half-secret kingdom. Look, I could say. I am very young but singularly acclaimed. This absentminded man, he's mortgaged his life to me. On me Bradley's pale light has fallen. I'm subject voluntarily to his gaze from here on. It's happy-ever-after time.

She sat on my other side. She had freckles in star-field patterns on the back of her hands, different patterns for each hand. On her right cheek was an odd dimple that appeared whenever she frowned, a dimple to break your heart. Her hair was mostly brownish but with a streak of something blond running through it to punctuate it. Up close I could see her eyes more closely, brown with a tiny flaw of blue in the right one. She was small-breasted like so many athletic girls and she held her shoulders together as if she were cold. She leaned forward and encouraged me to talk about anything. It was odd: she felt like the sun to me. I glanced down and saw Cassiopeia's chair in the freckles on her left hand.

Jenny and I did a conversational dance, something very formal. She didn't say anything about her leaping catch. She was talking about her cat instead. She had a calico cat named Ralph with urinary tract problems. She went on about this cat. Women often do. It's polite to listen. I don't like cats much but I listened to her talk about this cat Ralph and I hung on every word. She got the cat at the Humane Society, by the way. You might be interested in that literary coincidence. By listening to the stories of the cat I learned that she lived by herself in a sort of spare apartment on the north side. One of those apartments decorated with line-strings of plastic hot peppers up near the molding to provide cheer. I was imagining it. She kept her radio tuned to the jazz station. Too much traffic noise in her neighborhood made it hard to sleep. *Hard to sleep.* She said she tossed and turned. Uh-huh. I see. It would be sad to be alone in that bed with the ionizer buzzing in the corner.

And I was thinking: Oh, this is a wonderful moment. I have a new woman friend and I can talk to her about anything, by which I mean all the subjects that Bradley never managed to pay any attention to.

In the bar she was still lanky. Big feet. Long legs. And they all moved in a pleasing languid dramatic graceful performance. As if her body also were busy having a conversation. First it talked to itself and then it talked politely to me. Beneath that politeness glided schools of fish.

I told her that Bradley and I had just been married and that we lived in a basement apartment just as spare as hers, except for his paintings. She appeared to be quite interested in Bradley and so I told her about his work and his art and the jobs we did. She yelled across me to say hi to him, and they shook hands over my lap. Then I explained again about our apartment. Ours was just as spare and empty as hers, I repeated without thinking why. For some reason we got on the subject of female medicine and I gave her the name of my gynecologist, Dr. Moosbrugger. I said I worked a couple of dumb jobs. She listened to me as if every time I made a commonplace observation it was the most noteworthy event of the day. We talked about cloning, hair dye, and personal web sites. As if we were two musicians, we kept striking chords. I don't know how else to say it. She leaned forward toward me. She laughed and nodded. For the first time in my life I felt myself hanging on to somebody's words, hanging on for dear life. By her expression, you could tell that she hung likewise on mine. Tight-rope hanging, as we reached for each other's hearts.

You don't know that you've crossed a border until you're over on the other side. At that point you see where you've got yourself to and whether you're done for or not. Plenty of friendships have a latent erotic component. But before I had even quite realized that I was attracted to her—well, I knew I was because I wanted to be more like her than I was like myself—the old terrible magic coalesced into the air, and I realized with a sort of shock what I wanted to do. Dear God, I wanted to put my hands on her as a trial, just as a test. I wanted to put a hand on her face or on her arm because I thought that if I did that, I would be so happy. I just wanted to feel her skin but of course I wanted to feel the muscle beneath her skin and I wanted to get at the soul underneath that muscle because I could smell it. I had never gotten a whiff of Bradley's soul and at that moment at the table in the King's Armor I had a flash that I never would. The menu of sensations in this post-softball evening was mostly new to me. But at that table I could smell her soul and I wanted it. She being a woman, et cetera, it was scary. But it was uplifting too. That's what you have to know.

When she laughed she opened her mouth and I saw her teeth. Well, now, and hello. I had a new thought: *I love those teeth.* Never in my life have I felt so private to myself with those feelings banging around in my skull. They were white and straight, those teeth, and I thought of a line of French poetry I had learned in junior high: *God, how good it is to look upon her.* I can't remember the original, only the translation. I shuddered with the excitement and fear of it. I was inventing each moment as it arrived as if I were in a car shooting down the side of a mountain without brakes.

I also felt as if I had been shot. That's how strong it was. Or maybe punched. Poor Bradley, he had no idea what was happening to me. Poor me also.

Well, she said, I believe I will put some money in the jukebox. She stood up and sauntered through the cigarette smoke over to the Wurlitzer. Behind her the smoke swirled as it filled the space behind her. As I watched the smoke eddy in those patterns in her wake, I realized that my new friend was just about all that I wanted forever and ever and ever. You can't dictate to yourself what you want. You either want it or you don't. I suppose I was drunk by then. She put a dollar bill into the jukebox and started programming. She stood in front of that jukebox with her hip canted to the right. She was profiling for my benefit, I noticed.

She walked back slowly to the table. Her ponytail bobbed a little as she walked. I'd never seen a woman walking that *comfortably* before. Oh she was secure in herself, and in despair and exaltation all at once I wanted to be free of Bradley and secure in her, and I shocked myself so much with that thought that I quelled it. She did a promenade thing through the smoke and the noise. The noise quieted in my head when she walked. I had the sudden perception that she was my royalty. I would bow down to her somehow. I would do it without drawing attention to myself or to her. She cleared a path through the room and the smoke swirled in to fill the space behind her as previously. Nobody noticed her all that much except me. Majesty and control in a woman was for me a suddenly disarming sight. That, and the way she looked into my eyes as Bradley never had. She saw my eyes.

My grandfather was dying. He took showers fully clothed. Our time here is short.

WE'RE TALKING ABOUT an ordinary summer night in the Midwest now. In a bar. Peanuts fell to the floor. Drunk men roared with laughter. The TV was showing ESPN cars crashing and burning at the Destruction Derby. Inside my head the room grew quite still and warm. She sat down. She put her hand ever so lightly on my knee. I doubt you or anyone else in the known world would have ever noticed, her touch was that deft and soft.

She leaned toward me grinning wickedly. The co-conspirator grin. The we-are-in-this-together-now grin. I could feel her face close to me. *Feel* its presence close to me. I couldn't remember being flirted with by a woman before. Nor did I think that anyone was noticing. Here I was in the New World and no one had noticed I was gone even for a second from the Old World. How did I get here? How did it happen? Someone caught a line drive? Please. But the sequel wasn't the sequel. It was a prelude. Just then the song she had ordered came on. It was Springsteen's "Jersey Girl." Now this song happens to be about a guy who persuades a single mom to leave her baby somewhere with a neighbor so that he can take her—this young mom—out to the docks. They stand out there at the docks and look at the water together and they get gooey.

"This song is going out to Kathryn from Jenny," Jenny whispered. She smiled her mischievous smile.

Now if you're asking me I would say that at that point I could've just taken Bradley's hand and said *Hey I'm tired of this scene, let's go.* I could've told him that I had work tomorrow and had to hit the hay. But at that moment I felt I had some power too. In that little bar competence and majesty were the songs she sang over in my direction. Authority radiated from her, plus this pixie impishness that was both sexual and scarily adult. She had some sort of mean blank-check knowledge of neighborhoods I'd never been to but should have seen by now. I felt girlish. I smiled back at her. And then I leaned back into Bradley. He was stroking my arm with one hand and peeling the label off his beer bottle with the other. The kind of absentmindedness I was used to. He continued to stroke my arm. I was his wifely assumption. He was *still* stroking my arm when I leaned forward in the other direction toward Jenny and put my lips up to her ear and whispered my phone number to her. She smelled of sweat and crushed roses and the future. The lights in the ceiling illuminated the tips of her hair. Then I leaned forward again. Again the sweat and crushed roses. Two women in baseball uniforms, one of them nervous. And told her when to call.

I wasn't even drunk. I had sobered up instantly. I was scared.

At home I stayed awake all night and wondered what in the name of the living God I had just done.

JENNY SUGGESTED THAT we drive out to an apple orchard. This was a month later. She called me and asked if I wanted to get out for an afternoon. Innocent, innocent. She picked me up in front of our local McDonald's. I wanted a touch of anonymity and you can't get much more anonymous than sitting inside a McDonald's waiting for a woman to pick you up. I got in the car and said hi. I was scared but also not scared. *She* gave me confidence. She had girled herself up for the day. She was driving her car barefoot. A warm September, this was. Her painted toenails made a strong impression on me as they pressed on the accelerator pedal. I resisted her for a while by thinking that she was bullying me, erotically. Her clothes were carefully disordered with her blue chambray shirt slightly unbuttoned and her hair loose, and the sun drenched her side of the car.

We talked about books, how boring they were to read but how you loved them anyway.

A few miles out of town, geese patrolled the riverbank. I sat on the passenger side with my legs tucked under me. A couple in a canoe floated down the river. We passed a little Lutheran cemetery on the other side of the road where the headstones were all in German. *Hier ruhet in Gott.* A necklace of brilliant glass beads swung from Jenny's rearview mirror: red and purple and blue. She said she used the beads for navigation. She didn't explain how. One rose lay across the dashboard facing me. Freshly cut. Its stem was wet. She said it was mine. She said it was my rose. That I could have it. This gift was *ordained.*

She told me that she was the youngest of three daughters. I asked her if she had ever loved a woman before. *Loved? Loved?* she asked. She smiled and laughed. Is that what we're talking about? I thought we were talking about being a daughter.

I got scared again. Being teased that way. But then she grinned squarely at the passenger side of the car, where I was.

JUST OUT OF TOWN is an orchard and a cider press. We parked the car and made our way out to the orchard. There're paths between the rows of trees for the people who come to pick the apples themselves and on one of these paths you can tramp up a hill where you are able briefly to see in all directions. The humble soft modest landscape of Michigan surrounded us with indistinct vegetation: the farmlands laid out in their green rectangular symmetries until they faded into haze, then the ever-distant water towers and sky-poking radio transmission antennas. Down below us in the orchard the trees were being mechanically shaken one by one by a motorized device that clamped the tree around the trunk and then vibrated so that the apples fell into a spread piece of rough brown burlap cloth. We watched the apples raining down in a circle and then being gathered and loaded.

Jenny held my hand for a moment. Then she walked backward

and leaned against the trunk of the tree that happened to stand there. She reached up and picked an apple and pulled it off the branch. She bit into the apple and smiled. Then she simply handed it to me. I held the apple in my hand and gazed down at the marks her teeth had made. I raised the apple to my mouth and put first my lips and then my tongue on the spot where her teeth had been. It had a familiar taste. The apple's bright sweetness worried its way into me.

I hardly knew her. We hadn't talked all that much.

Guess what, she said. *I happen to know that this very tree is the very tree of life. What an amazing deal!* Then she laughed and said, Come on. And then she said, You know that you and I are going to be the two best friends ever. We'll share everything. The two of us?

Doing what? I asked.

Oh just being together. Having adventures, Kathryn. Kathryn and Jenny.

STILL BAREFOOT SHE WALKED into the barn where the cider press commanded the central room. They lowered the press over a layer or two of apples enclosed in burlap and held inside a wooden frame. They crushed the apples into mash and the cider flowed out through the slats into an immense wire-mesh drain beneath the press. The guy there operating it, his body looked like a sackful of gravel. The cider poured down into a containment tank. In the mass of details I lost my concentration because at that moment a dog happened into the room. A cocker spaniel. Jovial and harmless of course. That's what they say. Just sniffing around the edges of the room for some doughnut crumbs. I turned quickly away from this dog. I can't bear to be in the same room with a dog. I was on my way out.

Until then I hadn't noticed that the room was filled with yellow jackets and bees. They flew onto the press and made their way onto the Dixie Cups on the corner card table and to the doorway where the late afternoon sun was shining in. I thought: Oh they're just yellow jackets. But just then Jenny cried out. She bent down. She shouldn't have been in there barefoot anyway. We agreed on that later, when we were less dazed. She walked out onto the driveway and sat down. She put her hand to her mouth. Her eyes were squinting at nothing. They squinted as she wept.

Stupid stupid stupid she said. To be stung in there. I am so oblivious. Good Lord it hurts. She glanced up at me. It's just like being stabbed in the ankle with an icepick.

Then she said, I don't suppose you can do anything.

Oh yes I said. Just wait here a minute.

I ran out of the pressing room and went to the back of the barn, the shady side that faces the fields and the orchard. I checked to see if anyone was there within plain sight. Nobody was. I took the cotton bandanna out of my hair. I looked around again and lowered my jeans and my underwear and I squatted and peed a little into the cotton. Funny about what you learn in Campfire Girls. Then I hitched up and ran around again and found her and dabbed at the spot on her ankle where she'd been stung. Her skin was as red as a little cloud at dawn. After about fifteen seconds she smiled and turned that hothouse smile in my direction.

Ah, she said, girl, it turns out that you are the life of me. What's that miracle cure you've got there?

My secret.

I drove back. I drove her car. I didn't let her drive. I didn't drive to our apartment. Not to where Bradley and I lived. No. Not there. I drove to her building. Outside we sat down and talked. That was all we did. I was curious about conversation with her and the atmosphere of calm expectancy that it created. We told each other chapter-and-verse of our lives. What I'm saying is that we waited.

For days after that, I sat on the front stoop, my own, ours. I watched the sun setting while my husband Bradley sat next to me and we shared the small talk of that particular day. And then sometimes he would go inside and I would stay out there looking toward the west as the breezes wafted through the tree (there was only one) in the front yard. I was thinking about her and about the feeling that she gave me.

Two weeks later, after Jenny and I had done some gardening together at one of those communal gardens where you have your own section, collecting a few late-ripening tomatoes in brown paper bags we brought along, we went calmly up to her apartment. We took the tomatoes into her kitchen. I took two of them out and found a small plate and a knife, but my hand was shaking too hard for me to slice them. I put the knife down on the table and looked straight at her.

Then she took my hand and led me to the bedroom. She told me to forget about the tomatoes for a while. In the bedroom we lay down together and we shed our calm exteriors completely and I saw her and when she asked me what I wanted, I said: I want you.

Afterward she sang to me. What she sang was "Hail to the Victors." She meant it as a joke and as an anthem. I learned how to do that from her. Her cat, Ralph, watched us from the dresser. I was miserable with happiness. Our souls had merged. I lay there and stared up at the string of red pepper lights attached with tiny hooks up near the molding, the ones I had bought for her, and I exchanged jealous glances with Ralph the cat who in agitation had knocked over a hairbrush, and I felt the cool autumn breeze blowing across my body and Jenny's where our two souls were lodged, and I heard the Good Humor truck go by on the street, little glockenspiel notes.

Then we both went back into the kitchen and, naked, finished slicing and eating the tomatoes. They were delicious, and she had made me ravenous.

My idea was that I could save my marriage. In some respect I suppose I loved him still. Bradley took me to the Humane Society on a Sunday and we walked among the dogs as he held me, and I guess I named them individually even though I don't remember doing so. I don't see what importance it would have if I did do that, or if I remembered it.

We made love several times that day and each time I came—and I did, believe me—I thought of Jenny. I thought of the flower-garden smell of her soul and how I could just reach in and find her heart any time I wanted it and of how that would be the end of my loneliness here on earth. When he was on top of me, I would hold out my hands above him in the air and imagine that I was grasping her, her invisible spirit, in the air, terrible hypocrite that I am. No, actually, that I *was*. I stopped being a hypocrite. It wasn't the right time to let him know that my soul had flown out of my body and taken up householding in Jenny's. I sang "Hail to the Victors" to him because I missed *her* so much. I felt strong with her and weak with him. Empty and absent.

He said that he loved me but I don't actually think that he did. Or maybe his love just didn't manage to get into working order with me. By that time I had seen love in its final form. I knew what it looked like. It had freckles on its hands, the southern hemisphere on the left and the northern hemisphere on the right. And it wasn't him. Or him with me. Or any combination of the two of us. She was flying my flag by that time.

He said he loved me and I stayed quiet and still. He had married me. You have to remember that. He had ringed me.

Several weeks later I told him. I told him about my beloved. His face fell in all its possible directions, my little husband Toadie, but then he composed himself and called me the only word he could think of, a lesbian. A goddamn lesbian. Well, when something hurts you, you can always find some dumb label for your accusation. Not just dumb but *dumb*. I picked up one of our vinyl kitchen chairs and threw it at him. It missed, by the way.

Anyway, what I've just told you was what prompted the chair incident. I had grown big, and he was trying to belittle me.

YOU THINK THAT what I've just told you is an anecdote. But really it isn't. It's my whole life. It's the only story I have.

FOUR

"I FOUND KATHRYN," I say. "You know, she wasn't at all hard to track down. She's listed in the phone directory. She told me all about it. She told me about Jenny and how she left you and how she threw a chair at you. I'm sorry about that chair, I guess, but it's still a good story."

"Wonderful," Bradley says. "That's *just great.*" He scratches his hair. "But you should realize our marriage was a long time ago, all that stuff, her leaving me and all." He hops up and down twice, an odd gesture. "You didn't have to look her up, you know. You could have taken my word for it. Kind of a small-minded trick, if you ask me, finding people to bear witness to my past." He grins at me. "Isn't this an excellent fire?"

Bradley had called and arranged to meet me at a benefit for the Ann Arbor fire department. They'd be burning an abandoned house—two stories, an attic, and an attached garage, he said—out in the township. The firefighters would be showing the locals how they do what they do, and there'd be a suggested donation of four dollars to help the Firemen's fund. Now we're standing off to the side, in a ditchlike dogleg of the dirt road bordered by poplars and junipers, watching this old firetrap farmhouse burn, as the accelerants planted in the basement explode and speed the flames along. From this distance, the fire has a festive quality. Just ahead and to my left, one fire truck, a tanker of some sort, is spewing water entertainingly through a second-floor window, while the children in the crowd cheer and run around in circles. A Dalmatian sits on another truck, looking rather smug. On the right of us, the fire-fighters themselves, in their yellow coveralls, are watching with academic interest as the house burns.

"It's a great fire," I say to Bradley, feeling the heat on my face. "But as for looking up Kathryn, well, this whole thing was *your* idea," I tell him. "Having everybody give me stories. Besides, the two of us, Kathryn and I, talked in your coffee shop, the one you own. It wasn't secret or anything."

"Kathryn. She's still with Jenny?"

I nod. "She says men are really hard to love. Hard for her to love. We're not very lovable, she says. Do I look lovable to you?"

"I'm not answering that. You're going to have trouble with continuity, Charlie. By the way, you know what you should do? You should talk to my employees in Jitters. They're just kids. *There's* a cross section for you. Start with this girl Chloé. She pronounces it Chloé, not *Clow*-ee but Clow-*ay*—I don't have any idea where she gets that from. Quite a girl. Excuse me. 'Woman,' I suppose I should have said. She's got a boyfriend named Oscar. Chloé and Oscar. They're sweet kids, but I don't think they represent anything. You won't get them to stand as symbols of today's youth, too bad for you."

I give him a look. He ignores me and keeps on talking. "They met at that fast-food place, Dr. Enchilada's. She quit that job. She said she went home smelling of guacamole and that the karma was bad. The karma was bad! Really, you should talk to her. Incidentally, while we're on the subject, you should *stop* talking to me. This is getting much too personal. But as long as you're collecting stories, did I ever explain to you how I got the dog back?"

"No."

"You're going to think this is funny. I know you. It'll make you chuckle. But it wasn't funny at all. It's a comic story, just not comic to me."

———

MY SISTER AGATHA lives north of here, in Five Oaks. You've been there, I believe. She's married to a guy named Harold, who happens to be a barber. A really *incompetent* barber, by the way, just as a barber, though he's a nice guy in other respects, nice enough, anyhow, for what his daily life requires. "Nice" isn't much of a virtue, though; kindness and mildness aren't on the map anymore, not these days. They're trivial. As it happens, Harold learned how to cut hair when he was in the Army. Certainly that could explain it. His father was a security guard, worked for Brinks. You let Harold cut your hair and you'll emerge smelling of Clubman and looking like Boris Karloff out for a night on the town.

They have two kids, my nephews. Harold was in love with a married woman years ago, Louise, her name was, and Louise had a son I always thought Harold had fathered, but that's another story, and I think he's over that by now. He got over that when he met Agatha.

But this was about the dog, Bradley. I had taken Bradley out of the Humane Society and arranged to sneak him up to Five Oaks and to board him with Agatha and Harold, until I had accustomed Kathryn to dog householding, to living with a dog. My sister and Harold have a big house up there in Five Oaks, with plenty of room for a mutt. Their colonial is close to a WaldChem plant, and the house has five bedrooms and didn't cost them too much, because of the chemical fumes or the poisoned groundwater or something, or simply because they're located in central Michigan. It's a huge house. Anyway, I thought it would take about a month for me to talk my then-wife Kathryn into tolerating a canine companion. I thought we needed a dog, *required* one. I thought our *marriage* required a dog. Young married people crave dogs. It cements them together. It gives them baby practice.

But I didn't have to talk Kathryn into our having a dog because she picked up a chair and threw it at me and left me for Jenny.

When she threw that chair, she missed me, by the way. She could've broken my head open. Besides, what was so bad about what I said? Was she a lesbian? Or was it me? As a man? I wanted her to clarify my thinking. I was just trying to get her transformation lucid in my mind. She says I cursed at her but that is *not* the case. I may have raised my voice, but I did not curse. Anyway, after that climactic moment, I was alone by myself in the apartment, and I wanted that dog, Bradley, back. I shouldn't say this, but I felt grief. And I needed that dog. I had nothing to hold on to except that dog, that dog with my name on it, my secret sharer, you might say.

So on a bright Saturday morning in early winter I called my sister, Agatha. I told her I was going to drive up to her house in Five Oaks and get Bradley the dog and take him back home. Thanks for keeping him all this time, I said. I thought I should warn her I was coming, to ensure that she'd be around when I appeared on her doorstep.

"Uh," she said, "I don't know about that."

"What do you mean, you don't know?"

"You can't have Bradley back, is what I mean." There was a long pause, and I could hear domestic noise in the background.

"Excuse me?"

"I'm sorry, Bradley. But I can't do it. You can't have the dog back. We're keeping him."

"Agatha, Bradley is *my dog*."

"Well, not really. Not anymore. He's bonded with us."

"Bonded with you? Wait wait wait wait wait," I said. "We had a deal, Agatha. We agreed. The deal was, you were going to board Bradley for a month or two, you know, enjoy his company, like you would a foreign exchange student, and I would pay you for expenses if need be, and then *you were going to give him back*."

"I know, but that was then. This must sound like a surprise," Agatha said. "But, as I say, we're not going to return him. We're not going to because we can't. I'm really sorry, Bradley, but we're in love with him. The love is total and goes both ways. The foreign exchange student stays."

"Agatha, don't talk to me about love. Kathryn has left me, I'm alone here, I'm very upset, what with my marriage suddenly over, and I need a dog. That dog, that specific dog, and no other. Bradley."

"Oh, sweetie, believe me, I understand. My heart goes out to you," she said. "You know that. I think what Kathryn did to you was just unforgivable. And cruel. She was selfish. She was always selfish. Forgive me, but she was a real bitch, that woman, leaving you without so much as an apology. I'll never speak to her again. But Harold and I have talked about this, and we think that you should go back to the Humane Society and get another dog. I mean, something truly extraordinary has happened here with us and Bradley. I can't describe it. Besides, you can fall—"

"—Don't say that. Don't say I can fall in love with another dog."

"I wasn't going to say that at all," she said, although, of course, she was. "I was going to say . . ." But my sister is not all that quick-witted and couldn't think of a substitute for what she had planned to announce to me.

"Agatha, you gave me your word."

"Well, I'm taking it back. It's null and void."

"You can't take your word back after giving it," I said. "That's dishonorable."

"No? Well, unless I miss my guess, I just did. And honor: well, that's *such* a guy thing."

"Agatha, I want that dog. For God's sake. This is not a joke. I'm talking about my stability here." There was a long pause. Then I said, "Now that I think about it, I could never count on you."

"Bradley, really, I'm sorry, but as their mother, I have to think of the kids. They just *love* Bradley. He's a great kid dog. They can pummel him and he doesn't mind at all. He's what they call a nanny dog. This dog contributes to family values."

"Oh no. Jeez, this is like always. Damn it, you always took things and never gave them back. You took my toys and wrecked them. You wrecked the wind-up parking garage and then later you took my car, I mean my *real* car, the green Pontiac, when I was in college, and you dented it and you never told me until I saw the dent. I should've remembered how you do that. But I thought: *this time* I can trust Agatha."

"Let's not go over that dent business again. I am so tired of hearing about that famous dent. And about trusting me? I guess you were wrong. The dog is bigger than that."

"Agatha, is Harold there?"

"Nope, he's down at the barbershop. It's Saturday morning. Busy time for haircutting."

I heard Bradley barking. I sensed that he knew I was on the line, that I wanted him back. "I'm going to call Harold."

So I hung up on her and called Harold's barbershop.

"Harold," I said, "I want that dog back."

"Hey, bro," he said in his friendly way. "Whassup? I'm kinda busy right now."

"It's about my dog," I said. "I just talked to Agatha. She's being stubborn. She won't give me Bradley back, she says."

"Oh, that. Well, I know, but, understand, she's real insistent and everything, and she does have a point. She's pretty hard to fight with when she has a point."

"She gave me her word."

"Yeah, well. Your sister does that," he said with a sigh.

"Harold, I've *got* to have that dog. Kathryn left me and I'm a wreck."

"You sound like a wreck, I agree with you about that. But listen, Bradley, the kids have gone all crazy about that animal, and I don't think I can return him to you. It's not all that easy, taking a pet away from children." He waited. "You don't have kids. You don't know about how kids scream at you. I mean, they *really* scream at you. They know how. It's like their *job*."

I heard a sound from someone who was presumably in the barber chair.

"What's that?"

"Oh," Harold said, "that's my customer. Guy named Saul. He says I should return the dog."

"He's right. A deal is a deal." I waited. "There's honor at stake here."

"There is? Whose honor?"

In the background, I could hear the customer named Saul saying, "*Your* honor, Harold."

"Listen," Harold said, "it's a busy morning and I have to go."

"Harold, you and Agatha promised—"

"Good-bye, Bradley. I'm sorry. I truly am."

And he hung up on me.

I HAD NEVER REPOSSESSED a dog before. But that was what I would have to do. First I had to go down to Jitters for several hours to supervise and manage the staffing and work on the books. Also, we were still training Chloé—she'd left Dr. Enchilada's, as I said, to do bookkeeping for us at the main downtown Jitters. But by two in the afternoon I thought everything was under control in the place, the customers jabbering away on their caffeine highs, spraying bagel crumbs in every direction, and so I changed clothes in the back room and hopped in my car and headed up toward Five Oaks. I had taken along Bradley's old leash, some Milk Bones and kibble, a bowl for water, and some squeak toys, including a squeak cat I thought he'd like to chew on.

The trouble was that I had lingered over a bit too much caffeine myself, with the result that my nerves were on fire, and I was pulled over and ticketed on I-75 just north of Bay City for driving eighty-five miles an hour. Mr. Toad is a fast driver, I'll admit that right now. The patrolman was a squat, bullet-headed youth with a mean and forthright expression of contempt. When I pulled out my wallet from my sport coat, several nuggets of dog kibble cascaded out. The cop, seeing this, intensified his expression of scorn. His face looked as if it had been made of concrete.

"Officer, *everyone* was driving that speed," I said, sounding authoritative, like a war correspondent. "We *all* were. I don't see why you singled me out."

"Sir?" he said. Even his voice sounded concretelike. "Let me ask you a question. Have you ever gone hunting? Up north?"

"Hunting? Once or twice. But I don't see what—"

"—Duck hunting?"

"No. Maybe once."

"Well," he said, "if you've gone duck hunting, and you were *there* in the marshes, let's say in the early morning, you know, at first light? When you aimed your gun, would you shoot at the individual *duck,* or would you shoot at the whole *flock?* You'd aim at one of them, wouldn't you? That's what I did. I aimed at you. And it seems I landed you."

So he opened his book and wrote out the ticket. But I explained to him as he wrote that I had been in a hurry to get a dog, *my* dog, and I explained about my wife leaving me—the caffeine still had me in its grip—but he seemed quite unsympathetic, and unmoved, and certainly not about to eat the ticket on my behalf. He was a callow youth with a simple idea of lawbreaking and had suffered no setbacks in the wars of love. He wore no wedding ring, I noticed. He said to me, after I had finished my presentation, "Things will go very ill for you if you are caught speeding again soon." Where do they find phrases like that? He was still trying to act the part.

Also, to compound my difficulties, it had started to snow, and the snow reminded me of Kathryn and of how we had once stood in front of a window hand in hand after going to the Humane Society, and how she had betrayed me, and *her* betrayal got mixed up in my head with Agatha's, with the result that the dog started to seem like the solution to just about every aspect of my life. How pathetically low the stakes had fallen. So after getting ticketed the first time, I forgot about how fast I was going, with the result that about thirty miles north of my previous encounter with the law, I was pulled over *again,* about half a mile south of an outlet mall, but this time by a different guy, a *better* guy, though not Highway Patrol fortunately, but a local cop this time. He was a cop with soul, a midwestern rural African-American cop I'm talking about now, married this time, who was more sympathetic to my story, and who, with a downcast expression, issued me a warning.

APPROACHING FIVE OAKS, I took the Oak Street exit off the freeway and drove past Bruckner Buick and crept past the Wald-Chem plant where Agatha worked as an administrative assistant to the CEO, this guy Schwartzwalder. There was a smell in the air of slightly rancid cooking oil mixed with the odor emanating from the paper plant near the river, an odor of cardboard and vanilla, a numbing upsurge of profitmaking industrial aerosols. I turned off the car radio so no one would know I was coming. I drove into town on little cat feet.

Unlike the cat, however, my car was slipping and sliding. My helplessness had lost its sense of comedy. It had become inane. I saw my reflection in the rearview mirror, and the expression on my face, of outraged innocent depraved desperation, frightened me. My car skidded and slipped onto a sidewalk. Fortunately, no one was walking there or I might have killed somebody. I threw the car into reverse and resumed my undertaking, my car yawing down the avenue.

I arrived in due course on their block, Agatha and Harold's. It's actually a nice enough neighborhood, tree-shaded, large old houses, solidly middle-class, lawns spray-painted with herbicidal chemicals in the summer. This being late fall, they already had their Christmas decorations assembled and displayed outside, with an

enormous plastic sleigh and eight plastic electrified reindeer dese-
crating the roof. The noses on these reindeer blinked sequentially,
and below them the MERRY CHRISTMAS sign burned brightly
even in the daytime. The sleigh was cluttered with tinfoil gift para-
phernalia. I think Harold put this up in September, a foible of his.
Despite what you might think, I am not a cruel man, and I realized
insightfully that I could not knock on the door and take Bradley
the dog by stealth or force during the Christmas season. In front of
the children, Tom and Louie, the event would be traumatic, it
would spoil their holiday memories forever—Christmas would
from this day onward be the time of year when they had lost the
family dog—and I would eternally be the monstrous ogre uncle.

So I parked about two houses away and advanced toward the
perimeter of the house, glancing in every direction. My footwear
caused me to slip on the ice. I fell with a great snowy thump. I may
have looked like a comic figure but my insides were churning with
misery and gastroenteritis. Next time I fell, my coccyx would be
smashed into pieces. I stood up and pretended that nothing had
happened, wiping the tears out of my eyes, tears of pain and suffering and rage.

My inner life lacks dignity. There's nothing I can do about that.

My hope was that the dog would be in the back yard, romping,
alone by himself, available for capture.

No such luck. There was not a sign of Bradley. I checked the
windows and walked around the house twice, stumbling once over
the Christmas wiring. The house, despite its Christmas decorations, had an air of solitary warm security and the light of settled
domesticity. It glowed in a way to break your heart. So after I had
walked around the house twice, my spirit sinking, I saw Tom, my
nephew, looking out the kitchen window quizzically at me. His
scrubbed, freckled face appeared to float above a pot of dusty
African violets on the sill. When he saw me, he smiled and waved.
His hands had smears of dried chocolate pudding on them. I
pointed at the back door. He ran back to let me in.

In the mudroom, he gave me a hug, God bless him.

"Hi, Uncle Bradley," he said. "What're you doing here? Did they invite you?"

"Is your mother around?" I asked. I heard the sound of the TV set in the living room.

"Naw, she's upstairs, taking a nap." He pointed at the mudroom ceiling. "I've been watching *Power Rangers*. Wanna see it? Louie's over at a friend's house."

"Okay." I breathed out. Things were going my way. "Where's Bradley?"

"He's—" And just then the dog padded into the room, as if by thought command. When he saw me, he wuffed once, and leaped up and put his front paws on my shoulders and began licking me on the face. It was just demonstrably what I needed. Passionate dog kisses were better than none at all, and were in fact more sincere than quite a few of the human variety I had been getting lately. Dogs don't kiss you in public just for the sake of appearances. "*There* he is," Tom said, with a child's delight in noting the obvious.

I thought for a moment. I would have to explain a delicate matter to my nephew, whom I loved. And I decided that I would have to tell him the truth. I was on a rash mission, but I was probably not a despicable person, and I was not about to lie to a child, at least one who was my relative.

"Tom," I said, "I have to have Bradley back." I explained how Kathryn and I had found him in the Humane Society, how she had left me sad and alone, how she and I were getting a divorce, how I was feeling so awful that I couldn't sleep at night, and that Bradley had *always* been my dog, because I had found him in the Humane Society, and that he had been boarding up here at Five Oaks for a few weeks, but now, I really really *really* needed to have him back.

"But he's our dog now!" Tom said tearfully, and I felt my chance slipping away.

"You can get another dog," I said.

"Where?"

"They have places," I said, "right here in Five Oaks, Humane Society places where they have every kind of dog, especially sad homeless dogs. They're in prison there. They cry all night. They want homes."

"But they'll be expensive!" he said. "We caaaaan't do that!"

"Not that expensive."

"Oh, yes, I know they will be."

I took out my wallet and opened it. I showed him the money inside. "How expensive do you think another dog would be?" I took out a five-dollar bill. "Five dollars, you think?" I put it into his hand.

He gave me a measuring look. "More than that."

I took out a ten-dollar bill. "Fifteen dollars?"

"That says ten on it."

"But you already have a five. Five and ten is fifteen."

"Oh. No, more than that, I would just betcha."

I took out a twenty from my wallet and pressed it into his little child's palm. "This much?" I asked. In the background I heard the Power Rangers killing something that sounded like a giant worm equipped with buzzers. "Think this is enough?" I wouldn't do any more arithmetic to confuse him.

"Maybe a little more."

I took out another five. "How about this?" He grabbed at it. "A five, and a ten, and a twenty, and another five. You could certainly buy a dog for *that*."

"Not as good a dog as Bradley," he said.

"Oh, better, Tommy, much better. Besides, that's all the money I have. They have golden dogs, dogs who wait for you while you're at school, and dogs that fetch the paper, and dogs that sleep with you at night and watch television with you, any show you want, and dogs that'll sit at your feet at the dinner table and eat the food you can't stand to eat. You can just buy a wonderful do-everything dog now."

"Bradley does all that."

"Listen," I said. "You just go ahead and stuff that money into your pockets and then hide it and be sure not to let your mom put those trousers into the washing machine until you've taken the money out, and don't tell your mom or *anybody* else that I've been here until she wakes up, and I'll take Bradley with me, and he'll make me happy again, and then you and Louie can go down to the Humane Society and pick out a dog of your own with that money I just gave you. No more blue Monday ever again. Okay?"

"Okay. I guess." He scooped up all the bills and stashed them in his pockets, as I had instructed him. "Can I kiss Bradley good-bye?"

"Sure."

Bradley sat with me in the front seat all the way down to Ann Arbor. I drove the legal limit. It isn't every day that a toad can free up a dog. We listened to the jazz station from Detroit, and when he stood on his four legs on the passenger side, he smiled at me with his big dopey face, as friendly and as unsubtle as a billboard. His tail wagged, but not in time to the music. Let's not get sentimental. That dog never had an ear for jazz.

SHE CALLED ME at dinnertime, as I knew she would.

"I cannot believe you did what you did!" she shouted. I had to hold the receiver away from my ear. Enraged spittle was teleported over the phone lines and was spattering out of the earpiece. "You stole the dog! Damn you, Bradley. What is the matter with you?"

"Watch your language. You have children. I didn't steal him," I told her. "I *bought* him back. It was Dog Liberation Day."

"You bribed Tommy. *Who* would do that to a child? You *are* a monster. I am truly, truly angry at you."

"Uh, no. I didn't bribe your son. He shook me down."

"You paid him fifteen dollars for Bradley? That's a rotten trick. Goddamn you!"

"Honor is *such* a guy thing," I said. "Uh, what did you just say?"

"I said you paid him fifteen dollars. That's low. That's the lowest you've ever gone."

"Fifteen dollars, eh?" My nephew was a child of deep cunning, I was discovering. "You get what you pay for. What was Harold's reaction?"

"You called him at the barbershop! You brainwashed him. He's changed his tune. He never liked this dog anyway, he *says*. And now Louie is saying that *he* never liked the dog either. I think Tommy paid him off to say that. Only me! I was the only loving one! You guys are ganging up against me. You're all against me!"

"Now you're self-dramatizing," I said coolly. She slammed the phone down.

THE UPSHOT OF IT WAS, I kept Bradley. I fed him and petted him and I built him a doghouse and called his name when I came home, and in return he loved me. My sister and brother-in-law found another dog, as I knew they would. Whom they also named Bradley. Now there are three Bradleys. Their Bradley is smarter than this Bradley, but I don't care about that at all, not really, because at least with pets, and for all I know, people too, intelligence and quick-wittedness have nothing to do with a talent for being loved, or being kind, nothing at all, less than nothing.

FIVE

OSCAR AND ME, we had such good sex together we thought there ought to be a way to make some money out of it, to live off of our crazy ruinous love forever. Only we hadn't figured out how. Oscar's real good-looking once you get his clothes off and his body into its characteristic behavior. As a boyfriend he's kind of indescribable. Words violate him. And me, Chloé, I'm even more that way. There's almost no point in me saying anything about myself because the words will all be inhuman and brutally inaccurate. So no matter what I say, there's no profit in it.

Still: once upon a time he, Oscar, had been a stoner, sort of upwardly mobile from pot to hash and XTC and heroin, but it was just an excursion for him, Oscar being ambitious in other directions. He got fascinated by oblivion but discovered its secret, which is that it's boring. But on some days you could look at him standing and eating a cheeseburger and see from his eyes that he had been ruined for a spell. He had been briefly tragic.

He told me once that in a drug dream he'd seen the famous African whispering monkey. The whispering monkey told him awful things about his possible future, bleeding scabby death in garbage alleyways, and that was what sent him into rehab.

After his substance-abuse experiences he became advanced, a reformed boy outlaw. Plus, we were, as I said, both real lively between the sheets. We were swoon machines.

———

WE MET AT THIS fast-food place, Dr. Enchilada's. They'd just hired him, Oscar, he was new. He had to wear the little paper hat over his semiblond hair. It's the law in this state, for hygiene. He came in and he looked at the hat, turning it in his hands. When he finally put it on, he wore it an angle, like he was *not* wearing it. He had an *attitude* about the hat, which made it okay and unopinionated. He was above the hat, the hat wasn't above him. That day, they gave him five or ten minutes of training, and then he was working the register, Mr. Can-I-Help-You, but looking bad and cool and totally unhelpful, and I was on the taco assembly line gooping on the guacamole. I was only looking at him occasionally, in secret, him being the new boy. It isn't really guacamole, by the way. They call it guacamole to keep up appearances at Dr. Enchilada's, which is owned by Citibank or somebody.

Anyway, we took a break together. We went outside to the parking lot for a smoke. He was still wearing the hat. To make conversation, he pointed at my ear and said, "Your name's Chloé? That's cool. Well, hey, Chloé, you're pretty but you're way underpierced."

So I kicked the dead caterpillars in the driveway and said, *Fuck you* but, you know, giving it a friendly girlish inflection, a smile, an invitation, just the right tone to start flipping him out.

He said, smiling back, "No, no, really, just one isn't enough." And he raised his finger to my earlobe. His hand motion was halfway on its journey to being a caress. It was then I noticed how nice-looking he was. The blond hair, the snaggle-toothed smile, the bomb-shelter eyes. A cute guy who can look at a woman such as me directly and not turn away has the courage of a mountain climber. Sometimes they get scared off by the eyeliner and the mint-green glint in my cornea, and they worry that they won't be up to the challenge. But boys in recovery have that reentry calmed-down zombie look, which you can't buy in stores, and they do sometimes turn it to their advantage if they aren't scared of girls. Oscar looked burned away and rebuilt, like a housing project. Survivors are sexy, sort of the way secondhand clothes are sexy because they *hang* right, you don't have to break them in or get the sizing out.

When he looked at me, he was sending me a signal that extended into the future and made my teeth rattle. He said he was pierced all over the place. And he told me about *where* he was pierced, including his tongue stud, and also the secret tattoo he had, of the skull, which said "Die."

I was deeply impressed. Also he had nice shoulders, despite everything he'd been through. He had been an athlete once, before indifference took him over and he absolutely no longer cared who won anything. I felt no lust toward him at that moment but knew that I would within a few brief hours, the itch starting in my heart and moving downward into my hands.

We went back to work. That afternoon it was kind of electrical as I watched him take orders and fuck up when he gave change.

That night when I told my best friend, the Vulture, about it, the Vulture said Oscar and I would happen, that we were inescapable and inevitable. She's never wrong about things like that, the Vulture isn't.

HE GOT MY PHONE NUMBER, in that house where I was living with about sixteen other people. They were all from high school, and we were existing generically and domestically together before we found serious jobs and apartments and lives that we could claim as our own. Some of them were working at this coffee franchise, Jitters. For this guy Bradley. I ended up working there. I guess you know him, obviously.

At home there was this constant desperate party going on day and night, which can be depressing and effortful. You get tired of the burns in the furniture and how the bathroom is always locked, or, when you get in, there are potato chips floating in the toilet. Anyway, Oscar'd call and say, *I want Chloé*. Not, Can I speak to Chloé? Or: Is Chloé there? But every time: *I want Chloé*. I liked that, especially the "want" part. My roommates taught him to say *Please*. They'd imitate him, these girls. *Give me Chloé I want Chloé*, was their envious little whine. The Spice Girls I lived with—Dopey and Sneezy and Slutty and Bookish—they were so urbane that they pretended not to eat or to cook or anything—they subsisted on air and bulimia. So Oscar took me to some movies and we ate popcorn out of the same bag. As a gift, he gave me his syringe and his spoon and his rubber tubing thing. He put them in a box with a sort of rubber band around it. He told me never to give them back, that I was the new event in his life, the new car in his driveway. The old events were passé. Things developed between us. I'm summarizing here.

He told me that he was burning for me, and he meant it. When he was around me, he gave off a smell of young man musk, mixed of salt and leather and grass. He'd stare at me desperately, smoldering his life away.

To be more romantic than we were, you'd have to kill yourself in the middle of the street and then write about it. Shakespeare did that.

He took me out to dinner at the Happy Chef, for example. The Happy Chef himself is outside the restaurant on a concrete pedestal. He's ten feet tall and made out of plastic and wood and glue. He's the symbol of everything that happens inside. Oscar let me press the button at the side of the Chef that makes the Chef talk, from a recording. "Hello. While you're at the Happy Chef, you may notice that some of the water glasses have no ice in them. This is not because we forgot to put ice in the glasses—all of our water comes with ice in it—but because the water got hungry, and ate the ice." Like that. We laughed sadly at the lame-o humor, then went inside for hamburgers. Oscar put his foot between my legs, and he touched the inside of my wrist with his fingers. I loved it, how high he carried a torch for me. It was romantic, at least as romantic as my life ever gets.

But! He still lived with his father in Ypsilanti. He took me over there and showed me his knife collection stashed under the bed in this velvet-lined box. He wouldn't let me touch his knives. Because I would hurt their aura. He *said.* As if I could blunt a knife! Also I got shown his stamps, that he had collected in fourth grade. Those I could touch. He still had his track team medals up, and his track shoes on his windowsill, all this boy-holy shit. He had run the relays. That was the last thing he did before he tried out syringes filled with mind-soak for a little while. But what really got to me? Was that he still slept with his Bert. Or maybe it was Ernie. It was the one that looked like President Bush, with the pinhead, whichever. Oscar gave it to me when I asked for it because it smelled like him, grass and vinegar and musk. It had Oscar-aroma.

His father dynamited tree stumps for a living, then hauled them away. That's what Oscar *said* he did, though even Oscar wasn't sure about his dad's total occupation. Early on, I saw Oscar's dad a few times, through the window, coming home in his truck. He didn't come inside back then. I believed it: about the dynamite. Oscar's dad had the strangest name I ever heard of on a man: Batholdt. And that was only his *first* name. Everybody called him the Bat. Oscar had to hide the fact that he slept with Bert from the Bat. The Bat was scary. The Bat *is* scary. Oh, you who are reading this book, brothers and sisters, look over your shoulder, for the Bat crouches behind you.

OSCAR SAID, You won't believe this, but I think of sex all day long. I didn't while I was temporarily a teen junkie but now I do again. Sex has made me totally pointless in the human realm. I would know stuff like the capital of Mormonism if I wasn't Mr. Obsessed. My mind is a pornographic event. I'm an onionhead. Oh, Chloé, you set me on fire.

But I—me, Chloé—was sick that way too, though not about boys generally, just about love, and then sort of gradually about Oscar. He made me feel actual. When I was with Oscar I felt I was in prime time. So I told him that, and when I did, his eyes lit up as if we had a connection, a plug to a socket. Then a week or so later he said he thought of *me* all the time, how he wanted to be with *me,* and talk to *me,* and how he was distracted at Dr. Enchilada's, thinking about me, how much I was a car that he wanted to drive, no, not a car—*the* car. I would take him to heaven. It was so sweet of him to say that. He had a streak of romanticism, it turned out.

By then I had earrings all the way up and down my ear. He had done his vibe on me and I had answered. Also, we had talked all night long twice, by phone. We said that no matter what, we'd be there for each other. So then we did the inevitable and fucked happily several times and he sort of moved in. Not that he really moved in, he was just there all the time day and night, touching me everywhere. My roommates, the Spice Girls, tried to ignore him. As if they could ignore a boy that beautiful, good in bed, as I carelessly bragged, a boy in recovery and therefore almost glamorous, a knight in shining armor galloping out of rehab.

But then we decided we *had* to move out, this particular night when the noise level was extreme, a headbanger party, bodies everywhere, every room a mosh pit. This couple, these two sexual fascists, they were kissing and molesting each other unobtrusively —they *thought*!—in the kitchen, standing up. But it was show-offy, whatever it was they were doing, and unsanitary besides. I didn't even know them. They were friends of somebody. When I told them they should find a bed like everyone else, the girl stopped what she was doing and said that being a food-service professional had warped me and would I please keep my opinions to myself.

How'd she know about my day job? It had to have been that they had seen me at Dr. Enchilada's tricking out the tacos with the guacamole pistol. There and then I decided to get another position somehow. I don't know, maybe the Spice Girls had been talking about me. But these two, they were *blocking the refrigerator*. You just don't do that at a party. When you don't know the people who're doing it, sex, or whatever those two were doing, can be repulsive and karma-damaging, if I may be so bold as to say.

So me and Oscar decided to take a walk.

We went down the side streets in the dark. I could hear locusts, and the hot night air lay like a damp towel against my skin. I saw this pre-teen girl doing cartwheels on her front lawn, back and forth, slowly and sweetly, as if she were performing all those actions as absentmindedly as a Ferris wheel. She was wearing a charm bracelet, and tinkling came from her wrists. I said, "I used to do that. I used to practice back flips. I was into cheering."

Oscar said, "You?"

"Yeah. Once upon a time, I wanted to be a cheerleader. So I was. For the wrestling team."

"No kidding."

"Yeah. But I guess I got degenerate, or something. That was when people didn't believe my cheers anymore, I guess. My cheers weren't infectious."

We walked on quietly for a while, hand in hand.

Oscar said he'd read in the paper about the Perseid meteor shower. Because it was August or because it was time for them to die. The meteors were all suicidal. They were bored with space, he said, looking up toward the night sky. They were burning themselves up in the atmosphere. A meteor deathfest. It was romantic, the way trees are romantic, and the way Oscar could be romantic if he set his mind to it. Also cosmological, a word I once learned. He pointed out constellations to me, the ones viewed for centuries and named for kings and queens. We were walking hand in hand and then we were talking about this new music group, Castro District, that we both liked. Our conversations were getting deep and personal the longer we talked. I could feel his love entering me through my spine. And we'd look up to see a meteor, but, fuck and alas, all you could see was another street light.

So Oscar said, Chloé, we *gotta* sneak into the Michigan stadium.

Which was how we got in there, to see the meteors, because Oscar? he'd been there before, he knew the secret way which I can't reveal to you, it's like almost a CIA thing, they can *kill* you if they find out you know. He took me right to the fifty-yard line, and we looked up at the sky. It was pitch dark, extreme dark in there with only the grass under you. You could hear sounds of traffic miles away. Trucks shifting gears. People shouting and screaming. People contemplating murder. The usual summer sounds.

Oscar said, Man it's suddenly cold out here.

I said, Well, what d'you have on, one layer?

Yup. No kidding, it's like: nipples, air.

That was when, boom, I saw one, a meteor. It was a streak. Then, ten seconds later, boom, another one, another streak. I'd never seen anything interplanetary before, at least not in real life.

And Oscar, next to me, says, Honey, did you see it?

That was what he called me. Honey. An endearment! It blew a fuse in my brain because, for all the quasi-romantic encounters I'd ever had, no boy had ever managed to say anything sweet to me, at least that he *meant*. My life had entered a new phase then and there because I knew that Oscar loved me and not only loved me but was able to say so. So I got all hot all of a sudden, I felt like dancing in my bare feet on the grass almost, and so I said, Oscar, gimme a Slurpee. Please, please, please? I want to look at the meteor shower while you gimme a Slurpee.

Slurpee is a name we have for this sexual thing we do. So we got my jeans off and my underwear and I lay down on the grass. It wasn't cold anymore. I only worried about the grass. That it would tickle. But it was just doing what grass does, growing under me and photosynthesizing, so I didn't mind it at all. Oscar, he went to work with his tongue down there on me and before very long I was clutching at the grass and saying his name and cheering him on like the pom-pom girl I once was and looking at the meteors streaking across the firmament. He has this really talented tongue. The stud on it helps, too. I started coming and almost couldn't stop. It was the best Slurpee I'd ever had.

So after a little, you know, after I'd recovered, I thought, now Oscar gets his reward, now he gets a prize, so I took his clothes off with my hands and teeth thread by thread and laid him down on the grass and scrambled on top of him. He looked up at me, no kidding, with hunger and impatience and appreciation. It doesn't take much to make a boy happy, often the basics are enough.

So he was lying there, sky-gazing. Deep inside me was Oscar, big and hard as thunder, doing the reliable thrusts that keep life going, the meteors showering all around us. And I was working away on him, moving my premium American-girl hips up and down, and then I looked up at the stands, built solidly way in the distance and bolted into the concrete.

And that's when I saw some guy sitting in the stands and looking down at us in the dark. It gave me a karma whiplash, and an idea.

SIX

SINCE YOU ASKED, I live next door to Bradley W. Smith. I see him walking his dog, also called Bradley. What is this, that a man should name his dog after himself? The man runs a local coffee franchise, a modest achievement, in all truth. Megalomania can strike anywhere, I suppose is the point.

After he lost his second wife to another man, I decided to explain to him about Kierkegaard.

AS A JEW, I am drawn in a suicidal manner toward the maddest of Christians. Kierkegaard, being one of the craziest and most lovable of the lot, and therefore, dialectically, possibly the most sane of them all, is of compelling interest to me. All my life, I have tracked his ghost doggedly through the snow. Lonely, eccentric, and crazed, the man Kierkegaard worried continuously about the mode in which one might think, or could think, about two unknowns: God and love. These were for the hapless Kierkegaard the most compelling topics. They bound him in tantalizing straps. Of the two vast subjects about which one can never be certain and should therefore perhaps keep silent, God and love, Kierkegaard, a bachelor, claimed especial expertise. Kierkegaard's homage to both was multifarious verbiage. He wrote intricately beautiful semi-nonsense and thus became a hero of the intellectual type.

AS A MEMBER of the bourgeoisie, I live quietly in this midwestern city of ghosts and mutterers. Everywhere you go in this town you hear people muttering. Often this is brilliant muttering, *tenurable* muttering, but that is not my point. All these mini-vocalizations are the effect of the local university, the Amalgamated Education Corporation, as I call it, my employer. It is in the nature of universities to promote ideas that should not be put to use, whose glories must reside exclusively in the cranium. Therefore the muttering. There are exceptions, of course. The multimillionaire lawyers and doctors and engineers—how did they get into the university in the first place?—live here among us in their, to quote Cole Porter, *stinking pink palazzos,* and motor about in their lustrous sleek cars. The warped personalities, like myself, like my prey Kierkegaard, walk hunched over and unnoticed, or we wait at the bus stops, managing our intricate and tiny mental kingdoms as the rain falls on our unhatted heads. We wait for the millennium and for Elijah.

MY WIFE IS ESTHER, a tough bird, the love of my existence. She works as a biochemist for one of the local drug companies. It was Esther who years ago found out that the wonder medication Clodobrazole deformed babies in the womb, gave them unnatural shapes, took away toes and fingers and entire arms. If Esther's mother hadn't joined the Party as a young woman (and who else but the Reds was trying to desegregate the public beaches in those days? who else had a *single* social idea worth implementing?) and hadn't put Esther in red diapers, and hadn't signed Esther up for the Party as a child, she would have been proclaimed, my Esther, from the rooftops. But somehow, in the shower of publicity, some measuring worm looked up her background, and, though Esther as a youngster was blameless, and not a Leninist but a reader of Trotsky, that was that.

We live, in all truth, a tranquil domestic life. We have a year or two to go before retirement. Mondays, Wednesdays, and Fridays I cook dinner. My specialty is a beef burgundy, very tasty, you have to remember to cook it slowly, covered of course, in the liquids so that the meat and the onions and the potatoes become tender. Tuesday and Thursdays are the nights when Esther cooks. We read, we talk, we play canasta and Scrabble. We feed the two goldfish, Julius and Ethel. *They must live.*

As is proper, the children—all grown—have left home. We have three. The oldest, our beautiful daughter Sarah, is, like her mother, a biochemist. She is successful but, so far, unmarried. She would be a handful for any man. I mean this as praise and description. The middle one, Ephraim, is a mathematician and father to three wonderful little ones, our grandchildren. I have pictures here somewhere. Of the youngest, Aaron, who is crazy, I should not speak. And not because he blames me for the mess in his head. No: he deserves to be left alone with his commonplace lunacies—he calls them ideas—and given peace. He lives in Los Angeles.

AFTER KATHRYN, Bradley's first wife—a woman I never met, I should add—left him, Bradley became the manager of a local coffee shop and bought the house next door to us. He became our neighbor. He moved into a haunted house, haunted not by ghosts but divorce. A divorce dybbuk scuttled around inside the woodwork. Young couples would purchase that property, they would take up occupancy, they would quarrel, the quarreling would escalate to shouting and table-pounding, they would anathematize each other, and, presto, they would move out, not together but separately. They would scatter. Then back the house would go onto the real estate market. *Three couples* we saw this happen to.

I should explain. At first sight, each time they arrived, they were fine, scrubbed American pragmatists you might see photographed in a glossy magazine. Blond, blue-eyed Rotarians, fresh owners of real estate, Hemingway readers, they would unload their cheerful sunny furniture from U-Haul vans. By the time they moved out, they would have acquired mottled gray skin and haggard Eastern European expressions. Even the children by that time would have the greenish appearance of owl-eyed Soviet refugees stumbling out of Aeroflot. These young families emerged from that house bent and broken, like vegetables left forgotten in the crisper.

So, when Bradley arrived, alone except for his dog, we thought: the curse is over. The dybbuk will have to locate itself elsewhere . . . This Bradley, an interesting man, invited Esther and me to dinner the second week he was installed in that house. A courageous gesture. He was not afraid of Jews. He served veal, which Esther will not eat. In the dining room, she picked at it delicately. She left small scraps of it distributed randomly around her plate. I said later: at least no ham, no pork, no shrimp mousse, no trayf. But Harry, she said, veal to me is like a frozen scream. I can't eat it. So don't eat it, I said. So I don't, she said. So?

The man, Bradley, had a certain hangdog diffuseness characteristic of the recently divorced. But he was trying against certain odds to be cheerful. He asked me about my work, he asked Esther about *her* work, and he listened pleasantly while we did our best to explain. These topics do not provide good conversation. He listened, though. He had large watchful eyes. I was reminded of an extremely handsome toad, a toad with class and style and good tailoring. He seemed to be living far down inside himself, perhaps in a secret passageway connected to his heart. Biochemistry does not scintillate at the dinner table, however, nor do neo-Kantian aesthetics. Only when I mentioned Kierkegaard did Bradley perk up. From behind a locked bedroom door, his dog simultaneously barked. I assumed that the dog had caught sight of the dybbuk or was interested in Kierkegaard.

Prompted by his interest, I said that Kierkegaard, the Danish philosopher, had fallen in love with an attractive girl, Regine Olsen, and then he had concluded that they would be incompatible, that the love was mistaken, that he himself was complex and she was simple, and he contrived to break the engagement so as to give the appearance that it was the young lady's fault, not his.

He succeeded in breaking the engagement, in never marrying her. Cowardice was probably involved here. Kierkegaard wished to believe that the fault lay with the nature of love itself, the *problem* of love, its fate in his life. From the personal he extrapolated to the general. A philosopher's trick. Regine married another man and moved away from Copenhagen to the West Indies, but Kierkegaard, the knight of faith, carried a burning torch for her, in the form of his philosophy, the rest of his days. This is madness of a complex lifelong variety. He spent his career writing philosophy that would, among other things, justify his actions toward Regine Olsen. He died of a warped spine.

Esther says that when I am seated at a dinner table, plates and food in front of me, I am transmogrified into a bore. Yak yak, she says. At the table she adjusted her watchband and raised her eyebrows to me. I felt her kicking me in the shins.

Still I pressed on.

Søren Kierkegaard maintained that everyone intuits what love is, and yet it cannot be spoken of directly. Or distinctly. It falls into the category of the unknown, where plain speech is inadequate to the obscurity of the subject. Similarly, everyone experiences God, but the experience of God is so unlike the rest of our experiences that there, too, plain speech is defeated. According to Kierkegaard, nearly everyone intuits the subtlety of God, but almost no one knows how to speak of Him. This is where our troubles begin.

At this point I noticed Bradley's attention flagging somewhat. Esther kicked me again. She glanced toward Bradley, our new neighbor. Don't lecture the boy, she meant.

I raised my voice to keep his attention: Speaking about God is not, I said, pounding the dinner table lightly with my spoon for emphasis, the same as talking about car dealerships or Phillips screwdrivers. The salt and pepper shakers clattered. The problem with love and God, the two of them, is how to say anything about them that doesn't annihilate them instantly with the wrong words, with untruth. In this sense, love and God are equivalents. We feel both, but because we cannot speak clearly about them, we end up—wordless, inarticulate—by denying their existence altogether, and *pffffft*, they die. (They can, however, come back. Because God is a god, when He is dead, He doesn't have to stay dead. He can come back if He chooses to. Nietzsche somehow failed to mention this.)

Both God and love are best described and addressed by means of poetry. Poetry, however, is also stone dead at the present time, like its first cousin, God. Love will very quickly follow, no? Hmm? Don't you agree? I asked. After God dies, must love, a smaller god, not follow?

Uh, I don't know. I'll have to think about it, said Bradley, our new neighbor. Do you want some dessert, Professor? I got some ice cream here in the refrigerator. It's chocolate.

A very nice change of subject, Esther said, breathless with relief. Harry, she continued, I think you should save Kierkegaard for some other time. For perhaps another party. A party with more Ph.Ds.

She gave me a loving but boldly impatient look, perfected from a lifetime of practice. Esther does not like it when I philosophize about love. She feels implicated.

Okay, I said, I'm sorry. I get going and I can't help myself. I'm like a man trying to rid himself of an obsession. Actually, I *am* that man. I'm not *like* him at all.

Esther turned toward Bradley Smith. Harry is on the outs in his department, she said. He does all the unfashionable philosophers, he's a baggage handler of Bigthink. What do you do, again, Mr. Smith? You explained but I forgot.

Well, he said, I've just bought into a coffee shop in the mall, I have a partnership, and now I'm managing it.

This interested me because I've always wanted to open a restaurant.

Also, he continued, I'm an artist. I paint pictures. There was an appreciable pause in the conversation while Esther and I took this in. Would you like to see my paintings? he asked. They're all in the basement. Except for that one—he pointed—up there on the living room wall.

Esther appeared discountenanced but recovered herself quickly.

The artwork he had indicated had a great deal of open space in it. The painting itself covered much of the wall. However, three quarters of the canvas appeared to be vacant. It was like undeveloped commercial property. It hadn't even been compromised with white paint. It was just unfulfilled canvas. Perhaps the open space was a commentary on what *was* there. In the upper right-hand corner of the picture, though, was the appearance of a window, or what might have been a window if you were disposed to think of it representationally. Through this window you could discern, distantly, a patch of green—which I took to be a field—and in the center of this green one could construe a figure. A figure of sorts. Unmistakably a woman.

Who's that? I asked.

The painting's called *Synergy #1,* Bradley said.

Okay, but *who's* that?

Just a person.

What sort of person? Who were you thinking of?

Oh, it's just an abstract person.

Esther laughed. Bradley, she said, I never heard of an abstract person before. Except for the persons that my husband thinks of professionally. Example-persons, for example.

Well, this one is. Abstract, I mean.

It looks like a woman to me, Esther said. Viewed from a distance. As long as it's a woman, it's not abstract.

Well, maybe she's on the way to becoming abstract.

Oh, you mean, as if she's all women? *A symbol for women?* There she is, not a woman but all women, wrapped up in one woman, there in the distance?

Maybe.

Well, Esther said, I don't like *that*. No such thing as Woman. Just women, and *a* woman, such as me, for example, clomping around in my mud boots. But that's not to say that I don't like your painting. I do like it.

Thank you. I haven't sold it yet.

I like the window, Esther continued, and all those scrappy unpainted areas.

It's not quite unpainted, he informed us. It's underpainted. I splashed some coffee on the canvas to stain it. Blend-of-the-day coffee from the place where I work. It's a statement. You just can't see the stains from here.

Ah, I said, nodding. A statement about capitalism?

Esther glared at me.

You want to see my pictures in the basement? Bradley asked.

Sure, I said, why not?

Only thing is, he said, there're some yellow jackets nesting in the walls—or wasps—and you'll have to watch yourself when you get down there. Careful not to get stung.

We'll do that, I said.

ABOUT THIS BASEMENT and the paintings residing there, what can I say? I held Esther's hand as we descended the stairs. I feared that she might stumble. Wasps, likewise, were on my mind. I did not want to have her stung and would protect her if necessary. Bradley had leaned his paintings against the walls, as painters do, on the floor. Each painting leaned into another like a derelict reclining against other derelicts. He had installed a fervent showering of fluorescent light overhead. A quantity of light like that will give you a headache if you're inclined, as I am, to pain. The basement smelled of turpentine and paint substances, the pleasant sinus-clearing elemental ingredients of art, backed by the more pessimistic odors of subsurface cellar mold and mildew.

One by one he brought out his visions.

This, he said, is *Composition in Gray and Black*. He held up for our inspection images of syphilis and gonorrhea.

And this, he said, is called *Free Weights*.

Very interesting, Esther said, scratching her nose with a pencil she had found somewhere, as she contemplated our neighbor's abstract dumbbells and barbells, seemingly hanging, like acorns, from badly imagined and executed surrealist trees, growing in a forest of fog and painterly confusion that no revision could hope to clarify.

And here, he said, lugging out a larger canvas from behind the others, is a different sort of picture. In my former style. He placed it before us.

Until that moment I had thought the boy, our neighbor, a dim bulb. This painting was breath-snatching. What's this called? I asked him.

I call it *The Feast of Love*, Bradley said.

In contrast to his other paintings, which appeared to have been slopped over with mud and coffee grounds, this one, this feast of love, consisted of color. A sunlit table—on which had been set dishes and cups and glasses—appeared to be overflowing with light. The table and the feast had been placed in the foreground, and on all sides the background fell backward into a sort of visible darkness. The eye returned to the table. In the glasses was not wine but light, on the plates were dishes of brightest hues, as if the appetite the guest brought to this feast was an appetite not for food but for the entire spectrum as lit by celestial arc lamps. The food had no shape. It had only color, burning pastels, of the pale but intense variety. Visionary magic flowed from one end of the table to the other, all the suggestions of food having been abstracted into too-bright shapes, as if one had stepped out of a movie theater into a bright afternoon summer downtown where all the objects were so overcrowded with light that the eye couldn't process any of it. The painting was like a flashbulb, a blinding, cataract art. This food laid out before us was like that. Then I noticed that the front of the table seemed to be tipped toward the viewer, as if all this light, and all this food, and all this love, was about to slide into our laps. The feast of love was the feast of light, and it was about to become ours.

Esther sighed: Oh oh oh. It's beautiful. And then she said, Where are the people?

There aren't any, Bradley told her.

Why not?

Because, he said, no one's ever allowed to go there. You can see it but you can't reach it.

Now it was my turn to scratch my balding head. Bradley, I barked at him, this is not like your other paintings, this is magnificent, why do you hide such things?

Because it's not true, he said.

What do you mean, it's not true? Of course it's true if you can paint it.

No, he said, still looking fixedly at his creation. If you can't get there, then it's not true. He looked up at me and Esther, two old people holding hands in our neighbor's basement. I'm not a fool, he said. I don't spend my time painting foolish dreams and fantasies. Once was enough.

I could have argued with him but chose not to.

And with that, he picked up the painting and hid it behind the silly ugly dumbbells growing like acorns on psychotic trees.

WHAT A STRANGE YOUNG MAN, Esther said, tucked in next to me several hours later, sleepy but sleepless in the dark. Her nightgown swished as she tossed and turned. He seems so nondescript and midwestern, harmless, and then he produces from the back of his basement a picture that anyone would remember for the rest of their lives.

Oh, I said, you could say it's imitation Matisse or imitation Hockney. Besides, I said, light as a subject for contemporary paintings is passé.

You *could* say that, Esther whispered, but you *wouldn't,* and if you *did,* you'd be *wrong.*

She gave me a little playful slap.

I only said that you could say that, not that you would.

You didn't actually say it.

No. Not actually.

Good, Esther said. I realized that she was agitated. I turned to her and rubbed her back and her neck, and she put her hands on my face. I could feel her smiling in the darkness. I could feel her wrinkles rising.

Harry, she said, it was a recognition for me, a moment of beauty. How strange that a wonderful painting should be created by such a seemingly mediocre man. Our neighbor, living in the Dybbuk House. How strange, how strange. Then she sighed. How strange, she said again.

Then the phone rang.

Don't answer it, Esther quickly said. You mustn't. Don't, dear, don't, don't, don't.

No, I must, I told her. I must.

———

I PICKED UP THE TELEPHONE RECEIVER and said, Hello? From across the continent, on the West Coast, my son Aaron began speaking to me. In a voice tireless with rage he cursed me and his mother who lay beside me. Once again I was invited to hear the story of how I had ruined his life, destroyed his soul, sacrificed him to the devils and angels of lost ambition. In numbing fashion he found words to batter my heart. Indictment: I had expected more of him than he could achieve. Indictment: I had had hopes for him that drove him, he said, insane. Indictment: I was who I was. Crazy, sick, and inspired with malice, he described his craziness and his sickness in detail, his terrible impulses to hurt others and to hurt himself, as if I had not heard this story many times before, several times, innumerable times. Razors, wire, gas. He called me, his father, a motherfucker. He told me that he did not want me to be his father anymore. Then he broke down in tears and asked for money. *Demanded* money. From the nothingness and everlasting night of his life, he demanded cash. I, too, was weeping with sorrow and rage, holding the earpiece tightly to my head so that not a word would escape to Esther. Cupping my hand around the mouthpiece, I asked him if he had hurt anyone, if he had hurt himself, and he said no, but he was thinking about it, he planned every single minute in advance, he planned monstrous personal calamities, he needed help, he would ask for help, but first he had to have money *now*, this very minute, *my* money, superhuman quantities of it. Don't make me your sacrificial lamp, he said, then corrected himself, sacrificial lamb, don't you do that now, not again. I said, against my better judgment, that I would see what I could do, I would send him what I had. He seemed briefly calm. He breathed in and out. He pleasantly wished me good night, as if at the conclusion of an effective performance.

To have a son or daughter like this is to have a portion of the spirit shrivel and die, never to recover. You witness the lost soul of your child floating out into the ethers of eternity. Ethics is a dream, and tenderness a daytime phantasm, lost when night comes. Esther and I, eyes open, held each other until dawn broke. My darling wept in my arms, our hearts in ruin. We live in a large city, populated only by ourselves.

Kafka: *A false alarm on the night bell once answered—it cannot be made good, not ever.*

SEVEN

ONCE I HAD BRADLEY THE DOG returned to his rightful owner (myself), I saved a bit of money for a down payment—actually, I was doing pretty well, financially—and moved out of my basement apartment into a white clapboard house next door to Harry and Esther Ginsberg, who became my friends and neighbors. Everything I owned fit into one small moving van. I brought the dog, and my easels, my paint tubes, my paintings, and every other worldly possession that I thought was fit to survive, and I found places for them where they seemed comfortable. I was the only entity in that house that didn't have a place to be. Bradley had his back room and his dog bed, the paintings had the basement, the clothes had their closet, the clock had its wall, the audio system had its shelves. I roamed around the house trying to figure out my proper location. But I couldn't get comfortable anywhere, including the bedroom, and finally I decided not to worry and just to go on being relaxed and uncomfortable and myself. After all, I was a single, recently divorced man. I was both a problem and a solution.

A MAN LIVING ALONE is a king of sorts, but unfortunately only one minute at a time, and his kingdom is remote and typically unvisited and small, with few comforts. Moodiness and solitude are the order of the day. It's easy to control moods and the king's solitude as long as there is a royal project, a scheme, or narcotic drugs left over from root canal, but the drugs eventually run out.

Those first few weeks, I was making business arrangements (I went from being a salaried employee to being an entrepreneur), but once I had organized the business in the mall and saw that it was up and running, I went back to my painting during my free time at home. I'd paint canvases and take the dog for endless walks around town, and we would watch sports on TV, Bradley the dog and I, though I was very often indifferent to the outcomes. Why should I cheer these steroid-stupefied guys? I'd watch seven innings, or two quarters, and then I'd turn the whole thing off, too confused about my allegiances to care.

Typically on weekends I would go down to the basement and start with the brushes and the canvases. I had a battery-operated radio propped up on top of the water heater and tuned to the FM station, and some masterpiece from the repertoire would come on, let's say Brahms, one of those symphonies, and I'd be all right until I started to listen. Since I'm visual, I converted everything audible into a visual, and while I was listening to this heavy Brahmsian music—it sounded like excited lamentation to me—I'd imagine a leaf being blown across a field, and then I saw myself as that same leaf being windswept on a drift of snow, and then I'd see a dry creek bed and people at a party at dawn wandering home and feeling hungover and sick in the key of D major, and I'd think: This isn't about good emotional hygiene, this is about me. I don't want to be a leaf, hell with that, I'm a king and not a leaf, *I'm Bradley W. Smith,* and I'd snap off the music. But once you've got yourself successfully imagined as a dry leaf and you've got that particular image stuck in your head, it's difficult to get it out of your mental repository, and you're committed to it.

This is how people mess themselves up, getting obsessed with images.

I'd wait for the news to come on and announce some noteworthy global disaster to take my mind off Brahms, but sometimes no global disasters present themselves when you require them, just a scandal or two to keep people interested in the informational scene, and so I'd start painting the leaf that I had become, I'd put the Bradley-leaf into a corner of the painting, and gradually the rest of the painting would become unimportant and I'd overpaint it and make it abstract with the only resolution in imagery being that Bradley-leaf rising out of a dense fog of abstraction. After a while you wouldn't even be able to tell what it was I had painted exactly; it had rearranged itself very far from the familiar home truths. I didn't want it to seem melancholy—I can't stand pathos—but there it was, hopeless and crazily metaphorical, nevertheless still a leaf, abstract as it was. Rothko wouldn't have done it that way. Franz Kline wouldn't have done it that way. No one else would have. It was my own autobiographical leaf, shadowing me and showing up in my painting, in pursuit.

What's agitating about solitude is the inner voice telling you that you should be mated to somebody, that solitude is a mistake. The inner voice doesn't care about who you find. It just keeps pestering you, tormenting you—if you happen to be me—with homecoming queens first, then girls next door, and finally anybody who might be pleased to see you now and then at the dinner table and in bed on occasion. You look up from reading the newspaper and realize that no one loves you, and no one burns for you. The workings of nature are mysterious, but they do account for a certain amount of despair among single persons, the irrelevance you sometimes feel.

I would sometimes mention these matters to Harry Ginsberg. I figured, well, he *is* a philosopher, after all. He'd be shoveling snow off his sidewalk, and I'd be doing the same, and I'd come over to his side to help him out. This was March, when you're sick of the snow and the overcast skies, and the sickness also has a way of settling down on your self, particularly on those days when money, more and more money, doesn't seem like the solution to anything.

Harry was glum, worried about Aaron again. "Good morning," he would say, downcast.

"Aloha," I said this one time, to cheer him up, leaning on my snow shovel. "How've you been, Harry?"

"It does not bear discussion," he said, pushing snow in my direction. Then he propped his shovel on his arm as I had been doing. "Today I was thinking of a story. A poem, I think, that my mother used to recite." He looked at me and breathed in. "About a dragon with a rubber nose. This dragon would erase all the signs in town at night. During the day, no one would know where to go or what to buy. No signs anywhere. Posters gone, information gone. Interesting, isn't it? A world without signs of any kind. The poem was in Yiddish. Signlessness is perhaps a Jewish fixation. Very curious. I often think about that poem."

"Very interesting," I said. "Harry, where did you meet Esther?"

"At a political rally," he told me, a twinge of impatience darkening his face. "Why do you ask?"

"I sometimes think I need to meet someone."

"Ah," he said. "Are there not conventions and get-togethers in your coffee business?"

"Well, yes."

"Then go to one," he said, resuming his shoveling. "Meet someone. Meet *any*one." I could tell that in his present mood he didn't want to talk to me anymore, so I left him there, disappointed with the snow, the fact of it.

NEVERTHELESS, I DECIDED to follow his advice. A month later, I went off to a convention in Indianapolis of specialty coffee retailers, and I asked Chloé and Oscar to stay in my house, so that I wouldn't have to pay the expense of boarding Bradley the dog at a kennel. They would house-sit, and they did. They moved in with cagey smiles on their faces.

In Indianapolis, at the convention, I had a one-night stand with the assistant manager of a Starbucks in Minnesota, and the experience was extremely pleasant but quite hard to remember after it was over—she was, and I'm not this saying as criticism, taxing once you got past her superficial prettiness, and at breakfast we finally decided not to converse because of the difficulty in finding topics of common interest. Our sudden and surprising apathy toward each other made the time pass slowly, above the scrambled eggs and the toast and the coffee. With the haze of drunkenness having faded and sobriety taking its place, she apparently found me shabby and colorless in the way that people can often be in the morning. I do remember that her red hair smelled of smoke when we were in bed. Smoky red hair, as if the head were on fire.

When I returned home from the convention in Indianapolis, the house was spick-and-span, nothing out of place. I mean those two, Oscar and Chloé, looked like castoffs and flotsam, but, being in love, their inner lives were conventionally brisk, and they were fastidious and neat, as if they wanted the world to continue for a while so that they could be in it.

I'd only been back in the house for a day or so when I noticed that an imperceptible change had overtaken the first floor and the bedrooms upstairs. I was cooking dinner, a simple stir-fry, when I thought I heard some sound, a cry of some sort, coming from the living room. Thinking that it might be Bradley, I checked the room but found nothing out of place. Here on one side was the bookcase, and there against the west wall was the audio system. I shrugged to myself and soon forgot about it. As I was doing the dishes, my hands slippery with soap, the tap water splashing into the sink, I heard the cry again, more distinctly, and this time I knew that the cry had not been one of pain but of surprise. Pleasure was in it somewhere. I found this auditory memory quite perplexing.

Suspicious, I went into the living room and did a thorough search, the dog following me. Finally I turned up a slip of paper hiding under the corner of the rug. On it was some handwriting that I recognized as Chloé's. It seemed to be in code.

Living room §
Kitchen §
Kitchen table ¤
Bedroom ¥
Bathroom shower ≈
Basement √

It appeared to be some sort of checklist. At first I imagined that she had gone around the house checking to make sure that everything was where it should be. I tossed the paper into the wastebasket and went back to making my dinner.

After dinner I fished the list back out of the wastebasket and checked it again, peering at the arcane doodled symbols. These kids, what had they done in my house? *Living room,* they wrote, followed by the strange coupled § symbol. I walked into the living room and sat down, not on the sofa, but on the floor. I closed my eyes and imagined these kids, the house sitters, also in the living room, engaged with each other so that their bodies formed a §. They laughed, they came together, they were solemn, and then they rested.

I imagined them, these kids, these newcomers to love, doing what kids do, exploring a house, having sex in the rooms, then the girl making a list of where and how, and as I sat there I heard the happy cry again plain as nightfall, and I thought: this house isn't haunted, but *it does have a memory,* this house remembers what people have done here, and then it plays back those sounds like a bored and absentminded African parrot. I moved through the rooms, feeling my way through the passions these kids had had, how they laid each other in bed, forming a ¥, a tree with two heads and four branches, a yen. I heard their love cries. I was neither frightened nor surprised by this discovery.

In the basement I felt the two of them passing by me, felt the memory of their having been physically present there as the boy, Oscar, teased the girl, Chloé, while they looked at my paintings and talked about them, the girl leaning over and the boy, behind her, reaching over to touch her—there—at the base of her neck, a delicate spot for her. Then he extended his arms around her, still standing behind her, as if grasping for her animal heart. Words were spoken. They made love quickly, standing up, I think, and Chloé's back, when she came, got damp. Then they turned off the lights and went upstairs. They were still somewhat frightened and impressed by the size and the majesty of their attraction to each other.

I follow them up the stairs. I watch them go into the kitchen and observe them making a dinner of hamburgers and potato chips. They recover their senses by talking and listening to the radio. I watch them feed each other. This is love in the present tense, and finally I have had enough of them, and I close my eyes, and when I open my eyes again, they are gone, and the house is mine again, at least for the time being.

All the same, there is still no comfortable place for me in the house. I am not much of a king, in my present condition. Passion occupies a space that is not vacated until another passion occupies it.

EIGHT

SMELLING OF ONION and garlic, what we did was, we'd lie in bed together, jabbering about the future, Oscar and me. This was in *his* room, because I was moving out of my roommates' palace into my own efficiency and spending more time just now in Oscar's bedroom, except for those days we house-sat at Bradley Smith's. Oscar's bedroom: like I already told you: trophies with bronzed guys running in place up on the shelf, his track shoes still on their nail, and snow drifting down outside. On his bookshelf: board games like Monopoly and Clue, relay batons from his track team, and busted video cartridges, dead Super Mario circuits and dead Ninja Warriors likewise. And right over there, up above us, located on the wall, was a crucified bronze Jesus I didn't want to ask about, what he was *doing* there or anything. I was lying snug under the covers one day with my hand peacefully on Oscar's dick, you know, holding it, it being only half-awake, similar to Oscar himself, 'cause we'd already done our lovemaking a couple times, and he, Oscar, was talkin' about the future.

"I have this image," he said.

"What image?"

"You know how people when they're ultra-rich, they've got front hallways?"

I said yeah.

"There's a name for it."

"For what?"

He lowered himself down in bed and kissed me, a little tongue and lip thing, on my nipple. His tongue stud gave it, I don't know, metallic content. Next to the bed we had acquired a bowl of popcorn that we microwaved a little while ago. When he kissed me, he tasted inside his mouth of buttered popcorn. Sometimes burned popcorn. It was like he was cooking snacks in there. My nipples stood up, it was almost painful.

"They've got a name for that, that room inside the front door. Where they put the big grandfather clocks and shit. You know. Also those things they put the umbrellas into."

"Like, the foyer?"

"Fucking A." He nodded. "The *foyer*." He was so pleased with himself or with me, he woke up utterly and got a boomer Woodrow immediately. It lifted my hand up. His dick is like a human barometer that way. I started to go down on him but he said, "No, no, wait." He put his fingers on my face and drew it up back to the pillow. His woody didn't get discouraged. It stayed nestled in my girl-grip, and I could feel his heart beat through it. "See, here I am, comin' home. Here's Oscar. Oscar-of-the-future."

"Yeah?"

"Yeah, you gotta imagine this. Okay? Here I am, Oscar, and I'm comin' home."

"All right. You're comin' home. I'm imagining it."

"Right. From what am I coming home? From whatever shit it is that I do. From my *work*."

"Okay."

"It's, like, the end of the day. Quitting time. Factory whistles are blowing. And I'm comin' home. Right? And in my truck, I've run into a detour which takes me around that new drive-in bank and this pond where the ducks have already flown south and that mini-mall and the multiplex. I'm just drivin', my hands on the wheel.

And I'm like, I don't *care* about this detour. I am *not* bummed. We're thinking up the future, okay? Now? This is what we're doin'?"

"Okay." Outside, I heard the sound of an airplane or something taking off. The furnace in the house started up.

"I'm comin' home." He got distracted and kissed me on the mouth and our tongues swirled for a while. Tongue stud action again. He shook his head like he was waking up. "I'm not comin' home, I *am* home, see, and I'm comin' in the door. My truck's in the driveway."

"Where am I, Oscar?"

"Where are you? Oh, okay. Honey, you're inside. You're inside this big house, Chloé, you're doing household shit. How the fuck should I know? You gotta decide that for yourself, right? 'Cause you'd be totally adult and feminist and everything about it. You want something done in the house, you give orders and it happens. You're tough. You're a take-no-prisoners woman. A real tough chick. We're alike, that way. Tough, I mean."

"I'm in the house? I live with you?"

"Yeah, you're there."

"Wow. Okay." I moved over and slipped his cock inside me. He was ultra-hard like a broomstick, but softer, Oscar being human.

"Don't distract me," he said. "So I'm comin' in the front door, and I've got, like, the bills, that've come in the mail?"

"Right."

"And Chloé, these are fucking *huge* bills. You never saw bills like this! These are bills for mortgages and shit, bills for the fucking dentist, bills for—I don't know—the eye guy, and the shrink, and bills for the phone and the electricity, these are the biggest colossal bills you ever saw, and they came in the *mail,* and I've got them. I got them in my hand."

"What's so great about this?" We were lying side by side, doin' our thing with our hips sedately, but it's weird because it's so secondary, though I'm heating up? I was so wet down there but I was also trying to concentrate on what he was saying. "What's so great about getting bills?"

"Hello? You're not listening to me," he said. "'Cause I've got these bills, they're like, uh, you know, the national debt, but look at the look on my face."

"Now?" His eyes were kind of not-focusing just then. He was staring toward the Monopoly game, on the other side of the room, and his glass Mason jar full of pennies, and the other Mason jar full of old shoelaces.

"No, not now. In the future. Look at me, Oscar-of-the-future. Uh. Do I look scared?"

"I can't see you."

"Yes, you can. Look harder. Close your eyes."

I closed them.

"Okay, now imagine Oscar-of-the-future. That's me. That's me comin' home to the house, not-bummed by the detour. Look at the look on my face while I'm holding these huge bills I gotta pay. Do I look scared?"

"No."

"How do I look?"

I kept my eyes closed. "Like a man. Confident and like that. A hero, even. You're smiling?"

"Fucking A. I'm smiling. You know why I'm smilin'?"

"'Cause you can *pay* all those bills, right?"

"Oh, yeah. 'Cause I'm a big man and nothin' scares me and I can pay all the bills because we got plenty of money, and, uh, I'm fear-less—"

He made a yelp, and he suddenly came, to his surprise. When he comes, his shoulders sometimes jerk back, and they did this time, too. It made me so happy to see him that I came with him, right on the dotted line, but quick. Efficient. It's like we're connected with wires that way. Something happens to him, it happens to me. We're *concerted*. Is that a word? It should be. Now it is.

We took a minute out for a breather, though we kept ourselves together. No condoms, I don't like them, I'm on the pill. It's funny about Oscar, he can come and pretty soon he's got his hard-on back, standing up and smiling at me. Weird. Maybe this was, like, the month of his sexual peak. I mean, in some ways he was still a boy. You could tell how he was still treating sex like it was a drug and vastly illegal. He had that addict glint in his eye. But it could be tiring also, like shoplifting. It goes from being hip to being a chore. You get to where you want to do something else. The righteousness goes out of it. That can happen.

"Now you," he said.

"What about me?"

"The future, man. We were talkin' about the future." He put his finger on my earlobe, where it had been pierced, as per his suggestion, my earlobe where I wasn't underpierced anymore, thanks to him.

"I can't see anything."

"Sure you can. Chicks can always see the future, it's what they *do*. Guys don't, so much, except those weathermen, you know— meteorologists. Forecasters. So whattya see?"

"I can't see anything," I repeated.

"Don't be lame. Close your eyes." I did. "Okay. Whattya see?"

I put my head on his chest. "Well, maybe in that foyer we were talkin' about? With the, what do you call it? umbrella stand?" I was speaking real slow. Groping love-talk.

"Yeah?"

"There's a table made out of wood? And there's, like, this vase, and it's red glass, and it's got flowers and . . . wait a minute."

"What?"

"Your heart sounds weird."

"Oh, yeah, that."

I had my ear to his chest, where usually with humans you hear chunka-thoom, chunka-thoom, chunka-thoom. But! Oscar had this other sound, chunka-jazz-thoom, chunka-jazz-thoom, chunka-jazz-thoom.

"I've got this heart thing," Oscar said. "Valves and shit. Like a murmur." He shrugged. His dick went down from where it was, but he was working up the confidence look and the greaser sneer on his face, like what's-his-name, the movie star. Even in bed he was working hard on his attitude. "It's nothin'," he said.

"Fuck and *alas,* Oscar! It's something. You should, like, have it looked at?"

"They did already. And they said, *Forget it, he'll live.* So tell me about this vase, Chloé, that you mentioned."

But now, I sort of didn't want to do it, I didn't *want* to imagine the future. The righteousness had gone out of that, too. But I thought maybe I should, a favor to Oscar. "There's flowers, you know, people have flowers in vases."

"What kind?"

He had his hands now in my hair, which was tricky, 'cause my hair's so short. "I don't know." It was hard for me to imagine the fucking flowers in the damn vase while Oscar's heart was murmuring and death was taking a close look at him. "Roses," I said. I took a big breath, to imagine them. "Red roses, with petals? Like they have them."

"Okay. We've done this. What's upstairs?"

"Oscar, I'm sort of tired of this." I shined a big fakey smile at him, then dropped the idea.

"Come on, Chloé, what's upstairs?"

I shut my eyes. I was working at it. I was imagining. Imagining is hard work for me, at times.

"Well?" he asked.

"I'm still goin' up the stairs."

"Okay." He waited. "You up there, yet?"

"Yeah. Just about. I got my hand on the banister."

"So what's up there?"

I had this problem then. Because what I was seeing was, all the kids Oscar and I would have. Like three kids in their kid clothes, OshKosh overalls with spit-up on the bibs, and they're yelling and jumping up and down and breaking shit and having fun, like a kid party. And maybe a baby in a crib or something.

"Well?" he asked.

"Big bedrooms, Oscar. The thickest carpeting you ever saw."

"Right. I can see it. It's, like, gotta be white."

"Yeah. It's the second floor. White carpeting in the hallways. Thing is, Oscar, I've never been in a house with a second floor. So it's hard for me to know."

"I have," he said. "They got bedrooms up there."

"Okay." He closed my eyes with his fingers. *He did it real softly.* "Okay. I guess I'm, like, supposed to imagine the rest of it," I said.

"What's in the bedrooms, Chloé?"

"We are."

"And what else?"

I took a deep breath, from way down in, what do they call it? the diaphragm. By which I mean my heart. Because I have one, too. "Kids, Oscar. There's kids everywhere. They're *our* kids. We've got, like, three? I can't count them all."

His dick started standing up again. "I was hopin' you'd say that."

"Bull*shit.* You were? Really?"

"Yeah. On account of I am the person who is not scared, like I said. Fearless. So that would also include kids, right? I *like* kids, man. Gettin' into trouble and shit. *I* was a kid. Absolutely."

"Absolutely!" I said, so happy my toes were tingling, little battery-operated things zapping them. "So . . ."

"Yeah?"

I was thinking of his heart. "So I have this idea."

"What's that?"

"I brought it with me," I said.

So what I did then was, I got out of bed, naked, and I walked over to my backpack, and I was about to get the thing I wanted to show him out of there, but I had to clean myself up, I was dripping, so I said, like the Princess of Wales: *Excuse me, I'll be right back.*

I went out into the hall, I guess you'd call it. Oscar's bedroom is on one side, and his father, the Bat, well, the Bat's bedroom is on the other side, and that's it, in this little ranch house. Oscar's older brother, he'd moved out, and there's no mother because she's dead and everything. It was about four in the afternoon. I was going to the bathroom to clean the remnants of Oscar off of myself. And I did. But when I was returning to Oscar's bedroom, I thought I saw something way down out there on the corner of my eye. It was Oscar's dad, the Bat, in the kitchen, sitting at the table, peeling some kind of awful fruit, and I sort of thought he got a measuring look at me, without my clothes on. Maybe I was imagining it. That can happen.

"I think your dad's home," I said, standing there. My hand stayed on the doorknob.

"Fuck him," Oscar said.

"No, I think he's really *home.*" I waited. "He's peeling food," I said, to prove it.

"So what're you going to show me?"

I took the videocam out of my backpack. "This," I said. I hoisted it on my bare shoulder and aimed it down at him.

"Where'd you get that, Chloé?"

"I sort of stole it. The people who own it, they won't miss it." I meant my parents, who I knew pretty well.

"And what's your plan?"

I put the camera down on the floor and got back into bed with him, my forearm on his chest. "Well, this girl told me how, you make a tape, you know, us in bed, you sort of invent a name for yourself and a story and then, I mean, *we,* well, what we do is, we just make a tape of ourselves doing it, like what we usually do, maybe some additions, fancy stuff, costumes that we take off for the camera, and there's an address these sex industry magazines have where you send the tape, or, well, you send them a sampler first, then the tape, and they send you huge bucks. This girl I know, Janey, she'll do it all for us. She wants to break into the video industry."

Oscar didn't look that happy about it. You could see he was kind of divided. 'Cause after all we had just been talking about a *house,* and, like, *vases* and *stairs. And* so much money that you weren't afraid of anything in the world. It's hard to make big bucks at Dr. Enchilada's or Jitters. But *he* was the one who said our sex lives were so good we ought to be able to make some money out of it, but clueless as to how, leaving it to me. *He* was the one who said we were *magnificent,* or some word like that. I told him I knew he was smart and could think of a story we could act out. It would be harmless.

But. I also had a little disgusting feeling, even as I was saying what I was saying. I mean, Oscar's got a nice body and, me, I've got a nice body, but I could see these old men looking at our tape and drooling. Excuse me, that's not *always* the road to vases and flowers and kids upstairs. That's radically poor karma, guys drooling. Also, as a rule, guys who drool don't shave. Gargoyles! But I thought, hey, a few times, why not, hey, nothing ventured? And we don't have to *see* the guys. We'll be safely inside the television screen.

Anyway, this friend I had, this video person named Janey, would help us make it look cool. And tasteful. She was the one who gave me the idea in the first place. She said she knew what to do with it, to sell it. She had taken film and video classes at the community college. She knew lighting and how to focus.

This is where, out of the blue, Oscar said, "Chloé, it's weird, but I love you." He waited. "I never said that before."

And I said, "Oscar, I love you, you are everything."

"You think we can make some money out of this?"

"Maybe." Then I said my nothing-ventured thing and how we were so minimum-wage and actually desperate right now.

"It's way creepy," he said. "But it's okay. I guess. 'Cause of the money."

"Right."

"And it's not like *work,* either."

"No, it's not like that."

"Chloé, tell me somethin' about when you were a girl."

"Why?"

"I want to hear it. I just want to see you from then." He looked right in my eyes. He wasn't zoned. So I, like, got up and sort of straddled him.

"Okay," I said. "When me and my sister, we rode in the car? long trips? We sat in the backseat. *And time goes slower in the backseat than the front seat because the front seat gets everywhere first,* in case you haven't noticed. Just zombie slow. So what my sister Rhonda and me did was, we took Kleenex tissues, just plain Kleenex, from our mother, who had zillions of them in her purse, and we'd take them, and this was a *contest.* We invented this." I had my hands on his shoulders, pinning the boy down. "I'd open my back window, just partway, and put the Kleenex, just, sort of, the *edge* of it, into that groove that the window makes, and then I'd, like, close the window? Rhonda did that with her Kleenex on her side. So there was mostly Kleenex tissues flapping outside, but held in place, and the car's speeding along, with these white Kleenex ears on both sides of it. And Rhonda and me, we'd watch our respective Kleenexes, out there, as the landscapes flew by, cows and farmland and cities and landfills, and the one whose Kleenex lasted the longest, didn't get torn up by the wind, she was the one who won the contest. I know it sounds dumb. But I—you know—I kinda enjoyed this. It kinda passed the time." I waited. "Well, you wanted a story."

That was when I heard footsteps outside our door. I was sure I heard them.

"Oscar," I said. "Oscar, I think your dad's outside. I think he's listening."

Oscar looked toward the door. "Dad?" he said. "You there?"

I heard a floorboard creak. The Bat was standing, just *standing* out there, giving off ghoul-auras. Jesus. My philosophy is, if somebody's standing outside your bedroom door, not saying anything, they're *not* going to be good for you. They are going to be the devil's hatchlings.

"Dad?" Oscar sat up in bed. He lowered his feet to the floor and stood up. He reached down under the bed. He got a knife from the box he had under there. The blade was very shiny and pointed. I didn't like Oscar being naked, though, under those circumstances. A man's gotta have clothes on to be in a fight. Shorts, anyway, like in boxing. Just my opinion. Oscar could've probably taken him, though, he's so buff.

"*I tell you what,*" the ghoul-voice said. "You get that girl out of your room and your bed, Oscar, and you do it now. Or else," and here he coughed, just like a human-bat would, "I'll have to do it myself. I'm not running a motel here."

"You drunk dumb fuck," Oscar said under his breath. "Would you like that?"

"Did you hear me?" the Bat asked, flapping his bat wings, out there outside the door, where I couldn't see him.

"Yeah," Oscar said, real quietly. But dangerously, too, like he wasn't scared of mayhem. "He is one mean son-of-a-bitch," Oscar said quietly, turning toward me. "But I can be, too, if I gotta be. You better get dressed, Chloé. Just don't be scared. I'll kill the son-of-a-bitch if I have to. You know why?"

I was putting on my underpants—black ones, that I had bought for him to see—and my jeans, and then my bra, and my tee-shirt that said RAGING HORMONES on the front, right across my tits, and then my jacket and the backpack. I was doing it fast. "Why?"

"'Cause I'm so into you, I'd protect you." He leaned down and put his clothes on, but not fast like me. Slow and slick, the jeans slowly rising up his legs where you can see the muscles to his waist. Like he could take his time. That was Oscar all over. Then he put away the big knife and got another one out of his dresser drawer. This one was, like, all folded up. "I gotta move out of here. Outta this house."

"Cool. Move in with me. We can make space." My efficiency was tiny but I could always create room for Oscar, seeing as how he was saying he loved me.

"Are you doing what I said?" the Bat asked.

"Maybe we should climb out the window," I suggested. I could tell my voice was, like, shaking? "Out onto the lawn."

"Fuck that," Oscar informed me. "Come on." He took my hand and walked me to the door. "You ready?" he asked. I nodded. "Let's have the introductions."

Oscar put his hand on the doorknob and whipped the door open. There in front of us was the Bat, his dad, standing in the hallway, his grimy hands made into fists. His mouth was open, and you could see in there, most of the way down into his stomach. You wouldn't want to send postcards with this guy on the picture side. I had expected somebody older. And bigger. The Bat was shorter than Oscar, more kind of pint-sized, very ratty and low-rent, with long Brylcreem greaseball hair swept back in hoodlum waves, and this brown mole just to the right of his nose. He looked like one of those smelly little cigaretted guys who ran the Tilt-a-Whirl at a seedy backwoods carnival, just waiting for someone to barf. That'd give him a tickle. They had shaved the warm-and-fuzzy off this guy a long time ago. From the odors in the air you could tell also that he was, heads-up, a full-time drunk. He'd gone way past the hobby stage. He had stare-at-the-jury eyes and funny pointed bat ears to pick up screams. Also: the deadest expression I had ever seen on a human being was equipped into this man's face, like he was a *failed* rapist or something, and couldn't get over it. The small wiry guys are the meanest. He'd kill you for a nickel. Under the hall light, he looked at me and *panted*. He would be the first customer for the video we were going to make, I just had a feeling.

"Hello Missy," he said, lookin' at me, proportionating me.

"The name's Chloé," I said. "Pleased to meetcha." I was keeping up the civilities, because maybe someday this ghoul would be my father-in-law. Didn't hold out my hand, though. Give me some credit. Anyway Oscar had my other hand.

But what Oscar did, was, being brave, he just had my fingers in his and took me, like we were the cool kids, down the hall and out the front door, Oscar saying nothing. I guess he didn't want to start a fight exactly at that moment.

"Don't you come into this house again unless I invite you," the Bat said. "I don't want that stuff going on here. There'll be trouble I can't be responsible for. Real bad trouble." I heard his ineffectual voice fading, a mean-streak voice floating in the air, rising up to the atmosphere, and because nothing in the universe is ever lost, heading out to the galaxies, and I thought: *Jeez, what a bad ambassador for Earth that guy is!*

Short fathers can be so weird. There must be something about short-fathering that makes men so crazy. If you're middle-sized or tall you're usually okay as a father. Otherwise, it's mysteriously unreal for everybody and inexplicable, in addition.

We got into Oscar's junk car, this old AMC Matador, with doors that sang when you opened them. I loved that sound and feel I should mention it.

"That son-of-a-bitch," Oscar said. "I'm gonna kill him."

"You could try to never see him again," I said.

Oscar put his head down on the steering wheel. This old car, I loved it, and I wanted to cheer Oscar up but couldn't think of how.

"It's 'cause of him," Oscar said, "I was sort of a junkie for a while. How I got my start."

"Wow," I said. "I can see *that.*"

"I don't want to talk about it though." He started the ignition and the engine magically turned over. "Chloé," he said, "we *gotta* make some money. We just gotta set ourselves up. I'm gonna kill him otherwise. Who's this Janey person, this video woman?"

So I explained to him about it, one more time. When I finished explaining, he nodded. I figured that was the go-ahead.

Charlie, now you know. Now you know how we got ourselves into show business.

NINE

SOMETIMES I FEEL as if my life is a murder mystery, only I haven't been murdered yet, and I don't plan on being murdered at all, of course. But it's puzzling—my life, I mean—the way a murder mystery is puzzling, with something missing or dead out there where everyone can see it—what happened to Bradley W. Smith—only I don't know what *it* is, just this intimation of violence. I need a detective who could snoop around in my life and then tell me the solution to the mystery that I have yet to define, and the crime that created it.

For example: every morning, driving Turbo, my car, on the fifteen-minute commute to Jitters, I go around three curves. On two of these curves someone has planted little white wooden crosses to memorialize sudden vehicular deaths, and next to each cross, a display of artificial flowers. Artificial flowers! Petunias, these are, and violets, probably. Weeks pass, and they don't fade. I wait for them to droop as in a natural cycle. But they are stubbornly unalive and therefore unwilting, so they must be plastic, with machine-made blues and yellows and whites. Imagine that: plastic-flower sorrow. It's not ennobling. The quality of the grief has a discount aura, like a relic tossed haphazardly into a bin. I just mark it down and store it away every morning. I notice these things for my own protection.

It's a short drive that I have to do, each dawn of the working week, and there are few signs of violence on it except for these crosses. I watch for minute changes in the landscape. I steer a straight line past the reddish-yellow-brick high school, ease my way around one of the fatal curves, and there's the Tiny Tot Drop-in Day Care Center, its sign decorated with pseudofestive balloons and a teddy bear waving an American flag, followed by a few acres of scrubby farmland with two FOR LEASE signs planted near the highway.

The last cash crop on this acreage happened to be pumpkins. Just before Halloween two years ago, the pumpkins covered the lawn fronting the highway, and the farmer sat behind a card table, wearing his feedstore hat and collecting his money. From the farmhouse chimney, smoke rose day and night, from autumn till spring. Woodsmoke spread across the highway like a porous blue curtain and enveloped the passing cars in a domestic living room odor, also blue. The farmer, too, smelled of woodsmoke, and his skin looked like treated lumber. He dropped his meager earnings into a little steel box. He seldom smiled. Then we never saw him again. Another section of his land was bought up, and condominiums stand there now, a complex called The Polo Fields. No more fires, not now.

A drive-in bank is located near the second curve (you'd think the manager of the bank would try to remove the white cross and the plastic flowers from the edge of the bank's manicured lawn, but no), and then you see a strip mall where the office of my dog's veterinarian, Dr. Hasselbacher, is located. After the mall you would see, on this route, three separate apartment and condominium developments, one called Appleton Estates and the other One Pine Lane. At One Pine Lane, the eponymous white pine, a *token* tree five feet high, stands planted near the entrance. It's amazing that the kids haven't killed it by kicking it to death. What I mean is, day after day, freshly scrubbed schoolchildren wearing backpacks are lined up for the bus, jostling one another, early morning kids, dressed in bright-colored kid-clothes, yellows mostly, and nautical blues. The boys bravely kick the tree, ripping off the bark. The girls watch, some avidly.

I like seeing these kids, though I wish they'd leave the tree alone. I recall being a kid myself. I was a successful child. I count these multicolored schoolchildren each morning and try to remember how many are wearing backpacks and how many are carrying lunch boxes. Sometimes their parents come along and stand with them, smiling proudly and distractedly. This thought keeps me occupied and momentarily removes the image of those drive-by crosses and plastic flowers.

I drive with one hand on the wheel, holding my cup containing coffee mixed with vanilla and chocolate-chip ice cream in my other hand.

I pass by the health club. The manager is often outside, enjoying a cigarette.

SEVERAL MONTHS AGO, on one of our Sunday morning phone calls, when I asked my dad whether he had ever had trouble rising and shining at daybreak or getting motivated for his job at the agency, he became exasperated with me. He said, "Son, Monday morning is Monday morning. Everybody's got to do it. There are no solutions, there's only the work." My father, a gentle man, becomes somewhat abrasive on long distance. "Brad, you want food on the table, you have to go to the job like everyone else," he said, as if this thought had not occurred to me.

"I was just asking," I said.

My poor old dad: liver spots, seven years from retirement, quadruple bypass, still overweight, a weekly participant at AA meetings. He's got little scabs on his scalp, I don't know from what. I imagined him standing there by the phone, a graying, pudgy

Vietnam War survivor trying to offer sage-sounding advice to his son.

"Nobody likes a whiner," he wheezed. "What brought this up?" He didn't wait for an answer. "A man's gotta show up at the place where they expect you to show up." He coughed and hawked phlegm into the mouthpiece, or so it sounded. "You have a good job. But since you want advice, I'll tell you something to keep your spirits elevated. I just recalled this. Something your grandfather once told me. This was his cure for low spirits. When you pour your first cup of coffee of the day, if you're feeling crummy, put a dab of ice cream into it. It's festive. Then you gotta trudge off like everybody else, like I said, but you got the ice cream with you. Forget art. Put your trust in ice cream."

Booze once, ice cream now, I thought. Jesus, the poor guy, I should be the one giving him consolation and reassurance.

"No," I said. "Dad, it's just . . . you know, with my marriage breaking up . . ."

"Listen, Brad," he said. "Don't tell me. I just can't . . . I don't know. You're way past the age when you tell your parents much of anything. It's just what?" My father worries about long-distance costs almost as much as he worries about me and sometimes is short in these conversations. Really, he means well. I'm not presenting his best side here. "You don't like your job, managing that coffee store, then get another position." He waited, and his voice grew a bit quieter. "Son, believe me, I blow some of my brains out at work every day. My head's full of bullet holes. It's what work does to you. Life is suffering, as the major religions say. Face up to facts."

"Well," I said, "as long as we're on this subject of advice and everything, how have you managed to stay married to Mom for so long? What is it, thirty—"

"—Thirty-eight years."

"Thirty-eight years," I said. "How'd you manage that?"

"That's no sort of question. You can't ask me that. But since you've asked, I'll answer it. It's simple. You want to know the secret? I'll tell you what the secret is. Here's the secret. *I kept my mouth shut.*" He waited, a wintry pause. "That's the secret."

There was another long cessation of talk, during which I smelled rubbing alcohol from somewhere in my house (had Bradley the dog found a bottle in the bathroom and knocked it over? I would have to look), and then I wished my father well and hung up. Months and months ago, after he had first met my wife-to-be, he had somberly told me that my marriage to Kathryn would not work out. So far he hadn't reminded me that he had said so. He wasn't that kind of parent, not so far.

I ARRIVE AT THE MALL and park my car and check the sky for rain or snow. On this particular morning, the sky has a weird pinkish cellophane-like tint to it. The air smells like factory exhaust. I walk in through one of the service entrances. I am a service person.

When I go into the back entrance to our business, I smell the beans and the roasters and the antiseptic-lacquered-with-fruit smell of floor cleanser, and then, even more faintly, the strange bleary artificiality in the air, characteristic of enclosed shopping malls. The ion content in the oxygen has been tampered with by people trying to save money by giving you less oxygen to breathe. You get light-headed and desperate to shop. The air smells machine-manufactured, and the light looks manufactured or maybe recycled from previous light.

Above us in the mall's atrium, close to our entrance, is a skylight in a mystical geometrical shape like one of those Masonic emblems. Don't get me wrong: I believe in business and profit. Only . . . anyway, across from us is a clothes store, Snooker, specializing in clothes that have a slick polyester thug appeal, and next

to it on one side is Video Village, and on the other side is All Outdoors, where they sell what they call wilderness products—though
there's no wilderness within a thousand miles of here—hiking
clothes and such, along with alpha-wave sound-effect tapes of
breakers crashing on the beach and nearly extinct birds singing
their farewell songs. The place smells of cedar and burlap. Nearer
to us, down a sort of mall alleyway heading out to the north entrance, there's a cinnamon roll concession and a one-hour photo
lab, and a Fun Factory and a maternity store called Motherhood,
next to a nutrition store for bodybuilders. They sell megavitamins,
protein powders, and motivation magazines and tapes in there. The
last store in that alley is eXcess-ories ("Everything eXtreme you
want").

Out on the courtyard is a salad-and-snack store, The Marquis de
Salade. Next to our business is Heppelworth's, which sells weekly,
monthly, and yearly planners, and motivation posters and motivation books. They sell *motivation* in there, preachers of aggression,
hard-sell cures for Monday morning blues. Motivation! Almost
everyone at our end of the mall sells motivation except us. Everything around here is a cure for Monday morning. Well, I guess we
do that, too, with our coffee. The biggest-selling items in Heppelworth's are the framed posters with pictures of seagulls flying over
misty Pacific coastlines thick with lyric beauty and printed wisdom
underneath. There is an enormous markup for these items. Here's
a sample of what they print on the posters.

SUCCESS: *Every effort no matter how large or small contains the ker-
nel of its own reward. In every inventory your greatest asset is you.*

Then there's another one of a raging river cutting through a swath
of pine woods. Underneath that you would read the following
thought.

THE FUTURE: *I can go no higher than my hopes can take me. Therefore I must be defined by my hopes and the awe-inspiring practicality of my dreams.*

Sometimes I go into Heppelworth's on my break. I speak to the manager, Windtunnel—not his real name, I don't want him to sue me—about customer traffic and about business. Windtunnel occasionally visits us when he comes into Jitters on his break, though he always drinks the cheapest coffee we have. He has the murderous blank open-eyed look of a screech owl, and his breath smells of floor cleanser. Anyway, in Heppelworth's, I look at these posters Windtunnel has put on display, and of course I feel the onset of mall hallucination. I am so far beyond being motivated that I want to punch the nearest clerk. But I don't! *That's* discipline. I start to think up my own motivation posters. I'd put them just below photographs of automobile junkyards and clear-cut forests and gray skies sick with cloudy indifference. The Gospel According to Bradley. *The Book of Job,* pronounced "job."

DISCIPLINE: *I am a peaceful man. Peace is my mission: I will not smite any customers today. That is sound business practice and a sure path to profits.*

Then I go back to Jitters.

Following Kathryn's departure from my life, I'd go to work after giving Bradley the dog his early morning walk. I have to admit it: the business gave me a boost. I liked having a place to go in the morning. I liked having a purpose. I liked arriving there before the mall had opened. It's what you might call a dawn feeling. No doubt there is a word for this in German. Every day is a new day when filled with dawn feeling, a virgin day, until it gets fucked up by human activity and becomes history. I'd look out through the steel-mesh security curtain at the dim interior spaces of the Briardale Mall. You know, stores have a peculiar bitter vacancy when there's nobody in them, nobody wanting anything. They succumb to pointlessness.

I'd sit down and inspect our books and spreadsheets, then make sure the cups and saucers and equipment were all in place. I'd make the brews for the day and load the dispenser-thermoses with them. I'd open the cash register and do a count. I'd page through *Specialty Coffee Retailer*. I'd look out through those cell bars at the empty mall. Shiny surfaces. Every surface washed and polished. After an hour or so, the bakery would deliver our breads and pastries for the day. I'd chat with the delivery guy, Hans.

Jitters is meant to be inviting. We have wood floors and semiwood ceilings. We have tables and chairs, and large sofas and furniture— Pottery Barn knockoffs—scattered every which way. *Soft* surfaces. We have—well, we have my paintings on the wall. *The Feast of Love* is up there, in the back. A portrait of Bradley, my dog, is also up near the entryway, but it's very abstract. You can't tell whether it's a dog or a contraption or what, though it looks friendly in its abstract way, like *Nude Descending a Staircase* except with a dog. You can see Bradley in there if you know where to look. He's eating dog chow, the food suggested by drips and dribbles. It was cubism plus charm.

If I had everything ready for the day and a few moments free, I'd start to draw. I'd draw the Dragon with the Rubber Nose, the dragon that Harry Ginsberg had told me about. I got started with this art thing by being a cartoonist. I'd draw this dragon on little sheets of motivation paper I'd filched from Heppelworth's, the dragon rubbing out all the wording in Heppelworth's, all that motivation. Then I'd draw little pictures of him browsing and shopping and setting fire to JCPenney's and Nordstrom's and eating all of the cinnamon buns just down the mall from us and then eating the Mortal Kombat machine at Fun Factory. And then, resting. My dragon: like God, on the seventh day. Some of these drawings were technically quite difficult.

When the exterior doors of the mall open, the senior citizens arrive and start their mall walking. Smelling of antique cologne, they hold their elbows up and appear to be quite complacent as they grind by.

Chloé comes in right about then, Chloé who works at Jitters because she says there's a harmonic convergence right in this very spot in the mall. She says it's a sacred place, like Sedona, Arizona. Sweet girl that she is, Chloé gives my nerves a good shaking every day. Sometimes she comes in so yeasty with sex she's just had with her boyfriend that I feel like applauding. She gives off sexual odors like a flower out in the front yard trying to make a statement about gardens, which of course flowers don't need to do. Her shirt says RAGING HORMONES across the front. She's in love with Oscar now, it's gone beyond sex, and Oscar has told her (after consulting me: should he tell her?) that he's in love with her. They look so punk and disreputable, those two, but they're just a couple of kids, dressed and costumed to affect a menacing appearance.

On this particular day, she comes in and says, "So how's it going, Mr. S?"

"Oh, okay," I tell her. "The usual. Monday, you know. I kept noticing those little crosses on the curves on the way here."

"Monday!" she exclaims. "Right. And those crosses. Did I ever tell you I went to school with one of the guys who, uh, *got* one of those crosses? He was a *total* asshole. He wasn't even a fun asshole, which, you know, some of them are. Even dead, he's lucky to get a cross. I'm sorry. I wouldn't give that guy a shave."

"What was his name?" I ask.

"Bumford," she says. "Bumford McGonahy. A *loser*. With a loser name. Those crosses. Cry my eyes out. He was a mean guy. Guess I should have more sympathy, huh?"

She puts on her apron and starts arranging the pastries, like an art project.

"How's Oscar?" I ask. "What time's he coming in?"

"You should know that," she says. "I'm just labor. You're management." She smiles, and then she stops to think. "Around one." She stands up straight. "No. One-thirty."

We have overhead track lighting, five lights over the service area, and Chloé has a habit of moving back and forth behind the counter so that she appears sequentially under the lights like an actress on a stage. She's careful not to plant herself in the small shadowy vacant gaps between the lights. She's star-practicing. She flicks her head to highlight her hair. She'd be breaking my heart if she weren't my employee and a kid and Oscar's lover, besides.

"Do you think," she asks, rubbing her cheekbone, "that it's bad to do a bad thing if a good thing is going to come out of it eventually?"

"Beats me," I tell her. I'm staunchly stacking franchise coffee cups near the entryway. "What sort of bad things?"

"Well, not way bad, just bad."

Now she's positioned herself behind the display case so that she can see her reflection on it. The glass is at an angle, but when she's under the lights, she can see her face reflected there, although she doesn't know that I know she can. When she stands in exactly the correct spot, she looks down at herself and kisses the air as if her reflection is kissing her, she's that pleased with the stringy unkempt unofficial beauty of herself. No doubt each time she undresses she unwraps herself like a Christmas present. I have a feeling she blesses her body for her various wild gifts every half-hour or so, now that she knows what they are and she can use them.

"Well," she says, "like putting yourself on display."

"I don't follow you," I tell her, having lost my concentration. I've been setting the copies of the *New York Times* and the *Detroit Free Press* on the reading rack. "Putting yourself on display how?"

"Skip it," she says quickly. She's regrouping. "You hear the weather report this morning, Mr. S?"

I tell her I didn't.

"Mucho thunderstorms and mucho kaboom. Sky evil. 'Course, who'd know in a mall?"

"Who'd know?" I agree.

"What's the worst thing ever happened to you?" she asks, frowning downward at her purple fingernails. She's arranging the foods for our sandwiches.

"The worst thing?" I wait. "How come?" I come back behind the counter and adjust my manager's smock.

"Just curious. Yeah. Just curious." She gives me an odd square smile.

"Hmm," I say. "Hard to decide. I can't think of it. Well, I'll tell you one thing, it isn't the worst, it's just that I remember something, at this very moment. Here it is." I straighten up to scratch my eyebrow. "One time, in college, a bunch of us somehow got cheap airplane tickets to Paris for a few days. We were hitchhiking once we got there. Anyhow, when you're in Paris, you go to the cathedral, Notre Dame. Big tourist attraction."

She nods.

"So the four of us go into Notre Dame. And Notre Dame, you know, is actually a working cathedral. People, supplicants, I guess you'd call them, go in there and pray. They have Mass every morning, despite all these tourists milling around." She's stopped arranging the food and looks up at me. "Well, we went in there. We started at the back. In the back of the cathedral you can buy votive candles from some nun or other and light them for a loved one who needs help, and even if you're not a Catholic, you can still do this. And because someone I knew was sick, I bought a votive candle and lit it. I mean, a votive candle looks like a soul, doesn't it? And then I went over to put it on the stand."

"It's almost nine o'clock, Mr. S."

"I know. We're almost ready. I got here early. Let me finish this story." I could see some customers outside our chain security gate waiting for their morning coffee fix. "Well, we'd been traveling, so

I was tired, so my hand was shaking. And these stands they have, they're thin and spindly, like thin wrought iron, and delicate, because this is Europe. That's where we are. And because my hand was shaking, I reached down to the holder, this freestanding holder or candelabra or whatever of votive candles, and somehow, I don't know how this happened, my hand caused this holder of candles, all these small flames, all these souls, to fall over, and when it fell over, all the candles, lit for the sake of a soul somewhere, there must have been a hundred of them, all of them fell to the floor, because of me, and all of them went out. And you know what the nun did, Chloé, the nun who was standing there?"

"She spoke French?"

"No. She could have, but she didn't. No, what she did was, she screamed."

"Wow."

"Yeah, the nun screamed in my face. I felt like . . ."

"You felt like pretty bad, Mr. S. I can believe it. But you know, Mr. S, those were just *candles*. They weren't *really* souls. That's all superstition, that soul stuff."

"Oh, I know."

"No kidding, Mr. S, you shouldn't be so totally morbid. I thought when you were telling me about the worst thing you ever did, it'd be, like, beating up a blind guy and stealing his car."

"No. I never did that."

"Oscar did, once. You should get him to tell you about it."

"Okay."

"He was drunk, though." She prettily touches her perfect hair. "And the guy wasn't really blind. He just said he was, to take advantage of people. It was, like, a scam. Oscar saw through all that. It's nine o'clock now, Boss. We should open up."

"Right." And I unlock the curtain, and touch a switch, and slowly the curtain rises on the working day. The candles are nothing to Chloé; they're just candles. I feel instantly better. Bless her.

The processional begins, and we have employees from nearby businesses coming in to get a cup of coffee and maybe something else, a brioche. We turn on the music: cool piano jazz to counteract the Mozart the mall is always playing on their PA system to keep the mall rats out. I look at them all, all our customers, and I smile. I chat them up. Many of them I know by name. But really, Chloé's right. I'm too morbid. I need to work on it.

For example, when I'm conversing with people, checking out the young women coming in and out, these women, even while I'm doing these day-to-day things, I'm in a reverie. I'll be standing there, behind the counter, and first I'll think about women, possible women who might be my girlfriends or wives or something, you know, the usual fantasies, candlelit dinners, for example, and then, when I get bored with that, I'll think about my own funeral, which always cheers me up. I mean, I'll imagine the church, full of distraught supermodels listening to the eulogy and sobbing. All these supermodels boohooing over my death. And there in front of the church would be someone like what's-his-name, Robert Schiller, the televangelist, the one with the silver hair and the electronic smile, and he'd be going on and on about me, shockingly eloquent.

"Bradley W. Smith," he'd say, and he'd shake his distinguished head. "No one really understood Bradley W. Smith, except maybe his dog. And, yet, unbeknownst to many, he was a great person—"

"—Could I have a double decaf cap, *please*?"

"Sure," I say, pulling myself out of my imaginings. It's probably not healthy to maunder through a fantasy about your own funeral. Morbid, as Chloé says. But, as the song says, it's a hard habit to break. And it's harmless.

Around eleven o'clock my next-door neighbor, Professor Harry Ginsberg, comes in, mostly soaked, his remaining hair plastered to the sides of his face. He shakes out his umbrella, the one with the duck's head on it. He then waves at me—not to me, but at me—in greeting, before he says, "Have you seen it outside, Bradley? Really, this is something you should see." He smiles and shakes his head, and raindrops drizzle downward off his face onto the floor.

"What?" I say.

"Skies so dark, my boy, that you can't read under them, and this in the daytime! Go look."

"Harry, I can't leave the business."

He checks out Jitters and spies some of my art. "I see you've hung *The Feast of Love* there in the back. Your very best effort. Is it for sale?"

"No, Harry, it's hors de commerce. And it's—"

All at once there's a crack, like someone snapping a whip, and a low roaring, and a strange singeing smell, coming from I don't know where, and Chloé, who's been bussing the tables with the collection tray, looks up.

"Didn't you hear?" Harry asks me. "They've been predicting tornadoes."

"There's no weather in malls, Harry," I tell him. "Not even tornadoes. We're impervious—is that the word?—we're impervious to conditions."

"I should have such optimism," Harry says, opening his mouth and laughing silently, a gesture I do not care for. " 'Impervious to conditions,' an interesting phrase. I should have—"

Another roaring, longer this time, seems to be approaching us, silencing Harry's meditation on my wording, and when the storm sound starts to reverberate throughout the mall, like the echo in a bowling alley, my customers hear it, and they all look up, and at this point the lights blink, and the Oscar Peterson CD falls silent inside Jitters, and Mozart leaves the podium in the mall, and that's when I hear the shard-crack sound of shattering glass.

"My God," Harry Ginsberg says. He takes his espresso-to-go and walks out into the atrium.

At that point the power fails in Briardale. The emergency lighting flickers on, battery-operated evacuation spots, and all but one of my customers get up and leave. Why should they leave? They're safe here. One woman near the entrance is drinking her cup of espresso and reading the *New York Times,* and she doesn't so much as budge while everyone else scurries out. The light inside Jitters becomes emergency light: frosty and cold and glaring. But she just goes on reading, her head down, deep in concentration.

You can hear the wind shaking the Masonic emblem skylight, then hail assaulting it, and you can hear the gusts shaking the exterior doors, but otherwise it's gone very quiet in the mall. Windtunnel, looking imperturbably smug, saunters over from Heppelworth's and says, "Power failure, huh?"

"Yup, I guess so."

"It'll be back on, no time flat," he says, gazing at the ceiling. He has trained himself to be an optimist, a professional optimist, a success maniac, despite conditions. Look at his tie today! It has yachts on it!

"Hope so," I tell him. "You want anything?"

"Naw," Windtunnel says, breathing in my direction, his breath so heavy with wintergreen he could stun an ox with it. "Maybe in a little while." And he saunters back toward his darkened motivation market, all of whose customers have fled. His protective gate lowers until it is halfway down.

Chloé joins me near the counter. "This is freakazoidal," she says. "Quel rush."

"Yeah," I agree. "Come on."

We walk out toward the mall. You can hear the wind futilely attacking the mall's exterior, but you would need a full-scale level-five tornado to blow this place apart, and so far we don't have that. From here we can see into the depths of the mall. These cold emergency lights are giving all the merchandise a shakedown, and when you gaze into Motherhood, all the maternity-ware has turned ghastly. The clerks have their elbows on the cash counter, including Marilyn, a sweet babe, pure honeydew. I should talk to her. The orphaned shoes in the neighboring shoe store are like artifacts or clues to a crime. It's uniformly gray inside the mall now. What few customers there are seem to be distressed or disheartened. They're limping along, without purpose. It's as if, when you turn the power off, the merchandise somehow becomes nothing but a ruin. People lose the desire to buy. Their hearts go out of it.

Why is the light given? you think. Why is the light taken away?

Down at the center of the mall, the fountain has stopped surging into the de-ionized air, and the water sits there, gathering dust. Here and there in the far recesses of the mall, the customers move around, totally unmotivated, confused and abandoned, quite conclusively Monday-morning, and everything we've got here for sale loses its allure. Nothing but wallflower commodities, spinster products. Two old people, arm in arm, help each other walk toward the exit.

Across the acres of merchandise a vast silence prevails.

"Wow. This is amazing," Chloé says, and I nod in agreement. "You know what this makes me think of?" she asks.

"What?"

"Well, uh, your candles going out." She smiles at me, and one of her blond eyebrows lifts, as she thinks of what to say next. But she doesn't say anything, eloquently sexy in her silence.

"Hmm," I say, pretending to think this over. But actually I *am* thinking it over.

Chloé and I go back into Jitters. She ambles toward the back, taking off her apron, swaying as she goes, her hips alive to their possibilities. She sits down in a sort of wing chair back near the rest room, and seems to doze off. Oscar keeps her busy at night. I'll wake her up when the customers return. I'm a demanding boss but a fair one.

Then two things happen. I go up to the woman who's been sitting at a small table near the front, reading the *New York Times*. I say to her, "How can you read in this light? It's so dim."

"I'm used to dim bulbs," she says, not looking up.

"In that case, you'd be right at home here."

She seems startled by my witticism, and smiles at me, and in the dim light I can see that her eyes are blue. We introduce ourselves eventually, and I find out that her name is Diana.

Not to get ahead of myself here, but she becomes my second wife.

The other thing that happens is that before the lights go back on in the mall, a strange little man with greasy hair appears outside what I guess you'd call our doorway. He stands there and stands there, shifting from one foot to the other. He's not large, but he looks strong and wiry, and when I first see him I get the impression that he's not really looking over the brioche, he's searching for someone, and then he finds what he's searching for, which is Chloé. Even though she's at the back, taking a catnap, he's staring at her.

"May I help you?" I ask him, to fill the time.

He shakes his head. From where I'm standing, I can smell the whiskey on his breath. I can even tell that it's cheap whiskey, a Canadian blend, the worst of all possible whiskies. The next time I look over in his direction, he's vanished.

When I tell Chloé about him, and I describe him to her, all she says is, "Yuck. It's the Bat. Señor Creep-o-rama." Then she looks at her watch. "Where's Oscar? He should be here by now? Where's Oscar, Mr. S?"

I tell her I don't know. But right at one o'clock, on the dot, Oscar swaggers into Jitters. After soul-kissing him, Chloé tells Oscar about the Bat's mysterious apparitional appearance. All Oscar says is, "Dumb old man." Then he puts his apron on.

But I am not really thinking about them because I am thinking about Diana, having already obtained her phone number. I took courage because she hadn't been demeaned as yet with someone else's engagement or wedding ring, I had taken care to notice. Before the lights came back on in the mall, I was thinking of eating supper with this woman, Diana, whose blue eyes and stay-puttedness in the midst of storm and wrack had banished from my mind all thought of eulogies and votive candles and little white crosses accompanied by plastic flowers that poked up through the dirt and unfolded their zombie blossoms on a cheerless Monday morning.

MIDDLES

TEN

"LISTEN, UH, what did you say your name was?" Diana asks.

"Charlie."

"Listen, *Charlie*. I mean, I suppose this is all very interesting and everything, but it gives me the willies. First of all my story is *not* a story. Second of all, it's not yours. It's mine, isn't it? I thought my life was mine and not yours. Third of all, I . . . I just lost my train of thought. Oh, I know: it's all private. My life is not in the public domain. All right? Please don't write about me."

"Oh, I won't. Not exactly. But I'll invent a replica of you."

"I wish you wouldn't. I don't really have time to argue. I'm a busy woman. I'm an osteopath, you know."

"Oh, that's fascinating," I say without irony, because I mean it. "An osteopath? What do osteopaths do? Do you mind my asking? I've always been confused about osteopaths."

"No, sorry, I don't have time to explain. You can look it up."

"Okay. Maybe I'll make you into a lawyer."

"A lawyer? How can you do that? Incidentally, what did you say this project of yours is called?"

"The Feast of Love."

"Ah-*huh*. Just like Bradley's painting. I got that, didn't I?"

"Yes. Just like Bradley's painting."

"It's the best thing he ever did," she says.

"There you go," I tell her. "See, you have opinions to contribute, too."

"That wasn't an opinion," she says. "I didn't say anything. And I'm not going to say anything, believe me."

"Okay," I tell her. "But you'll wish you had talked to me."

"What does that mean?" she asks. "Are you threatening me? I should give you a piece of advice. As a favor. Free. Here it is. Don't threaten me." Her voice somehow manages to rise and to stay calm simultaneously. "Don't threaten people, especially lawyers. Don't threaten your own characters. It's for your own good. You'll wind up in a mess of litigation and . . . *subplots*." She pauses. Then she seems to laugh. At least I think it's a laugh. "You're probably an intelligent man. Let's not beat this shit to death. You get the point."

ELEVEN

THE POINT WAS, I didn't need a lover. I already had one of those, a married man who sometimes came over and who brought bunches of beautiful cut flowers, or soup he had made at home the night before.

He'd sneak the soup, carrot-leek being my favorite, out of his house in Tupperware containers, pretending he would serve it to himself for lunch. How he snuck the containers back was not my concern. He favored white shirts with French cuffs, lightly starched, though he sometimes wore a leather jacket and sunglasses to my place for his beauty's sake. The last time he tried that I said, "You look like one of the Village People, sweetie," kidding him, and he never wore those clothes again. As a back-door man he was devoted to me, and reliable. He wasn't a lawyer, thank God. He worked for a pharmaceutical company, and his hours were flexible. I wasn't in love with him so far as I could tell, but I liked him, sometimes to bursting, and I enjoyed talking to him, going to bed with him, and cooking meals with him, anything you could do inside four walls and away from public view.

He was athletic and fierce, funny when he wanted to be, and affectionate. As a lover, he was so companionable and enthusiastic, and he was clean as a knife. He had a thick head of hair, absolutely gorgeous features, and kiss-curls at the neck. I only saw him sweat hard when we were physically locked together, and his sweat had no odor, none, though his body did, a wonderful breadlike smell. We could have sex all day. He could make me come over and over again, but he didn't bring me to a boil. How can I put this accurately? As follows: I didn't have to sit up any further than normal for him and take more than the usual notice. Maybe I should have.

The only trouble with having an affair like ours is that the two of you can't go outside much. It tests the friendship more than it tests the sex. The old story: you can't be viewed in public, you're always Anna and Vronsky on this diminished suburban scale. You can't work in the garden, the two of you. You can't rake the leaves. You can't go to movies at the cineplex and you can't find yourselves at concerts or gallery shows. You have no opportunity to sit around on Sunday morning, funky and grungy and full of opinions, while you read the paper. You just stay in little rooms, those times when you can arrange it, the illicit playground of furtive and therefore heightened eros. The constraints challenge your sexual resourcefulness. Sometimes you have sex inventively all afternoon, in bed or on the floor or in the shower, for want of anything better to do. You do the fireworks. You light them and watch them go off. Of course, he didn't mind that, but, like me, he saw its limitations.

WE HAD ONCE TRIED to do what married people do: we went together to a department store to buy a pair of driving gloves. The whole event felt uncomfortably like a charade. At the counter, the salesgirl allowed me to try on several different pairs, and David smiled and frowned and exercised his discriminations and helped me choose the ones I bought, a very soft leather, light tan.

"Is that pair the one you really want, Diana?"

"Yes." I smiled.

"Sure?"

"Yes, I'm sure."

He wasn't the least bit businesslike when he was strolling the aisles with me; he was pleasant when he admired the sweaters and the watches and the diamond pins, and me, but the whole episode was like an amateur theatrical: Two Lovers Pretend They're Not Clandestine. But we were, even there, under the lights and surveillance cameras. Our eyes kept roving, on the lookout for anyone known to the two of us, including the wife.

She, the wife, hadn't managed to stay interested in him, he said, though they did make love somehow for the sake of appearances, and she put the radio on to a twenty-four-hour news station so that she wouldn't have to hear the sounds they made together, the creaks and the groans. He liked going to bed in my bed because he didn't have to listen to the news when I was on top and was riding him to kingdom come. Well, I mean: the poor man.

Despite all this, he said he loved his wife, et cetera. And of course there were the children, two of them, a boy and a boy. I'd say: You don't have to explain or apologize, honey; I *don't* want to marry you. I don't love you. But, oh, sweet guy, you're my friend, my buddy, and you're agreeable and adept in bed. He seemed wounded when I complimented him for these secondary virtues. And I said, No, no. A sane man who can be a friend and a lover to a woman is a *find*. You, David, are a find, I would say as we lay facing each other in my bathtub's hot soapy water and he slipped soap-rings over my fingers and then massaged my feet. You are a real find and you keep me satisfied, up to a point. After all, I'm a malcontent and you can't change that.

SO THERE I WAS, in Jitters at the Briardale Mall, drinking my morning coffee and reading the paper during a power failure. Housed in my gray suit, nicely and distinctly accessorized with a small gold pin David had bought for me, I was sipping a Tip of the

Andes specialty blend and checking the *New York Times* arts-and-leisure section, a feature on the choreographer Mark Morris whose work I happened to admire for its ritualized symmetries. In college I had aspirations to be a dancer, now done for. But I felt relaxed and very expensive, concentrating my forces. I had a large complicated case in the works and I was Zen-ing the whole thing, coolly distant but already imagining through strategy each step and each minute detail how I'd win. I was pre-victoring it. I had a couple of aces up my sleeve, and the anticipation of my winning—my future winnings—made me not happy, exactly, but contented with myself. The client was almost irrelevant by that time.

When the power went off in the mall, *I* was the power, so I didn't care. I thought about my four colleagues in their darkened law offices half a mile away. I imagined those contentious characters—nominally friends of mine—stuck in elevators or in conference rooms with no ventilation, trying to figure out who to blame for the loss of electricity.

If God appeared on this earth again, lawyers would sue Him.

I always have coffee before going to work. I tend to get to the office a bit late. I am quite successful—I do litigation—and can pretty much set my own hours except when I go to court. I have to be reckoned with. No one tells me when to arrive at the office. No can do. You don't dictate *anything* to me.

My days are segmented, very clearly divided and defined, and that is how I work it. I have a compartment for everything, including getting ready for the working day, down to the coffee and the paper and the arts-and-leisure section. And I have always orchestrated my romances with, well, an icy methodical self-interest. That's how I managed my affair with David.

As regulated by law, as soon as the power went off, the safety floodlights went on. Certainly enough illumination to catch up on the news. Sounds of meteorological strife resounded above me. From the sound of it, hail was falling out of the sky. I didn't care. I went on reading.

The manager of the shop appeared next to me.

"How can you read in this light? It's so dim."

I didn't bother looking up. "I'm used to dim bulbs," I said.

"In that case, you'd be right at home here."

Oh, a contender. Someone for whom some notice was required. It's always a key moment when you have to drop what you're doing to look up at a man who has initiated this sort of conversation. So, noting the paragraph where I had stopped reading in the Mark Morris article, I trained my blue eyes on him and took his measure. Before me, leaning against a chair, stood a tallish man of somewhat uncertain appearance. He gave me a guarded smile. He didn't flinch when I gazed at him. He radiated a sort of old-fashioned semisexy kindliness planted in the midst of a serviceable face. He had meditative, haunted eyes, a painter's eyes, as it turned out, widely set apart in his vaguely half-handsome head. I couldn't yet tell if he was being friendly in order to flirt, or to increase customer satisfaction. Or whether the flirting was specific to me or generic to women. I kept thinking: he's halfway there, wherever "there" is. Probably the kids in grade school had called him Froggy.

He stood, as if planted, in the cold trashy evacuation floodlight and smiled persistently. He didn't seem dim in the least. It was all a pretense. He was imagining us as comrades in a weather crisis, elbow to elbow as we faced a green sky. Meteorological solidarity. I heard the hail pounding atop the skylight. Weather is so nineteenth-century in its effects, I thought. "I've seen you here before," he said.

"This place is close to work," I said.

"I thought maybe the appeal lay in our atmosphere." He leaned against the wall. "Our way of making our customers feel at home. Not customers—*guests*."

"It's close to work."

"Or that maybe you were attracted by the paintings, the ambiance, all this comfortable furniture you see, or perhaps even the quality of the coffee."

"It's close to work."

"Okay," he said, "it's the staff, the friendly unassuming service people you tend to encounter periodically around here, like Chloé, snoozing there in the back." He gestured in the direction of a punkette half-asleep in a rear booth. I was about to get up and flee from his defective overtures when he said, "I'm sorry. You're exasperated by me, I can tell. You know, I don't mean to be exasperating. I'll let you finish your coffee. Sorry to bother you." He waited. "By the way, where *is* work, for you?"

"A mile or so away." I pointed a finger westward. "You're not *particularly* exasperating, you know. Not specifically. I've known worse."

"Thank you. What do you do? For a living?"

I told him.

"Ah." Sudden thunder crashed outside. We both moved, though I think I must have shuddered and surprised myself, because he told me a month later that I had shuddered and he had noticed and recorded it. That little movement, that tremor of mine, struck a flame. Bradley is interested in fears and phobias. He gestured toward the center of the mall, where there was nothing at all to see. "Violent weather," he said.

"Right."

"Well, you know . . . an improvement."

"Ah." I decided to nod, but not emphatically. An improvement to what? I would not inquire. A nod without enthusiasm, a nod that withheld final agreement, was what I gave him. I realize that my irony and my distance can become fatiguing, tiresome. But evasiveness is deeply erotic, at least to me. I can fight my own chilliness when the situation demands, when I rouse myself to charm and warmth. He smiled at me as if facing a strong headwind, which I had created and which collaborated with the storm outside. "You like it?"

"What?"

"The . . . the violent weather."

"Oh," he said, "sure." He was very agreeable.

"So do I, I suppose." I was trying to make a bit of a social effort. "When I was a little girl, I was afraid of thunder." I glanced down at my newspaper. Something by Paul Hindemith was being revived at Lincoln Center. And something else by what's-his-name, the boy genius, Korngold. What had happened to the Mark Morris article? "I was quite a cliché in those days," I said, remembering the conversation.

"But you're not a cliché anymore, probably. What are you afraid of now?" he asked.

"Now?" I thought for a moment. "You're very direct. Why do you ask?"

"Because you don't look like you're afraid of much. You don't look like the afraid type."

"The afraid type? Exactly right. I'm not. Well, since you ask, I *am* opposed, emotionally I guess, to open spaces," I said. "They get to me sometimes. Fields. They make me slightly loopy. Any place without a boundary. I have mild agoraphobia. Also I'm terrified of being bored. I get bored, and then I get scared of the way I'm bored. Nothing I can't handle, though."

"My ex," he said, "was afraid of dogs."

A pause. He didn't say anything, and neither did I. The thunder and wind outside made a theatrical sound-effects din, but externally, distantly, an irrelevance to people in a shopping mall, except those who wanted electric light and couldn't have it. "You know," he said, pressing his luck, "sometimes, when I'm working here, I look out into the . . . *recesses* of this place, and I see all these people walking by, and I think about what they like and what they're afraid of, and what makes them feel desolate." *Desolate.* I'd never heard anyone use that word in conversation. What would be next? *Disheartened? Forlorn?* What a strange counterproductive and counterintuitive way to flirt! The style beyond a style. He kept on smiling, despite the turn in the conversation and despite his ineptitude at this sort of talk.

I still didn't know his name. Shopping specters slid past us on their way somewhere. Winds belted the mall, whipped it.

It felt and looked weirdly sweet, that smile of his, and then I took the time and the initiative to glance at his hands. He had nice hands. There was a physical intelligence there. He didn't have—he would never have—the visible attractiveness that David had, the sexual power to make you painfully aware of his body's presence in the room with yours without your even having to look at him, and he would never have David's shoulders and his way with words, but David was beautiful and wrongful and already spoken for. He was as assuming as this guy was unassuming.

"And then I think"—he was still talking while I considered what he, this guy, might be like in bed, long-term, or on the sofa on Sunday morning, married, as it were, as the sun poured in the windows, how he would be behind the wheel or raking the leaves—"about how even that—what people are afraid of—can make them attractive. And after I've been through their . . . fears, I start to imagine, not that I have all *that* much time, how I'd get along with them, if we were ever a couple, you know, where we'd travel to and so forth, Bali or Fuji maybe or the Orkney Isles, and how—"

"You mean Fiji."

"What?"

"You said 'Fuji' and you meant 'Fiji.' One's a film. The other's an island in . . . well, you know where it is."

"Oh," he said. He was trying to smile, but it was a brave smile, a sickroom smile, and I was sorry I had caused it. I had apparently taken the wind out of his sails. His discouragement wasn't a good sign. Men should stand up to me more than that. They have to fight back to satisfy me. They have to face me down.

"—Here," I said, interrupting his silence. I took a business card out of my purse.

"What?"

"I'm writing down my home phone number. My name is Diana."

He took the card and stared a bit dumbly at the number on it. "Thank you," he said at last, as if he'd found an eyedropper of eloquence and was determined to use it.

"And now," I said, "as decreed by custom, *you* tell me *your* name."

"Well I'm Bradley," he said in a rush, as if the kids in elementary school had always made fun of that name, and it was a wound for him. "Bradley Smith. Could I ask you to do something?"

"What's that?"

"Could you stand up, so that I could give you a hug?"

Well, that was cute. But I'd rather have a tracheotomy than hug a man the first time through. "No," I said, "no, indeed, I certainly won't do that. Not yet. Nope. Too soon for hugs between strangers. Actually, I *will* stand up, but if there are going to be hugs, Bradley, they'll have to come a bit later. That's one of the things you'll learn about me. You'll excuse me, but I have to get to the office now, power failure or not. Time's a-wasting."

I shouldn't have said that, that minute condescension in tone, but I'm not sure he noticed. So I rose to my feet, and he watched me do it. He appraised me. Oh, the poor guy: I bet he knew he was overmatched already. I think he knew I would always be quicker, and not just verbally, my edges would be sharper than his, more acute angles, I was the superior animal and he was in for the time of his life. I'm good-looking, but I *will* come at you. I'm one of those women who can't see the beauty in any kind of weakness or pathos. Most men won't trade up from themselves, they'll walk away from a matchup like this, even if the woman is scarily beautiful, which I'm not, though almost, if you like intelligent eyes and gestures that correct themselves halfway through. But I saw him pocket my phone number and keep his fingers on the card, that little brand-new fetish curled up safely in its nest. He must have been a brave soul, in his way.

Then he went behind the counter and came back and gave me a slip of paper. It was an expertly drawn sketch of a dragon erasing, with his nose, the sign in front of Jitters. I was sitting inside the door, in his drawing, reading. Just a few strokes of the pencil, and you could tell it was me, just from my posture. I put it in my pocket. It had been signed by Bradley. An original.

WHAT WAS IN IT FOR ME? A relationship with Bradley Smith? Was this the classic instance of a smart woman selling herself short? As the weeks went on and I grew to know him better, I thought of all these default-mode negatives: he seemed not ignoble, not ill-spoken, not a bully, not inconsiderate, not obnoxious, not a boor, not violent, not distressing, not disdainful, not a bad dresser, not unmindful, not dirty or smelly, and not particularly ironic. He was not unhandsome. He was not unattractive.

In other words, he was husband material. Simple as that.

I didn't need a husband, I've said that. But I hadn't had one, not yet, though there had been half-hearted offers, and I was ready to have the experience, retro as it may have been, of being married, to say nothing of the fact that it seemed about time for one of them, one of these unattached default-mode fellows to wander into my life and choose me. God, I sound awful. Also, I wanted a baby sooner or later, and I didn't want to do the baby thing without having a husband. I didn't want the weird political progressivism and the faint pathos of the single mom label hanging over me. Myself, I wanted to do the whole scene in the old-fashioned way.

As my mother once said to me, *They're quite crazy, dear—men are. What you look for is one of them whose insanity is large enough, and calm and generous enough, to include you.*

I WATCHED HIM PAINT his canvases in his basement. We went canoeing on the Huron River. I played with his companion, Bradley the dog (a special-needs dog, I am sorry to say, cognitively challenged, and a slobberer). We took some weekend trips to Chicago and listened to jazz. He drew a picture of the Dragon with the Rubber Nose giving me a ride on its back. That picture actually made my heart do a back flip. How could he possibly know that I had wanted to ride dragons from the time I was a girl? We had candlelit dinners at his house. We had sex, successful sex, good-enough sex, though when I compared him to David in that category, which I could not help doing, he lost. It seems a shame to say so, but one orgasm is *not* as good as another. So what, I thought. We sat around on Sunday morning, funky and grungy, and traded opinions. We went to galleries, where he expounded his views on the art we saw (he rarely liked it and denounced and demeaned it in whispers to me). He showed me his copies of *ARTnews*. I met his neighbors, the Ginsbergs. We went up to Five Oaks and met his sister and brother-in-law, the barber. We worked in the yard, we went to my health club. There was a peacefulness to it. I would talk about the law, and he would zone out a bit as he pretended to listen. I scared him and, humbly, he tried to cover it up. I gradually settled down into him the way you settle down into an easy chair. I accepted, conditionally, the kindheartedness he offered me, though I thought it a bit dull, the way a comfortable familiar thing is dull, and its dullness is totally beside the point.

I found myself, at odd moments, leaning over him and kissing his bald spot, the one toward the back of his head. I met his parents. He met mine. He was always nervous around me, afraid that he would say something that would unmask him as a fool or a dolt. Poor guy, he was unmasked right from the start. If I loved anything about him, it was his plainness, his lack of mask, his failure of costume. This is the sort of man he was: he made balloon sculpture every two weeks or so to amuse the neighborhood kids who lived up the block and sometimes wandered into his yard. He criticized himself for not being better at it. What a midwesterner he was, a thoroughly unhip guy with his heart in the usual place, on the sleeve, in plain sight. He was uninteresting and genuine, sweet-tempered and dependable, the sort of man who will stabilize your pulse rather than make it race.

He proposed. And I accepted.

THE NEXT TIME DAVID came over—because peacefulness is insufficient—he brought wild rice chicken soup, along with a per-fectly chilled wine he liked, a sauvignon blanc. No leather jacket this time—he'd come from the office.

Somehow he'd gotten a streak of ink from a ballpoint pen on his face, the right side. (He's clean-shaven.) Once he was inside the door, but just barely inside, I curled my leg around his and licked my finger with spit and slowly and pleasurably wiped the ink off.

As I did that, we talked about our usual news, but somehow I didn't get around, at least not right away, to telling him about Bradley's proposal and my acceptance of it. After the soup and the wine, we went into my bedroom where he kissed me and un-dressed me, unsnapping my skirt smartly and kneeling before me, slowly lowering my underwear. He liked to get on his knees before me while I was still standing, doing homage to me. He would put his arms around me, kissing me, and then he would hold his face against my abdomen, and I would feel the nubs of his beard, and I would sigh with pleasure. He made me, I have to admit it, weak in the knees. After that, I took off his clothes. I noticed his body a bit more this time, caring for it, appreciating its musculature. I saw his reflection in the dresser's mirror, on whose side I had lodged Bradley's drawing of me riding the dragon.

David and I made love at some length. While we were engaged in this activity, I continued to study him, between gasps, the way you'd study a habit you're about to give up. This man, this particular one: all his adult physical features, all of them manfully occupied, not one of them boyish. Boyishness was not his style. We bucked and buckled and fought and ground ourselves into each other. First we made love—the quiet tenderness of it—and then we fucked brutally and mindlessly and then we went back to making love and then that lapsed into fucking again. He brought out a thing, a beast in me I hadn't known I had, and it always surprised me to see it, to see her as me. For the first time in my life it occurred to me that a guy who is really, really good at making love to a woman, the same woman, and who is inventively and exceptionally good at it time after time, who is carefully brutal at some moments and solicitous at others, who knows her sweet spots and concentrates on them and seems to be worshipping her body and is keen on driving her to a sweet distraction every time, is not someone to be ignored or otherwise taken for granted or dismissed on minor charges, even as a lover, a recreational human.

When we were done, I inhaled and smelled the rank and honeyed odor of our brute sexual heat, which, that evening, made me feel nostalgic for us, for the two of us. I cut it off, that nostalgia, but it kept seeping back.

After a rest, I was kissing him on his flat gorgeous stomach, seasoned with small hairs, letting my own hair tickle him, and moving downward toward where the smell was strongest. It was then that I looked up at him and said, "You know what, David? Bradley proposed."

He nodded. He knew all about Bradley. Apparently he had never taken him seriously. He had his fingers in my hair, my aggressive attitudinizing hair. He frowned. "Your artist? What did you say to him, Diana?" He waited as if he were actually curious. "What did you say in response? To his question?"

"I said yes."

There was a long silence after that, during which he kept his fingers in my hair, stroking my scalp. I was still kissing him, more as a delay to the next stage of whatever we would do or say to each other.

"You did, eh? Well." He leaned his head back. He was quiet. Sounds of the crickets came into the room, and the music from the CD player, Coltrane's "A Love Supreme," and the occasional car passing by on the street. "That's interesting. So you said yes." Then he said, a bit more querulously now, his face disagreeably restive, "Well, Diana. You agreed to marry him?" He was alert. He was quickening. "You actually did that?"

"Yup. That's right," I said.

"You *are* going to marry him. No kidding. Jesus, you're mean. You're doing this as a little prank. This is the joker side of you. But you know, you're going to wither him right away. Honey, you are going to eat him alive. You do that to the nice ones, and I know that because you have a past and you have me, and I've seen you in action. I *know* you. Don't say I don't, kiddo, I know every square inch of you. He won't stand up to you for longer than a year, you and your sharp edges. He's not your match. You've described him to me, here in this very bed. You're such a bruiser, Diana, what the hell are you thinking?"

"Oh, I'm not *that* mean—"

"Yes you are."

"Not to him, I'm not. Besides, you don't know him. He makes me into a nice person, sometimes. You don't know what he can and can't do. I'm different with him than I am with you. You know, now that you mention it, maybe I should apologize."

"To whom? To me? For being in bed with me?" he asked. "You're being vague. That's not like you. It's not me you should apologize to."

"No, no, that's not what I'm getting at. You're missing my point.

Deliberately. Well, Bradley . . ." Somehow I couldn't finish the thought. I couldn't remember whom I thought I should apologize to. He had confused me for a minute. That wasn't like me. My mind felt bleary.

Right about then the phone rang. He told me not to answer it, but I did, leaning over him so that my breasts brushed against his legs. It was a solicitation call, one for window treatments. I hung up briskly and looked over at David.

"What *about* Bradley?" he asked me, as if we hadn't been interrupted. "Speaking of whom, why are you here with *me*?" His eyes, I thought, were quite bright with something like curiosity. "Let me get this straight. If you're planning on getting married to this Bradley, this coffee guy, this sketch-pad fellow, what exactly are you doing here in bed with me? And how come you didn't tell me until now? You're supposed to be fat with your new love. You should be thick with it." He scratched his shoulder and frowned squarely at me. "You should be strutting around arm in arm with him. You should be nestled with him, listening to those Mingus albums of yours. Instead, here you are, and you're in bed with me. I thought this marriage idea of yours was a goof. You always *said* it was a goof."

"A goof? No, I never said that. I'm sure I never said that. I wouldn't use that word. I don't know. As for us, you and me, we're having sex. What do you mean, what am I doing here with you? I'm doing what we always do together. We talk and make love, and make love and talk."

"Well, if you're going to marry him . . ."

"I *am* going to marry him."

"Then you shouldn't be curled up naked with me like this, should you? Correct me if I'm wrong. You should be out there, wherever 'out there' is, with Bradley, this fiancé of yours, and being with him." He waited for a moment. "Exclusively."

" 'Exclusively'? Oh, come on. Don't be priggish about this," I said, collecting myself. "*Exclusively.* What a word. I don't see why. Why I shouldn't be here, I mean. *You're* married, after all. You're the married one. The guilty party." I pointed at his finger. "When we're both naked, just the two of us, you're still dressed in your wedding ring. I'm not even married yet. I'm just that plain old traditional figure, the other woman. The mistress." I had his cock in my hand. I was determined to keep this light, comic, social, and not insane, and I started to suck him playfully, but he wouldn't let me go any further, shaking me off, and he sat up.

"Stop that. We need to talk. That's different," he said. "My being married."

"No, it isn't," I told him. "It's exactly the same. You can't criticize me."

"You're wrong," he said. "You're going in, a first-timer to marriage, lecturing me on ethics while you go down on me. You're betraying him *before* you've even been faithful to him. What kind of scene can you call that? You haven't even tried to be faithful. There *was* a time when I was faithful to Katrinka. You're so restless, Diana, you haven't even given your own marriage a chance. You're pre-bored, for Chrissake. You're like a monster who wants me to play with all your toys, out of sheer boredom."

"You're jealous, David. That's sweet."

"No I'm not. I'm taken aback, is what I am. I'm really taken aback."

" 'Really taken aback.' Listen to yourself. Look at the words you're using. You're not one to give me lectures on faithfulness, buddy boy. Is this some sort of guy solidarity thing?"

"Well," David said. "Well." He gathered himself, sat up in my bed, and stared at me. I looked away. "Hey, Diana," he said, "look at me." I did. No problem there. "You're a pretty strong woman, you know that? And you're beautiful. But the trouble is, you're a thug. What do you think you're doing here, doing this lonesome-girl thing in bed with me? Are you just playing with this guy? Do you love him? This Bradley person? Do you love this guy you're going to marry?"

"It's not that simple."

"Sure it is. It's always that simple. So. Do you love him?"

"He's lovable, David. That's what counts."

"No. That's not what I asked. Lovable is different. *Do you love him?*"

"What a question. I don't know," I said. "Sort of." I grinned and shrugged.

He wound back and slapped me, hard.

I got out of bed, right then, right away. I stood naked next to the window. On the bedside table the little votive candles that we always light for lovemaking were blown out by the breeze of my passing. "You bastard. Get the fuck out of my house," I said.

"Oh, no, I don't think so," he said, a calm and sexy insolent look on his face. "Nope, I think I'll stay here for a little while." He snaked down under the sheet. "I'd like some coffee, if you please, Diana." He thought for a moment. "Decaf." He then gave me a strange look, one I can't describe, as if he'd been gratified by hitting me.

"Don't you ever do that again," I said. "Don't you hit me ever, you bastard." I said this calmly.

"You're marrying a man you're not sure you love?" he asked from where he lay, scary and calm. "That's what you're doing? You cunt, you deserve to be slapped."

"Don't you ever call me that."

"What?"

"That word. I hate that word."

"Yeah, I agree. It's an ugly word. But, you know, somebody should knock some sense into you. Honey pie, I should beat the living shit out of you." At once he was on his feet, putting on his boxer shorts. Standing there, he cut a figure (David's vice is his physical vanity), and I couldn't help it, I watched him. He has nice legs, powerful thighs, every inch of which I had kissed and put my tongue upon, and I didn't care anymore. "I've never hit a woman before in my life. Now I see the logic in it, if it's you," he said. His voice was heading toward a shout and soon would arrive there. "I would save you a ton of grief if I beat the living crap out of you, so you didn't marry someone you didn't love." His eyes were glistening and bright with rage. "Goddamn you." He was pacing. "You've just hired him as an entertainment. This is beneath you. Excuse me while I do the dishes. I have to calm down."

He went into the kitchen. When I heard the sound of running water, I sat on the bed and I cradled my face in my hands for a few minutes. My cheek was burning where David had struck me. I made small wrinkles in the bedsheets with my toes. I was trying to think but seemed to be out of basic cognitive resources. That was new for me. I'm good at the complexities of argumentation. Somehow I hadn't—I don't know why—expected him to react the way he had. At last I stood up and put on a nightgown and went into the kitchen.

David was standing there in his boxer shorts, washing the soup bowls and rinsing them, washing the wineglasses and rinsing them, all with his usual care and thoughtfulness. I looked at the curve of his spine as it plunged into his shorts. I thought of how I would miss his body, the soups, the wine, the talk—the whole of this beautiful fucked-up man. I would miss the commotion we made together. That more than anything. Making love to him was like going through a car wash, except you came out dirtier and more alive at the other end.

"You made that coffee yet?" he asked.

"Not yet. I thought you could brew it yourself."

"Why don't *you* do that right now? And go to hell, if it's no trouble, while you're at it."

"This coarse language isn't like you, David."

He turned around and gave me the display: he held his arms out operatically, and I was still so in love with him at that moment, I realized, so fevered, and I hated that. "Don't get fastidious with me. What am I like, Diana? What am I *like*? What do I do? Go ahead. Tell me, if you're so sure, if you're the expert on me. What am I, besides your friend, and the man who makes love to you when we can both arrange it? *Diana, I'm the guy who looks out for you.* Who else does that?" He was getting angry all over again. He was re-angering himself. "Who else *really* does that for you? Nobody. I think I'll go outside, right this minute if you don't mind. If I don't, I'll make a mess of you, I'll give you a shiner. And then what will the neighbors think? Why don't you make that coffee for me, while I'm outside?"

"You're not dressed."

"I have my shorts on. Besides, do you think I give a flying fuck about the neighbors?"

He crossed the kitchen, past the vase where his cut flowers—gladioli this time—were arranged on the breakfast table, there in the alcove, and then he stomped out toward the back entryway. As quickly as I could, I put on a bathrobe and ran out to see where he'd gone. I couldn't see him. In the living room, the CD player, rotating its carousel selections, had gotten around to the Miles Davis we had carefully timed for background to postcoital murmuring, *Sketches of Spain.* But no David in sight.

I put my face to the window and tried to see him. Oddly, for a moment Bradley's word *desolation* returned to me as I raised my hand to the side of my face and stared out into the darkness. Night birds and crickets chirped away madly.

The house I own is a large one, and I have an ample front yard with azaleas planted on the north side, and when I put my hands to the sides of my head to blank out the light, I could see him squatting in the back under a tree, in his underwear, pulling out random clumps of grass with his right hand as he swigged at a beer, which he must have found somewhere in the refrigerator. He was talking to himself, a novelty David-thing, absolutely new and unseen before by me, though I couldn't be absolutely sure what he was doing in that dim light aside from being actively upset with me. The face, though, was the classic male crying face even if there happened to be no tears on it. The son of a bitch loved me, and he had never told me about it. He was so rigorous.

He dropped the beer can and the grass he had pulled out and started to walk toward the garage. When he came around to the front again, he was buck naked. In his grief he had taken off his boxer shorts. God knows what he did with them. Thrown them up into a tree, maybe. He was in a state of erotic semicomic despair. At last he had well and truly surprised me. I was dumbstruck, and I was thinking of the nearest phone, but all David did was to come inside and return to the bedroom and slowly and almost shyly put on his beautifully tailored clothes, item by item, carefully, though of course without the boxer shorts. I wondered what he would tell his wife about their absence, but maybe she would be asleep when he came in, oblivious in her dreams. Maybe she never noticed what he wore. He attached his cuff links: David. If he lost his composure quickly and violently, he recovered it just as quickly. There's that particular man for you.

I had followed him into the room. My face stung. "David," I said. "This doesn't mean—"

"—You shouldn't marry someone you don't love," he said, his back to me. "Oh sweetie, it's a soul-error." He waited. He stared at the dragon drawing on my dresser mirror. "Yeah, and see if I'm right. Hey, where's that famous coffee of yours? The cup I asked for? Again and again and *again*? You never made it, did you? You couldn't bring yourself to do that, could you, for my sake? That little thing. Well, too late now."

And those were the last words I heard from him until after Bradley and I were married, when David and I started up our relationship once more. I was the one who called him. I was the initiator. Then he called me. Before too long, we were back to where we were before, slamming each other around. By anyone's standards, I suppose, I'm bad and ill-tempered, but David matches me in that and it's why we were so compatible. We go about our hypocrisy with aplomb. And we're complacent, too, mostly about what we have and what we can get. He is my other. But, you know, these are the cards I was dealt, and that's the way I played my hand, and I don't much care what you think.

TWELVE

BECAUSE THE NEXT MORNING was a Saturday, and my
Esther was sleeping at last, perhaps only for a few minutes, the
tossing-and-turning kind of sleep, I rolled quietly off my side of
the bed and took a shower. I took care not to drop the bar of soap.
I shaved my face (my features are porcine, coarse, and bristly—I
have a snout like a wild boar, and yet, I think, I am handsome), not
looking into my own eyes, avoiding self-commentary on the bags
underneath them. I cooked some oatmeal for myself and then fed
the goldfish, Julius and Ethel.

I went into my study and pulled out the checkbook from the
desk drawer. I am familiar with clutter, with the diffusion of philosophy into papers and bookmarks and the scatterings of thought. I
wrote out a check to the order of my son Aaron Ginsberg (it was
not for as much as he had asked). And then I realized: no no no, I
cannot send the boy a check with my bank account number on it.
He is wily, he and his strange dangerous friends. They will find a
way of ordering the bank to send them *all* the money in my account. I do not know how they will do this, but they will know.
These children of ours have befriended computers, and the terrible
dangerous computers will help them help themselves.

So I therefore drove, this bright sunny morning, to the branch
bank that kept its offices open on Saturday. By this time it was nine
o'clock, by the official clocks. The sun shone its burning rays on

the landscapes of my life, the real world that made Plato so un-happy. My bank teller's name was Theresa. I seem to remember that she wore glasses. I was beyond having any certain opinions on her appearance, however, this girl, her beauty or lack of it. Perhaps she belonged to somebody, in the amorous way of things. Perhaps she gave off an odor of lilac. What was that to me? What, may I ask, was the odor of sachet of lilac from a bank teller to me that morning? We were in separate galaxies. We were lit by separate lights and we cast separate shadows. I was managing a catastrophe, and she was working as a clerk in a bank.

Theresa, I said when I reached her window, my throat dry, I need a cashier's check made out to my son, Aaron Ginsberg. It must come from my savings. I handed the passbook and the with-drawal slip to her, and she checked my balance and quickly typed up the check on a machine. Thank you, I said. She must have smiled, such people do all the time, after all, but I must confess that it made no impression on me. I returned to my Ford car and drove home.

Back in my study I wrote a brief note to my son, asking for . . . asking for what? For his assurance that he would spend it wisely? We were beyond such tender father-son messages. (A mad-dening tune was going through my head, "Twentieth-Century Blues.") I asked my son Aaron not to make good on his threat to end his life. On my desk was a picture of him, smiling into the white-cotton sunshine on a tennis court, on a singular day when he was healthy and happy.

I enclosed the check with this note. On the front of the enve-lope I attached a stamp—the American flag. Well, I don't mean for these details to have an oppressive poignancy. I stamped the letter and wrote his name and address, a post office box number, on it. I walked to the corner and dropped it in the mailbox. In the dark it lay among the other fellow letters, whispering to one another their messages of love and longing and betrayal.

But almost as soon as I released the metallic lip of the box, I remembered that Aaron had instructed me to send the money by *express* mail, as a sign of his last-minute emergency condition, the bloodletting of his threatened mortality. What could I do? The letter had been thoughtlessly mailed. Briefly I considered calling the airlines to get a ticket immediately out to Los Angeles, to intervene personally. But by now I knew that to him I was worse in person and therefore more ineffective as a father than I was when reduced microscopically to a mere voice over the phone. In person, revulsion at the mere sight of my paternal features would settle over his face instantly, before I had committed the first father crime of the day.

Inside the house, Esther slept on restlessly, poor old girl.

ENWOMBED WITHIN MY FORD CAR, not knowing where to go but recognizing for my own good that I should not go anywhere near the Amalgamated Education Corporation, I drove to my neighbor's coffee shop in the mall. Bradley was not there in person. Instead, I found in front of me a young American girl whose tee-shirt was labeled RAGING HORMONES and who asked me for my order.

Coffee, young lady, please.

Any kind?

Any kind is fine.

Blend-of-the-day?

Fine, fine.

Comin' right up.

Excuse me, I asked, but where is the manager? Where is Bradley?

In back somewheres, she said. Ordering stock. You know him?

He is my neighbor, I informed her. In fact he lives next door.

Wow. You're Mr. S's neighbor. No kidding. Hey, you want a Kleenex? she asked. Here. She held one out to me.

For what purpose?

You look like you need it, she said. She pointed at my face. Like, tears or something?

I hadn't realized, I said. Thank you. Thank you very much. After paying her, I took the coffee and the Kleenex and found my way to a chair near the back. I dabbed at my eyes. My eyes were damp but not yet completely overflowing. I was the only customer. In desperation I glanced around for something to read. The newspapers, however, were in the front.

She came toward the back to clear the tables near mine.

So, she said, whattya do?

I teach philosophy, I said.

Oh jeez. I could use a philosopher, she said, like right this week. Right now. This minute. She stopped and put her hand on her hip. Like, I'm about to do something? Maybe you don't mind my asking. And this thing I'm about to do, it's bad? But it's going to result in something good? So, in your opinion, should I do it?

What's your name, young lady? I asked.

Chloé. Clow-*ay.*

Not *Clow*-ee?

Naw. I customized it. Everybody should customize their names.

The answer is no, Chloé. The ends never justify the means. Almost every ethical philosophy of consequence will tell you so. Kant's categorical . . . well, bad actions make the result turn out bad.

I thought that was what you'd say. Thanks. Uh, she said, do I owe you anything?

What?

Like money? For your opinion. Because it's your job as a philosopher to give advice, right? And besides, you live next door to Mr. S. Since it's your job to think, I should pay you. Anyway, do I owe you anything?

No, Chloé, you don't. But thank you for offering. I bowed my head. In silence, she went away. I drank my coffee. Never once had Aaron as an adult child asked me for advice. To my best recollection, never as an adult had he ever asked me so much as a single question.

Bradley returned. He stopped by my chair. He sat to make neighborly conversation. He asked me how I was. And I told him, the genial man, I told him everything, because I hardly knew him, and because Chloé was taking care of his customers, and because he had hung up *The Feast of Love* in the back, and because he was so vacant as a human being—I do not mean this as criticism—that I could fill him, that morning, with my difficulties, and not cause a flood condition. Toward the end, he put his hand on my shoulder. It was a consolation of sorts.

And how are *you*, Bradley? I asked.

I'm in love, he said. It's recent. I've met this wonderful woman.

And who is the lucky lady?

Her name's Diana, he said. We're going to be married, I think.

Well, you must bring her over to meet Esther and me.

And with that, I rose to leave.

THIRTEEN

I CAN BE *SO* UNMOTIVATED. For example. You know the dust that can, like, float in the air? Me, I was totally capable of sitting in a chair for *hours,* watching the dust-fuzz hanging in front of me. If there was sunlight in the room, just the particles of visible molecules or whatever, I was excellent and enthralled.

I'm not saying that I'm deep, I'm just saying I watch the dust, and I'm not stoned either, when I do it. Just observant. I'm concentrating on it, figuring out its mystery, its purpose for being here in the same universe with us.

When I tried to get Oscar to study the dust, he went: you're so, like, Looney Tunes, Chloé. Jeez, dust. He *was* smiling when he said that, criticizing my dust interest. But you could tell that he didn't get the profundity of dust at all. Poor guy. Well, some people can't sing, either.

But what I'm saying is, I can get motivated when I have to. I can stop dust-meditating and get off my ass and get the job done. Which means that when I had to figure out the future, I took steps.

Oscar's friends, these boy-men from his high school jock clique—Speedy and Ranger and Fats (who was not fat—where do guys *get* names like this?)—came by our apartment, grab-assing Oscar and demanding that he come out to play basketball, it being early summer, and the two of us, Oscar and me, not having to work at Jitters that day. Oscar! Hey, man, they said, first of all hollering up to our window, dude, you just gotta come shoot some hoop, doooooooode, Oscaaaaaaaar, we just gotta have another guy. Oscar hears the call of male needs, he barks his yes downward to them, so then he puts on his shorts and his Nikes and kisses me and gets his shoulders punched in the parking lot and his ass whapped and he is gone. Like poof, like a husband. Empty nest.

I had to figure out if Oscar and me had any prospects at all, as a couple, together. So there I was, me, Chloé, alone. But with the keys to Oscar's ancient AMC Matador, and I sat there, and I'm like, *I gotta find out the future from an expert.* So I took some money and put it into my pockets and my shoes in case I got robbed, and I drove over to Ypsilanti, where the psychics are. You can't do psychics off of TV. The TV psychics are mostly wrong, and way too expensive besides.

I had been reading my tarot cards on Oscar and wanted a second opinion. And I figured I'd need to take something of his, so I took a mungy sweat sock and his track team relay baton and one of his knives, which he had told me not to touch, but which I did touch, for his own good and mine too.

YOU GOTTA GO TO YPSILANTI to find out the future. Or Willow Run. See, what you do is, you leave the ho-hum middle-class environs of Ann Arbor and Pittsfield Township, and then you explore your way down the strip, past the used car lots and the Arby's and the Dairy Queen, and then there's Eastern Michigan University with its stiff-dick watertower (but there's a brick condom on it—go see it for yourself if you think I'm kidding), and then downtown Ypsi, but then, when you get east of there, *that's* when it turns really interesting and nasty over there in the Twilight Zone, that's where the future-experts ply their trade.

I mean, most cities have got their own Twilight Zones, right? Where the old wrecked factories and warehouses live? 'Cause East Ypsi has got these ancient car assembly plants, these old humping kickass grounds of steel and scrapyards, and the scrapyards sort of find their way next to topless bars and tattoo parlors, and these freakazoidal video stores where you don't want to know *what* or *who* they're renting in there, and outside on the curb the underfed cats and dogs are staring at you and begging for puppy chow when you drive past, and then there's razor wire around most of the warehouses, so you just know the karma's really complicated there. It's like the future has already happened, and it's all past by now? Like that?

Anyway, you gotta drive over there on a sunny day. Otherwise it doesn't work. You get bad head colds in your psyche if you go there on a cloudy day. Then your psyche sneezes your good karma out into the ozone layer, where, of course, it burns away.

And that's how come I was driving the Matador in the sunshine past Odd Lots Supermart and a pawn shop and a gun shop and then a vacant patch of struggling grass, with a thing in the middle of it you couldn't identify except it was metal, and no one had ever found out how to work it, and it was ultra-dead. Rust never sleeps, said the bard. I'm bummed. Where's the professional psychic whose office I thought was here? I saw it once last time I found myself located in this locale. In this hyper-slum there were, like, *shoes* everywhere, shoes without anybody standing in them, old shoes. On the sidewalk here and there, brown leather shoes. Very *Plan 9 from Outer Space*. So how come people, such as men, leave their shoes out here? What's going on with these shoes out on the pavement? My advice is: Guys, find a wastebasket.

And now I'm near Willow Run, where they made the big World War Two bombers back when life still had a purpose in this area and people knew what their work was good for, and I'm seeing more pawn shops with iron bars on the front, and bunched-up tallboy-beer-in-the-brown-bag guys standing but mostly sitting on the sidewalk doing their smiling openmouthed but no teeth chicken-shit thing, *har har har, hey man, there's a girl in that big ol' Matador, is that door on the driver's side unlocked,* and then I see the place I was looking for, that I'd seen the last time I was over here. And which I knew was here. Which had to be here.

Professional Psychic
Fortunes Told
Tarot or Palm Reading
Walk-in

I park the Matador out front, which is a dangerous move to start with, but I figure the psychic has got to have some control over what goes on outside her store and in the neighborhood—she's psychic, after all, right?—and I go inside.

It's dark. No crystal balls. She's in possession of this gross cor-duroy sofa that smells of spilled meatloaf and cat food, and over to the side there's a partially assembled table and two chairs, and a church rummage sale table lamp with birds and bunnies painted on it, and over on the walls there's a Laurel and Hardy clock, with their eyes moving back and forth, like pendulums except not quite. There's other Laurel and Hardy stuff in the room: L&H porcelain cups, and a souvenir L&H dinner plate mounted on the wall, and a one-foot-high L&H statue set in the corner. On the other wall is a picture of down-by-the-old-mill-stream that you'd buy at Wool-worth's. By my ankles a black vampire-cat is stroking against my legs and purring. God, I hate cats. I'm the only girl my age I know who hates cats.

Meanwhile, country-western, moron music if you ask me, Tricia Yearwood or somebody, your-cheatin'-this-and-your-cheatin'-that, is playing off some staticky AM radio in the back. I hear this voice, "I'll be right with you," and then the sound of a toilet flushing and somebody gargling.

In comes Mrs. Maggaroulian, which I know is her name because her business card is out on the table, and her name is also in little print on the front window, and she says, "Hi, I'll be with you in a minute, honey."

I look at the wall. She's posted the prices. Tarot readings are twelve dollars, and palm readings are twelve dollars, and the guaranteed predictions of the future based on psychic determinism, which she happens to know how to do, are also twelve dollars. It's all twelve dollars each. If I get everything she's offering, one from column A and one from column B, plus dessert on column C, this is going to cost me a full day's salary.

But! you can't get your hands on the future for free, fuck and alas, so I shell out almost every piece of folded money I have, and I give them to Mrs. Maggaroulian, and she puts on her reading glasses that she has on a beaded chain around her neck, and she locks the front door and puts my money in a little steel box underneath the table, where it's hiding. By this time I am noticing that Mrs. Maggaroulian is big, I mean she is really big, the way a giant is big, at least compared to the way women usually are shaped and sized, and she has a mohair wig, it looks like, and something there on her jaw that looks like facial hair. Her nose looks like it's made out of modeling clay. Her dress didn't even come off the rack, 'cause it's a tablecloth fastened together with safety pins. She wears black nail polish, not the sexy black but the scary black. She's got big hands and feet, big hoppers and big choppers. This Ypsi chick is not the Better Business Bureau's idea of a respectable psychic. But, duh, if she were prettier she'd be broadcasting on the Dionne Warwick psychic network at forty dollars per minute and she'd be whispering predictions to Oprah. Hey, I don't give a shit if she *is* a drag queen, I'm cool with that, she could be the fucking Queen of the May for all I care, I just want the future out of her, provided it's one hundred percent accurate.

She sits me down at her table and says, Honey, whatcha want to know about? So I say that I've got this boyfriend, Oscar . . . and Mrs. Maggaroulian nods, 'cause of course she knows what I want to know, being able to read my mind. She says we'll do a palm reading first.

She takes my hand, opens up the fingers and studies my palm like a road map. She frowns. "This is your love line," she says, tracing her finger along a crease. "Notice this."

I look at it. "What?"

"You have a relationship with this Oscar? This Oscar relationship," Mrs. Maggaroulian says, "is soon going to be over, it would appear."

"How do you mean, 'over'? You sure about that?"

"We could ask the cards," Mrs. Maggaroulian informs me, as if she really doesn't *like* my hand at all and doesn't want to read it anymore, and she takes out her tarot cards, which, get this, she kisses first, on the box. Me, I would never do that. I would never kiss a deck of cards. She tells the cards in painful detail the questions she wants to ask and she proceeds to lay them out on the table. I will not tell about the cards that came up—that is *such* bad luck—but it was, like, a magical mystery train wreck.

"Well," says Mrs. Maggaroulian, in a sort of guy-imitating-a-woman Monty Python bagpipe drag queen voice, "I've certainly seen better cards, I'll say that."

"Is there any hope?" I asked. "For the two of us, Oscar and me? 'Cause I love him and everything."

"Did you bring any item of his?" Mrs. Maggaroulian asks, emphasizing the word *item* like it was word-candy. "Any of his possessions? That he's touched often?"

"Besides me, you mean? Yeah. This sock," I say, plopping it down on the table, "and this track team baton." I wait for a moment, and I do my very best to grin. "And this knife."

She takes the sock in one hand, and the relay baton in the other. She looks up at me, and the wig on her head shifts a little, to the right, toward one o'clock. I can hear Laurel and Hardy ticking my precious time away. I'm afraid she's going to tell me about her glory days when she was on the track team herself. "I don't have to hold Oscar's knife," Mrs. Maggaroulian says. "You can hold Oscar's knife. I can see everything clearly enough without it. Honey, what did you say your name was?"

"Chloé."

"Chloé, honey, you know we're not always right. Sometimes it's a good idea to take the future with a grain of salt. We psychics, well, I don't know. Psychics have bad days, too. We have our up days and our down days." She puts the baton and the sock back on the table.

"Is this your bad day, Mrs. Maggaroulian?"

"Yes, it is, dear. I have a headache. I have a very terrible headache. All those little hammers."

"What do you see about Oscar, Mrs. Maggaroulian?"

The room really filled up with the smell of meatloaf right about then, like a freight train of meatloaf just went by. I was beginning to want to get out of there, in the worst possible way. I could feel the cells of my skin revolting against the room. My individual skin cells wanted to get free of me just for being there. Mrs. Maggaroulian kept trying to smile at me, and she kept failing at it. "Well, honey," she said, "everything I see about your boyfriend is not so hotsy-totsy. Both Laurel and Hardy are telling me that his future prospects are not bright. Did you say he was still alive?"

"Oscar? Oh yeah, he's still alive." I decided not to ask her about Laurel and Hardy, or how she talked to them. Some things don't stand much looking into.

"Well, that's wonderful. You go home to him and give him a big kiss and a bear hug, honey. That's what I would do if I were you. You know, I haven't seen all that much in your future, so I'm going to . . ." She stood up and went over to her little steel cashier's box and took two fives out of it and handed them back to me. "I'm going to give you a little refund. Ten dollars. Think of this as a re-fund on your future. You should stop and get a cheeseburger on the way home, honey. Get two cheeseburgers. And some fries. Take it all to Oscar. He'll be so grateful, I can guarantee. If you love him, he's bound to stay alive for a while. Then go out bowling tonight with him like a good girlfriend. Do you like bowling? You do go bowling, don't you?"

"I guess."

"Okay. Go bowling with Oscar. 'Cause what I see is . . . you want something to eat? I'm making some meatloaf back there, in the kitchen."

"No thanks." *I figured I had to ask.* "Is it bad, Mrs. Maggaroulian, what you see? You gotta tell me. I paid you all this money. It's like this week's savings. Wages and even tips, that our customers put in the jar on the front counter? I have to know. About Oscar?"

"Listen to me." She gave me a moment to look into her eyes. There was another person living in there, at least. You couldn't tell if what was inside Mrs. Maggaroulian was human or just an honorary human. Maybe she was a resident alien. The IRS wouldn't dare audit her, 'cause they'd find out she was an alternate life-form, and they don't have income tables for that. "I can't be-lieve he's alive, this Oscar of yours," she said. "But if you really love him, he'll stay alive for a while longer. Trust me on that. People can keep other people alive, you know. Now go, honey. You drive home."

"I will." I stopped at the door. "Mrs. Maggaroulian," I said, "are you really a girl?"

She didn't even look up. "No, dear," she said, sniffing. "I am a lady."

WHEN I CAME INTO the apartment, Oscar was all over the bed, half-asleep after his exertions and his shower and his beers. He had the TV on to baseball, and his eyes were closed, and I figured, worst-case scenario, that he was dead. So I took my shoes off and I put the two cheeseburgers and the big thing of French fries on the kitchen table, and I went running over to where he was, and I gave him a good shake. And, just like that—presto—his eyes open.

"Hey, Chloé," he says, "whassup?"

I'm straddling him, and shaking him, and he smiles at me. "How was basketball?" I ask.

"Great," he says. "Man, I was so hot, I was like an action figure. Hey, I see you took the car. Wheredja go?"

"Ypsi," I said. "I went to a psychic. Mrs. Maggaroulian. I wanted to find some things out."

"Yeah?" he says. "Cool. What'd she say?"

And that's when I took a deep breath, and I looked down at Oscar, and I said, "Oscar, I've got this idea. Don't get mad at me, okay?"

"Naw," Oscar says, "I wouldn't get mad. What's your idea?"

"Well," I say, "I know it's early and all, and maybe we should go slow and everything, and I know that girls aren't supposed to say this, but after talking to Mrs. Maggaroulian I've been thinking that maybe I should. I mean, this is going to sound real weird, 'cause here it is Saturday afternoon . . . anyway, what I was wondering was, Oscar, maybe we should get married. Oscar, would you marry me?"

And Oscar, who's said that he loves me about a thousand times in the last week alone, he doesn't even stop to think about it, he just sits up a little in bed, and he says, "Oh, *yeah*." Just that, "Oh, *yeah*." Like it's a great idea that he hadn't thought of recently, but should have. Then he says, "That's a real cool idea, Chloé. You and me married. Like I'd be your husband, and you'd be my wife, right? Wow. I'd *like* to do that."

Some things you think can't ever happen, and then they do.

I gave him the hugest kiss he'd ever had, and then I went over and got the bag, and we did a four-alarm fuck, and afterward I fed him the cheeseburgers, both of them, his and mine too, from my hand to his mouth, bite after bite after bite after bite after bite.

FOURTEEN

YOU KNOW WHAT I HATE? I hate it when someone turns to me and says, "What're you thinking, Bradley? Tell me. What're you *thinking*?" Well, no. If it's a-penny-for-your-thought time, here's your penny back. Because, first of all, it's private, whatever my thoughts are—and don't think I'll tell *you* all my thoughts, either—but secondly, most of the time I don't, in the way of things, *have* any thoughts. There aren't any *thoughts,* per se, is what I'm saying. Day after day it's a long hallway up there, just a yard sale, interrupted with random images of my paintings, or my dog, or the coffee store, or memories, or a woman, her face or her body or something she said, all of it in free fall through the synapses.

And I don't care if I'm mixing my metaphors. This is my second marriage I'm talking about now. I can damn well mix my metaphors on that marriage if I want to. I've got my rights.

The reason I say all this is that I couldn't stop asking Diana what *she* was thinking. We'd be somewhere, like a restaurant, before or during our engagement, and she'd drop into these states, staring off into space or down at the breadsticks in the glass container. Then she'd look at the butter plate or the hors d'oeuvres instead of at me. And I just knew she was carrying on a serious conversation with herself. You could all but see her lips moving.

So I'd say, "Hey, Diana. What're you thinking?"

She'd smile, suddenly. She'd sort of pick at her engagement ring. "Nothing." As if she had been recalled to Earth from some asteroid belt or other. "Nothing. Why do you ask, Bradley?"

When they—women—are serious about you, they'll use your full name. *Bradley.* "You just looked deep in thought, that's all."

"I'm thinking about us," she'd say, and reach for my hand. Another big smile, like a smile you'd do for a flashbulb, a smile like arriving in France after seven cramped hours on the plane, that's what she'd give me. But those smiles of hers didn't even have a half-life. They were on her face, optically illusional, and then they'd be gone so quickly you couldn't be sure you'd seen them at all.

She'd go absent without leave at meals, she'd go absent in the car, and she'd go absent after our lovemaking. She looked like a woman gazing out from the railing of a cruise ship toward an island of some sort, and her bangs would fall over her eyebrows while her feet twitched in time to an interior melody. She was a great one for examining the ceiling. The molding fascinated her. Lying beside me, she could carry off her fleshly existence away from me, but, after a moment, she couldn't. I mean, my God, I was so in love with her that I almost didn't notice. I thought I was made of plutonium, I was that powerful. Radioactive Man. I would imagine Diana walking toward me, looking at me with *recognition*—I am your woman, you are my man, we are mated—and I'd think: How did I get this lucky? Not that I'm selling myself short.

Other men envied me, I was sure. I longed for her. I looked forward to her, not to her sweetness, because she didn't have any of that, but to her acids and spices, the way she made me feel more alive. To hear Diana talking or to kiss her, to wake up beside her, you'd just know, I mean any man in his right mind would know, that she was a goddess, and not one of those New Age goddesses either, but one of the old ones, the genuine kind of goddess, the sort they don't make anymore, with lightning coming out of her eyes. She filled my eyes with her beauty; her eyes put me on trial.

I mean, Diana was a handful, but after one of our largish moments she would lie in a still, solemn posture while her feet beat in time to her inaudible music and her fingers touched my ribs like a fretboard, and she would stare off ceilingward, as if . . . well, it was then that I'd ask her what she was thinking, and she'd turn to me and give me a flashbulb smile, and she'd say, "I'm thinking about you, honey."

And I didn't know whether that was good news or bad, given the fact that she was almost frowning, and her lower lip beginning to stick out, pouty, as if she were reading poetry or something like that that's more trouble to figure out than it's worth. I didn't really want to know what she was thinking after such moments. I just kept that door shut. Bluebeard kept one of his castle doors shut too. Well, I said to myself: she's a lawyer, and she's contemplating her next case.

At our wedding, which was not at a church, because she and I didn't believe in anything that large, but which occurred in the expansive back yard of a reception hall near the Saline River, she had said, "I do," with considerable force. We were under a large white canopy and there would be dancing afterward. But she had seemed almost surprised when at the conclusion of the ceremony I leaned down to kiss her, the way you do when the ritual is finished. She was made light-headed by my kiss, the fact of it. You could tell from the way she looked at me. Her eyes grew wide and she seemed frightened for a split second as my lips attached themselves to hers. She said later that she had been studying the pattern of the woodwork in the bandstand and had been distracted. Distracted? At our wedding? For the kiss? I used to think that technically the wedding doesn't happen unless you kiss each other.

After the kiss, though, she remembered to smile. She could be polite. And following the reception, we had a horse-drawn carriage take us to the motel. The carriage was antique-elegant, with inlaid wood though it had a wet bar inside, and a TV, and as we got into it, we were pelted with rice and flowers by her lawyer friends and my artist-and-coffee friends, and by our parents and relatives and hangers-on. Chloé and Oscar were there in thrift-shop formal attire, and they threw flowers at us, too. My sister Agatha was there, and Harold, and my nephews, my friends, and my father and mother, and some of Diana's friends including an old boyfriend of hers named David, whom I didn't exactly get to meet, not then.

The sun was out, not a cloud in the sky. The driver wore a top hat. This was unlike my first wedding to Kathryn, which took place in city hall, where people do not typically wear costumes. We clip-clopped away from the reception hall, and I kissed Diana again, and she didn't seem so surprised this time. The horse smelled of straw and oats, I remember.

My best man had said, long before this, *You may end up like the happiest man on Earth, old Buddy, or you may end up like someone on daytime television.*

During the first night, after we had made love as man and wife, as wedded partners, instead of just lovers, Diana said, "Bradley, you're such a nice guy," as she drifted off to sleep. I thought: Well, I'll take my compliments where I can get them, but "nice" is not what a man wants to hear under these particular circumstances. I mean, she had nothing to complain about. I had satisfied her. She *looked* satisfied. We had groaned together during our lovemaking. But "nice"? When you make love to a goddess, you want a fierce compliment. Or speechlessness. Speechlessness will do just fine.

DIANA'S AGORAPHOBIA PRESENTED a bit of a problem as regards the honeymoon.

Her idea had been that we should remain in Ann Arbor and perhaps, as a kind of respite from ordinary life, stay in different motels and hotels around town for a week or two. We could laze in lounge chairs near the indoor pools and order vast crazy meals complete with champagne from room service, if there happened to be room service. We would make love a lot and metaphorically cement ourselves together. We would go to movies if we felt like it. Despite its attractions, however, I found this entire prospect unappealing. It lacked, I don't know, the charisma of the exotic.

She didn't like open spaces at all, and she didn't care for locales she'd never been to before. She did not like to travel and did not care for airplanes, except when her legal business required rapid transit. Nevertheless, I suggested that we drive to Michigan's Upper Peninsula and spend our honeymoon at a bed-and-breakfast on Lake Gogebic, near the Porcupine Mountains. Eventually I wore her down. I asserted myself, and she shrugged—Jesus, she had a beautiful shrug—and agreed. I'd been to this B&B, the Porcupine Inn, before, alone, and thought she'd like the vistas. We held hands as we talked about what we'd do there.

We boarded Bradley at a kennel. Chloé and Oscar would mind the store. Harry Ginsberg said he'd keep an eye on the house. Diana hadn't sold her house. She had rented it out.

I suspected that we were in for trouble when we began to cross the Mackinac Bridge. Diana began to breathe hard, and she put her hand to her face and smoothed her eyebrows. I shouldn't say this about my ex-wife, but she farted, I'm not kidding, out of sheer fright. The sky and the bridge and the water far below her were oddly and intensely *incorrect* to her at that moment, or so she reported. You can't see much from up on that bridge except the infinity of fresh water and some uncommonly distant islands. Spatial malevolence. She felt this wrongness surrounding her and ganging up against her. The empty air was unpleasantly interested in her. Funny to find this phobia in a woman so strong in other ways. I turned the radio on, thinking it would help, but the radio was tuned to an oldies station, and the first line out of the speakers was, "Well, I would not give you false hope, on this strange and mournful day . . ." and of course Diana reached down and snapped off *that* song.

It's not unusual for people to go phobic on that bridge. Sometimes they just stop the car at one end and have to be escorted, or driven, to the other side. We made it intact to St. Ignace, the first town you meet up with in the Upper Peninsula, but her episode of horizon panic had established a bad precedent.

MOST HUMAN BEINGS have never been to Michigan's Upper Peninsula. It retains its somewhat mysterious origins. Cartographers have mapped it, all right, but there are places up there where visitors have been maybe once or twice but never returned, because they didn't want to return, and never would want to. I'm not talking about Marquette, where they filmed *Anatomy of a Murder,* but places like Matchwood, where there's a busted American Motors dealer sign standing near an abandoned farmhouse, and not another habitation for miles, and large fields where they gave up farming years ago, and dense forests filled with trees—I do not exaggerate—of a kind you never saw before, probably hybrid trees resulting from the mating, it could be, of white pines and willow trees, grafted together out of sheer loneliness. I mean, these are odd-looking trees, barbaric and sad, and there are entire forests of them growing unobserved and unlabeled up there.

For the tourists, there are little tiny zoos scattered just off the main highways, with animals tucked away inside cages the size of carry-on suitcases, and other visitor attractions, like mystery spots and restaurants where they make pasties that the locals eat. You drive across this expanse of peculiarity as all the radio stations fade, all of them, Brahms and the Ronettes and Toad the Wet Sprocket and Hank Williams, and you start to wonder what got into you, that you brought your brand-new wife up here, the goddess whose scary wondrous beauty put you on trial. The broad open vistas fill you with second thoughts bordering on consternation. When you get to the waterfalls, you have to pay to see them; you have to pay a guy chewing a toothpick who somehow managed ' to buy the whole goddamn waterfall and is now going to sell you the view.

As we crossed the Upper Peninsula, Diana and I tried to be cheerful—we were both wearing jaunty hats and sending postcards to our friends every seventy miles or so—but by the time we reached Lake Gogebic, the distant aroma of a mistake was in the air, and it was my mistake, and it seemed to be going in several different directions at once. But after we unpacked at the B&B and tried out the bed, my spirits improved. We had an upstairs room filled with interior decoration antique bric-a-brac, and a bed close by a window just to the left of the headboard, and some cut flowers there on the bedside table, next to a simpering porcelain tabby cat. The window's glass was flawed and antique, so that the lake outside asserted itself in several visual dimensions, several different geometrical planes.

"Look," I said, pointing outside. Early evening, and the sun had given the lake a golden tint, the kind you see in bad paintings and bad movies, though this, I should quickly add, had been a good day and not a cheap imitation of a good day. She raised herself in the bed and lay across me, so that her breasts brushed against me. I was sitting there, propped up against the pillows and the headboard, reading a local tourist guidebook. It was so friendly and so erotic at the same time, Diana draped in that manner over me. And I thought: this is what marriage should be, this intimacy, eros and friendship, Diana and me, exciting and calm.

"Oh yes," she said. "Very beautiful." She just rested there, stretched across me, gazing languidly out through the window, elbows on the bed next to my legs, and I looked down at her back and felt like touching each one of the bumps of her spine consecutively. I traced designs on her back. I drew, with my finger, a dragon rising out of the valley above her waist and flaring upward with powerful wings toward her shoulders. "What're you doing?" she asked.

"I'm drawing a dragon."

"Hmmm. Tell me when you're finished."

I drew some scales on its sides, and some fire from its mouth. She was giving me pleasure as I drew it, so I slowed down my draftsmanship. "I'm done," I said, after a minute or two.

She turned over. I cradled her head in my right hand. I put my left hand placidly on her rib cage and then on her breast. She gazed up at me. We were loving and familiar. "You're so sweet," she said. "Tell me you love me."

"I love you, Diana," I said. "I love you very much." The truth was easy for me to say.

She smiled. "Yes, that was nice," she said. "You know, I love you, too. What do you love about me, Bradley? Really?"

"How beautiful and smart you are," I said. With my thumb I twirled her hair. "I love that. I don't know," I said. "It's like love doesn't *have* any reason. I can't stop looking at you." My voice had dropped to a hoarse murmur. "I go to sleep with your image in my head, and when I wake up, it's still there. I think you're a goddess," I said, meaning it. My cock had stayed up, and the way we were positioned, she could probably feel it beneath her, tickling her back, right where I had drawn that dragon. "Why do you love me?" I asked, still in a whisper, a little frightened by the way she might answer. We'd never had this discussion before.

"I don't know," she said.

"You don't know?"

"You're a better person than I am."

"You love me for that?"

"Bradley, I don't think people should talk about these things."

"Why not?"

"Some matters you shouldn't verbalize. I mean really, Bradley" —and here she raised her hand and caressed my cheek—"all this love business is just nature's way of getting more babies into the world. The rest of it is just all this romance nonsense." She struggled for the word. "The rest of it is just *superstructure*."

"Well, maybe. But what if," I said, still gazing at her, with her sly sexy smile like a little dawn on her face, "what if the love we feel, what if it's central, what if it's what makes the world's soul possible, what if it's what made the world and keeps it running, and the babies, the babies are also a product of that, our soul-making, not the only product, but . . ."

"That's what I mean," she said. "You're so weird and metaphysical. For a coffee guy."

"About what?"

"That you would say that. That you would say that love isn't just a necessity for . . . biology." I had my hand cupped around her breast, and she had her hand on my cheek, and we were having an argument, though it was still sounding like love talk. "Bradley, what are we going to do here? At Lake Gogebic?"

"We're on a honeymoon," I said, noting the obvious, which I had hoped at that moment I wouldn't have to do. "We'll have meals and make love. That's about all." She turned, so that now her back was to me again. "And we could go outside. We could explore. We could take hikes."

"You know I don't like hikes."

"You're in shape, Diana. You run in the gym."

"You know what I mean." She gazed outside. "This doesn't have anything to do with *fitness*. The outdoors gives me the creeps."

"But look," I said. "Look what I've brought." I pulled myself out from under her and went over to my suitcase, from which I pulled two whistles, the kind that football coaches use, with the little balls in them. They really make a racket. "Hey, hey," I said hopelessly.

"What're those for?"

"You get lost in the woods, you just blow."

" 'I get lost in the woods, I just blow,' " she repeated. "What is it about my agoraphobia, Bradley—does it make you feel better that I have it? An advantage? *You brought those along?* I mean, why now, of all times, do you want to worry it?"

"I don't want to worry it," I said. "It wasn't that. The thing is, I saw the two of us, walking outdoors, and I thought: What can I do for Diana? I can help her get outside, I can help her with the wide open spaces." I handed the whistle to her.

She took it and tossed it in her hand. Then, sweetly, she raised her other hand and put her index finger on my lower lip. She played her finger back and forth on my lip. "We're not compatible, you know," she said. Her eyes hardened and for an instant looked through me a little. I thought that was such an odd thing for her to say that I refused, almost, to hear it. I just felt her finger on my lip.

"It's not compatibility," I said. "It's how you manage it. How loving you are."

"I'm loving with my friends," Diana said, "and I'm mean to my lovers." She caressed my mouth. " 'Just put your lips together and blow,' " she said, quoting from somewhere. "Oh, screw it," she said. "Put that whistle down and make love to me again, since you want to." She pointed to me and what was obvious, my well-meaning and innocent erection. So I did, I made love to her, because she asked me to, and because I wanted to, even though—and it's hard to explain this—my feelings were hurt and I was angry, so I was meaner to her in bed than I usually am, rougher, more abrupt, and slowly it dawned on me, as I watched her respond, that she liked me that way, almost as if she was used to it, and I thought, *Uh-oh,* and kept it to myself.

You can have good sex on your honeymoon and still suspect that there's something fishy going on.

THE NEXT DAY we went over to the Porcupine Mountains. They're worn down in that region and the state forests and parkland have been crisscrossed with paths, but it's a moody landscape given to early morning fogs and indescribable forest sounds. They tear through the silences every now and then. Out of nowhere, a half-mile behind you, a baby cries once, then quiets. Tree branches snap and fall in front of you. These seemingly harmless nature scenes fill you with premonitions of bucolic doom.

We veered off the main highway onto a county road and continued driving until the pavement turned to dirt, and then parked when we found a stand of woods with a marker for a path. I myself had grown interested in the mushrooms. I'd brought a sketchbook and sketched a few. They caught my attention with their red caps and their structural mockery of flowers and umbrellas and sexual organs. Diana wouldn't touch them and seemed puzzled, or even saddened, by my interest in them.

Diana's hair was swept back and held under that cap, and she was wearing a light yellow tee-shirt. She'd brought along a jacket in case it started to rain, and after we'd been out there for an hour or two, it began to drizzle. The drizzle was so fine that the water couldn't even be glimpsed as it fell. You could see its presence as a graying factor in the air.

I'd also brought a small field guide—my jacket was full of pockets —and was checking the identifying marks of what I thought was a destroying angel when I heard Diana blowing her whistle. I tripped my way over several dead logs and through some underbrush that I couldn't identify until I found her standing near a stump. She was shaking, but it didn't quite make sense, because she was smiling that tough smile of hers. Her breasts heaved under her tee-shirt.

"I heard something," she said. "Also, I think we're lost."

I told her that we weren't lost, that my map said that a road existed on the other side of the ridge ahead of us. She shrugged— God, I loved that!—and agreed to follow me.

As we were walking on the path I saw a small bronze engraved plaque that someone had affixed to a tree.

On this spot in 1983
E. L. Orlan discovered that the meaning of his life
lay in learning, friendship and love,
and service to others.

I pointed it out to Diana, but she just laughed. She was personally way beyond the meaning of life. She was making, I thought, heroic efforts to love the outdoors, but she had her limits. I took her hand.

Behind us and then to our right came a two-note call, neither bird nor animal. More like the rubbing of an agitated branch against a tree trunk.

Nobody was around. "You wanna make love here?" I asked. "You wanna mess around in the woods?" She just looked at me. We walked down a slope toward a patchwork clearing. She was not about to get herself laid in the woods. What had I been thinking?

A road became visible ahead, opposite the clearing. A white farm house, with a wide front yard dotted with objects too small to be seen from a distance, stood sagging and in need of paint on the other side of the dirt road.

We crossed the road and looked down at the objects for sale in the front yard: several bright blue Virgin Mary shrines, wooden deer and rabbits, and a nondescript collection of other creatures made out of ceramic God-knows-what, all of them with big eyes, all of them smiling without sincerity. They had the mean cuteness of painted souvenirs. The phrase *blunt instruments* came into my head. I imagined a disgruntled wife pitching one of these skunks at her husband after a long weekend. I almost tripped over a sign.

EVERYTHING HERE
FOR SALE
RING THE DOORBELL

"Of course it's awful," Diana said. "But that's why we're here." She held up a possum, aimed it at me, and made terrible kissing noises.

Sometimes she enjoyed slumming around in junk stores. Cast-offs and ripped, dented things flashed a spark in her. She fever-grinned at me. So *I* shrugged. "This makes good taste seem easy," I said. "Dull, too."

"Oh, I don't know." She put the possum back down on the ground. "You know, we *could* make love right here, right on the ground, now, and it wouldn't help at all. This stuff is more compli-cated than you realize."

I was thinking about what she could possibly have meant by that when the screen door slammed and a blind woman came toward us down the porch steps. I knew she was blind because her blue eyes were milky and she looked in no particular direction. Like the ani-mals, she too was smiling. And like them, her eyes were slightly too large for her face. Her brown hair sagged, if that's the word, under a hair net.

She wore a brown cardigan sweater, and as I watched she fished a cigarette out of the left pocket and a Zippo lighter out of the right. She illuminated the cigarette and took a long stagy puff. She had the pleasant formal manners of a troll under whose bridge you have just wandered. "Can I be of any help for you?" she asked. "Is there any assistance I may be of?"

"Oh, no," Diana said, and she glanced in her perturbed stylish way toward the horizon. "We were hiking. Now we're here."

"Now you're here," the troll-lady said in an echo-chamber voice. I gazed at her with great uneasiness. I have never liked men or women who live on dirt roads. It's a matter of temperament, mine or theirs. I looked to my left and saw a gorgonzola-green automo-bile in the driveway. "You're both so young," she said. "Well, cer-tainly take a look around. Take your time."

"We were just married," Diana said quickly. The proprietor of this lawn exhaled some smoke straight up. I wondered if it might be a signal to someone we couldn't see, some message or other. Emotional health is a relative matter once you're away from the cities. I thought it was time for us to go.

"My name is Mrs. Watkins," the old woman said. She held out her hand, and I shook it for the god of politeness. Then Diana did. "Yes, that's a good woman's grip," Mrs. Watkins muttered, taking another puff from her cigarette. "I'm so pleased you've visited me. But you must come into the back yard. You must see the children. These," she swept her hand in the direction of the animals, "are just for show."

Then she turned around and walked toward the back of the house. She seemed to know where everything was. We followed her. I wanted to take the whistle out of my pocket and blow it. Diana reached for my hand. She appeared to be having a perfectly good time. The huge air and the horizon weren't getting on her back and weighing her down in the conventional ways.

I decided to be tactless. "You manage so well," I said to Mrs. Watkins. "Considering." Then we saw the back yard.

"You think I'm blind, but I'm not," Mrs. Watkins said. "I have cataracts and things, but I'm not blind." As she said this, she stared at my right elbow. "I can see all the colors, and I can see you have many pockets in your jacket. It looks like you've been picking mushrooms."

I wasn't exactly listening to her at that moment, because I had fixed my attention on her back yard. The children were in front of me, stone children and plaster children, in various postures of disarray.

One boy stood with his hands in the air, appearing to hold a kite string. Another lay on the ground with his head propped in his right hand, gazing blankly off into the distance, but in my direction. Those children had been there forever. Mrs. Watkins walked toward the kite-flying boy and put her hand on his head. "My husband made these," she said. "He made all these children on weekends."

I noticed the past tense. Close by me was a girl on her knees with her hands together in prayer and her head tilted upward. She had been outdoors for as long as these mountains had been here. Part of her face was wearing away, probably from rain or from the blind woman's caresses. Although it's probably a shame for me to admit it, I'll say here and now that I don't think statuary is any form of art. You can put it in a museum, and I'll walk right past it. I don't want to look at or touch those things. Rodin, Michelangelo, Degas: just clutter to me.

On the other side of the praying girl was another girl—very white and also plaster, my guess was—bending down and looking for a worm. There was a price tag on one of her fingers. It had smeared in the rain, and I couldn't tell what her asking price was.

"They're all of them very sweet," Mrs. Watkins said. "My husband loved making these children. It was a constant love and occupied his daytime leisure hours, such as they were." She looked up at me but her gaze missed my face and focused on the gray Michigan sky. Quite possibly she was kind. I had no way of knowing. She reached behind her and put her hand on a boy with an open mouth. He appeared to be singing rather than shouting. "Anything interest you here?"

"It all interests me," Diana said. And then she put her hand underneath my shirt and reached for me around the waist. I could tell she wanted to kiss me in front of Mrs. Watkins, and I wasn't going to let it happen. Diana's hand went up my back and I felt the shivers coming on. Being among all these cement children bothered me. It was too much like being with Kathryn at the Humane Society.

Mrs. Watkins stubbed out her cigarette in an open space between two children and deftly reached in her left pocket for another one. I admired her Zippo. Those things could really light cigarettes, and they closed with a satisfactory metallic smack. "We get all kinds of people here," she said, exhaling more smoke from her freshly lit cigarette. "Most of the children have been sold, though, as you can see."

"Do you have names for them?" Diana asked.

"Oh no," the old woman said, leaning back. "That would be sentimental."

"I think we have to go now," I announced. All this was more than enough for one day. "Our car is parked on the other side of the ridge, and we need time to get back before it gets too dark to see. We're on our honeymoon," I added, without thinking. It was still midday. No one paid any attention to me. I was noticing that most of the children's faces had worn away a bit too much, and the loss of detail was unnerving. No doubt there would be a clearance sale fairly soon.

"I want that one," Diana said, pointing toward the reclining boy whose head was propped up by his arm. "How much is it? No, I mean, how much is *he*?"

"I could let you have him for thirty-six dollars," the old woman said.

"Bradley, you'll have to bring the car around here to pick this up," Diana said, smiling curiously at me and scratching her scalp as if in thought. "We can't lug it back."

"You didn't ask me if I wanted it."

"Oh, this is for me," Diana told me. "I'll just put it somewhere." She was counting out dollar bills into Mrs. Watkins's hand.

"What mushrooms you got there?" Mrs. Watkins asked me, pointing toward my jacket pockets.

"I don't know their names," I said.

"Hand them to me," she said. "I know mushrooms."

"No, no, I don't think so," I said.

Diana put her hands into my own pockets and pulled all the

mushrooms out. She turned them over to the old woman, who dropped them on the ground. Then Mrs. Watkins picked up one with a red cap in her left hand—her right hand still held the cigarette—and sniffed it several times. "This is called a pungent russula," she said. "It's not poisonous but it'll make you vomit. *Emetica,* they call it. Very delicate structure though." She passed her fingers around the mushroom's gills before handing it to Diana. Then she reached down for another one. I wanted to get out of there but Diana was watching all this with considerable attention. Something was happening, and I didn't know what it was.

More sniffing from Mrs. Watkins. "This is a club foot. It's no good for eating. The woods are full of those." She threw it on the ground near one of the boys and reached down again. "Ah," she said. She stubbed out her second cigarette. "Now this one is something. This one's a parasol. This is one of the best."

Then, and I can't say I was prepared for this, Mrs. Watkins— with her cataracts—bit off a tiny piece of the mushroom and chewed it. "Yes," she said, smiling, like the ebullient hobgoblin she was, "that's indeed what it is. Here." She held it toward Diana.

"No," I said. "Absolutely not. Don't you do that."

"Shut up, Bradley," Diana said. "Just shut up."

"No no no," I said and forced it out of her hand.

"Give it back here," she said. "Or this will become very serious."

"This is serious right now," I said.

Mrs. Watkins looked at us with her inaccurate smile. Perhaps she meant well.

"You don't know what that is," I said. "You don't know what this is all about. Stop all of this, please, Diana."

"Oh yes, I do," she said. She pulled the mushroom out of my hand. "This is about us." She bit into the mushroom. I watched her chew and swallow. Then she leaned toward me. She whispered. "It's a feeling. This is about this exact moment and where we are exactly right now." She was biting off more mushroom, and chewing and swallowing. "This is about a favor that is being done to me. This is a spell. This is a charm. From one woman to another."

"Oh, dear," the crone said. "A quarrel." She turned around and went back into her house. She stumbled on the stairs going up.

ON THE WAY HOME, with the reclining boy stashed in the trunk, Diana said to me, "When we get back, I'm going to make such love to you, it'll take your roof right off."

When we arrived back at the Porcupine Inn, the bedroom smelled of lilacs, even though it was the wrong season for lilacs. We left the statue, or whatever it was, in the car. I wasn't about to carry it up to the bedroom. It might have been a joke, that boy, but I couldn't stop thinking of him, all thirty or forty pounds of him, ensconced in the trunk gazing through the darkness at the spare tire. Up in the bedroom, between us, Diana brought more fever to our lovemaking than she ever had before, but it was the wrong fever, as if she were trying to get rid of an internal pressure through physical means. She would ride me and close her eyes, and she would bend down to kiss my eyelids, and there wouldn't be a sprig of affection in it, not a single solitary sign of love. It was just something she needed. She churned away and when she'd whip her head back and forth, the sweat from her forehead fell on my face. She slapped me several times as a sex thing, and as often as she came, it wasn't enough, she wanted to come more often, and harder. She knocked the porcelain tabby cat off the bedside table, and the flowers too. They lay insensate on the floor in a puddle of water. She told me we were going to skip dinner. The mushroom didn't make her sick, but I guess it gave her some sort of permission. It went further and profoundly into night, all this mushroom sex, and then on and on toward morning. I'd fall asleep and wake up to feel her working on me. She wouldn't let me sleep. We had bruises. I never imagined this happening, but no matter how naive you sometimes think I am, I knew that whole night, by then, watching her, that she was in love with someone else, intensely, and had always been, and been tormented by it, and now she was taking it out on me, and making it obvious and those were her thoughts, the ones she couldn't tell me, not for a penny, not for a pound.

We had some great times, Diana and me, but we couldn't last, and we didn't. We brought the statue of the boy home, and Diana put it into the garden close by where the petunias and pansies had been despite my protests.

FIFTEEN

THERE'S A STORY of Kierkegaard's that I especially like. A philosopher builds an enormous palace, but to everyone's surprise he himself does not live in the palace but establishes his residence in a dog kennel next to it. The philosopher is invariably offended when it is pointed out to him that he lives in this ludicrous manner. *But how else could I have built the palace,* the philosopher asks, *if I had not also lived in the dog kennel?*

It is like a Jewish joke. Kierkegaard made great efforts to live in the palace of thought he himself had built, but of course he could not manage it, given to polemical rages as he was, and to a peculiar kind of spiritual unhappiness driven by heart-spite. Besides, one eventually grows attached to one's own doghouse and the daily bowl of scraps. Stubbornly we stay on in the dog kennel to prove that we were correct to have established ourselves in there in the first place.

The story *about* Kierkegaard I like is the one in which he falls drunkenly off a sofa at a party. Lying on the floor, he starts to refer to himself in the third person when the other guests try to help him up. "Oh, just leave it there," he says, speaking of his body. "Let the maids sweep it up tomorrow morning."

———

THE NEXT TIME Aaron called on the telephone—like the secret police, the terror experts, he always made the bell ring in the dead center of the night—he informed me that the money I had sent him was an "installment." In consideration of emotional crimes against him, he said, he would regard his intentional death as postponed until after the next such payment.

I was braver this time. I told him he was talking nonsense.

Between us in the electronic ether, the thousands of miles, a silence brewed and thickened, was salted and seasoned, mixed with the sounds of his breathing.

Nonsense? he asked. *Nonsense?*

Just so, I said bravely, touching with tenderness the crease in my pajama leg. Esther likes to iron my pajamas, it relaxes her. Utter nonsense, I said with a fatherly rumble. And furthermore, I said, to nettle him, You sound like a schoolgirl, all these theatrics about killing yourself. Please. Get yourself some grit. If you want to kill yourself, Aaron, you are free to do so. But prior to that you must not blame us. It is too late for these complaints. You are an adult now. Your life is a gift to do with as you choose. Such blame as you enjoy directing at me, at your mother and me, no—it is baseless, and I cannot accept it. We are two mild people, your mother and I, who love you dearly. For true villains, Aaron, you must look elsewhere.

I was frightened out of my wits, saying these terrible condemning words. But the sentences came out of me as if I meant them.

You've done it this time, he said. *You've done it this time, there's no going back* . . . Gently, my broken heart thumping, I hung up the phone, laying the receiver in its cradle.

I entrusted his life and his soul to God at that moment, placing my son in His hands, this God in whom I do not believe.

AND KIERKEGAARD? Kierkegaard himself says that the gods created humankind and its troubles simply because they were bored.

SIXTEEN

WITHIN A MONTH after our return to Ann Arbor, we were talking about a divorce. Diana lived with me for a while, a few desultory months, and then, once she had the renters removed from her house, she moved out of here and back in there. She took the stone child she bought in the Upper Peninsula and put it in her back yard. Snow fell on that child all winter long; drifts blew up against it, and gradually it disappeared into the snow. She also salvaged the pictures I had drawn of herself on the back of the dragon. Those she saved. That dragon erased the two of us.

That's all I'm going to say about the subject for now. As Chloé says, some things don't bear much looking into. If you want something to read, then read the white space on the rest of this page. That's me, down there in the white.

SEVENTEEN

I COULDN'T GET Mrs. Maggaroulian out of my head. I'd be sleeping, and there she'd be in my dreams, pulling up a chair for an intimate girl-to-girl chat. Her wig'd be edging down toward her forehead and her nail polish would sort of be flaking off. I mean, she looked like a human pawn shop, Mrs. Maggaroulian did, but she never was one for appearances anyway. The whole point of Mrs. M as a person was inner truth. The outer Mrs. Maggaroulian was a horse that somebody should have let out to pasture years ago; you could see she didn't even have a game plan for contemporary life. She was post-makeover and just about post-human. You could have, like, set her on fire, and I don't think she'd even have noticed or minded.

But in my head and my dreams, she made sense. She talked to me about Oscar and myself, us as a couple, and she told me to get my marriage license signed immediately, because time was running out on the two of us. She said we had to get married right away on account of our personal eternity was contracting rapidly into a space the size of a dime. We had just about no eternity left, Mrs. Maggaroulian told me. If we weren't careful, we would be forcibly tossed out of a time window. She couldn't elaborate. She went on about how you can't name names in dreams. She had all these disclaimers, how she knew everything there was to know but only had an operator's permit from the universe to tell me a tiny percentage of it before I woke up.

I told Oscar some of this. I trusted him.

She was a soul-antique, Mrs. Maggaroulian. You could see that she believed in marriage by the way she talked about it. A sacrament, she quoted from somewhere, rubbing her big hands together. Mrs. Maggaroulian talking about marriage was weird. It was kind of like a dog talking about being the mayor of Cleveland. But if the dog does it long enough, talking on and on about the difficulties and the responsibilities of being mayor and how he has to keep track of everything and not slip up, you start to believe him. Well, she could have called it—what Oscar and I had—anything she wanted to, because, as you know, we were getting married. Mrs. Maggaroulian was telling me what I already knew. I mean, I knew we were holy and would only become more so. She was just saying to get holier in a hurry, to put it on the fast track.

JANEY, MY FRIEND the video artist, called me and said she wanted to have coffee, so I met her at a rival caffeine establishment, Goodbye Blue Monday, that was more downtown Ann Arbor than we were at Jitters, out there at the mall. They had GBM decorated to look Eurochic, with posters on the wall of people wearing berets and Woody Allen in French and all that other Parisian high life everywhere. Janey was sitting at a back table reading the current issue of *Bust* magazine. She was all grown up but you could see where her pimples had once been when you approached her. When she smiled at me, it was wolfish. Untamed, though not in the good way. She had brown hair like a wolf. Some girls, it almost doesn't matter if they wash their hair or not. Shampoo won't help these ladies. I can be a bitch, I got to watch that tendency.

You just knew from the radar that she was a woman who dug other women physically but wouldn't do anything about it, and she had spent her young life hemming and hawing, lighting cigarettes and putting them out in frustration. She had an inventory of failed gestures. Being modern, I'd slept with other girls once or twice myself but that was all over now that Oscar loved me and we'd have a life together. Janey, she was pretty in a predatory way, like that pianist, Liberace, but without the clothes he wore to keep you confused and off the scent. She just wore jeans and tee-shirts, like me. You could see by peering at her why she wanted to film porn all day. She stared with these dead-fish eyes at whatever was swimming by her. She was a hungry ghost, sucking people up in her karmic vacuum cleaner and storing them in the dustbag. Also, she chewed her fingernails. I *hate* that. Still, we were friends, maybe out of convenience or something.

Anyway, she was sitting there with the videotape on the table. She gave me a sort of bored wave of hello, like I was already a disappointment to her before our first words had been spoken, very Hollywood agent, and she flipped her head back with this girl-of-the-world shake, accompanied by her patented wolf smile, which looks better on guys than it does on her. "Hey, Barlow," she said. Barlow is my last name. "Whassup?"

"Not much," I said. "How 'bout you?"

She shook one of her hands like there was water on it. "Do you ever get bored with weather? The weather is *so* sobering around here." I didn't know what she was talking about, so I pretended to smile, which came out as a real smile. "I'm going to move to Seattle or somewhere where they have some goddamn actual weather. You know: *real* rain? Rain and heroin. As opposed to what we get here? Oh, and guess what. I'm discovering something," she said, sipping her cappuccino. "Guess what I discovered."

I leaned back. "No idea."

"Try to guess."

"Janey, I gotta be at work in a coupla hours. I don't have *time* to guess." She was staring at me like she wanted to dine out on me, and she flashed me a quick thing, an event-horizon thing lowering and happening on her face, and then it was gone, and she was normal again. "Why don't you just tell me?"

"Okay," she said. "The video we made? The one with you and Oscar, that I shot and directed? We're not going to make any serious money out of it. In fact," she said, "we're not going to make any money at all, almost."

"Like how much?"

She leaned back. "Like almost nothing. Like zilch."

"Jeez." I felt that punch in your arm you feel when you're disappointed. I hadn't minded Janey taping us doing our mating dance because I figured we'd get enough for a deposit on a better apartment. Besides, you could tell straight sex just bored her silly, when it was happening in front of her, and she wasn't paying attention, except technically. "I was expecting a lot more," I said. "Considering how easy it was, doing it."

"Well it just goes to show. I guess it's harder to break into the sex industry than I thought. They're sort of going for the details, those guys. People are bored with what we served up. They want exotica. They didn't say anything about exotica in the ad. But get this. They said the video was too *dull*. I have to tell you, I was offended. I mean, hey, I *worked* on that video. I put a lotta effort into it."

"How do you mean? Dull?" Suddenly my pride got up. Oscar and me, dull? In bed? No way.

"They called me." She leaned her head back and her eyes went up just like a shark after a bite of leg and shoe. "They said they could maybe, *maybe,* use a few minutes of it someday in a video anthology devoted to today's youth. They said the marketing would be tough, though. There's no target audience for watching people like you and Oscar. The only thing they liked was Oscar's skull tattoo and the 'Die' underneath it. They said the sex was too midwestern. And they said the setting was bad. *Unimaginative.* I asked them what was bad about it, and they said it was just a bedroom somewhere. When I asked them where it was supposed to be, they said, well, someplace different, like an office at a used-car lot." She thrummed her fingers on the table. "And no offense, Chloé, but they said you were pretty but not voluptuous. What do they expect? And they said that the costumes you and Oscar were wearing weren't any good. They were *very* critical, these people."

"What do you mean, the sex was too midwestern? And what was wrong with the costumes?"

"Well, like I told you, they said it wasn't exotic enough. Like, track star and cheerleader aren't exotic? But they said they weren't. Your bodies were okay but nothing special. You took your shoes off. That's a no-no. What's the big deal with feet? Anyway, you're supposed to keep your shoes on. And they claimed you guys didn't have a 'look.' Hey, I *argued* with them. Chloé, I really did. I defended you. And they said there were other problems."

"Like?"

"The love thing."

"What's that?" I asked.

"They said that it looked like you and Oscar were in love."

"So?"

"They said the love thing makes the video off-putting. That was the word the guy used. 'Off-putting.' It wrecks it visually. That you can just tell by watching. It kinda takes the kick out of it. It makes it creepy to watch. The way you two look at each other was alienating, like you had a thing going. And he really had a deal about the way you went at it. Creepy, he said, too plain-style and also too midwestern. Can you imagine? Fuckin' mondo. This guy on the phone, working for who he works for, tellin' me about *creepy*? I got a little indignant. He blamed the pacing on me, as the director. He said it would a better video if you guys had used your imaginations."

"No way."

"That's what I figured. Well, he was one mean guy, and I guess the result is, I'm not going to make my fortune with you and Oscar." She poked down at a bag. "Here's your videocam back. I'm getting another one."

"What about the money?"

"What about it?"

"You mentioned a figure."

"First I have to sign an agreement. Then he said the check would be in the mail. It's not here yet."

"He said that?"

"Those," she said in a kind of weird half-whisper, "were his exact words."

"So you haven't got the money?"

"Chloé, would I lie to you?" She pouted for a split second.

"I don't know. I guess not." It occurred to me just then that Janey hadn't talked to anybody, that she had made the tape for herself.

"There's this other thing."

"What other thing?"

"I've been asking around town. I made a few inquiries. I found someone. You wouldn't believe some of the people I talked to. But I guess the Midwest is like anywhere else. I know someone here in town who'll pay you and Oscar a lotta money if you do something. I brokered it, so I'd have to get fifty dollars out of that."

"What?"

"Well, it's pretty, uh, slight. All you and Oscar have to do is make love to each other. You can do that, for sure. All you have to do is sex, and all you need is love." She looked disgusted.

"Yeah."

"There's a catch."

"What's the catch?"

"Well, this person here in town wants to watch."

"Watch us?"

"Yeah, I guess. You know, he'll be there in the room, sitting on a chair, watching you. That's all. It's not exactly what you'd call a *job*, Chloé. I mean, it isn't *work*. You just make love and then you get paid."

I got instantly depressed. Ordinarily I have high spirits. This scene was getting worse and worse and worse and worse and worse and worse and worse and *worse*, like an event out of somebody else's life that you don't even want to hear about in a story. What had happened to how holy we were, Oscar and me? I had fallen low, I could see that, thanks to economics, the hunger for money in a hurry, and I was worried about dragging Oscar down with me. Thinking about foyers can corrupt you, I guess. "Janey," I said, "did you ever think when we were in fifth grade that we'd be having this conversation?"

"I didn't think we'd be having this conversation *last week*."

"So who is this guy?"

"I don't know. Just some ordinary horrible guy I met. He's harmless. Some typical man with eyes. The world is full of them."

"Is it safe?"

"Sure. Nothing'll happen. This guy is all middle-aged and bald and a wimp and a loser. Besides, honey, Oscar—well, I've seen him naked, right? That boyfriend of yours is strong. He may have done drugs once, but he can sure handle himself. I mean, he looks like a tough motherfucker." She stopped to sigh admiringly. "Though I know how sweet he is and everything." She reached around and scratched her back and looked annoyed, like I should be doing it for her, the scratching.

"That money," I said. "How much was it? I want to get this right."

She named the sum, and then she said, "Maybe I can get it higher, but I doubt it. It's already a huge lot."

"Well, I'll ask Oscar. But I don't think so. I really don't think so."

I waited. "I mean, we're broke, and we could use the money and everything . . ."

"Well, it's like being sex workers for one night. One night only. Putting on a show for a lonely guy. Hey, I hear you guys are getting married. Wow. You're so traditional."

"You heard that?"

"Yeah, word gets out. Congratulations." She started to shake my hand, thought better of it, and stopped in midair.

"Thanks. We're gonna do it in a week or two."

"Where?"

"Well, my boss, this guy, Bradley Smith, he's offered us his back yard for the reception."

"Who's going to perform it? Like, the minister?"

"We're going down to city hall first. You know: the clerk. The clerk does it."

"Hey," she said, "you remember that guy, Buddy Preston, from school?" I nodded. "Well, he's made himself into one of those ministers you become if you send in a matchbook application and twenty dollars. He could marry you, and it'd be legal. He's married a couple of people lately." She ran her fingers through her hair. "A couple of people we knew from school. I forget their names. He does it as a sideline. He makes a little money from it. I saw one of his weddings a while ago. It was a real wedding. And he's a friend of ours. Well, not a friend. But an acquaintance. I mean, you remember him, right? He lives out in Dexter now."

I gave her a long stare. I was super-irritated. "Do I look zany to you?"

"Well, no."

"This is my wedding I'm talking about. Jesus, Janey. I want a proper city hall wedding. I don't want some quack minister. Come on, Janey. Have some respect for my feelings, would you please?"

"Okay, sorry."

I took a sip of my lemonade. I don't drink coffee, it's bad for you. "Oscar and me, we don't go to church or anything, so we gotta settle for city hall."

"Let me see your ring." I showed it to her. I held out my hand in her direction, and she put my hand in her hand. I knew that was the thrill for her, my fingers touching hers, not the ring. "Wow. It's real pretty. A stone and the whole nine yards. Is that gold? Where'd you get it?"

"I didn't get it. Oscar got it. He bought it for me."

"Where'd he get it? Is it, like, an engagement ring?"

"Sort of. It's a real short engagement, though. He bought it at the jewelry department at the mall. He made a special trip." I didn't want it to seem like I was gloating, so I didn't say anything more about my ring, which had a genuine zirconium diamond in it. It wasn't glass, if that's what you're thinking.

She leaned back and examined the ceiling. "Your parents coming?"

"My parents hate me," I said. I tried to find what she was looking at on the ceiling but couldn't. "My dad threw me out, you remember that, back in my party-animal days. They think I'm a loser. Plus my dad is taking orders from my mom about ignoring me. So I'm pretty harsh on them, too, now that the ball's in my court. What I do is, I exclude them from stuff, such as my wedding."

"Yeah. You gotta be radical," she said.

"So anyway, I'll tell them after the wedding. But they're not invited. Rhonda, my sister, you remember her? She's coming. She'll be at the reception."

"What about Oscar's parents?"

"He's only got one parent. The Bat. Very scary individual. Don't know if he's going to show up or not."

"Am I invited?"

"Well, yeah." I gave her the time and the address, but you could see she was pissed about not getting a written invitation, of which there weren't any.

She tried to recover herself by getting girlish. "You guys goin' on a honeymoon?"

"Yeah. We're going to a School of Velocity concert the next day and we'll spend the night in a motel in East Lansing."

"Chloé, you are *so* hot. You're going to be *the* happening married couple. So what about this guy who wants to watch you two love-birds fuck?" She was going back to street language, back to business. She smiled at me like she had indigestion and was trying to cover it. "Like all that money?" She named the figure again. "Now there's a fortune. What about him?"

"It's way creepy. But, like I say, I'll ask Oscar."

THE THING WAS, I wanted to buy Oscar some medical insurance, because Bradley couldn't afford to give us any benefits at Jitters. And I thought that if we had it, and something happened to Oscar, we'd be covered. But! I knew, alas, that you can't get an insurance policy for five hundred dollars, but you almost can. What I was worried about also was the pre-existing condition thing, how they never cover that. Well, maybe we could put a deposit on a better apartment.

As for us, I didn't want anyone watching us ever, exactly. But I also thought: Hey, this customer wants to watch Oscar and me, it's *his* problem, right? It's not *our* problem. We're not watching. We're just doing it the way we always do, being in love and physically endorsing it. Some poor loveless unloved excuse for an American human wants to watch from the bottom of his particular barrel so we can pay for Oscar's health insurance or a down payment on an apartment, well, hey, there's a possibility for positive gain here. I guess everybody wants to watch, sort of. Except: you don't feel like *doing* it quite so much, maybe you don't feel like it at all, the air goes out of that particular tire, any of the things you usually do, when somebody's got their gloating eyes on you.

And then I thought about what sort of man would want to do this. I mean, he had to be pretty desperate, calling up some service somewhere, just because he wanted to watch. I took a walk in Allmendinger Park to think about it. I watched the dogs and the parents and the kids. I imagined him coming home from work, another lonely guy doing the dishes, standing under a lightbulb and listening to the radio, trying not to be a creep but being one anyway, and one night he realizes, bingo, that he's in hell, he just lives there permanently, helllllooooo, he's never getting out. The fix is so in, you can't get more in than that. So what he wants is, he wants to look at what it's like in heaven, where we are, he wants to see two representatives of the youth culture, which is us, Oscar and me, just lying around and making love, and maybe he could get clarified that way, you know, sitting there, looking at us yelping with happiness the way we do.

It'd be sort of like bringing a dog to a person in an old-age home. Therapeutic. Except you can pat the dog. Us, he wouldn't be able to touch. I'd insist on that.

Seeing is believing. Seeing is different from telling. I mean, it's different from me telling you about it, right? Right?

Well, I think so.

But suppose Oscar starts to give me a kiss. When nobody's watching, he's, like, doing it for me, and for himself, because he likes to. He likes the way I taste to him. He just breathes me in up here and down there. Would he give me a Slurpee? Maybe not if we were being studied. He'd get shy. But when you've got this golf-playing lonely polyester hyper-wimp sitting in a chair watching, this guy who's bought, excuse me, a fucking ticket, then you're doing it, like, for him. The whole deal changes. It turns into a show.

That's not healthy.

THAT NIGHT, WE WERE MAKING hamburgers at the tiny stove, so close to everything that it's not even in a kitchen, and I told Oscar about it, Janey's proposal, and you know what he did? He sat there. So I just sat there. Then we both started talking. Eventually he yelled at me and I yelled at him. He and I fought and we ended up crying together, but by the end of the dinner hour we'd decided.

We told each other it wasn't a big deal.

After all, everybody likes to watch. I mean, I like to watch Oscar, I even like to watch him shave when he's naked, and he likes to watch me.

We decided to do it. But we wouldn't go to anyone else's house, we had to do it here. The guy would have to come in and we would close the door. Those were the conditions. And we did. I called Janey and Janey called him.

THE GUY CAME OVER, just this anonymous middle-aged small-ish bald guy with asthma, wearing an old-fashioned gray fedora hat. You could tell his upper lip had been surgically reconstructed. There were flesh fault lines heaving upward from his off-center mouth.

Anyway, this citizen sat on our chair, our *furniture*—and that was almost the worst part—and we did it for a while, for long enough, anyway. The trouble was, it was an act. And I never felt that Oscar and me were an act before. I couldn't look back at the guy watching us. I just concentrated on Oscar. I never took my eyes off him. I held on to Oscar like you'd hold on to a lifebuoy that keeps you afloat. At one point his eyes said he couldn't go on, and my eyes told him he had to, so he did. It was the low point of my life so far.

When we were finished, the guy said he wanted to see us do it again, with some variations.

Oscar sat up in bed. He said okay, sure, in a minute. Then he said he wanted to talk about a movie he'd seen. Did the guy like movies? The guy shrugged. So Oscar said he'd just seen this movie called *Cyber Catch* or something, and in this movie there's a vast evil megacomputer that the super-secret government owns that can analyze your DNA from a blood sample. And the computer, the big mainframe, has some people all predicted from here until infinity, their lives laid out and everything based on the DNA, even their afterlives are predicted by the computer before they're born, in their pre-life. The computer also knows if you'll go to hell or not, even before you're born. Your entire post-life is completely mapped out. What it doesn't get from blood it gets from handwriting samples. The computer wants total control for a consumer society, including the afterlife. The hero and his girlfriend are trying to get *at* the computer, but the computer knows all about them, so the guy-hero has to think his way into being somebody else in order to defeat the computer, and the girl-hero has to change her identity into, like, this minimum-wage cleaning woman. They've got to *imagine* their escape.

Oscar sat up in bed naked doing this plot summary for about ten minutes. I never knew he could make up stories before that. Then the bald guy with the facial fault lines said, "That's nice, kid. But if I wanted to go to a movie, I'd go to a movie. Maybe you could do what I'm paying you for, okay?"

"Okay," Oscar said, and he shrugged his naked shoulder. He turned to me and gave me a peck on the cheek, like the show had to go on.

The second time was harder, that's all I'll say. We earned that money. At the end of the show, when we were finished, we got paid. I'd almost never seen so much cash in my life.

I swore off life for a day or two after that. My New Year's resolution was to bag it.

I won't even tell you about how I vomited the next day. Or how I got rid of the chair the guy had sat in. My life isn't sad, I have a good life, so I won't convey that it's pathetic or anything. But I did get rid of that chair.

The funny thing was, after all this happened, and before we actually got married, I stopped thinking of myself as a girl. I *had* thought of myself that way, on and off, up until then. But after that, no. No more girl. The girl was out of me. It didn't apply. The word sort of made me flinch from then on.

EIGHTEEN

THE LITTLE MARRIAGE EXPERIMENT with Bradley hadn't worked out, and so here I was, doing a recently divorced debutante show.

It was Saturday. I had drifted into this summer evening party, a back yard gathering with pinprick clouds of gnats disturbing the air, in that space where the other guests were drinking and talking. Farther back, near the garage, a wasp nest was hanging from a maple branch just above the phone lines. I didn't see any wasps, but the guests were windmilling their hands in front of their faces to keep the gnats away. "Hi, Diana," they would say, waving as if to say good-bye. The hostess, Lydia, smiled with relief when I came in. I am rarely a disappointing guest. I tend to spice up whatever social gathering I am invited to. I create small harmless scenes.

The weather seemed untroubled. I heard birds crying out, somewhere above us.

These two people, my friends, the hosts, had constructed this back deck a few years ago, parallel gray boards nailed to a frame. Lydia's taste was for a certain easygoing informality that thrived on summer parties but not winter ones; this marriage, the one with Don, was her third, and all sorts of children and stepchildren and semi-orphans had been dressed up and were serving condi-

ments and hors d'oeuvres. One of them, whose name was Edgar
—you don't expect a small child to be named Edgar—was playing
the piano in the den. The windows were open, and the music—
beginner's Mozart—mixed with the sounds of conversation.

People lazed around. They came and went. Coolers full of beer
lay open for inspection and slow bluesy jazz arose like candle smoke
out of the stereo and was combined near the house with the sound
of Edgar's Mozart, the minuets he was playing. Their house, which
was stuffed with scratched-up antiques, was set back far enough
away from the street for privacy, and the hedges were littered with
kids' toys, tricycles, and broken plastic battery-operated games.
Walking in, you'd see this wreckage, and it was comforting, familial.
Then you'd get to the back and note a treehouse falling to pieces
close to the nest of wasps. And down there, in the yard, under the
wasp nest, the guests had assembled. The invited guests and the
more or less invited guests, people like me, our laughter mixing with
the sounds of the crickets and the outcasts, the cigarette smokers,
huddling in the back corner, grumpily inhaling.

Lydia is a tall, straight-lined woman with curly black hair that
sweeps in a tangle down both sides of her face and her neck. She's
not beautiful, exactly, but her eager, smiling intelligence greets you
at the doorway, and before very long you're divulging your small
wickednesses to her, and she's telling you hers, and she takes on the
attractiveness of anyone for whom every sub-minor detail is interesting. Interesting events cling to her. She's a perfect hostess for a
party. She'll just pry the outrageousness out of you for the sake of
a story. She wants to hear about everyone, and it's only later that
you remember that you neglected to ask her about herself.

She writes and illustrates children's books, all of them about a
family of goats who are given distinctive individual features like
reading glasses, distinctive smirks, uncombed forelocks, and scowls
that Lydia has picked up from her two ex-husbands and her own
children. I have often wondered what her children thought about

finding their own features located in these goats, but I never found the right moment to ask.

The guests were all from Burns Park, a rumpled academic-professional neighborhood, mostly made up of professionally paid know-it-alls, people with opinions and the leisure to express them.

They—we—had a certain party varnish on. Depending on whether I've had enough to drink, I usually don't like ironic friendliness as much as homely glitter. Because it's the Midwest, no one really glitters because no one has to, it's more a dull shine, like frequently used silverware. We were all presentable enough, but almost no one was making any kind of *statement*. Out here in Michigan, real style is too difficult to maintain; the styles are all convenient and secondhand. We're all hand-me-down personalities. But that's liberating: it frees you up for other matters of greater importance, the great themes, the sordid passions.

I hadn't planned to come at all. I knew people were going to take a sort of friendly interest in me and my novelty marriage to Bradley and its quick aftermath. I was prepared to be snarly in a provocative and sexy way, provided I could manage my smiling and witty quarrelsomeness within acceptable limits. I didn't want sympathy. Well, these people were too hip for sympathy anyway. To be honest, I had this image of myself: I was the tree that a drunk driver slides off the road into. The tree doesn't move. It doesn't do anything except stand there. It kills the person just by standing there. That would be me. I've got my attitude: lethal neutrality and immobility.

"Hi, Diana." A voice out of the party air.

"Oh, hi." My voice back to it. A glassy indifferent smile.

"You look so cute in that."

"Thanks." I turned to freshen my drink. I said something about the weather.

I *had* been back in my house, refurnishing it, preparing one of my cases, and thinking about David now and then, just before this party. Bradley, who was a mistake when conjoined with me, did not occupy my thoughts, but David did, and the other preoccupations I had were the probable duration of our affair and his probable attendance at this back yard social. The statue of the little boy reclined in my back yard.

If you're recently divorced, and you're a woman, you don't know what to wear for a while. You put on the pale blue sundress but you don't like the boniness of your shoulder blades—people will comment on your eating habits or your level of fitness because they're terrifically eager to know your mood—so you take off the sundress and you put on the jeans, but that's physically vain and indulgent unless they're new and the exact right fit, and so you take them off for the simple skirt, but that's *too* simple, that and the blouse: it turns you instantly into one of the clueless off-the-racks, hopelessly unstyled and unaccessorized. So what you do is, you put on one of David's shirts that he left behind, one time, one summer afternoon in your bedroom, escaping in his undershirt from your presence, bloated and mind-numbed from sex, the undershirt with the bookstore logo on it. Then you put on your jeans. You don't tuck in the shirt, David's blue denim, you let it hang down. Then you do tuck it in. You wonder if the wife, the ill-named Katrinka, will recognize it. It has started to seem, in your meaner moments, to be an interesting prospect that she might recognize it. She could make a fuss and stage an outcry. That might even be quite wonderful, that prospect. It would enliven the party.

Before the itch started, I made a social effort. I conversed with one doctor and one accountant, one electrical engineer and two remedial educationists, one professor of economics and one landscape gardener, another person who as far as I could tell was gainfully *un*employed, very proud about it, too, and one person who had in a former life-phase programmed computers and now, following a personal crisis, contentedly made furniture. I talked to an aging personnel manager who wanted to take up jazz piano. Some of these people were women and some were not.

Then I felt the itch on the sole of my right foot, a poison ivy rash or a mosquito bite. What I wanted to do was to remove my sandal and start clawing. Sometimes my whole body feels that way. When that happens, I can claw at myself anywhere, I turn into a woman-rash, head to foot.

I put down my plate of barbecued ribs and barbecued chicken right there on the green and fuzzy lawn, without somehow noticing that the clouds had formed and rain had begun to fall and then was insistently falling. Soon everyone except for myself had gone inside. There I was. Preoccupied, I took my sandal off to scratch my foot. Intent on my little task, I just dug at it. I love to do that, it's one of my bad habits when I have an itch. I was sitting behind a tree guarded from public view, near that wasp nest. No one saw me, or so I thought, enthralled with myself as I was, dazed and thoughtless and fugued. That's why I didn't notice this lightly damp business from the sky, this airy show of droplets. I wasn't paying attention. I was under that tree. The party had gone inside, the people and their food and Edgar's minuets, and I hadn't noticed, and it had been reciprocal. No one had collared me. I was uncollected.

At that point I was facing away from the house, with my back hunched over, and I had the sensation on my back of a man looking at me. That particular feeling's like a humming on your skin.

And what I remember next was this guy, David, of course, his arms folded across his chest like a park ranger, bending over me and putting his jacket over my shoulders and saying, "Let's cover you up. Let's shelter you."

"Hi, David."

"It's raining, Diana. Didn't you notice?"

"Apparently not."

"You don't pay enough attention to the present conditions." He looked up at the sky with gentle gloominess. "You never did. You don't pay attention to the conditions at hand and then you get soaked and someone has to come and clean up the mess you've made of yourself. You're so willful, but in you it isn't courage, it's obstinacy. Diana, Diana, Diana." I noticed that he liked saying my name.

I said, "Ah. I see that I have been explained in full. Where's your wife, by the way? Where's Katrinka?"

"Kat? Well, she's inside, of course, with the other guests." He looked toward the house. "They sent me out to get you. They said it was raining. And it is, Diana. It *is*."

"I hadn't noticed." I looked up at the sky and rain fell into my eyes.

"Exactly right. That's just what I'm saying." He gave me a sweet look, and my heart crashed in my chest, at least a little. "The weather reports had predicted rain."

"Well, I was scratching my foot. I think I have poison ivy."

"Let's see." He sat down and lifted my foot. "Ah." He fingered it. The itchy spot was right under the arch. "Yes, there's a dermatitis there, all right." Then he bent over, shielded by the tree trunk, and kissed it, kissed me, right there on the rash. The nerve of him! My lover.

I don't remember anything else about the party except for a conversation I had twenty minutes later with Katrinka, there in the corner by the upright piano. Having come inside, I had given the jacket back to David, and he had disappeared into the kitchen. Katrinka and I, old acquaintances, were talking about the politics of the local school-board election, and then we were discussing poison ivy (she, too, had it growing at the edge of their yard), and as we held our plates (I had a new plate with new food) and ate, the conversation swerved like a slightly out-of-control automobile toward the proven or unproved benefits of Vitamin E, and all this time, through an act of will so resolute and brave that it can scarcely be imagined, she kept her eyes on my face after having looked, *locked on* is maybe a better phrase, once, twice, and then a third time, at the denim shirt I was wearing. You could see, from a telltale movement of her eyebrows, that she was struggling to remember the shirt, trying to ascertain if she did remember it, whether she thought or could think that it might be the shirt she suspected it was, her husband's blue denim shirt, hanging on me two sizes too large. I watched, not without a trace of pity, as a small gauze of sweat broke out on her forehead, tiny spindles of perspiration.

FOUR DAYS LATER, as in a farce, a comic opera, a nighttime TV half-hour comedy written by a committee, David developed poison ivy rashes on the backs of his hands and on his face, near his mouth.

I don't remember the last time poison ivy was considered a sexually transmitted disease. Actually, it can't be transmitted from foot to mouth or even from hand to hand. But it was certainly what you might call a catalyst, accidental though its appearance was on him. Anyway, Katrinka had been thinking about my shirt for days and at last deduced that it was David's—a wife does not forget her husband's shirts, not a suburban-four-bedroom-home wife like Katrinka. And when she put one and one together, the two they added up to was us, David and Diana, and that was the night when David moved out, and where he moved was over here, his little boys desperately crying and clutching as he walked out the front door. It doesn't matter the least little bit that you can't really pass poison ivy back and forth. She thought you could. So they had an opportunistic fight, which resolved matters. Remember the song? It became our song.

You're gonna need an ocean
Of calamine lotion

Which we daubed on each other with little tender gestures, our first night as an official couple, unclandestine, David miserable and relieved and miserable again and somehow relieved again, not knowing at all what he felt when I kissed him wildly. He stayed awake all night in his joy and misery.

HE HAD ALWAYS LOVED ME and kept that love a secret from me. Every man likes to pretend that he's in the CIA, a holder of vast dangerous secrets. This is why they suffer so in telling you that they love you. But once he was here, in my bedroom, the truth having come out, he talked about it—the love—openly, wretched as he was after leaving the boys. As I said, he was rigorous about that. I was the person you had to pry open with a crowbar.

By late summer, a month later, this particular evening I'd been out watching him play basketball with this kid Oscar and some other guys at a city park. The men were vocalizing, I have no idea what they were grunting to each other, this guy-yelping, and their shoes were squeaking on the asphalt. Actually I loved that sound. I was lounging on a park bench off to the side, sitting there, studying him. He was just in shorts and shoes. Earlier in the day we'd been doing yard work. I thought he was kind of beautiful. I liked thinking about him. My tastes had changed. My concept of male beauty had altered: he was now the definition of it. He'd lunge for the ball, he'd use his elbows, he'd do his layups. I sat there, just watching. I'd thought of playing and decided not to, for now. I had shorts on, too. I thought my legs might distract him from time to time. My legs were prettier than they'd been a month or so before. Smoother and nicer-looking. I don't know why. They just were. Oh, actually I do know why: he loved them.

Behind me, the dogs barked at passing fire trucks, and in another section of the park, two softball teams were shouting some sort of encouragement to their batters and pitchers. The sun sank under the horizon.

When it was finally too dark to play, he joined me. I stood up, and Chloé, Oscar's fiancée, who was sitting on the other bench after jogging around in her Joy Division tee-shirt and whom I had sort of befriended, well, she stood up, too. David came over. David's skin was so sweaty that his hand slipped out of mine at first. Then he reached for me again. He laced his fingers between mine. I could smell his sweat. It was rank. I wanted to have him immediately. He put his arm around my shoulders. I hitched myself to his waist.

We got into his car and drove back to my place, which was gradually also becoming his. We went into the bedroom and lay down together. He was still wet and as his sweat dried he had a sweet heavy smell, like overripe blueberries. God, I loved that.

When we were naked, finally, we were standing up, and then he had his hands on my breasts and he was kissing me. I felt star-spattered. And I was thinking: he can have every inch of me. Sweet Jesus, he can pick my bones clean.

I told him I loved him. It escaped me, just like that. And he was cool: he pretended I hadn't said it or that he hadn't been listening, though he had heard me say it plenty of times before.

Just about then I heard an ice cream truck going by on the street, the Good Humor Man. With those distant prerecorded bell chimes. They're supposed to sound cheery, but they sound unearthly and preoccupied, like death's angel.

And then we were making love, calmer than we usually do it, and I'm looking at David, and my soul—I can't believe I'm saying this, but it's what happened—became visible to me. My soul was a large and not particularly attractive waiting room, just like in a Victorian train station with people going in and out. In this waiting room were feelings I hadn't known I had, discarded feelings, feelings with nowhere to go, no ticket to a destination. It turned out that I was *larger* than I had known myself to be; there were multitudes of feelings in there. This can happen any sort of way. I don't care if you disapprove of what I'm telling you or the means I used to discover it. I warned you: I'm not an original. But at that point I felt like one. I'm just telling you how it happened with me. I was a different person than I had planned to be. My soul was not particularly attractive, but the surprise was that it was there, that I had one.

I loved him and we fused together. He didn't save me from anything. I was the same person I always was. But as they say: one phase of my life was over, and another one began.

NINETEEN

FOLLOWING THE DIANA marriage incident, Bradley the dog took over my affairs. He urged me onward to take walks with him, eat regularly, and make noises at strangers. This did not include Harry and Esther Ginsberg, who came by from time to time with baked foods of various sorts, and who informed me that the cause of my divorce was not actually myself, or my happenstantial faults, but the house I lived in. At first I thought they meant this metaphorically, but no: the reference was to the physical enclosure, the walls and windows and ceilings. They claimed there was a dybbuk living in it. I had never heard of such a thing, and they refused to explain, claiming that to speak of the thing itself was, like the uttering of the unutterable name of the divinity, bad luck. I checked it in the *American Heritage Dictionary* and couldn't believe what I found there. He was a philosopher and she was a scientist, and they were both alleging that Diana and I had been done in by some sort of Jewish phantom.

Well, they're my neighbors, and I suppose they mean well. I listened to them talk about their son Aaron, and they listened to me talk about Diana. Let them have their dybbuk. Or, excuse me, my dybbuk. After all, I had heard Chloé and Oscar yelping with love cries in my house long after they had been there, house-sitting.

I had felt the breath of themselves, the memory of their bodies crisscrossing down the hallways. Who was I to scoff at a dybbuk?

LATE IN THE SUMMER I was walking around town with Bradley. I wasn't feeling too bad. This song, "My Funny Valentine," as sung by Ella Fitzgerald, was going through my head as I walked. I always liked her; I liked it that she sang jazz while wearing glasses. I came to the park. There was just enough light to see by, Magritte light. These guys were playing basketball, as usual, including Oscar. Chloé was jogging around the park, wearing her Joy Division tee-shirt and keeping a distant eye on her beloved. And there next to the basketball hoops was a bench, and on this bench sat of all people my ex-wife, Diana. Of course I knew she hadn't moved out of town. She still occasionally showed up at Jitters, just to say hello and to have coffee. She had changed her hair color. It looked as if it had been dipped in blond ink or something. She looked nice. She was resting on the bench with her arms crossed just under her breasts. I watched her—I was some distance back, on the other side of the street, in the shadows—as she slapped at a mosquito. Her legs looked prettier than I remembered.

After ten minutes, it was too dark, and they stopped playing. And this guy, David, came over to where she was, and Diana stood up, and he put his arm around her shoulders, and she put her arm around his waist, and they started walking toward his car, that way, his arm around her shoulder, her arm around his waist. It couldn't have taken more than fifteen seconds for them to get to that car. But I'll remember how they looked all my life.

I'd never seen Diana with that settled contentedness before. It's funny how you can tell when people are in love.

They passed under one of those streetlights they have near the parking area. Bradley tugged at the leash, but I was not to be moved. And I saw Diana clearly, leaning into this fellow, her head bent to the left so that it was resting on his shoulder, and this insane eventuality happened. I felt this punch in my stomach. Standing there, across the street, in the shadows where it was possibly my fate to live, forever after, I felt this punch in my stomach.

I could see instantly what I was missing. That she was beautiful in a way I hadn't noticed before. Suddenly I missed her lazy manner of reading the editorial pages aloud on Sunday morning and I missed the way she said good night by whispering it in my direction and I missed everything about her, including how mean she could sometimes be. I remembered the way she blew the bangs away from her forehead by jutting her lower lip outward and blowing a stream of air, perfected by her years of playing the oboe in high school, upward. Sick with memory, I was in love with Diana, genuinely, still, or maybe for the first time, at least this way.

They got in the car and now she put her hand on his chest and started kissing him. They kissed for a while. I should have turned away. I tried.

A fire truck went by a few blocks away, howling. Chloé came and collected Oscar and they went home together in Oscar's beat-up Matador.

I staggered home and couldn't sleep. It occurred to me for the first time that I had smashed my life with a hammer.

THE JOB AT JITTERS became a different job.

Couples, plain-style Americans, would come in, hand in hand, arm in arm, treating each other as delicacies. They'd order a pound of coffee or they'd order decaf cappuccino, and they'd sit down at a table and talk, leaning toward each other, their secretive knees slowly but ever-so-surely touching. Every day this familiar tableau that I myself had painted in *The Feast of Love* was presented to me as a done deal, an actuality. In truth, there are only two realities: the one for people who are in love or love each other, and the one for people who are standing outside all that.

The mere sight of happiness made me groan inwardly. Now, when I walked in the parks, all I saw were couples, Chloé and Oscar types of every description. At intersections I would find myself behind couples necking in the backseat, or some woman next to a guy in the front. I would watch. I would see her toying with the back of his neck. Twirling her fingers there. Playing with the little curls. Sometimes I'd see people smiling for no reason. Just smiling, happy with life. This enraged me. I suffered from the happiness of others.

It helps that in Michigan everyone goes inside from November through April. But from May until October they are outside, on display, and all of a sudden if you are single, you have a window to heaven and no way at all to get in.

My attitude toward my art changed. Now I didn't paint my canvases; instead I vandalized them. Harry Ginsberg came over one evening and said, "I have heard of action painting, but this is new. Bradley, you are at last a pioneer in the visual realm. You are post-action and post-Pop. This, what you are doing, is devastation painting. You are the first painter of the new millennium."

I was pleased by his comment.

ONE EVENING I LEFT Bradley behind in the house, and I drove to Jackson, Michigan, which is about thirty miles west of Ann Arbor. I had no idea what I would do when I arrived there. It was just a place to go. Jackson is one of those hopeless-case cities that are cited in magazines at the very bottom when they list America's most livable communities, one of those working-class locales where they're all repairing cars in the front yard and otherwise having fights and breaking beer bottles over the nearest head. The houses aren't painted, and the siding is falling off. They'll kill you for a nickel and steal anything that isn't nailed down. What can I say? Folks there are enjoying themselves any way they can.

When class warfare erupts in America, as it must within the next decade, it'll start in Jackson, probably. Those citizens are not being fooled.

Anyway, I found myself driving to Jackson's one tourist attraction, the Jackson Cascades. This guy named Sparks built it in the 1930s. He was a radio tycoon. He thought Jackson needed some waterfalls, for the view. It needed *something*. But there weren't any visible waterfalls except for the ones that Consumers Power had already dammed up. So he built this thing in the central city park. It's huge, the size of a football field. Water gubbles out at the top, where it's been pumped, and it flows down these ten or so artificially built cascades, like a display in a hotel lobby in Las Vegas, and you sit in the chairs they have, having paid your four dollars, while computer-controlled lights play over these cascades—it only opens after dark—and the speakers they've attached to telephone poles play Mantovani and Neil Diamond and the 101 Strings. This is where I decided to go to collect my thoughts.

The water doesn't flow during the day. It sits there. Mosquitoes breed in it. At night they hatch and go insane. They go after you.

This was a Tuesday night. I bought my ticket and sat down in a sort of bleacher chair. The management gives you a fly swatter, a little one with *Jackson Cascades* printed on it, and you're supposed to swat the mosquitoes with this device. Neil Diamond's "Song Sung Blue" was blaring over these internment-camp speakers, and I was sitting there with my head in my hands wondering what I was doing in Jackson, Michigan. The colors on the water were turning from magenta to a sort of hot pink, and I was having this insight that my parents had let me loose in the world without explaining anything of importance to me.

Down below me were some families, likewise sitting, likewise watching this spectacle but perkier than I was. One child wearing Oshkosh overalls was running in widening circles. He was yelling, "I'm gonna explode!" I nodded at him. Okay with me, kid. You just explode right there. I'm watching, and I've got the good view.

The music switched to Mantovani, this string slop, pouring molasses over hapless George Gershwin.

In front of me this picture-perfect high school couple was sitting on a bench. He looked a little bit like the guy that Diana was seeing, and she looked a tiny bit like Diana. The resemblance was close enough to indicate God's trickster pranksterism. They were talking. Then, God help me, they were kissing. *Everywhere I went I saw people kissing.* It was this smooch conspiracy. These two were holding hands, and with the hand that was free, she was swatting mosquitoes on his back, and he was swatting mosquitoes on hers.

I found them unbearable. Another couple in love, this time at the Jackson Cascades, swatting mosquitoes off each other's backs, and they both looked dirt-poor, knowing the system was rigged against them, and they didn't care because they were both sedated with amour.

Down with love, I thought, and all its theatrics. I felt a sort of energetic, visionary despair.

I raced back toward my car. As I drove home, typically, I was arrested for speeding. I, Mr. Toad, was traveling eighty-five miles an hour on I-94. I was given a breath test. Sober sober sober. Oh, I am a sober man, and the state trooper wrote me a ticket to confirm my sober crime.

Back in Ann Arbor, Bradley greeted me with great joy, which for once was not contagious. I walked into the kitchen and turned on the overhead fluorescent light. It snaps at you when you do that, before it begins to shower glare and that flickering corpse-blue illumination on the sink and the Formica counter and the red dish drainer. For once I believed Harry and Esther; there was indeed a dybbuk living in the house with me. I saw it in the living room. It had the appearance of an easy chair. Demons can disguise themselves cleverly.

I sat down. My head was full of wild ambitious urges to hurt myself. I tasted the ambrosia of maddened impulse. I wanted my interior pain out in my body somehow. I wanted this vague pain to be specific. That's how I explain it.

I took out my sharpest knife and cut off the very tip of my little finger. On my left hand.

I sat there and bled while my dog whined and barked at me. Then I called my neighbor, Harry Ginsberg, and he drove me in my car down to the hospital. He did not comment or ask questions. He's a good man. Philosophy has taught him how to keep his mouth shut when necessary. I insisted on taking my car because I knew I would leave bloodstains soaked into the leatherette, and indeed I did: great expressive blotch-stains. At the emergency entrance, Harry dropped me off to park the car. Eventually they put me into a room with this black woman, this doctor, who introduced herself as Dr. Margaret Ntegyereize, and she was the one who bandaged me up. She asked me how I had done such a thing. I explained. She had beautiful eyes, Margaret did, and no wedding ring, and I fell in love with her on the spot. I couldn't tactfully get her phone number right there but resolved to obtain it by stealth.

Driving me home, Harry told me—how could I not know it?—that Jackson Pollock had cut off the tip of *his* little finger at the age of seven. Seven! Jesus Christ. Not even my pain is original.

TWENTY

IN THOSE DAYS, before I fell in love with Diana and married her (which was after Bradley had met her, married her, and she left him for me)—before all that, I used to hunt in the forests and marshes up north. Deer, in particular, but ducks also, and pheasants. Now that I've lost that passion, I remember my prey with an odd clarity. I see all the individual animals I killed and cleaned and prepared for meals, crossing my line of sight one by one like mechanical birds in a shooting gallery flipping up from one side and sinking down on the other. I see their eyes, small glintings there. Sympathy for these animals? Why should I feel sympathy? That's for others. They were one form of life, I was another. I was never one of them.

It could be that I didn't think at all. The cells of my body collectively strained to be outside with a weapon in my hand, in pursuit of them.

Every part of this pursuit made me edgy and alert. I didn't say to myself: I like to hunt. Liking had nothing to do with it. It was much more simple: I was a hunter, and that simplified my identity. I didn't really have to consider the matter at all. I hunted the way an apple tree produces apples, as if it was purely second nature. My father had taught me how. I felt his presence there in those woods and fields, the weight of his flesh and bones on my shoulders, the sound of his gruff voice in my ear.

I counted the days until hunting season opened just as other men counted the days on the calendar until baseball or football season began. My hunting clothes were stored in a basement closet, the bright orange for deer hunting, the camouflage for the ducks. I'd go to that particular corner, open the door, yank at the pull chain for the light, and just look at the clothes, hanging there, swaying sometimes in the draft I had brought in, or from the furnace vents, swaying like ghosts dangling on the clothes rack. I'd have a beer in my hand and I would drink the beer as I gazed at the contents of the basement corner, an expression of suspended animation on my face.

I had a succession of girlfriends who tolerated this behavior. Then I had Katrinka. I married her.

I gave it all up when I left her and moved in with Diana, when I left my boys, Carl and Jeremiah, and took up with her. Once Diana belonged to me, and once I had begun to experience what it was like to live with her, and to live without my sons except on weekends, to have lost or at least be separated from my children, I abandoned all my interest in hunting. I took all my guns and my hunting clothes to the dump. I had no intention of selling them or giving them away. I didn't want them to fall into another man's hands. I wanted their history to end with me. I loved her, I loved her with some kind of violence, and that was all that mattered.

THERE'S ANOTHER STORY I want to tell you, and then I'll be finished. I don't think people should talk about their health, but this story is more about love than medicine. I had gone to the dentist for a routine cleaning. The dental hygienist, a pleasant woman about my age with whom I conversed easily, had just about finished the job when, as she was examining my throat, she said, "Hmm." She asked me to open wider and to say, "Ah." I did. She looked. I gazed out the window at the view. She did not say what she was looking at. I stayed calm. She called in the dentist, who also took a long look at me—at my tonsils, it turned out, and the uvula, on which were spots of some sort.

"There's something there," she said with maddening nonspecificity. "I don't think it's serious, but I'm sending you to a specialist. Just for a look."

"What do you see?" I asked.

"Probably nothing," she said. "Probably just a couple of papillomas. Which are like warts, a wart on your throat." She looked at me carefully. "Really," she said, "that's all I think they are."

She gave me the name of the specialist I was to see, a Dr. Hovhanessian. When I called his office, I discovered that I would have to wait for a month for an appointment. It was August, *and Dr. Hov would be on vacation,* his secretary told me, so I—and my throat and its contents—would have to bide the time until he returned.

On the day of the appointment, I drove over to the medical complex, checked in at his front desk, and sat in the waiting room reading old copies of *Time* and *Newsweek*. Eventually the nurse called my name and ushered me into an examination room that at its center featured a chair like a dentist's chair. Up on the wall were various posters about deafness and throat cancer. I had thought about throat cancer and about the possible choking or pain that might accompany it, I thought of speaking with an artificial larynx, but the truth is that until that moment I had really done my best to be a man about it and to keep the whole matter out of my mind. I'm quite good at such denials and exclusions.

Bad health is for others. I'm not supposed to get sick.

But in that examination room with that black chair in front of me, my heart began to pound, and because the chair I was sitting in was a simple metal one with stainless steel sleighlike runners resting on the slippery blue-speckled linoleum tile, I found myself moving slowly across the floor, powered by the pounding of my heart against my back. Fear has a certain horsepower, I discovered.

Dr. Hovhanessian eventually arrived. He was an oval-faced man who affected an authoritative air and who presented a general and perhaps inflated aura of competence. We exchanged pleasantries and he was kind enough to show interest in the research work I do for the drug company (I'm a molecular biologist). Then he said, "Let's have a look at you."

When the exam was over, he leaned back and said, "You don't have anything."

"I don't have anything?"

"You had your tonsils out once. Those are lymphatic deposits. They've been there for years."

"Oh." Then I smiled. "I guess that's a relief."

"I'm sorry to have kept you waiting," he said. Then he rubbed his face. "You know, when I first started to practice medicine, I thought my patients wanted me to give them a clear diagnosis of their illnesses and a clear course of treatment. But that's wrong. What my patients really want is for me to tell them that nothing is wrong with them and that they'll be fine and that they'll live to be a hundred."

I nodded.

"Nothing is wrong with you," Dr. Hovhanessian said, "and you'll be fine. You'll live for another fifty years, give or take a decade."

I thanked him and walked out of his office and got into my car. What I didn't do was drive back to work. Instead I drove along the river for an hour or two and then went into a bar downtown and ordered a double scotch. Instead of making me drunk, the scotch brought me to a higher pitch of lucidity. I made a resolution, the only one I can remember making and keeping. I decided not to tolerate, in my life from then on, any form of trivial unhappiness.

This thing had been a lesson to me. Our time here is short.

That night I told Katrinka that I would be leaving her, and I informed her about Diana. Diana's story about the denim shirt is her invention. I was the one who initiated all this.

I CAN'T TALK about love directly. I never have been able to. The only way I can talk about it is by talking about hunting and visits to the doctor.

TWENTY-ONE

I'D BEEN AT THE GROCERY BUYING, I don't know, food, for example orange juice, and a candy bar and ice cream for Oscar, and I had come out to the parking lot to unload all this stuff into the Matador and take it home. That was when I saw, over there in the corner by the dumpster, my future father-in-law, the Bat, leaning against his truck, an open-sewer smile on his face. He was taking his own time, the Bat was. He had his wings folded up but he was calamitizing me with his evil.

I figured that word had finally gotten out to the Bat about Oscar and me getting married. Maybe Oscar had invited him to the reception as what you'd call a friendly gesture.

That must've just shoved the Bat's psyche down to the barroom floor among the peanut shells and the sawdust. His short-fatherhood was obsolete now, he had no necessity for being alive. Nobody wanted him here on Earth. Anyway, explanations aside, his little greaseball head nodded at me directly over the space of the cars in the parking lot. Like, recognition. He hoped! Maybe he thought . . . shit, why am I saying this? I don't *care* what he thought.

I pulled the car out onto Stadium but fuck and alas, there trailing behind me, still at a distance, was the Bat himself, busily hunched over his steering wheel smoking his Camels and drinking his no-brand beer while he kept me in his line of sight. Well, now at last I had a one hundred percent genuine stalker, and not a handsome one like some women get, with a killer smile and Continental manners, but a genuine blue-ribbon humanoid rodent. I turned by the Dairy Queen, hoping to shake him, but his intentions, being impure, were strong. He hung on to me from his distance. I could feel his puny rat's eyes boring into the back of my neck.

I drove downtown and parked in the police station parking lot. I figured some proximity to the law would give him the willies. Plus you put human refuse next to courts of law and the human refuse will get anxious and crazy, and eventually they will go away. I thought I'd got rid of him. I waited and then I drove over to our apartment.

But when I got there, the Bat had already arrived and was parked across the street, like we had an appointment. I eased the Matador into the parking lot and hefted the grocery bags into my arms and made my way to the front door. I was not about to run away. The ice cream would melt, wasting my hard-earned money.

Oscar was at work. I should mention that now.

I was trying to open the door with my hand, holding all the groceries. From behind me I heard the Bat say, "You want some help?"

"No," I said, trying to get into the building.

"Hey, maybe you and me could have ourselves some lunch?"

"Well," I said, "Lunch? I don't know. Maybe."

"Or dinner? Not that I need 'em. You been standing against me," the Bat said, getting closer. There was this odor in the air that preceded him. "You been back in my house."

"No, I haven't." I wasn't going to get inside of my building in time. I'd have to face him directly.

"You been in my house and you been takin' my things over here for your own self."

"No, I *haven't*," I said. I put the grocery bags down on the stoop. He wasn't going to hurt me in broad daylight. Bats don't do that. Not here. God, he stank. I could hardly breathe. Evil has got a smell. Don't let them tell you otherwise.

"You been takin' my things, girl. You could have got you your own things but you took mine and you kept them for yourself. You even took that souvenir glass dish I like. I want the things back, all the valuables that you got your little bitty hands on."

"What glass dish? I don't have your *things*," I said. "Except Oscar, and he's not yours."

"I oughta punish you for your smart mouth," he said. "Wouldja like that?" He smiled, making a joke. "Some do."

"No."

"I been thinkin' 'bout how I might just manage it. The punishment." He put his chin in his hand like a demonstration of thinking. "It'd hurt. And you, with them nice pretty features you got there, it'd sure be such a shame and a mess." He waited in a posture of thoughtfulness. "I'm still pondering it, considering the right and the wrong." He smiled again, and what an awful sight that was. Demons smile, as a rule, before they force themselves into you. "You showin' your naked self to me in my house and then stealin' my son the same breath, and takin' my valuables, I oughta just cancel your rights right on the spot, missy."

"What spot would that be?" Maybe I could get him on technicalities.

He looked confused for a microsecond. "Any spot."

"Like this one?"

"You're tryin' to turn me around. All's I'm sayin' is, you return what you stole. Meanwhile I'm keepin' my eyes on you, so's you don't take you any more of my belongings and then smile yourself up like the little weaselly piece of tail you are."

He did this little swivel thing and walked back to his car before I could correct him on his dirty language. It's sad when youth has to reprimand the elders. I could hear him chuckling to himself. I felt relieved that he wasn't going to try anything violent on my front stoop. He couldn't have done anything anyway because that week, being totally in love, I was immortal. Also I was relieved to see evil in such a pure form and to see how *stupid* it looked. The thing about Oscar's dad was, he was a moron. God himself could've tried to tutor the Bat and He'd've gotten absolutely noplace. Still, he was Oscar's dad, and I was sorry we'd never have cheery Thanksgivings around the turkey, family reunions, photo albums, and suchlike. We'd have this dumbfuck drunk meanness, instead. We'd have forty miles of bad road always stretching out in front of us.

It just amazed me that Oscar had come out the way he had, with a father like that. It just goes to show you how inexact a science genetics is.

I took the groceries upstairs and got the ice cream into the freezer before it melted.

Oscar'd been gone a lot, working at Jitters during the day and taking classes at the Arbogast School of Broadcasting at night. He wasn't going to do coffee all his life. Oscar was not a loser. He had a future in broadcasting. He would be Radio Man. We both *agreed* on that. He would practice his glottal thrust in the bathroom where the echo was good. In the shower with me, while I was washing his back or his chest, he'd recite commercials that he had written himself in his broadcast voice. He wrote commercials for products that didn't exist. He wrote a commercial for a pair of scissors with three blades instead of two. You could efficiently cut two things with it simultaneously. He wrote a commercial for a pocket furnace that you'd carry in your overcoat during the winter. Oscar had many many ideas, several of them amazing.

He made an audition tape for a radio show he wanted to do, a mix of Goth, techno, and progressive rock. I listened to it at home. You'd never guess that it wasn't already on the air. His DJ name was Bone Barrel. He had a medium-low voice and could sound scary and crucial.

We had to do *something,* since the sex thing hadn't been lucrative and had been a morale drain besides. We were starting to map out our future. He would be in radio, and I was going to do something utterly else, only I hadn't decided what yet. Oscar said I should be in the movies as a screen star, and I did consider it. I figured I was so good at so many things, I could kind of pick and choose. I was beginning to think that maybe I could go into social work. I didn't mind being in the service sector. Anyway, Bradley had asked me if I wanted to learn bookkeeping so I could keep the books at Jitters. So maybe I would do that. I had many options.

For the next couple of days we didn't see the Bat. He went back to his cave, I guess. And then it was the day of our wedding.

IT WAS A SUNNY DAY in August, the thirteenth. We dressed casual. Bradley Smith was going to meet us at city hall to be our witness. We wanted him there because he's like an official adult, and he'd always been ultra-nice to us. Also he was going to have a reception for us that afternoon in his back yard, and we wanted to let him have the honor of being at the ceremony, the authorized witness.

On the way to city hall, I went down on Oscar, right in the Matador, that's how much I loved him. I started at a red light near that new tellerless bank and finished about a mile and a half later, near a minimart and a dry cleaner. I don't know if anyone saw me. I don't think so. Oscar said, "Honey, I'm just amazed." I *believe* he was. He just let out a little mew when he came, and then he accelerated accidentally. It was straight from the heart, him and me, whatever we did. I kind of hoped you'd be able to smell his splurge on my breath an hour or so later after I said "I do," but I don't know if you can detect that smell conversationally. I didn't leave any stains on him; I swallowed it all down, neat as a pin as I am, though there wasn't much to swallow, since for good luck for our marriage we had made copious desperate love about two hours earlier on the floor, before we got dressed. Oscar's cum tastes like wheat beer with a dash of Clorox, by the way. We were a couple of wild childs, that's for sure. Everything we did was holy instead of scandalous. You have to trust me on that.

Bradley was there, grinning, at city hall, when we arrived. His left hand was all bandaged up. We went in, and when we came out an hour later—there was another couple waiting, and that slowed us down—with Bradley as our witness, the mayor officiating, Oscar and me were man and wife. Once we were married we kissed, even though it was redundant, the two of us being who we were.

I was Oscar's wife. In the olden days I would have been Mrs. Oscar Metzger, but since we were living in contemporary times, I was still Chloé Barlow. Anyhow, it was time to celebrate.

WE SET UP THIS BOOM BOX in the boss's back yard, and a collection of CDs, and he'd taken some tables out there and covered them with food, and over to the side were coolers filled with beer, and jugs and jugs of wine. We would never run out no matter how much we drank or who we invited. I didn't know why Bradley wanted to do this for us except that we had started as his employees and stuck by him or something. We were Bradley Smith loyalists, Oscar and me, despite our almost minimal wages and the oppression we experienced by having to work hard.

The sun did what it's done for decades: it shone. First thing I did when I got there was toss my shoes off so I could dance. I wanted to dance on the grass and feel it on my bare feet like an African woman approaching her new husband. I wanted to be that fierce. I took Oscar's shoes off myself by hand and I started to feed him food by hand from the table including the cake that Bradley had remembered to buy. I would breathe oxygen into him if I had to.

My sister Rhonda was there, and the Vulture, and Janey, taking her videos, and a bunch of my big-haired friends from high school, and a couple of the Spice Girls I used to live with, plus some of Oscar's friends like Ranger and Spinner and Fats, and a guy whose name was unimaginatively just plain Don. Bradley's dog, Bradley, was racing around, barking conversationally to everybody and eating the hors d'oeuvres out of your hands. Bradley the human, not the dog, had invited this new woman, this doctor, who was black and amazingly superchic. I was drinking a fair amount, and Ranger had brought a big number that he lit up on the other side of the house, and although I was the new bride, I got high anyway.

Funny stuff happens to me when I get stoned. Two years ago, before I met Oscar, in my wild-girl days, I went to a summer party. Here's how high I got. At that party I saw Jesus, the real one, also in attendance at the party. Not all that many people have that honor. He was glistening. Glistening! I mean, he *looked* like an average Joe, but you could tell he *wasn't*. This guy, just standing there, waiting around for I don't know what, was the Son of Man, so-called, and you could tune in on that without asking anybody, it was so obvious. He was dressed in white and was wearing sandals, and He was so beautiful you just wanted to, like, eat him. He had a million watts of candlepower. He didn't have to introduce himself because his divinity was so blatant. He didn't stay. He had business to do. He drank some lemonade and then asked for directions. Jesus nodded while I told him where he wanted to go. It wasn't the Celestial City, just a street address on the west side. He thanked me. And then he left. Jesus was on an *errand*, if you can believe it. I wished he'd stayed. He's probably busy all the time. Everyone in the world wants to talk to him constantly, not just the prison population—*everybody*.

My point is, I saw Jesus once, and I'm still alive, I'm still here. Talk about luck!

I WAS THE MOST BEAUTIFUL woman there at the wedding party that afternoon. No one could take their eyes off me. I drank and danced and smoked Ranger's weed and kissed Oscar, and if a man or a woman wanted to dance with me and get high by being near me for a moment or two, okay, but then I'd go back to Oscar. Bradley's next-door neighbors, Harry and Esther Ginsberg, they dropped by. Harry and I have a lot in common. We're both interested in philosophy. We compare notes. He asked me to dance, and I did. He's a gentleman, and sweet, and he's so smart you can tell thinking bothers him and takes up a great deal of his time. He gave me a little speech while we danced, ordering me to be happy, which I explained I was anyway, and he said, no, I had to be *aware* that I was happy. I asked him about evil, and he explained. He wanted to waltz, so I waltzed with him. He showed me how, and I picked the moves up right away.

At one point I looked at the street and saw the Bat just standing and watching, but then he vanished. I should have been concerned, but I wasn't.

Bradley danced with this black doctor, Dr. Ntegyereize, and she was a much better dancer than he was, but she didn't seem to care. They looked nice together. You got the feeling that all his life, Bradley had been looking around for an emergency-room physician, and at last he found one, and she was beautiful, besides. People who said that Bradley was unmarketable as a boyfriend and husband would just have to eat their words with a fork and spoon from now on.

He had drawn a picture of Oscar and me riding a dragon, and he put this picture up on the back door into his house, so you'd see it in passing when you went in to the bathroom to do your business.

Late in the afternoon a lot of the guests—our relatives and friends—were getting pretty drunk and/or stoned, but that was okay and totally acceptable behavior at a wedding party. I came out of the house from the bathroom, and I looked at this table, the one Bradley had set for us. The light was shining on it in a certain celestial way, blazing blazing, and for a second the table turned into a bonfire, and so did the food and the wine. The party became, like, incandescent, right in front of my eyes, and I heard voices saying my name, Chloé, like the air was saying it, or God saying it, celebrating me. This table in front of me, the party, was so bright you could be blinded by it. It was just like one of Bradley's paintings, the one of the table he'd put up in the back of Jitters.

Oscar started dancing with me, whispering love-and-sex stuff in my ear, wrapping himself around me (for a sometimes inarticulate boy, he could sure be eloquent, at least about me, when he whispered to me), and I was afraid I'd take my clothes off there and then, in front of everybody, shameless and crazy with love as I was, giving myself to him body and soul on the lawn, so we excused ourselves from the party and got rice thrown on us and we thanked everyone and we remaindered our sweaty selves into the car (I forgot my shoes in Bradley's yard), but instead of going to the School of Velocity concert and staying at a motel in East Lansing, we went barefoot back to our little apartment, where we did our lovemaking all night long, my legs wrapped around him oh sweet sweet sweet fucking, like happy birds, which is sort of what you should do anyhow, given the circumstances, newlyweds and everything. We were legal now. We fell asleep at sunrise, birds chirping outside, all our limbs intertwined and confused.

"Sweet dreams, girl," he said to me.

"Sweet dreams," I said.

———

I'D HAD MORE HAPPINESS than most people do in a lifetime, so when Oscar died four months later, I wasn't ready for it, but I tried to be. I was pregnant by then, and I had memorized every inch of Oscar so I'd never forget any particle of him, inside or out. I didn't think Mrs. Maggaroulian could be wrong about something that big, and she wasn't.

ENDS

The Soviets made me change *Romeo and Juliet* so that it would have a happy ending, a barbarism, because living people can dance, but the dead cannot dance lying down.

——SERGEY PROKOFIEV

TWENTY-TWO

THIS BAREFOOT YOUNGSTER, Chloé, wearing her bridal blue jeans, approached me to make a few inquiries at her wedding party, which happened to be next door at Bradley's. Why, she asked, did love—by which she appeared to mean sexual love—attract so much, her phrase, *weird badness* to it? She said that as a philosopher I would know and that she needed to have the answer in a hurry. (I am not a philosopher; I teach philosophy of the antique and out-moded variety, and there is after all a difference between making philosophy and teaching it, a difference of stature and modesty.) Her question was not entirely clear. She stood there beautifully young in the hot sunlight. She referred to "scumbags," but I grasped her intention. She was holding a beer and grinning quizzically. Her lips were so chapped it must have hurt her to smile.

When I asked about the scumbags, she referred to pornography in a general way and then pointed to a strange little man staring at us from a distance near the street. Who was he? She didn't say. But he, the strange man, appeared to be the scumbag problem to which she referred.

Oh, I said—I had had some wine myself by that time, my syntax was not of the best—the force of eros, which is godlike and has been known to be such since ancient times and therefore does not have to include morality, being outside of it—think of the Bacchae, the unleashing of this force, the goatish caperings, well, any force as powerful as that is premoral. Eros, I told Chloe, is a devil as well as an angel; the faces are the same but the expressions are dissimilar. Every positive attracts a negative and must contend with it. I mentioned *The Marriage of Heaven and Hell,* Freud and de Sade, the mingling of the angelic and the demonic, the control of these forces by means of ritual, of which her official marriage was one. I was prepared to speak of Spinoza and Plato, the *Symposium* and the *Phaedrus,* but she asked me to dance just as I was about to pontificate.

I taught her to waltz, this young woman in bare feet. Esther danced with the handsome groom, who was similarly unshod, if otherwise decorated with earrings and a necklace of animal teeth. The music was not waltz music, but I hummed it into existence. Her delicate bones under my hand unleashed in me an unexpected surge of protectiveness. She was someone's daughter. Of her parents, nothing was visible at this party. I took this to mean that at the ceremony itself, her father had not given her away. She had given herself away, courageous girl.

FOLLOWING MY SON Aaron's last call, I had decided not to interfere again with the misconstrued ironies of his life. I would not bother him with my fatherly intentions. I would not call to ask for his news. What news he had always tended toward the apocalyptic. Let him call me. This was my plan.

I failed to carry it through. Afternoons, I worked in the garden, planting snapdragons and petunias, or weeding, and while I did so, I thought about my son. These thoughts were tormenting, buzzing gnatlike around my head, because they had no content except by way of the images they presented. I added fertilizer to the soil. Aaron on a swing set, Aaron playing touch football, Aaron slouched in a chair reading Churchill's ghostwritten history of

World War Two. I remembered his shy tokens of affection toward his mother and me, pen-and-pencil sets he had bought us, home-made birthday cards, school projects from the elementary grades we had never had the heart to throw out.

I remembered how he got the scar on his forehead and the scar on his knee. I remembered his face as a Bar Mitzvah boy.

I tried to think of my new project, the book about Kierkegaard and his admirer Wittgenstein, but my attention continued to turn in the direction of my son.

At last, giving in to my own myopic affections one Thursday around dinnertime, I called his apartment in Los Angeles. From the phone came the mechanical message that that particular number had been disconnected and was no longer in service. I dialed information and asked for Aaron Ginsberg on Ambrose Street. There was no longer such a person at that address. I obtained the numbers of all the Aaron Ginsbergs without street addresses, the new listings, but none of them were him.

I called the florist in Los Angeles where he had worked intermittently as a delivery person. He had quit, they said. He had moved. To where? He hadn't told them. He had been soaked into the ethers, and there he was dispersed.

That evening at dinner I broke the news to Esther.

Aaron has disappeared, I said. I tried calling him but his number's dismembered. Disconnected, I mean.

Oh, honey. No one disappears. What do you mean?

I explained. Maybe no one disappears. But *he* has, not to the world of course, but to us. I told you: his phone's disconnected. He's not working at the florist anymore.

Esther put down her fork. He's just moved, Harry. He'll tell us where he has moved to as soon as he can. We have to be patient with Aaron. His maturing is taking its time.

Maturing! He is one of these never-never land Americans who will never grow up. Intellectually he is still in diapers. I feel like calling Los Angeles missing persons. I feel like calling the Martian embassy.

Don't do that yet, she said. He's not missing.

I could hardly look at her face.

He's not missing, she repeated, to succor me. He is somewhere. He is always somewhere.

But he *was* missing. The police could find no trace of him. They recommended a private detective who at great expense to us found a few sniffs and scents of him in the Pacific Northwest but not the person himself, not Aaron, our son.

America, as everyone knows, is large enough to lose a child in. The tendency of the country to absorb its inhabitants and to render them anonymous and invisible had gone to work. He was now a runaway, a runaway from us, and was effectively erased.

My vice is the comfort of abstractions. Concrete events as a rule disable me. When my son disappeared from the face of this earth, I was willing to try out sociology, I was willing to commit a social science the better to know the patterns of mislaid children in a post-industrial economy. I was willing to try out religion: Judaism, Christianity if need be. An exceptionally developed capacity for abstract thought does not preclude a consideration of the soul, a word I do not surround with fussy quotation marks. But *I did not know how to look for him,* and I no longer knew how to think about him, either. Concerning Aaron, I could find refuge in no known set of ideas. Aaron had gone to work on his own invisibility with zest and imagination, as if he had finally discovered a calling, which was the eradication of himself.

We have, Esther and I, two successful children, Sarah and Ephraim. We love them and think about them. But we do not think about them half as much as we do Aaron, who is unsuccessful and invisible besides. As the tongue goes to the missing tooth, so do we poke and pry at his absence. He is our null.

He is not a boy, but a young man. We must—we had to—give

him over to the mischievous criminal attentions of the world. And now he had taken his heartfelt leave of the public realm. He did it to hurt us.

When Esther and I are alone together in the evening, we avoid looking at each other's faces. Aaron's disappearance is much too visible in our eyes for us to bear the mutual sighting of it in ourselves. Esther and I know each other so thoroughly, we don't even have to confirm our thoughts back and forth anymore. I know her moods; she knows mine. Aaron has achieved his purpose. I mean this: When you break the heart of a philosopher, you must apply great force and cunning strategy, but when the deed is completed, the heart lies in great stony ruin at your feet. If you succeed in breaking it, the job is done once and for all. It will not be repaired.

Thus encumbered, I taught Chloé to waltz on her wedding day, humming to her tunes from *Die Fledermaus*.

TWENTY-THREE

IT DOESN'T SEEM FAIR that I've spent all this time telling you about Kathryn and Diana, who made me unhappy, but not about Margaret, who did the opposite and filled me with joy, a word I don't trust and have never used in my life until this moment. When I met Margaret, I wasn't inclined to tell anyone what was going on between us. People don't go to psychiatrists and pay good money to talk at length about how happy they are. Talking can spoil it. As a rule you don't settle down at the end of the day with a beer and tell your friend the particulars of how you lucked out and how well the day and the week and the year went, unless you're the gloating type. You just don't do that. It's provocation. You find some other neutral ground. If you're smart, you keep happiness to yourself.

THE FIRST TIME I called Margaret to invite her out, she asked me why I had called, and I told her that I had admired the color of her yes. I meant *eyes* but said *yes*. I think she was touched by my dazed friendliness. She wasn't inclined to go out with me—she had an on-again, off-again boyfriend—but at last she decided to take a chance on me, just for coffee at first, at Jitters.

I gradually learned that she's so used to emergencies that she's relaxed and urbane about the rest of life. Almost nothing fazes her.

She has a calming effect, as a human being, as a person. As a doctor, she's used to the sight of blood, gunshot wounds, broken bones, and the other norms of calamity. A daily diet of emergencies puts existence itself into a steady and calm perspective. She told me a few weeks after our first date that I looked like someone who had offered love to a lot of people but that I hadn't had any takers so far. Then she said that I was an unusual man, and when I asked her why, she said I was "openhearted," which made me look down at the ground, not knowing what to think. Women use such words at the oddest moments. No, that's wrong. Only Margaret ever used that word, maybe because she's a doctor. Then I was gazing at her face with such concentration that I could hardly hear what she was saying. When I realized what she had said, I kissed her, and she kissed me back. Bradley stood nearby watching us and wagging his tail. She never called me a Toad. Perhaps she had never seen one.

We were standing in the kitchen. It was raining out. She leaned back against the kitchen counter. She said, "I've heard about men like you, but I never actually met one until now."

I went to her dripping blood, my heart in tatters over Diana, and she cured me of that in a week.

She was born in this country. Margaret's parents were African diplomats who sent her to schools in the United States, where she decided to remain after she'd finished her internship. She didn't dislike white people. She liked emergency medicine and wanted to practice it in a large training hospital. That's all I'll say about that.

HERE'S A PROFUNDITY, the best I can do: sometimes you just know. Chloé and Oscar knew. You just know when two people belong together. I had never really experienced that odd happenstance before, but this time, with Margaret, I did. Before, I was always trying to make my relationships work by means of willpower and forced affability. This time I didn't have to strive for anything. A quality of ease spread over us. Whatever I was, well, that was what Margaret apparently wanted. I wasn't sure that she'd want a white guy like me, a service person afflicted with modesty, but she said she didn't care about my color or my temperament one way or another because they were fine just as they were. She hadn't thought she could love a man of my race, but once I showed up in her life, I turned out to be the man she loved, what is the word, regardless. To this day I don't know exactly what she loved about me and that's because I don't have to know. She just does. It was the entire menu of myself. She ordered all of it.

We do what you do in tandem when you belong together. We go to movies, we go dancing (she's a better dancer than I am), we go to the grocery store and hold hands in the aisles (scandalizing the racists), we decide about furniture, we cook, we make love, we talk about the future, we play with the dog and take him for walks, we talk about our plans to get married, where and how and when. We fit together. (I avoid saying these things in public; people hate to hear it, as if I'd forced them to eat raw sugar.) There's nothing to talk about to strangers anymore, if you know what I mean. Everything I want to say, I want to say to her. Life has turned into what I once imagined it was supposed to be, as complacent and awful as that sounds. In fact, I don't really want to talk about this anymore. As the poet says, all happy couples are alike, it's the unhappy ones who create the stories.

I'm no longer a story. Happiness has made me fade into real life.

THE ART. First I sketched her in charcoal and then I did a portrait of her. I hadn't done human figures in years. I drew and painted her nude and clothed, asleep and awake, wearing her amused expression or the thoughtful one, frowning. I did each portrait, each study, quickly. Inspiration made me confident and efficient. Besides, she doesn't like to sit very much for these portraits. She's too nonvain. So I do most of them from memory. Her skin tone was very hard at first for me to get, the way light hits it. But through trial and error I learned the tricks of shading flesh the color of hers, first in charcoal and then in oils. You should see what I accomplished, but I won't let you, because I will not show any of these pictures in public, ever. They're not for sale.

I'M TALKING ABOUT gains and losses here.

When Oscar died, it was a Saturday in mid-November, and he was out playing touch football with his friends and with Chloé. Just before that, during the afternoon, they'd been watching the televised University of Michigan Wolverines as they defeated the Ohio State Buckeyes on the gridiron, and the sight of it inspired them and brought their blood up to a boil. I was working at Jitters with another assistant I'd hired, Stusnick, and had given those kids, Oscar and Chloé, the day off. Harry and Esther Ginsberg were strolling around the edge of the park with Bradley the dog (I'd given them a set of keys to my house), worrying about their missing son, Aaron.

They'd gone to the park, this group of people, and they'd found others from our neighborhood there, out for a stroll, out for a physical release after the tension of that game, and these neighbors, these keyed-up fans, who happened to include Diana, my ex, and her new love, David, who was athletic and who—I believe I've said this already—liked to hang out near the park for pickup basketball and touch football games, they were there too. They were invited to join Oscar's game. Oscar and David knew each other from previous basketball. The more the merrier. For all I know, Kathryn was out there, with her partner, Jenny. Pregnant as she was, Chloé was on the sidelines watching and cheerleading. This is a small city. All these spokes of the wheel came into place that afternoon, all these gears meshed, everyone drew together at that moment.

It's February now. I've taken my dog out to that field, out into the snow. Bradley and I walk over the field, crusted with winter. In February the overcast sky isn't gloomy so much as neutral and vague. It's a significant factor in the common experience of depression among the locals. The snow crunches under your boots and clings to your trousers, to the cuffs, and once you're inside, the snow clings to your psyche, and eventually you have to go to the doctor. The past soaks into you in this weather because the present is missing almost entirely. I stand in the middle of the field, right about where I imagine Oscar ran out for that pass, and then, I mean now, with Bradley running after a winter squirrel, I imagine Oscar leaping up, out of the range of everyone else, and I can see him, even at this moment, in the middle of winter, catching the football the way he did in November, and then falling, still holding it, to the ground, and lying still.

I can see them all bending over him. Even Bradley the dog has come over to examine him. Oscar's friends are talking to him, or what's left of him. I can see Chloé running out to the field. Someone—it's his friend Scooter—nudges him. They say someone must have hit him and knocked him out cold.

What hit him?

I dunno. He got the wind knocked out of him. That's all. Or, hey, maybe not. Maybe it's something else. Oscar? Hey, man, Oscaaaaaar. Jeez.

Maybe we gotta get him down to the hospital.

Naw. He's okay. I'm pretty sure he's okay.

Somebody take his pulse? He doesn't look like he's breathing.

They bend down. They listen. Diana takes his pulse. Chloé pushes her aside and starts shouting that they have to get him to the emergency medical thing. Come on, come on, come on, come on, she says. Pick him up, you guys. Pick him *up!*

So they load him into the nearest car, which happens to be David's, and David and Diana and Chloé prepare to take Oscar—*Oscar's body*—to the University Hospital, where Margaret has just, as it happens, finished work and is headed in the opposite direction, back to me.

But they have all forgotten about the football traffic after the game. Every street in Ann Arbor is snarled with cars. This is a small city, and it takes a long time to empty of traffic. The stadium holds over one hundred thousand human souls. When David honks and waves his arms frantically, the drivers ahead of him and to the side honk happily in return and wave their arms and make the V-for-victory sign, or, using the same gestures that David has used, hold their fists in the air, unless they're Ohio State fans, in which case they sit and glance around sullenly, hands clutching the wheel. No matter how much he honks, no one moves aside, no one lets him proceed with the body of Oscar to the hospital. There is no space to move. In both directions the traffic has halted, like blood in a blocked artery. He cannot shout. What good would shouting do, in this crowd of happy shouters? They're all shouting. He's one of many. He can't get out of the car because that would accomplish nothing: the cars in front of him are stuck as well. His sedan with its occupants moves by slow increments toward the hospital.

What's worse is that the cars to the right and left of him have stopped in the same traffic jam he's in, and their happy inebriated passengers witness Chloé bending over on the seat and breathing into Oscar's mouth. They misunderstand what they are observing. They think it's passion. They think it's the feast of love in the back seat. Apparently they don't see her clamping his nostrils shut, as she breathes her breath into his lungs, because they give her smirks and grins and smiles, honking in great amorous collaboration at what they take to be Chloé's celebrational mouth-to-mouth. Go for it, girl! Go Blue! And they don't stop giving her the high sign until she turns her face away from Oscar's. Then she fixes her eyes on them, and she screams, but the scream is swallowed up in the tumult. She then brings her mouth back to his, to keep him alive.

It all takes a long time.

AND STILL HE ISN'T ALIVE when they arrive at the hospital, and nothing that is done to him there can bring him back. He has had (we learn these helpful terms later) hypertrophic cardiomyopathy, the medical slang for which is "hocum." Goddamn these doctors anyway, with their jargon, their jauntiness, damn them all except for Margaret, who is my beloved exception. Ventricular fibrillation dropped him down. Eventually he was declared dead, Oscar was. An autopsy showed an abnormally enlarged murmured heart, from the track and the basketball and the genetic code, though I refuse to give up the metaphor and think it enlarged itself from his love of Chloé. Margaret explained all this to me in her calm, horizon-greeting African Zen style, using terms like *commotio cordis*. Against the terrors and sorrows of death, only the multisyllabic Latinate adjectives and nouns for protection, the know-how, and then the prayers, for those who have them.

TWENTY-FOUR

THERE I WAS, CAGED. I sat in the front seat next to David, with Chloé bending over Oscar in the back, trying to breathe her life into him. All around us people, these fans, these monkeys, hollered. They whooped. They celebrated. On their faces were all the manifestations of *glee*. Being of a difficult and combative nature, I wanted to kill them early in their lives.

I sat in the car, containing myself but wild with sanctioned fury, and then I thought of whom I would sue.

Oscar and Chloé, these two kids, who had served me coffee day after day out at the mall—I had taken a liking to them. I enjoyed the spectacle of how they felt about each other. I thought it was rather inspiring, actually, those two orphans, with nothing, really, to their names. They weren't middle class in any of the tiresome customary ways, and they didn't have two nickels to rub together. You could tell from the fatigue lines under their eyes that they'd been around a few blocks. Sometimes, seeing them working together at Jitters, I thought: David should marry me. We could have that. Except, possessing money, we would have it easier, we would do it with a little more style and a little less emotion.

And now, in the backseat, Oscar looked, to all appearances, no longer living, no longer even dying. His dying had been successfully accomplished. Watching Chloé trying to keep him alive, putting her lips to his, I started to cry. I *never* do that.

I'm a lawyer. I reached for the car phone. I called the emergency number. I explained the situation. The dispatcher told me that no ambulance would be able to move faster in this traffic than we were able to do. No helicopter would be able to land where we were located, the congestion being what it was. Such a maneuver, I was informed, would be unsafe. It would be faster if we just continued to drive.

So we stayed in the car.

I'm a lawyer. I think about responsibility. And in my ire, I thought: I'll sue the university, for staging the game; I'll sue the city of Ann Arbor, for having clearly inadequate plans for controlling and siphoning off the traffic. Within Ann Arbor, I'll sue the police department and individuals within that department, standing at intersections and misdirecting the cars, buses, trucks, and vans; and then I will organize a suit against the city manager, for permitting the congested and overfilled parking lots to block proper egress from the city; and the zoning board, for the proximity of the buildings. I'll sue the architects, for the design of those buildings. I'll institute proceedings against the automobile manufacturers, for the size and shape of these vehicles. I'll sue the athletic department, no, I've already done that; I'll sue the advertisers who have supported these games; and I'll sue the Wolverine Fan Club; I'll sue each and every one of the businesses lining this street, for being located there and for blocking our way. I'll sue the driver of the car in front of us and I'll sue his drunken girlfriend—I already have their license plate number committed to memory—and the two passengers in the back, waving at us while David gives them the finger and then leans on the horn, they'll all be penniless by the time I'm finished with them and sorry that they were ever within living proximity to me. In my wrath I'll sue the drivers and passengers in front of *them*. I'll sue the manufacturer of the football that Oscar caught, that proximate cause, I'll drag the officers of that company into court and pull their names through the mud, so that even their children will refuse ever to speak to them. I'll sue the makers of the clothes Oscar wore, including his shoes (he may have slipped! he may have lost traction! he may have fallen because of the shoes!); I'll find out what he ate while he watched the game, and I'll sue the brewers of the dangerous beer he drank and the makers of the arteriosclerotic snack food he consumed; I'll sue the tattoo artist who tattooed the skull and crossbones onto Oscar's back (Chloé told me about it) with the word "Die" underneath it, goddamn it, I'll sue them for *prophecy;* I'll sue Oscar's father, the Bat, for not taking care of him, for not preventing this eventuality, and for generally endangering Oscar and Chloé's welfare; I'll sue the doctors, I will take their fat-cat medical school asses to court and nail those asses to the wall, for *whatever* they give him, for *whatever* they do, in their wisdom and knowledge, oh, let them try anything, fuck them all, for I shall see to it that their efforts could be construed as unprofessional, mistaken, foolish, and wrong. I'll sue the doctors and the drug manufacturers for not bringing him back to life; I'll sue Jesus, who is acquainted with Chloé and who once met her at a party, for not being here, when we needed Him; and I'll sue God, who passes out misfortune with equanimity.

Such were my thoughts as we motored, inch by inch, toward the university hospitals.

Oscar had been a young man, physically beautiful, and in wonderful condition except for his now-defunct heart. After they were done with the electrical defibrillation, the intubation, the epinephrine, the lidocaine and the procainamide, and the chest compressions, they harvested him. They sold him off for parts, down to the skin and bones. He helped save the lives of others, et cetera, et cetera.

CHLOÉ NEEDED SOMEONE SMART, mean-tempered, and bad-natured to accompany her to the funeral home and to take care of things. I was that person. We had womanly solidarity, Chloé and I. First off, I called Oscar's father, the Bat. Ah, now there was a charmer. He had a German name, Metzger, though he said his friends called him Mac. I doubted it. Such a name wasn't plausible. He wouldn't have had friends. Co-conspirators maybe, but friends, no. I would *not* call him Mac, as per his request. I asked if he wished to have a hand in the funeral arrangements, and he said he would not. He appeared to be lacking in grief; I couldn't hear a trace of it in his voice, and his lack of grief managed to enrage me. He, this dreadful example, explained that Chloé had *killed* his son, at which point I pulled out some of my verbal knives and went to work on him. Some of my meanings went over his dull-normal head, but he was stunned by my vicious eloquence into hostile silence. Then he tried a retort, but, unused to the arts of argumentation, he tripped over himself, and I threatened him again. Things, how shall I put this, had quickly become acrimonious, and I will admit that I finally hung up on the man, who was, judging from his slurred speech, as drunk as a church sexton.

We had better luck with the funeral director. A pleasant enough person, a Mr. Kleinschmidt, broad-shouldered and athletic and a go-getter as most funeral directors are, he took us through the possibilities, and Chloé decided on a closed-casket viewing and a cremation. Then we were ushered into the cavernous casket showroom downstairs. Some of the caskets, particularly the ones with brushed aluminum exteriors, looked like huge kitchen appliances dedicated to obscure purposes. They didn't appear to be caskets at all. Though I had offered her money for the funeral costs, Chloé didn't want my money. She was prideful. She made arrangements for installment payments, but I examined every charge that Kleinschmidt put on the bill, down to the dime.

For the closed-casket viewing, Kleinschmidt had something in mind. He walked over to a cherrywood casket and pointed to it. "I can give you something of a bargain on this one," he said. "But I'll have to explain something about it."

"It looks nice," Chloé said, a bit uncertainly. "What's the deal?"

"Well," he said, "it's used."

"Used? You mean they buried somebody in it?"

"Oh no," he said. "We would never do that. No, this is the casket we used last time we had a viewing, prior to the cremation. The body is laid out in it, and then removed and cremated. All the inside cloth and padding is removed—okay?—and replaced. It's just the wood that's the same. So it's not *really* used, not the way you might think. It's never been *buried.*" He waited. "In the ground."

"I dunno," Chloe said. "A used casket." She turned to me. "Diana, whattya think?"

"I think it's all right," I said. "I don't think Oscar would've minded."

"I guess not."

"Good," Mr. Kleinschmidt said, "that's settled. Now we need something for the cremains."

"The cremains?"

"Well, that's the word we use. You know. The . . . ashes. The urn." We followed him to the back of the room, where there was a display of these commodities in an alcove. It looked like a sculpture collection of Bakelite canisters and wooden boxes. One of them was green ceramic of some sort, with a bronze dolphin frolicking on the side.

"Not that one," Chloé said. "I don't think Oscar liked dolphins." She waited. "Well, he never met one." She pointed. "That one. That's the one I want." She had indicated a polished and gleaming mahogany box about a foot and a half in each direction like a knickknack box that happened to be a bit too large for the dresser. "He'd like that one," she said.

Just about then Chloé's forehead began to get damp, and she put her hand on my shoulder. Her eyes, which are unusually bright, had gone stoned-or-bored-gauzy. I was about to ask her how she was feeling when her eyes rolled up, and she fainted. I grabbed her around the shoulders in time before she hit the floor.

Kleinschmidt and I managed to haul her upstairs, he carrying her by the shoulders, while I took her legs. It wouldn't do for Kleinschmidt to carry her alone. We laid Chloé out on the sofa. He pulled out some smelling salts from his desk. "Happens all the time," he said. "Men *and* women. You'd be surprised."

"No, I wouldn't," I said.

After she came to, she rubbed at her scalp and said, "Hey." She tried a smile. "Hello, again. Diana, I was just wondering where Oscar was. I guess I was wondering that when I passed out."

"He's dead," I told her. "Oscar died, Chloé."

"Oh, yeah, I know that. I meant his body. You know: what's left of him."

"Downstairs," Kleinschmidt said. "In the rear of the building."

"Can I see it?"

"Why don't you come back after lunch?" Kleinschmidt suggested. "We'd need some time to get it ready."

"Okay," Chloe said. "I could eat about a month of cheeseburgers anyway. Gotta keep my strength up, right?"

I took her to a restaurant where, I'm glad to say, she ate like a horse, shoveling it all down, cheeseburgers, fries, salad, and a chocolate malt. She didn't even stop to talk. "I'm nauseous in the morning but by lunchtime I'm starving," she said, munching on a ketchup-covered french fry. I liked almost everything about her, including the way she chewed with her mouth open and how she disapproved of the meager dieter's salad I had ordered. "You could just go outside and eat *grass*," she said, pointing at it. "It'd be cheaper. Maybe more nutritious, too, except for the herbicides." When we returned to the funeral home, she was ushered toward a viewing room. "Want to come along?" she asked me. I said no.

About twenty minutes later, she came back out and said, "Well, that's done."

"How'd he look?" I asked her.

"He didn't look like himself anymore," she said, working up to a concentrated scowl. "So what I gotta do is, I gotta remember him, instead."

AFTER THE VIEWING and the cremation, Chloé and Oscar's friends had a party-wake for the two of them. There was a controlled tumult of drinking and dancing and stories about Oscar. She took the wooden box containing his ashes along, and put it on a shelf near the stereo system. I asked her about drugs. She told me—I was being the starchy big sister—that, pregnant as she was, she wasn't drinking or smoking anything at the party. She had made a resolution about that. After all, it was Oscar's baby too she was carrying, and she didn't want to fuck it up with anything toxic, she wanted it to come out big and strong. Those were her words. *Big* and *strong*.

The next time I went back to Jitters for my morning cup of coffee, the box with Oscar's ashes in it was sitting on the shelf on the back wall, near the signboard listing the varieties of coffees and drinks. That box looked as if it belonged exactly in that spot. There he was, Oscar, a bit more anonymous now, back at Jitters, following his death leave.

Bradley and I had gone back to being wary friends. Whatever had gotten into us, to think that we would be successful partners? It was an embarrassing interlude, our marriage, of which we were both slightly ashamed. Still, we greeted each other with pleasure, those mornings when I came into his shop for coffee, and he was there, the Toad, behind the counter.

Chloé managed her grieving in an absentminded way, but she managed it all the same. She told me that she knew Oscar was dead, but she didn't believe it. I didn't ask her what she meant by that, but I should have.

—

I DON'T KNOW if David and I will stay together. Our lovemaking is so stormy and theatrical that we keep tearing into each other, and when we do, we tear holes. Sometimes what we do is more like fighting than love. We slam each other around. I think we're trying to find each other's souls, knowing they must be in there somewhere, close to our undernourished hearts. You shouldn't envy us, sexy as we might appear to be. It's not sustainable. No one could endure it. This intensity can't continue forever. But it's the way we are, hard-assed and mean and a bit selfish, and yet the main point to make here is that we're obsessed with each other and are willing to admit it now, for all the good it does two people like us to be in love, if that's what it is, which is very little good at all. We probably shouldn't be in love. Dragons shouldn't be characters in love stories. We should turn our attention to something else. The orgasms I have with him go up to my shoulders and down my arms and leave me beleaguered for hours afterward. The thing that we create when we're together is wondrous but certainly not wonderful. I hate the idea of marriage. I hate seeing couples in cars going the other way on the highway. It makes me cringe. I go into rages.

On some days I'd like to be more like Chloé, who has star quality, but I'm not like her, and I won't be. I'm bad, because I lack usable tenderness and I don't have a shred of kindness, but I'm not a villain and never have been. That's what you should remember about me.

TWENTY-FIVE

BEFORE I MET OSCAR, I was fine. But then I met him, and I knew him, and I loved him, and he died, and after that, in an Oscarless world, I couldn't go back to the way I was before I knew him, because I wasn't the same person anymore. He mutated me.

First off, I had to do some serious crying. It got me nowhere, but I did it anyway. It felt like work, like building a fence or doing hard labor. I was okay during the day, most days, but I'd wake up crying and go to sleep crying, first in chairs, then in bed. I'd wake up and the pillow was still wet. In the morning I'd cry into my cereal, my tears dropping into the milk. I'd cry in the shower, and then I'd cry at work during my breaks. At home I watched TV and wept all the way through an infomercial for exercise equipment. So I guess I wasn't okay during the day after all.

It didn't help that Oscar showed up in my dreams constantly. Talking and jiving, his cap on backward, wearing his wedding ring, he'd go on and on about bands he liked and games he wanted to see, curious about my news just as if nothing special had happened. I kept telling him to get actual, that he'd *died,* and he'd say, *No no, honey, you got it all wrong. Oh, man, look at my hand.* And I'd look at his hand that he held out, and I'd grab it, reaching out in dreamtime, doubting him, and it was there all right, but the touch of it, the tight tough skin exactly Oscar's, would startle me with terror and love, and I'd wake up by myself in my apartment in the dark like a flashlight you've just switched on, with the traffic moving on the street outside the window and the headlights lighting the ceiling, and this big broken hole in me that Oscar had left behind, by dying.

Sometimes I'd get mad at him for leaving me behind here in this life on Earth, but that didn't work either. It was counterkarmic. Okay, I admit it: I only pretend to know about karma. I read in this magazine about it and I made up the rest. I don't even know what language it comes from. So there I was. All day I was baffled, and all night I was sweating and shivering. Only I wasn't sick, unless you count being pregnant and abandoned as sick.

It's funny what being pregnant does for you socially, though. People such as your parents, who couldn't be bothered calling you up or saying that you were an interesting person, who were alienated from you, suddenly do start calling and showing up as if you *were* interesting all of a sudden. They found out my whereabouts from my sister and drove forty miles from their home downriver to see me. They brought cooked chicken on a tray.

On this Sunday, my mom came in dressed to the nines, wearing her church dress and plum-colored lipstick and some sort of hair thing tottering on her head, and carrying, like I said, the chicken, which she deposited on the kitchen counter. She shrieked when she saw me as if I was the surprise of the month. "You're so grown up!" she said. Yes, I was. She planted a kiss on my face and put her hand on my tummy, which you could tell she was dying to do. Then she looked around at our apartment, Oscar's and mine, and said it was cute, and she took my hand to look at my wedding ring, doing an *ooh* and an *aaah* five months late, long long long past the deadline when I could've used it, that admiration. She asked me where he had bought it, and I told her truthfully, at the jewelry counter. She nodded wisely.

My dad, Chester, was behind her. I don't know if I love my

mom, but I have loved my dad even when he was angry at me and was a misogynist when he said I was no good. I go back and forth about him.

He's confused all the time about life and doesn't pretend to know anything except his job—he works on the line at Ford—and how to fix household appliances and moving-parts things, and he knows sports. With my sister and me, and how to raise us, I think he took his orders from Geraldine, my mom. He would've been okay with sons, but with two daughters he was clueless and sweet and so generous it was a compulsion with him. Anyway he was standing there in the doorway as if I hadn't invited him in, wearing his hat and cleaning his glasses with his shirt flap, very shy and embarrassed about his previous anger toward me. So I said, "Come on inside, Dad," and he walked in, all two hundred and twenty pounds of him, wearing his sheepish look. A sheepish look on a dad can bring you into a state of startled puzzlement. You could tell he was ashamed. Ashamed that he had once hypercursed me, but mostly ashamed that he had never met Oscar and had taken no interest in my life for the last year or two, because his wife had told him not to. He didn't even look around at our little apartment. I guess he thought he didn't have the right to look around. But I'm not squalid. Neither was our apartment. I couldn't stand it, so I ran over to him and gave him a hug.

My dad smelled of grease and dime-store aftershave. Hugging him, you kind of collide with his stomach before you get to his face, but that was okay. My dad's stomach is like the *foyer* to the rest of him.

That Sunday afternoon proceeded in a normal fashion until my mom asked if I had a picture of Oscar. I went to a drawer and pulled out his high school graduation photo, where he's smiling in a smug way I never saw him smile, and his hair is watered down, and he's basically pre-me, pre-Chloé, so he doesn't look like himself, he doesn't look transformed, except by the drugs he was using right about then. He was a little gaunt in those days, at least in the off-season, away from the track team, feeding his body with drugs. Later, Oscar in love went out of two dimensions into three or four. We made love in the fourth dimension, for example. But anyway this graduation portrait's the only picture of him I have, except for one of him that Scooter took at our wedding, in which me and Oscar are kissing and Oscar's got his hand planted on my tits, which I wasn't going to show to my parents, the picture I mean, for safety's sake.

"He looks very nice," my mom said.

"Kinda thin," my dad said.

No point in telling them about the drugs, so I said, "He'd just had flu."

They nodded.

They spent the rest of the afternoon with me, making mature efforts to reconcile. We talked about boring stuff like my dad's job, my mom's job (she's sort of a cashier-receptionist at a car dealership), and how the house was empty these days and if I wanted to move back, just before or after the baby was born, I could do that, and I could use the crib for my baby that they used for me. I almost said, "Thanks very much, that's very sweet, but, you know, it's too late for that," but I didn't, because they were trying to be solid and correct with me, turning over a new parental leaf, now that I was my own woman and not their little girl anymore. Besides, I wanted to show them how mature I'd gotten by not saying *fuck* all the time, a habit that's hard to give up. That's scary for parents. You have to be careful with parents once you're grown up into mature adulthood. They get *sensitive*. Almost anything you say, you hurt their feelings. Their aging hearts get broken. They just crumple up. Besides, I was about to become one of them.

THERE WAS ONE OTHER CALL I was expecting, and sure enough, eventually it came. I was expecting it to come at about two in the morning, but the phone rang at seven at night, and I just knew it was *him,* I had known all day at work that it was going to be *him,* it was a little gift that Mrs. Maggaroulian had given me, knowing when my father-in-law the Bat would call me before he actually did. Maybe I knew these things because I was carrying his grandchild, but I don't think that's it. I think I picked it up from Mrs. Maggaroulian, what *Weekly World News* calls "precognition."

After I was a full-fledged married woman, the Bat had stopped stalking me, and Oscar and me, we sort of forgot about him, just figured that he had retreated into his bat cave for a while until he decided to be decent. Oscar didn't need anything from the house —he'd taken all his stuff out of there a long time ago—so we were what you would call out of touch with the Bat.

Anyway, the phone rang and I answered it.

"This is Mac Metzger," the Bat said. "I thought I had better talk to you."

"Oh, hi," I said.

I waited for him to say something. Then he said, "Lot of water's over the dam, ain't it?"

"I guess so." Then I asked, "Uh, water?"

He ignored the question. "I hear tell you're in the family way."

"Yes," I said. "How'd you know?"

"Word gets around. Well, besides," he said, "I guess I got some apologizing to do."

"Apologizing? For stalking me?"

"No. On account of I was drinking so much, last time I saw you. Well, finally I quit it, praise God."

"You did?" It seemed we were both doing New Year's resolutions, without the New Year to help us out.

"Swore it off. Had to. The long arm of the law caught me falling down, you might say, and they were going to confiscate my truck and my license, so I had to go into this treatment group. I did it. I swore it off and I'm making amends. Hardest thing I ever managed to do."

"You sound different."

"Well, I am different. Ashamed of the way I acted. I don't know what-all got into me. And besides I forgave you for all the stealing, you loaded down with my stuff. I didn't care about that worldly goods anyway. It was castoffs. You could have had it, you being Oscar's wife, if you'd asked."

"I never stole anything. Really."

"Okay." He waited. "I know that was what you said. Well, you got your story and I got mine. Difference of opinion. I guess everybody's got a story, right?" He waited for me to agree with him, and when I didn't, he said, "Anyhow Oscar's gone. Poor kid. I guess I was angry at him way too much."

"That's right."

"I was so surprised and done in by events that I pretty much got dead drunk when you asked me for help on the funeral arrangements. I don't know what got into me, what I done or said. The devils, I guess. I got a problem with the devils, I can tell you right now. Sorry I couldn't do more. A kid his age, he was too young to have a heart attack. You told me where you put his ashes, but you'll have to tell me again. I blacked out on everything after he died."

"In Saginaw Forest," I said, lying to him.

"That's a pretty place, I been there. Well, now he's dead, Oscar might do the trees some good, the way he did you. He was a handful. And sometimes he sure acted too smart with me. That boy was constant trouble."

"He did me some good," I said. "He was the best person I ever knew." I could have hung up, but I didn't. "Yes," I said. "He was."

"Well, is that a fact? I'm sure glad. You know, Oscar was so often a terror, and when he wasn't a terror, he couldn't be moved off the sofa. The drugs did that to him. They made him lazy, and then he had a mouth on him when I'd get on him. We had quite a household. Between us, it was like a war, so I'd make myself scarce, and when I was around, he could be as mean as my own daddy had been. 'Course I miss him. You always miss your children."

"Yes," I said.

"It must be there was a side to him I almost never saw. I was mostly proud of him when he was running. That boy could run the relay as fast as anything, and that was when I was happy to claim him as my own. But so much of the rest of the time, I just had to put up with him and his drugs and troublemaking and his smart mouth, but like I say, maybe there's another side to matters and I'd like to hear your side. You probably saw things I never saw. You got a side?"

"Yes," I said. "I have a side."

"Well, see, that's just what I'm saying. You got a side. You've got a story. You probably got a story about Oscar. You probably know something about him that even I never got me no idea of."

"Probably."

"So what I was thinking was, you should tell me your side, since I want to hear it so much, with my son dead and gone and his ashes in Saginaw Forest." The Bat waited, and all at once I thought I had caught his drift. "We oughta you and me meet face to face, so you can tell me your side," he said, as if thinking it over. "I want to hear about Oscar from you."

There was a long pause in there, while I waited. "What're you suggesting, Mr. Metzger?"

"You mean I'm not being clear? I sure thought I was. Goddamn if I'm confusing you. I was kinda hoping you'd invite me over that apartment of yours."

"I don't know," I said. "Maybe a restaurant'd be better."

"You want to come over *here?*" he asked. "It's kinda dusty. I'd have to clean up and mostly I'm too tired at the end of the day to do that." He sighed. "I could, I guess. Okay, you're invited."

"No. I'd rather not come over there."

"Well we got ourselves an impasse, then," he said. "I don't want to go to a restaurant, myself. I don't ever do that. So we've got a failure of the meeting of minds."

"I know what we'll do," I said. "I just had an idea. Why don't you come over here and meet my parents? I'll invite them, too. You know, like how the in-laws meet when their kids get married? The grandparents, now. Just 'cause Oscar's dead doesn't change that. What d'you think?"

I had outfoxed him and he knew it. "It's your side I want to hear, not theirs," he said, all of a sudden somber.

"You'll get mine *and* theirs."

"I was never much for relatives," the Bat said, "of the conversational variety."

"But that's what I am."

"Oh all right," he said angrily, like I'd been beating him at a game. "Invite your parents if you want to. Sure, I'd be happy to meet them."

I had sudden shooting pains in my stomach, which the Bat was causing just by talking to me.

"So," he said. "When should I come? How about tonight?"

"I have to work," I said. "It's too soon."

"You don't think much of me, do you?" he asked me suddenly, a question I wasn't about to answer.

"You're fine," I said. "I don't think of you one way or another."

He cleared his throat, an awful sound. "Sorry," he said. "I got this thing caught in my throat. So, how about Saturday night?"

"Well, I'll call my parents and then call you back."

"You do that. I will wait right here by the telephone for that call-back from you."

I called my parents, reached my mom, who was overjoyed that I was inviting her and delighted to be meeting Oscar's father, and I called the Bat again. So as a plan it was accomplished.

I bought bags of potato chips, and pop, and beer, and some potato salad, and hamburgers, and the hamburger buns, and the ketchup and relish and pickles. Good-time food. It wasn't a picnic but I figured picnic food would put everybody into a better disposition and help them get along with one another.

I guess I should have been afraid, but it didn't occur to me to be, with my parents there.

That night it snowed, this being December, and I'd invited my parents early, but they didn't come when they were supposed to. I kept checking my watch as I buttered the buns. It was one of those best-laid-plans deals. When the phone rang, sure enough, it was my dad saying they had slid off the road and had to call a tow truck, and they'd be there eventually, but they were going to be late. "De-layed" was the word he used. And had I seen the snow, my dad asked, how it was coming down?

That was about when I heard the Bat's knock on the door. With this building, there's a front door that's supposed to be locked, but no one ever keeps it locked, they've always got bricks propped against it. Anyone can get in. Anyone *did*. And he was knocking at my door right now.

No point in looking through the peephole. You didn't need Mrs. Maggaroulian to tell you what was on the other side. The only thing was, when I opened the door, he didn't look bad or mean, but more like a loser standing in line at the unemployment office, hum-bled, ready to ask the passers-by for a quarter.

He had a layer of snow on his head. Snow was on his shoes. And he was, all over again, small. I kept expecting Oscar's father to look like Oscar, but instead he was a miniature, shorter than me, and the only feature Oscar'd got from him was a sort of cheekbone thing, which, for a second, made me homesick for my late husband. The Bat was holding a tallboy, and he didn't look sure of himself. Car-rying a beer? What had happened to his promise to swear off the alcohol? He was half-smiling, almost panting with the effort of it, wearing a jacket, a wrinkled necktie, and snowy shoes.

"Hi," I said.

"Hi there, daughter." His voice rasped and rattled. He moved from foot to foot. "You gonna invite me in?"

"Sure," I said. I helped him out of his jacket and hung it in the closet. He kept his cap on. I turned around and walked back toward where the three chairs were and the hideabed. I heard him following me. He let out this cough that went on and on and sounded like the end of the world. I sat down in one of the chairs and waited for the coughing event to cease. Finally it did.

"I got phlegm," the Bat informed me. He looked around my apartment. Then he sat on a chair and gave me a look in which cheerfulness and meanness were mixed equally. He cocked an eyebrow at me. "Snows get into my lung cavities and I can't get 'em out." The coughing started up one more time. When he stopped, he said, "It's bad. Don't really know what it is. Don't *want* to know."

"You should see a doctor," I said.

"You think so? All they have is bad news and bills you can't pay. No, I'd rather see myself in hell first," he told me. He tried to lean back, and when that didn't work, he leaned forward. He smiled at me. "Here, you want this beer for your party?" He handed me the tallboy and reached into his shirt for a cigarette, which he proceeded to light. "You want to know what I do? For the lungs?"

"Sure," I said.

"I go to a healer. We got this healer in our church. He lays his hands on me."

"Does it help?"

"Wish I knew. I couldn't say. I'm neither dead nor alive. You got an ashtray?"

I brought over a dish I kept under the sink and handed it to him. "There."

"Thank you," he said, fingering the ashtray and then peering at me. "I reckonized it. But that's not what I'm here to talk about. I want to get to know you. A little, anyways. You don't know me. For like an example, you don' know I'm a Christian man. Go to a church, go to a healer." He crossed his arms, holding the cigarette, and touched his forehead. I was watching the snow on his cap and his shoes. I was waiting for it to melt.

"No, I knew that. The church part."

"How come?" He looked at me, squinting his eyes.

"Oscar told me."

He shook his head, and water dripped down from his hair, but the snow remained on his shoes. He laughed. "I was born in Kentucky where we had a healer living on the same street. Old woman named Gladys—there was a scary and amazing power she had, so I've always believed in it more than medicine. She happened to be a great-aunt of mine. She called me Little Mac."

"Like the hamburger."

"Hunh?"

"You know. The Big Mac."

"Oh, right." He turned his eyes upon my apartment. He looked long and hard at the window. "Did you ever happen to come to Jesus yourself?"

"No, actually, he came to me. At a party. He asked me for directions."

He stared at me for several moments. He stood up, went to the window, then sat down again. "That's blasphemy. Well, I forgive it. Where's your parents that you said was coming?" He scratched at a scar above his left eye. I couldn't help it: I was watching him closely.

"They're late."

"I can see that. It must be they had trouble on the road. Weather reports give, I dunno, five-six-seven inches of snow."

He threw me a look, the very same one I saw him give me when I walked past him out of Oscar's bedroom into the hallway. I couldn't say for sure, but I thought he was calculating his chances.

"Now you tell me about yourself," the Bat said. "Let me hear your story. I'd like to hear that, where you come from and everything."

I talked for ten minutes, yakking away, hoping my parents would arrive to get me out of this mess. But they didn't come and didn't come, and meanwhile, in the middle of my life story, the Bat went to the refrigerator and found himself a beer, not the tallboy he had bought but another one, which he opened and drank in about five seconds. I remembered that he wasn't supposed to drink, that he had sworn it off and was supposed to be clean. Then he opened another beer and brought it over to his personal chair. He was, like, proportionating me all over again, his eyes like lizards crawling up and down my arms and legs. The phone rang once more and I ran to answer it. It was my dad, calling from his car phone, saying the axle was bent and they couldn't drive it, seeing as how the car had gone into the ditch and the front end was broken open. I didn't want to sound desperate so I just went uh-huh, uh-huh. My dad said if he could figure out a way to get over here in the next half-hour, they'd come by cab, if the cabs were running.

I went over to the boom box and put some music on softly, radio-type tunes.

"Who was that?" the Bat inquired, from his chair.

"My dad."

"Still late, those two. Am I right? Well well. Just us, you and me, Missy and Mac. I kinda like the sound of that. 'Missy and Mac.' Do you believe in Jesus, Missy?"

"Back to that topic? Sure," I said.

"Me too. You know why?"

"No."

"'Cause he's interested in me the way he's interested in every-body. Being the way I am, big trouble in a small shape. Hey, I got a riddle for you. What'd the elephant say to the naked man?"

"I don't know."

" 'How do you eat with that thing?' " He smiled fiercely. "Get it? 'How do you eat with that thing?' I think that's funny. You know, Oscar always said you were pretty, and I guess you are, but it's more like country-cute." He studied me for a moment. "With that toothy smile you got."

"Thank you."

"I can see why Oscar'd want to sleep with you and even marry you. All that marriageable cuteness in one package and such."

"What was Oscar's mother like? He's told me—"

"—Do you mind me saying what I just said, a dirty word or two? Sometimes I cain't help it."

"Well, no."

"You should of. You should of said, 'Mac, don't talk that way, it's nasty.' Like that time I called you a dirty word. I shouldn't remember doing that, but I do."

"Well, it is nasty, I guess, but—"

"—Not as nasty as the act, y'know. Which you did in my house, can you remember it? Walkin' past me on display? That got me started."

"I'm sorry for that."

The Bat reached down and took a swig of his beer. He appeared to think for a moment. "So you can apologize after all. I liked it though." He stared at me. "Seeing the features of yours. You sure are pretty." He appeared to think for another moment. "Your parents ain't comin', right?"

"No, they'll be here any minute."

"I don't think so. I think you're puttin' me on. You're just actin'. That's all you ever done with me, was pretend. I had high hopes, drivin' over here in my four-wheel. Missy and Mac, I thought, maybe we can be friends." He stood up and walked toward the kitchen area. He scratched his scalp with the beer bottle. "You think I'm a bad person? Honestly? Tell me now."

"I don't know what you are," I said.

"That's the ticket." Now he scratched his ear with his index finger, then examined the finger. I wanted him to stop all the scratching. "That's the ticket right there. I don't know either. I just don't know what I do from minute to minute. Goddamn, I am confused." He stared up at the ceiling. "Lord, I am confused and tired.

I am forever gettin' tired. You think, Missy, we could, y'know, somehow, well, be friends, and I could someday, when your baby comes, help you out? I'd like to do that. Babysitting. I might help."

"I think so."

"I think so too. We could start all over. Like nothin'd ever happened between us. 'Cause I'll be a granddaddy. We could give it a baptism. Wash it in the blood of the lamb. What you gonna name it?"

I told him I didn't know.

For a moment this thing happened on his face. I had never seen it there before and I couldn't be sure I was seeing it now. His face calmed down for a few seconds, settled into itself. He was peaceful and quiet. I saw at that moment that all my worries about the Bat were mistaken. He was just a harmless little middle-aged guy who drank way too much and who had once followed me around and who had trouble with demons.

"You wanna give me a hug?" the Bat asked. "A hug for the father-in-law?"

"Well, not quite yet," I said, softening. "Maybe later. Soon. In a little while."

"Okay," the Bat said, scratching himself higher, on his chest. His face was getting dazed again, maybe from the beer. "If you'll excuse me, I gotta go for a pee."

"Be my guest," I said. The Bat disappeared into the bathroom and I reached under the hideabed for Oscar's knife box, and I took a knife out and hid it under a magazine. I reached over to the bowl where the potato chips were, and I grabbed some and ate them.

The door to the bathroom opened an inch or two. "Hi," he said, from behind the door. Here things get a little hazy, a little unclear.

After another minute or so, the Bat walked out, with his pants off, and his underwear off, and his shoes and socks removed. His dick swung back and forth like an inspection tool, as he made his way in slow motion toward me. I remember looking at the window quickly. Maybe someone would see this. He stood there for a moment, naked from the waist down, as if he couldn't decide on his next move. Then he said, "How 'bout that hug now?"

"Mac," I said, trying to hold my breathing steady, "you left your underwear and your pants off." I couldn't run; he was closer to the door than I was.

"Yeah, I guess I did," he said, clearing his throat. "Maybe I oughtta put 'em back on."

"That's a good idea." I stood up. My knees were shaking. My face had gone ice cold. "Why don't you do that? Just turn around and go back in there."

"I forgot," he said. "Thought I was home. Thought it was Missy and Mac, quiet evening at home."

"No," I said. "It isn't that." I was measuring the distance to the door. He started to walk toward me, his dick swinging again a little.

"I'd like that hug now," he said. "Then I'll put the pants back on."

I couldn't think. I didn't have a single good idea to help me out.

"The shades aren't down," I said, feeling my tongue rattling. "People will see." The Bat turned around to lower the shades, and when he did, I reached for the knife under the magazine and held it behind me. I took a deep breath. I'd never been so scared in my life, but I was also not scared, which is harder to explain. But I am going to explain it, because I've thought about it ever since. I mean, I knew he could kill me, or rape me and kill me, but I also knew that I could probably kill him, if I wanted to, and that maybe at any moment any of us could do any of that to anybody. He hadn't decided what he would do, not yet. But the more amazing thing is, I felt Oscar's spirit pass through me right at that same exact instant, and I almost cried out, *Oscar!* 'cause there he was, my boy and my man and my husband, he had just walked inside of me out of nowhere, out of death, and I could think like Oscar and move like Oscar and be strong like him, strong and fearless. Maybe all I was doing was thinking of Oscar. That's probably it. Thinking of being fearless. Which I wasn't, scared to death as I was, but I was also this other person, right at that moment, like that person was on one side and the scared person was on the other. I was going to give room to the fearless side. Oh Oscar, I thought, be in me.

The Bat walked over to me, calm as a cucumber, but drunk all the same. Concentrating on his every move, calculating the odds. "Shades're down now."

"Get away," I said. "Don't come any nearer to me."

"You sure are pretty," he said, getting closer. "Prettiest little thing. Always were. I can be pretty, too. I can be a kindly man."

"Put your clothes on, Mac," I said. "Besides, I'm pregnant."

"I get so confused," he said. "Help me. There isn't anybody I can talk to. I get so tired. Help me out, little one." His arms reached out as he got next to me. "I'm not askin' for much. Please. I'm askin' please. From politeness. Just a little hug. And a kiss? The tiniest bit of love."

Then the air unfroze itself.

The Bat put his arms around me and he pressed himself against me, and my hand came down once, stabbing him through his shirt into the upper arm with Oscar's knife.

He looked hard at his arm for a second, then howled in surprise and dropped to his knees. Some blood appeared on my blouse, as the knife sort of worried its way out of his arm, and with its blade shiny with blood fell to the floor, spattering the linoleum. I got to the doorway and grabbed my jacket and ran outside. I turned the lights off as I went. I thought: *I'll get the neighbors. No no no: he'll be here in a minute, he'll accuse me of something. Assaulting him.* I should've gotten the neighbors, but I wasn't thinking so clearly. I just wanted to get out of that building. I raced down to the Matador and started it. I had a few minutes on him, but no particular place to go.

If you're in your right mind, you drive straight to the police, but I wasn't in my right mind, and besides, the roads were terrible. I was thinking: I did the wrong thing, and now they'll arrest me, Chloé, for what I did. I saw myself, arrested, ruined, panhandling on the street. I thought of Rhonda, my sister, too far away; my friends, too unhelpful and stoned; and then I thought of Bradley, my boss and my friend, and his girlfriend, Margaret, because maybe I was still thinking of Oscar, I could still feel him, and I was thinking of our wedding day, and the party that Bradley had thrown for us, the feast of love he'd laid out on his table. I thought of that, too.

THE ROADS HADN'T been plowed yet, and this thick snow lay over everything, and the Matador had rear-wheel drive, plus it was old and rusty, and the first thing I knew I was going down my street sideways, and then I wasn't going anywhere at all, just spinning and spinning at an intersection. I thought of the Bat and his four-wheel truck gaining on me, and that was when a face appeared on my driver's side window, and I screamed.

But it was only a passing pedestrian walking his dog, and, like, offering to push me. It's amazing he stayed when I screamed like that. But he did, and he pushed my car, and I was off again.

I made my way around the city trying to get to Bradley's street, over by Allmendinger Park, and at one point the engine died and I had to start it again, and at another point I found myself on a dark street with the snow falling and I had to stop the car because I was crying and shaking and shivering. But then I faced up to things and got strong, and I made another New Year's resolution two months early that I wouldn't give in to cheesy panic or anything, even though it made sense to panic, and was the easy, logical thing to do, lame though it was.

The street lights passed over me, and I felt myself getting faint and helpless, and I had the sudden recognition that I didn't know where I was, but then I passed the football stadium where Oscar had once given me a Slurpee, and I made a right turn, and another left, and another right, and I started skidding down Bradley's street, and suddenly I felt my baby kick, although it was way too early, it couldn't have been the baby kicking, so I guess it was my heart thumping, which is how I knew Oscar was leaving me, because I was having this little tiny heart attack, just like the one Oscar'd had, except very small, so it was time for Oscar to go. And then he was gone, out of me entirely, having helped me in my time of trouble. He re-died.

I parked in front of Bradley's house, which was, like, totally dark. I opened the Matador door with its formerly satisfying squeak. I ran up to his door, and when I did, the snow got into my running shoes, and I rang the bell, rang it and rang it and rang it, and Bradley the dog started barking inside, but there was no Bradley the human there, or Margaret either, and I thought, oh please, someone save me now before the Bat gets here.

So I ran over next door, where Harry and Esther Ginsberg were, and there was more snow in my shoes, and I thought I would faint, but I pounded on their door knocker, and I said, "Help! Please, help! Somebody, please!"

And I heard Harry coming toward the door, and as he opened it, he said, like he didn't know it was me, like my voice wasn't my own but a man's voice, like he thought it was someone else, "Aaron? Is that you? Aaron?"

TWENTY-SIX

I KNOW ONE UNASSAILABLE TRUTH: *Help your friends and those whom you love; hurt your enemies.* The very banality of this formulation ensures that most academics—who enjoy hurting their friends—will ignore it.

For days, in any case, I lay awake, thinking of Aaron and of how I might have done him indeliberate harm. I awoke, nocturnally fevered, my forehead sweating, perspiration soaked into my pajamas, in my unforgiving mind's eye the spectacle of Aaron being ill served by my negligence. On my son's behalf, I had performed no heroic measures, the ones that, bright with prudence, you wisely do not perform in the daytime but whose nonperformance terrorizes your conscience following the arrival of dusk. Disquieted, assailed, I would rise out of bed and aimlessly walk down the hallway to the bathroom. I would switch on the light. All bathrooms, whatever their minute variations, are overilluminated at night, just as, at night, all telephones when they ring are too loud. The existential nocturnal glare of bathrooms has a certain ghastliness built into the shadowless illumination. Under such lights one discovers the first signs of cancer.

Moody and forlorn with middle age, baffled by the enigmatic Christian knight of faith, Kierkegaard, who nevertheless came to grips with spiritual psychologies as few thinkers ever have, battered with visual memories of Aaron, I would walk back to the bed, comically abandoned by sleep. It occurred to me that my lifelong tramps through the landscapes of philosophy had set Aaron off in the direction of counterphilosophy, of Scientology and Theosophy and Anthroposophy and the other occult sciences he favored. Who knows, who knew, what set him off? Perhaps he loved men and not women. But who would care one way or another about such a choice, in this era, except the unenlightened? We would have accepted him gladly, accepted his homosexuality, if that's what it was. We would have welcomed him back to the house. He knew that. He could have come back, our own beloved prodigal, bedecked with strange clothes and jewels, dressed like a gypsy, and we would have swung wide the door and hugged him and kissed him. But no, he preferred to hate and to be hated.

This is the only cure for insomnia I know. Lying on my back, I would imagine myself in a cosmopolitan but still rather lethargic city, a city that had long ago given up worldly ambition, a city in genteel decline, Lisbon, for example (which I have never visited), where I am sitting at an outdoor café during a mild summer afternoon, drinking bitter coffee and reading the paper in Portuguese. Esther sits there with me, commenting on the architecture of the square—shabby Baroque—and on the passersby. Some are solitary. Others, the lovers, walk arm in arm. They all have an inaptitude for work. The women wear bright scarves tangled around their necks, the young men wear peacock-colored shirts. Occasionally we witness a group of three or four, laughing quietly as they pass in front of us. Then I revise the city so that the square faces the estuary. Boats sail in and out past the anchorage, near a breakwater at whose end is a harbor light. I am also on some of these boats (I am subdivided), and I wave to myself affably. No one has to go anywhere, no one has to accomplish anything. One has, it seems, an entire lifetime to sort through the major questions and to develop a coherent set of opinions and judgments on these matters. The meaning of everything will arrive in due course.

Gulls land and then take flight from the quay at Alcântara. The waiter brings another cup of coffee, a boat toots in the distance over the lapping waves, there is a hint of rain beyond the wharf, a bank of clouds developing over the horizon suggests but does not threaten the relief of a storm. At the next table over a man feeds olives to a gray pet parrot perched on his finger. Esther murmurs something to me, a consoling phrase, I don't quite attend to it, though I may register the words later. I look around again at the harbor and now at the buildings behind me. Nearby, children are playing hopscotch. Two scholars of the Talmud stroll by, arguing in Portuguese flavored with Yiddish. A small band of musicians is tuning up, a trio of vagabond string players enjoying the outdoors, intending to perform Rossini. I am not particularly hungry, but when the solicitous waiter comes by I order a plate of the local delicacy, a rolled pastry with honey tucked inside.

I take another sip of coffee.

Usually this little nighttime fantasy is enough to send me off to sleep. But on certain nights, following fierce committee meetings at the Amalgamated Education Corporation, I must calm down by closing my eyes and reading the imaginary paper in imaginary Portuguese at length. I don't read Portuguese, but in my insomnia cure I do. I scan the paper at my sidewalk café near the harbor. The paper I imagine has trivial matters reported in a lively and almost comically beautiful prose. This is paradise, to read a newspaper containing matters of no consequence written by vainglorious prose stylists. A woman has her purse stolen in a leather shop, all this reported in a fashion that would have done honor to Gibbon, if the great man had written in Portuguese. A man falls off a balcony, breaking a bone or two, and the account has the melancholy wit of Saint-Simon. In another section of the paper, a cat is reported missing, but the story has been written by G.W.F. Hegel, and one can barely discern the cat. Well, no one admires Hegel's prose style, but it is pleasing and relaxing to imagine Hegel, humbled at last, having to write for a newspaper. Hegel also reports on the doings at the racetrack. Elsewhere, a soccer match is narrated by Proust, an apartment is offered for sale by Heine, a quarrel between two neighbors is accounted for by Colette. Virginia Woolf has control of the financial columns, which, in this newspaper of mine, detail how money should be spent, and on what items, not how it should be invested. In this city of my making, my imaginings, there are no major investments. Savings are minimal. The bankers are as poor as mice. They must go begging, organize bake sales.

But then, or now (I am still awake), I lower the paper and look into the harbor, and there, in a rowboat without oars or motor, is Aaron, drifting away from shore, and shouting. Behind me the great clock tower in the central square sounds its lugubrious and melancholy bells. These are large bells, with a complex layering of overtones, and their announcements dictate the timing of the social life of the city. It is four in the afternoon. Aaron is shouting or screaming. The bells clang repetitively, going past the hours into tollings of sorrow. I cannot make out any of his words. *My son is shouting at me.* He is drifting out to sea. He is gesturing. My G-d, I must help him. I am sweating, I have a fever.

Somebody save him.

ALMOST EVERY RELIGION obsesses over the sacrifice of a son by a father. For the Jews, it is Abraham and Isaac, an example appropriated by Kierkegaard for the purposes of irrational faith. For the Christians, of course, the son, Jesus, is sacrificed, is donated as an offering for the first and last time by the father-god; Gentiles cannot get over this. There is Absalom. Elsewhere, we find Prometheus, understood as a young god, who must be killed time and again. These myths I find more compelling than the tales of the father's death, organized by the primal horde, an idea whose commonplace vulgarity was so aptly taken up by Freud, a vulgarian of the clinical variety.

When I was in college, my father, a gruff undemonstrative man, died of a stroke on a ladder one Saturday afternoon while painting the house. When he tumbled down to the ground, the can of white paint went tumbling with him, splashing over his face and torso. My father died stretched out on the green lawn, the nearby grass and my father's face painted white, clownishly, as if by an action painter. I believe it gives me no pleasure to tell this story, but Esther says that it does, I have told it so often and so compulsively to anyone who would listen. He, my father, thought me bookish and unworldly. He sold copper pipe in Chicago and wanted me to go into the business, which I refused to do from the age of seven onward. My father was given to rages, as is Aaron. He suffered from a metaphysical anguish without any apparent cause. I see my father in my son. Both have a talent for withering cryptic conclusive remarks. I never said Kaddish over him. I am not that sort of Jew. It complicates things.

THIS SATURDAY NIGHT, I was pacing through the house while Esther did her sewing. I was trying not to think of Aaron but could not help myself. To block my worries, I had taken up Kierkegaard and was deliberating over the Wittgensteinian pronouncement in *Repetition* (Wittgenstein, who admired Kierkegaard enormously, was the Knight of Rules) that "He who knows how to keep silent discovers an alphabet that has just as many letters as the ordinary one." What does it mean, knowing how to keep silent? What *kind* of silence would this be? How do such silences differ from one another? How does this particular silence contrast with being morosely mute? What is a knowledgeable silence? How would we know or for that matter recognize this knowledge? And what, if I may ask, is the nature of this silent alphabet?

Wittgenstein regarded metaphysics as the lint on a suit. However, after he picked off the lint, the suit itself vanished.

Perhaps these musings would find a chapter in my new book, a refutation of the tendentious and mannered arguments concerning Kierkegaard and Wittgenstein in Herbert Quain's *The Labyrinth of the God.*

Outside it was snowing, a dreadful December snow, wet and clumped and cumulative. Sitting in my study, mulling over K's notice that all life is a repetition—these silent alphabets must have existed before us—but actually visualizing Aaron's wanderings over the face of the earth, I peered through the window.

I imagined my son pursued by barking dogs.

Helpless in my imaginings (where was Lisbon? my city had faded with the pitiless evanescence of all fantasy), I imagined Aaron, hapless and lonely, an orphan of this midwestern storm, pelted by wet snow, one of the wretched. I would like very much to say that I did not think of Aaron at all and that my thoughts were free, but my son, having disappeared, commanded my thoughts entirely in his absence and silence. At that moment it occurred to me that *Aaron had discovered Kierkegaard's secret alphabet and was writing letters to me, employing it.*

A car rumbled out on the street. It was not Bradley's car, which I recognized, but one of an unknown pitch and timbre. The driver stopped the car, opened the door—it squeaked—and slammed it.

I am not inclined to magical thinking. Nevertheless my breath quickened, I must tell you, at that moment. My heartbeat increased. I stood up and approached the front hallway. Aaron had at last come home, was my intuition. He had given up his rebellion and had returned, remorseful, quite possibly drug-free, and grateful for our forgiveness. Perhaps he would bring someone with him. There would be wildfires of contrition on all sides. Fine, fine. I made my way toward the foyer.

A fist knocked against the door. A hoarse boyish voice called out for help. I opened the door a crack and sniffed the winter air. Aaron, I said. Is that you? Aaron?

Pulling the door open, Esther standing behind me, I saw not

Aaron but Chloé, the coffee waitress and recent widow, her face pale and airless and stricken and terrified.

CHLOÉ, I SAID. What is it? Come in. Please come in.

He tried to rape me, she cried out. And I stabbed him and now they'll arrest me and take me off to jail. I'm done for.

Esther brushed me out of the way. She reached for Chloé's ungloved chapped hand. Come in, dear, she said, come in right this minute. Esther pulled Chloé inside and shut the door behind her, turning the lock. She did not let loose for a moment her grip on Chloé's palm and fingers. Esther unzipped Chloé's jacket—the girl did not at that moment seem capable of this simple action—and took it off. Then she unlaced and removed Chloé's big shoes and led her into the kitchen, where she sat her down at the dinette table. Shoeless, the girl scattered snow from her jeans down the hall, past the ticking clock. Don't say anything, Esther instructed her. Just warm up for a moment, and I'll make you some coffee. No, not coffee. Tea.

He tried—

—Just a moment, please, Chloé. Just wait, Esther said. Then she turned to me. Harry, you must leave us.

Nonsense, I said.

It's okay, Chloé said. He can stay.

No, Esther insisted. Harry, go back to your study. Please, open a book.

Open a book?

She took pity on me. Do as I tell you, Harry. Open one of your books. Ten minutes. Give us ten minutes here.

Who tried to rape you? I asked. We must call the police.

Harry! Esther said. She rose and with a will of iron pushed me with both hands out of the kitchen. She pushed me into the living room and then down the hallway to the stairs. She would have pushed me up the stairs to my study, but I had agreed in my mind to go up there anyway.

Nevertheless, at the landing I turned around and waited. I could not help but be curious. What rape? And who the perpetrator? The door to the kitchen closed behind Esther, and I heard from in there female murmurings. Chloé said something, Esther said something in return. Women have this way of excluding men from discussions of domestic importance. Around the house we are befuddled by their private plans and strategies. I trudged upstairs.

THEY WENT TO THE POLICE, leaving me behind in the house. But Chloé, having not been penetrated or otherwise assaulted by her father-in-law, declined to press charges for criminal sexual assault or to testify against him, although she was encouraged to do so. They calmed her fears of being arrested, Metzger having all the bad unsavory cards in this particular deck. Late that night, she returned to our house and called her parents, who had made their way home by tow truck and taxi. Esther would not let her drive herself home. She gave Chloé a spare nightgown—they were the same height, Esther and Chloé—and put her to bed in Aaron's room. Much of the night Esther sat there on the edge of the mattress, until Chloé slept.

The next morning Esther rose, I won't say "joyfully," but with serious intent. She called in to her job and to her boss, informing everybody that she would not appear. In the kitchen she prepared orange juice, scrambled eggs, toast, and bagels. Chloé came in wearing Aaron's too-large green bathrobe, and I must say it was a shock, seeing her dressed that way, barefoot in our kitchen as she had been at her wedding reception, dressed in our son's robe, then a priestess of Eros, now brought low.

She managed a smile for the two of us, one of the more heartbreaking gestures of politeness I have ever witnessed.

Good morning, she said, and she started to cry. Esther rose up faster than I did and took the girl in her arms. I can't eat scrambled eggs, Chloé said, huddled inside Esther's arms. Because I'm pregnant, they make me sick or something.

You don't have to eat anything.

Hard-boiled eggs're okay, she said. Still she continued to weep.

Please sit down, Chloé, I requested of her.

I'll try.

She sat successfully at the table and dabbed at her eyes with a napkin. What are you going to do now? I asked.

I can't go back there, she said. That little shithead—pardon my French—is gonna be followin' me around. I can't . . . She shook her head. I can't think, for starters.

Well, you'll live here, then, Esther said. Until you think of something to do. For the interim, you're right here. You can move into one of the bedrooms upstairs, or we can make up an apartment for you in the basement. You could have privacy down there. You could come and go as you please.

Esther looked at me, an expression on her face not of inquiry— *Was this plan acceptable to me?*—but of unarguable confirmation—*We are going to do this.* Why would I argue? I just nodded.

Here, Esther said, and she pulled a green bracelet off her arm and put it on Chloé's.

What is it? the girl asked.

Malachite, Esther told her. It gives courage.

Later that day, I drove with Chloé over to her apartment and helped her collect some of her household gods: her clothes, her radio and CDs, her little TV, her late husband's track shoes and baton, pathetic odds and ends. In two carloads we brought them over. The chairs and table we left behind for a later trip.

Eventually she broke her lease. She is now our tenant.

She decided that she wanted to live in the basement. I don't want to have windows, she said, even though the basement did have glass-block windows up near the ceiling, through which the light strained into the room. Chloé's living in our house was Esther's idea; before anyone had thought the matter over, it was done and completed. Consequently: there she resides in what was once our rec room. Where Ephraim and Sarah and Aaron once played Ping-Pong, Chloé now lives. She reads Dr. Spock's *Baby and Child Care,* watches television, goes to work, listens to music, sleeps, and prepares for her delivery. From time to time she comes up the stairs to the kitchen. Now and then she joins us for dinner or breakfast. Mostly she keeps her own hours, does whatever youngsters of her generation do. (I don't inquire.) Sometimes, from down there, I hear singing, Chloé's intermittent solitary warbling.

She has swelled up. She radiates the preemptive procreative heat of pregnancy. Esther accompanies her to the Lamaze classes. They come back laughing and whispering. My wife appears to be regressing to presumptive girlhood and to be enjoying it. She often has on her face a pumpkin grin. Myself, I have agreed to be godfather to the baby. This is all inappropriate—a Jew as a godfather? —but I have decided to indulge what Kierkegaard calls "the blissful security of the moment." Even baptisms hold no terror for me. It is simply what the Gentiles do.

Bradley's new girlfriend, Margaret Ntegyereize, has promised, if she's available, to deliver the baby. As Jimmy Durante used to say, Everybody wants to get into the act.

Bradley Smith and Margaret Ntegyereize—how will it end? This coupling is no more preposterous than the others, and perhaps less than most of them. It is possible that Bradley will fall in love with a new woman every two years and marry her, like, what's-his-name, Tommy Manville. I see them together, Bradley and Margaret, walking hand in hand, trailed by the dog. The days of my pestering Bradley with conversation appear to be over. If I am going to be lucid, I must talk to myself.

But the father-in-law, Metzger, what of him? Do I remember my German? A *Metzger* equals a butcher. This Metzger, of dubious humanity, he is a more difficult case. Chloé calls him the Bat, but I prefer his name without metaphoric trappings. We have not, I think, seen the last of Metzger. As long as there is Cupid, as long as there is Venus and for that matter Adonis, there is Metzger, the broken wheel, the nail rusty with infection.

Feeling that she should not do it herself, I returned alone to Chloé's apartment, intending to pick up the remaining furniture. There was not much to take, very little substance. The hideabed I left there. She didn't want it.

Oscar and me fucked our brains out on it, she said crudely but straightforwardly. I don't wanna see it again. Its career is over.

But I recovered a lamp, a chair or two, a table. I brought back her books—Edgar Cayce and the prophecies of Nostradamus— and one or two small items she'd missed, including, to my surprise, a tea strainer and an egg coddler. I resisted the pathos of this small collection of kitchen fixtures. Girls leave home every day, set up house, and buy dish drainers, colanders, and garlic presses, thus bringing a version of themselves into existence. It is their rendition of a late afternoon in Lisbon reading the paper near the quay, except for the reality of it.

On one of my trips out to the car I encountered a man I took to be Metzger, there on the sidewalk. He had an inescapably trashy look. Pallor was mixed with incipient disease on his remarkably ignoble features. He was both pre- and post-venereal. Apparently the knife wound had not slowed him down. He nodded at me and grabbed at my elbow. I believe in the great courage and perseverance of the working classes, but this Metzger was an exception, a step down from the lumpen proletariat into the ash can.

That chair yours? he asked me.

I put it down on the sidewalk. I don't believe we've had the pleasure of meeting, I said.

I don't believe we have, he said.

Harry Ginsberg, I said, holding out my hand.

Howdy do, he said, shaking it.

And you are . . . ?

Friend of the family, he offered. That chair yours?

Yes, I said.

Lookit, he said. I think it got stole from me. I got my truck over there for it. You'll wanna take it for me?

Sorry, no, I told him.

Perhaps I have not mentioned: I grew up on the streets of Chicago, and despite my abstracted and somewhat airy ways, am not a physical coward, quite the contrary, in fact. In my youth I fought the boys and men who wished to fight me, some of Chicago's best, mostly Irish bullies affronted by Jews. Many of these Americans went home Ginsberg-bruised and bloodied. It had been years since I had found myself in a brawl, but the prospect of one with this man of doubtful probity filled me with cheer beyond measure. I had not practiced my pugilism for years, but I was ready. I felt happy and truculent.

I had taken hold of two of the chair's legs, for carrying. The little greasy-haired man now grasped the other two legs. We began a grotesque dance on the front sidewalk, a shoving match. He muttered, while I kept silent. My blood, somewhat dormant at the Amalgamated, began to boil.

Greedy fucking kike, said the smelly diminutive shegetz. I put the chair down and popped him one. He stood for a moment, as if surveying the sky for blimps. Then his knees gave way under him and he appeared to sit down, dazed, on the sidewalk. How easy it had been! And how pleasurable! I had expected to expend more effort in subduing him. He stood up. Again I slugged him, an easy uppercut this time. Fistfighting is like riding a bicycle: you don't forget how. Down he went again. But there he sat, fingering what would soon be his shiner. I carried the chair to my car, returned to the building, messaging my knuckles, locked up Chloé's mostly empty—except for the hideabed—apartment, and returned to the front sidewalk.

He was standing up by now, but not steadily.

You'll hear from me, he said.

By phone or telegram? I asked. I reached the car, lowered myself inside, and drove away.

ONE DAY, I THINK, Metzger will find us. Chloé's enemy is now mine, however, and my feeling is: Let the lamebrain Metzger do as he pleases. I am ready for him. I am pleased to have an enemy who is not symbolic.

We must collect our thoughts, for the unexpected is always upon us. Who said that? Beckett? Kierkegaard? I am no longer sure of my quotations.

Every night I take up my watch by the front window. I have my lamp and my book. I listen to Schubert on the phonograph. Next to my family, Schubert is the love of my life; if he were to return to Earth, he could come to my house and take any of the objects here he wanted. Nearby, Esther reads or knits. Certain nights of the week, we play honeymoon bridge or canasta or Scrabble. On other nights, when Esther is Lamazing with Chloe, I am alone here, guarding the house. Aaron continues not to call. Our son has vanished into the maw of this vast continent. But I continue to think that one night, for it will surely be an evening (all reunions occur in the evening), probably one in the spring or summer when the cool breezes are blowing through the maple and linden trees in our front yard and the birds are uttering their consolations, a car door will close softly, and within moments the tread of a man will become audible as he makes his way toward the front door. The air will be clear and crisp. He will step tentatively up to the front entryway. He will make his hand into a fist, to knock. Or perhaps he will extend his index finger to ring the doorbell. Dad? he will say. Daddy? It's me. It's Aaron.

But perhaps the person at the door will be Metzger, the butcher, having found us out, having discovered our place in the world, our location and locale, our modest lives. From the street he will hear Schubert. The music will enter his ear and have no effect. It will fall like a seed upon stone. He knows as much about music as a pig about oranges. Perhaps he will bring along his thuggish and nitwit friends. Perhaps they will bring firearms. Fine. Let them come. I will be here. I will be ready.

I think of a poem I had to memorize in college: "Love makes those young whom age doth chill,/And whom he finds young, keeps young still." Something like that.

The unexpected is always upon us. Of all the gifts arrayed before me, this one thought, at this moment of my life, is the most precious.

TWENTY-SEVEN

LOOKS LIKE I GET the curtain speech.

Some nights I walk around town, protected by my malachite machine-made bracelet that Esther gave me and by Oscar's track team relay baton, which I could use as a weapon. The obstetrician said I should exercise for the baby's sake, and when I do that, I sort of accidentally see into people's living room windows even though I don't always want to. But because it's spring, the windows're open and the curtains are pulled aside, flufftering in the breezes, and it's that movie, *Rear Window*, by Hitchcock, except in my case everything's out front, *Front Window*, by Chloé. Generally people are just practicing their slumping vegetable life by watching TV, or they're mowing down the lawn or grubbing in the grub garden, but what's amazing is how often you see people sitting on the front stoop staring off into space. I guess you're not supposed to do that, stare into space, because it's not-for-profit, but believe me, that's what people do with their unapplied leisure time. They look like human-sized possums. And when they see a pregnant woman walking by unaccompanied, pregnantly huge like me, carrying a track team relay baton, they usually give me a smile or a wan wave, like I'm contributing to the Gross National Census or the enlarging welfare of humanity. People go by, things go by, such as me. When people are staring off into their neighborhood infinity, before they see me, what are they thinking about? That's what I'm trying to grasp. I think they're stupefied, thinking about love, mostly, how they once had it, how they got it, how they lost it, and all the people they loved or didn't love, how they ended up royally hating somebody, like, the weirdness and wetness of it. Bradley says they're thinking about money, but I know they're not. Love comes first. They're humming their love songs, for example as sung by Frank Sinatra or the Beatles or Madonna—did she ever sing one? a love song, I mean, and not just sex and money? I guess so—and they imagine about how they'd like to be with somebody else, or truly the person they're actually with, sitting there on the stoop, accompanying them on life's journey by talking, talking about nothing special, just talking. Or sitting in the kitchen, making turkey club sandwiches for each other. Or watching TV together. Or dancing. Or in the bedroom, having sex merrily or maybe not so merrily as the case may be. One thing I never mentioned so far was that once Oscar and I made love so hard that I got out of bed with a sunburn. It's true! If he hadn't died, he could vouch for me. We had tried something we hadn't done before, I won't go into harmful detail, and when he was doing me he asked if I was happy and I said I was. We did it for as long as we wanted to and then when we were finished I went to the bathroom and I had acquired a sunburn. And I thought, *this is totally inexplicable.* But I had it. Making love with Oscar gave it to me. I wish I still had it. Now I'm as pale as a sheet. Maybe I'll get it again when my baby is born. I'll give birth to the baby and get a sunburn in the delivery room in the process. Positive ions will darken my skin and I'll look like a native. So, as I said, I walk past these houses and I see all these domestic arrangements, I guess you'd call them. Women living with women. Women living with men. Men living with men. Women living alone. Men living alone. Sane people and crazy people, people who have lost what once remained of their minds. The crazy ones are mostly crazy because love made them that way. I believe that. Dan Cupid's arrow can make you one bubble off-level, is what I'm saying. Love has some ingredient for flat-out lunacy in it. Everybody knows that. Look at the Bat if you need proof. I mean, you can say that love is obsolete and retro, okay, but everybody comes home at night wanting somebody there, even villains come in the door and say hopefully, "Honey, I'm home?" and either somebody is there to kiss you, or somebody isn't. And if somebody isn't, if there are no kisses, you've got to deal with it. Maybe you get a dog so that the *dog* kisses you, like Bradley did once. Maybe the cat dances around your feet, meowing with happiness. That happens. It's no disgrace to kiss a dog in the evening. Dogs don't mind. I'm not saying you can't manage one way or another, I'm just saying you have to cope, such as the dog solution. So anyway, I come home to my basement that I rent from the Ginsbergs and of course Oscar isn't there. Oscar isn't there because he's dead. I mean, I know that he's dead because I saw his dead body, close up, but even though I know he's dead, I don't *believe* it. I don't *believe* he's dead. He's around here somewhere. I just know that, don't ask me to explain. I sleep with his Bert or Ernie doll, and I can smell him on it. And so that's part of the reason I'm out there walking. I'm gonna find Oscar. It's partly because of what I did to him, how I changed him. That boy befriended me. I suppose that I made a man out of him, but I don't think that's really much of an accomplishment. Oscar could've made it to manhood on his own, without my help. I keep talking about all the sex we had, but what I forget to mention is what *else* we did together. We danced and listened to music and played cards (I taught him gin rummy) and went to movies and we talked *all the time,* complete with our opinions about things. Oscar had a lot of opinions. Some of his opinions were unique and experimental. He said that the universe was expanding, it *had* to expand, to make room for all the souls, human and animal, that had died in it. Each soul took up considerable space. The universe had to accommodate that. He thought that the rich had invented poverty in order to get poor people to do terrible and stupid jobs no one would consider doing unless they needed the money. Money, he said, was God's worst invention, the only way he could think of to get people to work. Get out! I said, but no, he meant it. He thought that when the world came to an end, everybody would sort of forget about Australia, and it'd survive the end of the world through sheer negligence. He didn't believe in cars, Oscar didn't; he thought cars would contribute to the end of the world as we know it. He thought that there were time zones on the moon, but only two. If it was midnight on the dark side of the moon it'd always been noon on the other side. Two time zones on the moon, two times of day or night. You wouldn't need daylight savings time on the moon because you couldn't save the lunar daylight just by adjusting your watch. He wasn't zany. He used common sense. He could be old-fashioned despite his tongue stud and his outward appearances. Like, he once brought me flowers in a vase. He once brought home a lobster for us to eat, but we couldn't put it in the boiling water to cook it—we didn't have the heart—and so we put it in the bathtub with some water for the night and returned it, alive, to the grocery store the next day for a refund. As for sex, except for when he got excitable, Oscar believed in extensive foreplay, he was a real traditionalist in that respect; the drugs had helped him to see there was no point in ever rushing anything. He didn't ever beat me up. I can't remember him ever hitting me once. Oscar the Gent. When I think about him now—and I think about him way more than I ever think about myself—I think of him like he's standing on a hill somewhere, this cow pasture, looking into the future, and telling me what he sees. I have my hand on his dick and I can feel his heart murmur through it, his blood bounding joyfully. I'm sorry he didn't make it to the year 2000 because he thought for sure there would be major changes in the cosmos, everything, down to physics, would be revamped. All the same, despite his radical-traditional belief system, I think *I'm* more of a visionary than he was. After all, I once saw Jesus at a party. There was another thing I saw there, which I'll tell you about eventually, once I get up my nerve to describe it. This thing I saw, it was probably the whole point of the party and of Jesus being in attendance and alerting me to it. But back to my walking around town. My point is, Oscar is here somewhere and that's why I'm strolling hereabouts looking for him. You can't have a body and a soul like that and just die and disappear. It's much too wasteful, psychically. God won't permit that. God's no hambone: God believes in soul ecology. Something has to happen to you after you die, something mysterious and so far unexplained to us humans, and I'm determined to find out what it might be. I'm the woman to do it, I'm the woman for the job. I think maybe Oscar has taken up residence in some other guy, or he's going to, and I have to find him there, though the search will be hard, because the guy will deny that he's Oscar, of course. He'll claim to be himself. I won't know if it's Oscar at first, because it'll look like someone else, but it *will* be Oscar, the guy will have Oscar-essence. That can happen. I'll strip him of whatever girlfriends he has and get him into my arms, as long as he isn't dismayed by my having a baby. He won't know what hit him once I go to work on him. I have enough goddess stuff in me to manage. Because he'll be Oscar without knowing it. That's why I go in search of him. Sometimes, when I don't want to walk, I get into the Matador on evenings when the car agrees to start, and first I head down toward Ypsilanti. I drive past where Mrs. Maggaroulian once worked. She isn't there anymore. She isn't anywhere. Mrs. Maggaroulian has disappeared from our planet. She can't tell me where Oscar is. I have to do the search by myself. Wait a minute. I have to take a breath. Just a minute. I need to breathe in.

There. I took a breath. Sometimes I get light-headed and I think I'm going to faint. Anyway, you can't figure out love without figuring out death, too, but the effort it takes can knock the wind out of you. Love is the first cousin of death, they're acquainted with each other, they go to the same family reunions. Mrs. Maggaroulian's office is empty, her sign's been removed, and another sign, THIS SPACE FOR LEASE, is up there instead. I wish she were still there, with her Laurel and Hardy clocks. I could use some help and advice from her. I could use a few e-mails from the future, a few pennies-per-serving tidbits from the prophet of Ypsilanti, where the three Christs once lived. We're constantly getting bulletins from the future, in case you haven't noticed, but mostly we ignore them because of the unsightly messengers, the slobby crackpots who get the information and have to pass it on with their bad breath and missing teeth. Harry Ginsberg, the professor who lives upstairs, is always going around saying, "Chloé, the unexpected is always upon us," but what he really means is that the future wants us to know what is about to happen and it, the future, sends us people like Mrs. Maggaroulian to help us out. I suppose he really means that *I* am the unexpected and that *I* am always upon him, but maybe he wants to say that he expected his son Aaron to show up one day and what he got was me, instead. He lost a son but he gained a sort of daughter, which was myself. You can't always get what you want but sometimes you get what you need—truer words than that *have* been spoken, but not much truer, and for sure not in my lifetime. Here's what I think: every once or so often, the Mrs. Maggaroulians appear in your life to help manage your most exciting and troubled times and to help you get through them. Ever notice how drag queens and street people and madmen typically show up at your doorstep just when you're about to take a new job or go on a long journey? They're there, as a rule, to tell you how it's all going to turn out. You've got to cock an ear in their direction, despite the bad oniony smells they give off. If you ignore them, good luck, you're on your own, that's all I can say. Here's another example of what I mean. Oscar had a cassette player installed in the Matador, so he could listen to music dimensionally when he drove to his various destinations. After he died, and I got the car, being his widow, I started to motor around town listening to the audition tape Oscar made at the Arbogast School of Broadcasting, where he was, like, practicing to be a DJ. On this tape, Oscar tries out different names for himself during his broadcast. Sometimes he's Sam Loomis. Sometimes he's Mister Van Damm or Bone Barrel. Oscar didn't think "Oscar" was a good name for a radio personality, it had something dreadful about it. It's funny. He plays music and does the weather and reads commercials that he wrote himself for clubs and used-car lots and window shade companies. God, I love hearing his voice. He's *mellifluous*. I found that word in a dictionary, where it belonged until I used it just now. He announces songs but he doesn't play them, not on this tape, except for one. In the middle of the tape he says that the next song is going out for Chloé. He doesn't say who's singing it. It's not rock or Goth or heavy metal or anything like that. What happens instead is, this old bluesy guy comes on and sings it. It's an old blues song, I guess. "Ain't No Grave Can Hold My Body Down." I guess Oscar liked it because of the title or the tune. Anyhow, on this tape he plays it, and it's for me, and the reason it's for me is that Oscar knew he was going to die, but that he would come back some way or other and find me. No grave would hold his body down. It's also a sexual boast. I have to take another breath here, I'm feeling a little faint.

Okay. I know it's audacious for Oscar to say he was going to be resurrected. But why shouldn't he be? Resurrection is a form of recycling. There's an efficiency to the cosmos. Souls don't get thrown out in the garbage dump. They get reused. The universe does not believe in waste, as you have no doubt noticed from observing the stars and the way they're always right back in the same places night after night, on the job for stellar occasions. One Sunday morning I was driving around on the other side of town and noticed this little church, the African Baptist Hope of Resurrection Church, and I figured, okay, sure, it's true that I'm white, but, hey, it's a church and that happens to be the place where people think about souls

being recycled. It was, like, February, when you really *need* a resurrection or two. So I parked the car and quietly crept in, trying not
to track in the snow. Inside they had an organ and a choir singing, they were so beautiful in their robes, and near me there in the
back was Dr. Ntegyereize and the only other white person, her
boyfriend, my boss, Bradley the human. Bradley the human, being
white, couldn't dance around and hold his hands joyfully in the air
the way the black people could, but, and this is the important thing,
he was doing these little steps, like he was concentrating on them.
He was concentrating on joy for once. He was doing it in a white-
guy way. It was because he loved Dr. Margaret and had resurrected
himself for her sake. You could hear the shoes of the celebrators
tapping on the wood floor. He and Margaret noticed me, but
somehow they also *didn't* notice me, they were so into the spirit
world, so I turned around and got back into my car and drove to
Harry and Esther's, with the singing still in my ears and the sight of
Bradley the human doing his little dance inside my mental frame-
work. Hey, sometimes I've wanted to throw off my clothes and
dance in the street out of pure happiness at the holy spirit moving
inside of me. I understand dancing. Harry was reading the *New
York Times* when I got back, which I guess is his form of Sunday
morning joy. It reminded me of something Oscar and I had done
after we were married. It was Halloween. Oscar and I didn't have to
work that night. We decided that you're never too old to go trick-
or-treating, and besides we both liked candy, the same brands.
Oscar decided to dress up as a big powerful dragon, the one with
the eraser for a nose, and I decided to dress up as Venus. In day-to-
day life Venus the goddess wears tight sweaters and skirts but, and
this is the most important feature, you can recognize her because
there's usually an invisible star in the middle of her forehead, a silver one, that she hypnotizes you with. I wore that. Oscar had a big
eraser attached to his nose, held there by a rubber band around
his head, and a green cape, for scales. We went to a few homes of

friends we knew, and we collected treats. It turned into a party. I kept thinking about the Dragon with the Rubber Nose, in Bradley the human's drawing, because actually the poem is about things about to disappear and not just signs and billboards being erased, it's about death. The Dragon with the Rubber Nose is found in most mythologies. We were Venus and the Dragon, and it wasn't until November or December that I realized that Oscar's costume was another form of prophecy, because the Dragon with the Rubber Nose self-erased Oscar. In another month he was gone.

But no dragon ever dies, either. That's how I know I'll find Oscar somewhere. I don't want to tire you out, so I'll finish this as soon as I can. Diana says I should sue the Bat in a civil action, but I won't. Suing the Bat would be like trying to collect damages from a cold virus. The Bat is just there, in whatever form he takes, such as Oscar's dad, and because I haven't seen him lately, I think he's gone in retreat back to his cave. Soon he may appear in another shape. That's Oscar's plan as well, of course. I know you're wondering why I dressed up as Venus and why I think the Bat will appear in another shape. It's because the shapes we have are, like, fragile. I once *was* Venus. I didn't look like her. I *was* her. These friends I had, these dropouts, they lived out in this rental farmhouse west of here, and a summer or two ago they decided to throw this summer solstice party, and as the night went on, it got pretty wild. We were all drunk or stoned, which helped. People were getting naked and running through the woods and the fields, and the girls had braided garlands for themselves and the boys had God knows what, and there was dancing and gallons of wine and beer and outdoor fucking and singing most of the night. That happened in my party days. Around midnight I went out into the woods and someone naked ran past me in pursuit of someone else who was also naked, and I thought: This sure is old-fashioned.

And I could point to a boy and then point to a girl, and they'd look at each other and it'd happen, they'd be locked, helplessly locked, and I had the power to point to a boy and maybe another boy, and even if they had been straight they'd decide, that very night, to try it, to try love on each other just once, flesh against flesh. To see two guys kissing is sometimes a big relief, for a girl. It takes the burden off womanhood. Or it might be girl on girl, because it was the summer solstice, and that's what Venus requires, though Venus prefers boy on girl because Venus is into procreation. I *ruled* that party. I had a star in my forehead. People saw that it was me, that I was making it happen, and they were in awe. Look out, I'm coming, it's Chloé, and I'll make you come, too, and I'll point at you and you, and you can just try to ignore it, but you'll be helpless. Ha. Slowly and then more quickly you will approach each other, you'll make these efforts at conversation, and your mouth will be dry because you're so scared and excited. You'll have your heart cut out with a grapefruit knife; love does that. You won't have a chance against me until you're very old, if then.

The dawn arrived and we all dressed and went home and took showers and then went off to minimum-wage work, dressed in our clothes of the day, our workers' uniforms, like the worker bees we were. Mostly we all had crummy jobs and mostly in our day-to-day lives we're irritable and humble and bummed. We just sit around and watch television and argue about who's going to go to the store to get potato chips and ketchup. I'm on, like, the bottom of the socioeconomic scale, as they call it. I can't do the money thing. That's not where my power resides. But that night, that summer solstice, we traded in those costumes of nothingness we usually wear for our nakedness, and that's how we became gods and goddesses for a few hours, and of all the goddesses, I was the supreme one and everybody knew it. They bowed down to me. You would too. Okay, give me a chance to get my breath, one more time.

There. I think I'm all right. I was going to tell you about this other party, this one other party, where I saw Jesus and then saw this other thing. I won't say that I was clean and sober that day, be-

cause that would be, like, false. Jesus had already come and gone.
I was sitting outside, almost passed out, in my chair, smoking a
cigarette and eating a chunklet of cheese. I don't believe I ever
bragged about my virtue or my party manners. Anyway, I was sitting there with, I don't know, a beer to wash down the cheese, and
a cigarette there somewhere, and because it was a Sunday afternoon, I thought I would check out the sky. Which was blue, with
clouds. I'd just said something really dumb and nonsensible when I
looked up. There was something up there. It was scary. I looked
and looked. This thing was made of cloud matter, but the longer
you looked at it, if you were as high as I was, the more it became
circular. I know you'll say, Get real, Chloé, you saw a cloud. Hey,
that's all you saw. Okay, okay. Maybe. I said, "Hey, look at that
cloud," but no one looked up, they were all too out of it to bother.
So like I said, it was circular, white and burning, like a fiery merry-
go-round, with, if you looked closely enough, people attached.
And cogs. You could see them, these people, getting on and off
the inflamed cloud wheel in the sky, and they'd be strapped in facing out, and they'd be turning slowly because it turned slowly. It
turned slowly like a huge grinding thing, and there were other
wheels and gears in the sky, and they were all meshing together.
And these people, they were all naked, walled up in the sky, attached to the wheel. I wished I hadn't seen it, the wheel turning in
the sky, because even if you're stoned as I was, it fills you with
majesty and terror, but that was the day I knew I had a goddess in
me, because I had seen that. Oceans and rivers and fires of light,
and I swam in that river from then on.

I asked Harry Ginsberg: Who saw the burning wheel? Because I
knew someone else had. Harry is very educated, he would know.
He was reading something else, a book, and for a moment he
looked up. And he said, Ezekiel, Chloé. Like two people had seen
it, Ezekiel and me. I know he was speaking to me, addressing me,
but I took it another way, that it was a list of two people, very ex-

clusionary, a tiny club in which I was one member, Ezekiel being the other.

So now I work at the coffee shop where Oscar's ashes are in a pretty wooden urn on a shelf up near the listings of coffees we offer, and nobody except Bradley and me know that he's there, my husband Bone Barrel. Down here in my basement—I'm doing Harry and Esther a huge favor by staying here, by the way, because they're lonely and they need contact with the youth culture—I've set up a crib and a changing table and I have baby toys ready. My breasts, they're huge, they're ready for lactating and nursing. I smell of milk. I'm careful about what I eat and drink: lots of milk and Caesar salads and steak and fruits and vegetables. I quit smoking. It wasn't needful. I wait for the baby and I wait for the return of Oscar. Oscar wasn't unsung. *I* sang him, so he'll be back. In whatever form he takes this time, I'll welcome him. Sometimes I think of what Harry likes to say, *The unexpected is always upon us,* and I think, Yeah sure it is, but maybe he's right, and one evening I'll be down here, and, who knows, Charlie, I'll be gazing toward the ceiling, just thinking about nothing, feeling my baby's kicks as she or he gets ready to be born, this baby that's half Oscar and half me, and I'll be thinking about the baby's name, and I'll hear somebody outside, somebody who's, like, approaching the front door, and maybe it'll look like Harry and Esther's son Aaron, who they've been waiting for all this time, who had previously invisibled himself but now has reappeared. He'll come to the door, he'll come in, they'll welcome him back, but it'll be me who'll know who he *really* is. Once someone has bound your heart, he's the only person who can let it loose again. I'm waiting, Charlie. I'm patient. I don't ever want my heart unchained, except by him.

The song was right, sweet Jesus. Here's your lemonade.

Ain't no grave will hold his body down.

Our life is no dream, but ought to be
and perhaps will become so.

—NOVALIS

POSTLUDES

"YOU'RE NOT *really* going to start your book with a character waking up in bed, are you? That's the first rule, isn't it? Don't start a story with a character waking up in bed?"

Bradley's words.

But yes: I am going to do that. I am going to break that particular rule.

I RISE FROM THE BENCH and start to make my way back around the periphery of Allmendinger Park. Year after year I have come to this spot to wait out the particular nights that are radiant with the moon, and voices, and wakefulness. Here and there, mostly on the other side of the street, are the restless joggers, who I first assume are all insomniacs but who on second thought are probably night workers, nocturnal laborers, home from their jobs and eager to get some exercise before they shower and bed down for a day's sleep. Overhead, a slight breeze riffles the branches, and the air smells of the white pines to my right through which the wind has passed. One of the lyrical consolations of insomnia is that the sufferer becomes acquainted with the special luminous emptiness of 4 A.M., these spectral stirrings when, just before dawn, the spirits seem to be abroad and are moving slowly toward you for reassurance. As I walk, I notice that the few joggers who are out here are all men. The women are afraid to jog at this time of night, wary of assault. No, I'm wrong: there's one very slender woman wearing a Toledo Mud Hens baseball cap and clutching a small can of pepper spray in her right hand. She jogs by, hardly bothering to look at me, intent on her times, probably a marathoner.

> *I fear we shall out-sleep the coming morn*
> *As much as we this night have overwatch'd.*
> *This palpable-gross play hath well beguiled*
> *The heavy gait of night. Sweet friends, to bed.*

Interesting that that play, *A Midsummer Night's Dream,* like *Macbeth,* has insomnia as one of its many dramatic subjects, though the comedy is concerned with summer love insomnia and treats it with calm sweetness, while the tragedy's sleeplessness, by contrast, is a container for guilt and has the feeling of desperate and cursed winter about it: insomnia as icy cold criminal mania, the arrival of the moving woods, the stalking trees, the hoarfrost. Not all insomnias are alike, as any victim of this condition knows very well.

I TURN THE CORNER and approach Michigan Stadium. A grandiose new cast-iron and brick fence surrounds it, and a high gate. You can't get into this place anymore without a ticket and certainly not at night. These days, you can't wander in and out during the summer or any other off-season. Too bad. Large construction machines block the west entryway into the stands. All this construction work has to be completed by the time football season begins. During the day I can hear the machines, distantly churning, from my study window. This stadium has become even more monumental, with enormous steel girders poking up above the current highest tier to support an additional section of new seating and a seven-million-dollar scoreboard. Around the upper reaches of the stadium's exterior are some words in gigantic maize-and-blue-colored lettering, but with most of the phrase invisible from here:

HAIL TO THE CONQUE

At the corner, the stoplight is blinking red in one direction (north-south) and amber in the other. It's too late even for the skateboard rats to do their practicing, their beautifully risky and ankle-busting curb jumping at this corner. No one driving by seems to have the slightest interest in me. They don't even bother looking in my direction as they whiz by on their errands. I have the sensation that *I've* become invisible. It's very quiet. All the voices have died out in my head. I've been emptied out.

Before I turn to walk toward the woods, I check the eastern horizon, where I detect the faintest glimmerings of dawn. My glimmerlessness has abated, it seems, at least for the moment.

I enter the Pioneer High School Woods, bordering our house. It's darker here than before, because the gypsy moths have not come back this year. The forest was sprayed with moth-attacking bacteria. I no longer remember the Latin phrase for it. I'm too tired for that and no longer moth-crazy. The trees have consequently leafed out and now block whatever moonlight might have filtered down to the path. But the path is exactly where it has always been, of course. *The mental map,* a phrase that psychologists use to refer to the means by which we conceptualize the home territories with which we're familiar, also applies to my imaginings. My mental map will get me through these woods and get me home. It's dark, almost pitch dark in here, but I can see.

A pleasant weariness overtakes me. It's a moment of drowsiness that promises a few hours of sleep. Birds—which one is that? I don't recognize the two-note song—are calling above and behind me.

———

AT THE OTHER SIDE of the woods, coming out onto the street, I walk past the vacant lot, on which no one will ever build a house because of the drainage problems.

I enter the house soundlessly. The dog does not wake or bark at me. I pass by the mirror that is so old that it can't reflect anything anymore, and I head up the stairs. How tired I am, how quiet these sentences have become, drifting slowly out of me, outward and away. The cogs are turning together, synchronized at last in the dark. I am dazed with sleepiness. Our time here is short. I can hardly stay awake. In the bedroom I take off my clothes and lie down under the sheet and the summer blanket, and she puts her hand on my back and says, "Where were you?" but already I am drifting off to sleep and cannot formulate the words in time to name aloud those places where I have been.

In loving memory of my brother

THOMAS HOOKER BAXTER
(1939–1998)

ACKNOWLEDGMENTS

Earlier versions of three of the chapters in this book appeared in *Boulevard, Ploughshares,* and *TriQuarterly.* Thanks to the editors of these publications. Grateful thanks also go to Mark Ricciardi, William Wiser, Dick Bausch, L. M. Daniel for his dragon, Eileen Pollack, Carol Houck Smith, and Dan Frank. Martha H. and Daniel J. saw it through and deserve more than a mention. The title and the summer solstice party in Chapter Twenty-seven were suggested by Virgil Thomson's translation and musical setting of the anonymous second- or fourth-century A.D. poem the *Pervigilium Veneris.*